The
Order
of the
White Boar

Books 1 and 2

'A wonderful work of historical fiction . . . altogether a very enjoyable book for both children and adults.' Isabel Green, *Ricardian Bulletin* of the Richard III Society

'This engaging and exciting story has the power to captivate readers of any age . . . extremely well researched and a pleasure to read.' Wendy Johnson, Looking for Richard Project

'A really gripping historical novel . . . well written, vivid and absorbing.' E. Flanagan, author of *Eden Summer*

'Exciting and appealing, accurate and well-researched . . . I can honestly see this becoming a classic.' Joanne R. Larner, author of *Richard Liveth Yet*

Also by Alex Marchant

The Order of the White Boar
The King's Man
King in Waiting
Sons of York (pub. 2022)

Time out of Time

As editor

Grant Me the Carving of My Name
Right Trusty and Well Beloved…
(both sold in support of Scoliosis Association UK)

The
Order
of the
White Boar

Books 1 and 2

Alex Marchant

To Margaret
Loyalty binds me!
Alex

Marchant Ventures

Contents

Author's notes
Translations of coded text (marked with an asterisk*)

Cast of characters

The Order of the White Boar
Matthew Wansford, a page
Alys Langdown, ward of Queen Elizabeth
Roger de Kynton, a page
Edward, son of Richard, Duke of Gloucester*
Elen, companion to Alys

At Middleham Castle
Richard, Duke of Gloucester, brother to King Edward IV*
Anne, Duchess of Gloucester, his wife*
Sir Francis (later Lord) Lovell, the Duke's friend and
    companion*
Sir Richard Ratcliffe, the Duke's companion*
Lord Scrope, a neighbour*
Master John Kendall, the Duke's secretary*
Master Guylford, the household steward
Sir Thomas, the estate steward
Sir William, the chaplain
Doctor Frees, tutor to Edward and the pages
Master Fleete, the weapons master
Master Petyt, the dancing master
Master Reynold, the horsemaster
Master Gygges, the chief huntsman
Hugh Soulsby, a page
Lionel de Bruyn, a page
Giles Pynson, a page
Robert, a page

The royal family
Edward IV, King of England*
Elizabeth Woodville, his Queen*
Edward, Prince of Wales, their son*
Elizabeth, their daughter*
Cecily, their daughter*
Richard, Duke of York, their son*
Thomas Grey, Marquess of Dorset, the Queen's eldest son by
    her first husband, half-brother to Edward, Prince of Wales*

Richard, Lord Grey, the Queen's younger son by her first
    husband, half-brother to Edward, Prince of Wales*
Anthony Woodville, Earl Rivers, a brother to Queen Elizabeth*
Sir Edward Woodville, a brother to the Queen*
Henry, Duke of Buckingham, a cousin, husband to the Queen's
    sister*

At court
Lord William Hastings, Chamberlain of England*
Margaret Beaufort, Lady Stanley, mother to Henry Tudor*
Thomas, Lord Stanley, her third husband*
Sir William Stanley, his brother*
John Howard, Duke of Norfolk*
Margaret, Duchess of Norfolk, his wife*
Sir James Tyrell, Master of the Henchmen*
Lady Anne Tyrell, wife to Sir James*
Walter, Lord Soulsby, a knight
Ralph Soulsby, his son
Master Cornish, the Abbey choir master*

In London
Master Ashley, a merchant
Mistress Ashley, his wife
Master Lyndsey, his steward
Master Hardyng, his secretary
Master de Vries, his print master
Simon, his apprentice
Friar Shaw (or Shaa), a preacher*

In York
John Wansford, a merchant
John Wansford, his son
Frederick Wansford, his son*
Agnes Wansford, his daughter
Peter Wansford, his son
John Burton, a chorister

Known to history…
Henry Percy, Earl of Northumberland*
John de la Pole, Earl of Lincoln, nephew to King Edward and
    Duke Richard*

Henry Tudor, 'Earl of Richmond', Lancastrian claimant to the throne*

Lord Strange, son to Thomas, Lord Stanley*

Sir Robert Brackenbury, Constable of the Tower*

In the past...

Henry VI, one-time King of England, deposed by Edward IV*

Richard, Duke of York, father of Edward IV*

Edmund, Earl of Rutland, brother to Edward IV*

George, Duke of Clarence, brother to Edward IV*

Richard, Earl of Warwick, cousin to Edward IV, known as the Kingmaker*

Eleanor Talbot, daughter of the Earl of Shrewsbury*

* Historical figures

The
Order
of the
White Boar

To

Philippa Langley

and

the Looking for Richard Project team

1

Middleham Castle, 1482

The sword smashed down just an inch from my nose, spraying my face with gravel as I sprawled on the dusty ground.

I rolled away in desperation, hoping to scramble to my feet, my hand flailing to grab my own sword.

But he was too quick for me.

His heavy boot kicked away my arm, then my sword, flicking it out of reach. Then he stamped down on my chest, winding me.

I gasped at the pain stabbing my wrist, my chest. At the fear crushing me from head to toe.

I struggled to catch a breath, glanced from side to side, seeking a way out, any way I might escape him.

But now he brought his sword down, down, down, in a slow deliberate arc, lining up the point between my eyes.

The tip almost touched my nose, unwavering.

Sunlight glinted off the length of its polished blade.

White knuckles clenched about the hilt.

Above, his eyes were dark slits, his mouth a pinched line. His face, usually so handsome, was deformed by hate.

'Upstart!' he hissed. 'Runt!'

I writhed, to left, to right, desperate to get away. But his foot still pinned me down. I was helpless beneath it.

My breath came in short, ragged bursts. My mind raced.

I had never seen such spite before. Why did he feel that way? What had I done?

I had no idea, could not even guess why he hated me so.

And still his sword was pointed at me as I lay there, gazing up at him.

Alone.

Defenceless.

Hands clapped twice.

'Boys, boys. Enough.'

The weapons tutor, Master Fleete, was hurrying over.

'Put up your sword, Master Soulsby.'

13

Hugh didn't move at first, as though he hadn't heard.

Then, slowly, slowly, his eyes holding mine, he lowered his sword from my face. Its tip traced down my throat until it rested upon the open neck of my doublet. My chest was still heaving from my fear and the fight, but I felt the tap, tap, tap as the sword point rose and fell there three times – as though mocking me in its triumph.

Hugh stepped back, nodding his head towards me, where I lay still in the dust at his feet.

'And that, Master Wansford, is how a gentleman wields a sword.'

A smirk on his broad face, he swung round to his audience, our fellow pages. A smattering of applause broke out and he swept them a most magnificent bow, his arms wide, his knee deeply bent, his rich crimson mantle tossed elegantly over one muscular shoulder.

He was the very picture of nobility as he stood there basking in their admiration. And I had been reminded of my place. According to Hugh, it wasn't here, at Middleham Castle, training to become a knight.

I eased myself to my feet and went to retrieve my sword. My shoulders were stiffening already after the battering I had taken and the light cloth of my undershirt caught painfully against bruises where Hugh's stinging blows had landed. As I picked up the sword, I weighed its burnished chestnut blade in my hand. They might be made of wood, but these play swords could cause damage enough when wielded by someone with so much hatred in him.

I slunk off to sit on a mounting block by the stables while Hugh joined the throng of pages and Master Fleete set another pair of boys to skirmishing with their wooden swords. Sweeping the dust and grit from my front, my fingers found holes again in the woollen fabric of my doublet where it had already been patched. My eyes stung as I remembered all the mending my mother had done before I came to my new home.

Feet scraped on the gravel, a shadow fell across me, and to my surprise other hands began brushing dirt from the back of my doublet.

'There,' came a voice. 'We'll have you clean enough before the Duchess returns.'

I blinked away my tears and looked up.

One of the other pages stood there, a fair-haired, open-faced boy, with freckles and laughing eyes. I knew him only by sight. No older than myself, he was of course taller, as were most boys my age. He was smiling down at me.

'You must not mind Hugh,' he said after a moment when I did not speak. 'He doesn't mean it.'

I grunted.

'I fear he does.'

'He is only jesting. He's like that with all the new pages.'

'Jesting?'

I drew up my doublet and undershirt. As I thought, the bruises were growing livid, the dark reds, blues of a deepening sunset.

'A fine sort of jest that leaves marks such as these.'

But he was the first boy who'd spoken friendly words to me since I'd come to the castle.

So I forced a smile

'But perhaps he just doesn't know his own strength. Like an ox that could break down a gate with one kick and be free, if only it had the brain.'

The boy laughed.

'Maybe. Soulsby the Dumb Ox. It has a certain ring to it. Perhaps when he is a knight he can adopt it as his badge. Vache noir on a muck brun champ.'

I frowned up at him.

'That sounds like very poor French.'

'Well, I'm not much of a scholar.' He sat down beside me, making me shuffle along the block to make room. 'French, Latin, scripture, it's all the same to me. I am made for dancing and sport, hawking and hunting, not classroom learning or weapons training.'

That last was true. I had seen him fighting before my bout with Hugh and he was little better than myself.

'And you, Master Wansford, what do you do well?'

'I'm Matthew,' I said. 'Or Matt if we're to be friends.'

The words sounded to me as sharp as a dagger's stab, but it was too late to bite them back. But the boy only smiled again.

'And I'm Roger, Roger de Kynton, son of Sir Denys de Kynton of the King's household. Perhaps we will be friends. So long as you don't outshine me in all our lessons.'

'I'm not sure I do anything well. I've been here such a short time.'

15

'But Master Guylford said you were at the Minster School in York. Doesn't that mean that you can sing like a bird?'

My stomach lurched as though I'd been hit again. I had hoped that no one would discover where I had come from.

I tried not to show it, but Roger must have seen something in my face.

'Don't worry. No one else knows. I overheard Master Guylford speaking with the chaplain before you arrived. He said you left under a cloud, but nothing more. What happened? Or do you wish to keep it a secret?'

'I would prefer to. I came here to get away from it all.'

'There are all sorts of rumours among the other pages about why you're here – none of them to your credit, of course. But they'll soon fade – rumours always do, even here. They'll get bored of them. And if we're to be friends, perhaps you'll tell me another time.'

I could have kicked myself again. No other page had spoken to me like this, and my secret could ruin everything. But I had to keep it, at least for now.

'Perhaps. It's not so very interesting.'

'In that case, I'm sure I can wait.'

A trumpet blared in the distance. Roger jumped down from the block.

'But maybe our dinner can't. Come on – we'd better hurry – they'll be clearing away early today before Her Grace's return.'

He grasped my elbow, pulling me with him across the outer courtyard. The other pages were already streaming through the grey-stone gatehouse into the smaller inner court. Several eyed us with curiosity as we joined them in the shadow of the massive keep beyond. But Roger only winked at me as we all filed up the covered stairs that clung to its outside wall.

We washed our hands in the basins held by servants in the wide doorway of the great hall, then made our way to the pages' table. As we sidled between table and bench, Roger nudged me and pointed to the high table beneath the tall arched windows at the far end.

'It's Hugh's turn to serve Master Guylford today. See?'

Master Guylford was the steward who ran the castle. When the Duke and Duchess were away, he sat in the Duke's own place to preside over mealtimes. Hugh was standing very straight behind the carved oak chair at the centre of the table, his chin up, looking neither to left nor to right.

As I watched, Master Guylford strode into the hall and on to the raised dais. In his livery of deep red and blue embroidered with the Duke's badge of a white boar, he was an imposing figure as he stood there, raising his hands for silence. Hugh stepped up smartly, ready to push the chair forward for him to be seated. The chaplain, Sir William, was standing in front of a similar chair alongside. As the hubbub of the busy hall subsided into quiet, he bowed his head and folded his hands on his rounded belly to say grace.

Roger put his lips close to my ear and whispered,

'Hugh will become squire next year and hope then to do the same service for Duke Richard. The likes of you and me will have to settle for serving lesser men.'

'But didn't you say your father is one of the King's knights?'

'True, but lords trump mere knights. Did you not know that Hugh is nephew to Lord Walter Soulsby?'

I shook my head. The name meant nothing to me. But after grace finished and we all sat down, Roger carried on, seeming unaware.

'His lordship may have fought for the Earl of Warwick against the King, but that was more than ten years ago. Now his loyalty is not questioned and his family enjoy high honour at court. My father says Hugh and his cousin Ralph are destined for great things.'

I glanced again at Hugh, now helping the steward to his meat. He might be only a year or two older than me, but he was far taller, broader, almost a man already. With his fine manners and rich brocade tunic, to my eyes he looked every inch a knight in waiting. I could only dream of reaching his position in life.

I turned to my own trencher, now filled for me by a servant, and began to spoon up my mutton stew from the bread.

2

The Return of the Duchess

After the fruit and last crumbs of cheese were finished, we pages all stood while the greater members of the household filed out of the hall. As we were hustled out in their wake, the chamberlain was ordering the servants to clear away the trestle tables and strew fresh rushes on the stone floor.

Outside, there was more commotion. Everywhere serving men and women were running to and fro, fresh white linen being carried from the laundry, clouds of dust being beaten from great tapestries. Garlands of flowers fresh from the castle gardens were draped around the buildings of the inner court and jewel-coloured pennons fluttered at windows. I had never seen so much activity since I had arrived at the castle.

The other pages scattered as usual, the younger ones to play at tops and balls in the outer court, where they would get under the feet of the grooms and the servants. The older boys usually found a quiet corner to lounge about and chat, or went riding, or took up their bows to practise archery in the butts.

Not belonging to either group, I generally hid myself away in the chamber shared by all the pages. There I read my books alone or, once, begging ink and parchment from the chaplain, wrote a short letter to my father. I had of course told him all was well.

But now Roger took my arm and drew me with him, strolling under the steel teeth of the portcullis into the outer courtyard. Despite my prickliness, he seemed determined to make me his friend.

Beyond the inner gatehouse was yet more bustle and busyness. Several wagons drawn up close by were being unloaded of chests and barrels and bundles. The horses were blowing and sweating as though they had pulled their burdens far today through the high summer warmth, and they flicked ears and tails at the clouds of flies buzzing around them.

When the first two carts had been emptied, then led away by lads towards the stables at the far side of the courtyard, I screwed up my courage to speak.

'What's all the fuss about?'

'Don't you know?' Roger asked, an eyebrow raised. 'The Duchess returns today and everything must be made ready.'

I remembered Master Guylford and my father talking about the Duchess and the Duke on my first evening at the castle, but I had been too excited to take anything in.

'Where has she been?'

'Up at Barnard Castle. She went there to see the Duke off to the Scottish wars after his meeting with the King. She's stayed there since. I think perhaps she feels closer to him when she's there.'

'And when will the Duke himself come home?'

Roger shrugged.

'The last we heard, he had captured Edinburgh, but Berwick Castle was still under siege. It could be weeks, or months. The border castles always hold strong, though the town itself fell at the Duke's first attack.'

There was pride in his voice. I had heard it also in the speech of castle servants when they talked of their master. When my father and his friends in York had praised the Duke I had never paid attention – why should I listen to council talk, merchant gossip? But now he was to be my master too, I wanted to learn more.

'Is he such a great warrior then?'

'A great warrior? My father says there is none better in the kingdom! Well, not since King Edward turned to politics and pleasure.' He glanced about him and lowered his voice, as though afraid that someone would hear.

'The King was the finest general of his day, but it's no secret that he now prefers life at court to campaigning. When the Scots started to cause trouble again, my father says he was planning to march north to deal with them. But he never came. It was Duke Richard who had to muster the troops and ride to battle. Do you hear nothing of events in York?'

'Of course we do,' I retorted. 'Those troops he mustered – many of them came from York. And on his way to the war the Duke stopped in the city and was greeted by all our important men. My father was amongst them.'

'So you have seen His Grace more recently than us. He rode from here in the spring and hasn't returned since.'

19

'No, I – my father was angry with me and wouldn't let me out of the house.'

I heard again the great key turning in the door's lock and saw him walk away in the early morning light, clad in his council robes of twilight blue. I hadn't dared climb out of the back window as I had so often before – his fury was still too fresh in my mind.

Roger was watching me closely.

'Ah, your little trouble? I'm sorry for you. You will have missed a fine spectacle. I hear the men of York admire the Duke above all others, even more than the Earl of Northumberland. He says they treat him royally when he visits – and we all enjoy the gifts they send here. Rabbits from the town warren, loaves of fine wheaten bread, barrels of wine…'

Was he mocking me – he the lad who belonged in this castle, me the lowly merchant's son from the city? But his smile appeared genuine and he clapped me on the shoulder.

'Come now, no more moping around. Let's go to the kennels – I hear the Duke's favourite hound has had her pups.'

He set off across the court, weaving a way between horses, carts, hurrying servants. I trailed behind him. After a moment he stopped, waiting for me to catch up.

'Come on. You do know where we're going?'

'I've never been there.'

'Never? What about the mews?'

I shook my head.

'What on earth do you do with yourself all day? I don't think I've seen you at the butts or out riding.'

'I read, mostly. I —'

'You read? You have books?'

'My father is a merchant. He imports books with his other goods. He even has printed ones from Germany.' Despite our recent differences, I was proud of my father. 'He lets me choose one for myself from time to time.'

'Really? Do you have any romances?'

'One or two. Also poetry and histories.'

'You must lend them to me – so long as they are not in French. But no reading today. In weather this fine we should be riding or at sport.'

'But I have no horse.'

'There are plenty in the stables for us to use. You know where that is? We'll find the one for you.'

I was not so sure. I had seen the other pages riding out from the castle on their beautiful mounts. My old pony, the one I had learned to ride on, would look no better than a mule alongside their shining flanks and dancing hooves – if my father had not taken her home with him. Would I be able to handle such a horse?

To my relief Roger said, 'But not today. We must be here when the Duchess arrives.'

'Why?'

'To give her a proper welcome, of course. The whole household will turn out. But before that we have time to see the hounds. Hark, perhaps they sense something is happening. Or maybe it's just their dinner time.'

A great clamour of barking rang out from the building next to the stable as we approached. Outside, the great carthorses stood all in a row, their steaming coats being rubbed down by grooms and their noses buried deep in bags full of oats. We dodged past their stamping feet and into the open doorway beyond.

Inside, in rows of wooden pens, scores of dogs were being fed. Several boys, barely older than me, were passing along the building, dropping meaty bones into each pen. A few hounds quarrelled for a moment, but all soon settled down to gnaw contentedly. A warm, musky smell hung everywhere, overlying even the sharp scent of the raw meat.

Tossing a word of greeting to the kennel lads, Roger led me to the back of the building where several pens housed dogs on their own. In one at the very end lay a large lean white hound, a cluster of tiny puppies snuggled up to her side.

Roger unbolted the gate to let us in and we crouched down on the straw beside the dog. She raised her head and licked the hand Roger held out.

'Good girl,' he said. 'Six healthy pups. Well done, Florette.'

The puppies were so small that their eyes were not yet open. Their mother nuzzled them, then rested her head back as though exhausted. Among the tumble of brown and white bodies one pup was a curious red colour. I stroked its soft fur with a finger and it mewled pitifully, nestling closer to its mother's flank.

Roger laughed.

'That's a strange one for a white hound to whelp. Small too. It looks like the runt of the litter.'

'There's nothing wrong with being small,' I shot back, conscious that my new friend stood at least three fingers taller than me.

'No, indeed,' he said. 'Nor with being differently coloured to your fellows. And those who are small to begin with often grow greater than many others.'

'I'm sorry.' Yet again I regretted my words. 'It's just that...'

'No matter.' He straightened up. 'Shall we go to the mews? It seems I have plenty still to show you.'

He let us out of Florette's pen and in a moment we were outside once more in the blazing afternoon sun. On the far side of the stables, snug against the mighty outer wall of the castle, crouched a long, low building, its windows all shuttered against the glare.

A man with a huge leather glove on his hand was coming out. He stood aside and held open the door for us, bowing slightly to Roger as we passed.

Once inside, my eyes adjusted to the gloom. Ranged on all sides were perches of varying heights above the ground. On each stood a falcon, its strong-clawed feet fastened to its wooden rest by a short leash. As we walked between the rows, every bird's head turned to watch us pass, their dark eyes glittering like cut flint.

Roger stopped by a perch on which sat a small mottled-brown bird that bobbed up and down as he approached. Tiny bells sewn on leather straps on its legs tinkled at the movement. Roger clicked his tongue as he reached out a finger to smooth the glossy feathers on its back.

'Hush now, Lady.'

With his other hand he slipped from a pouch at his belt a small morsel of something and offered it up to the bird. Bending her head, she took it delicately with her cruelly curving beak.

'She's beautiful,' I said. It was the first time I had seen a falcon so close.

'So she is.' In the half-darkness I heard rather than saw Roger smile. 'And I hope one day she'll be mine. I helped to catch her in the spring from a nest up on Pen Hill. The Duke has promised her to me if I help train her well. Most days now I come to see her flown, and sometimes the falconer lets me take her out. No, don't touch her!'

For I had raised my own hand towards the bird and too late did I hear his warning. Her head darted forward, the beak stabbing. The pain was needle sharp before I could recoil.

Roger drew me away towards a shuttered window and held up my hand to the chink of light that crept through. Blood was oozing from a deep cut in my forefinger. I put it to my mouth, trying to stem the salty flow.

'She doesn't know you. Never approach a strange hawk. If she had been a large bird like a gerfalcon or peregrine, rather than a merlin, she'd have had your finger clean off. I should have warned you. Perhaps you can help me with her and she will become used to you.'

I took the none-too-clean kerchief he offered me and tied it round my finger. Sore it might be, but I was grateful it was still attached.

Roger gave another tidbit to the bird, who began her bouncing routine again, before leading me back to the door. I was careful this time to steer well clear of the perches, especially those holding the larger falcons.

Back outside Roger's head went up, as though a questing hound sniffing the air for a scent. From beyond the castle walls came the sound of many hooves and people were hastening towards the inner gatehouse.

'I think they must be coming,' he said. 'Come on, we'll have to hurry. We mustn't be late for Master Guylford.'

Together we joined the flow of people across the outer courtyard. Some stopped to make way for us. I wasn't used to this. On the streets of York few would allow me to pass first. I was just one among many merchants' sons in the town. But here, groomsmen, servants, men-at-arms all stepped aside. I guessed it was Roger, with his costly, bright-coloured doublet and hose. They recognized him as a page of the household, and while I was his companion, perhaps I was entitled to the same respect.

Master Guylford was arranging crowds either side of the gateway and waved to us.

'Pages to the inner court. Hurry now!'

Roger and I passed through the dark tunnel and emerged into another throng of people, domestic servants and higher officials, surrounded by squires and our fellow pages. Master Fleete was barking orders while Sir William, the chaplain, just flapped his hands at the excitable boys milling around him, laughing and calling to each other. As we arrived, somehow the masters together managed to form everyone into lines, with the youngest pages at the front. I just about made it into the second row, to my relief. I had no wish to be lumped in with the seven and eight year olds. Roger stayed with me, though by rights he should have been with the taller boys behind us.

Master Fleete hustled the final stragglers into place. Among them was Hugh Soulsby. He strolled to the back of the ranks, chatting with a friend, one hand resting casually on the pommel of the knife at his belt, refusing to be hurried. Then the trumpet sounded, a peal this time rather than the more usual single or double blast.

Shouts began in the outer court and rippled towards us. Those nearby wearing hats of any sort took them off. Roger craned to see round the taller servants between him and the gateway, as everyone around us broke into raucous cheering.

'Is the Duchess coming?' I had to yell to Roger though he was so close beside me.

'Yes, of course,' he shouted in reply. 'And so I hope, at last, is my best friend.'

'Your best friend?'

'Yes. She went away with the Duchess. And now, I trust, will return with her.'

'She?'

'Yes, she.' His smile flashed again. 'Is that so very strange?'

I remembered my sisters, closer to me in age than my brothers. I had missed all of them so much these past days.

'Perhaps not.'

'You'll see when you meet her.'

A small procession of carriages flanked by horses and riders trotted through the gateway, the grating of wheels and clatter of hooves drowned out by the cheers of the crowd.

'There she is! Riding of course.'

My eyes followed his pointing finger.

Among the foremost riders, the rest of whom were men, was a girl of about my own age, straight-backed upon a high-stepping chestnut pony. She spotted Roger at that moment and flung up her hand to wave. I caught a glimpse of light reddish curls and sharp green eyes, before the horses passed by us, further into the courtyard.

The cheering grew louder and my gaze was drawn to the first carriage, eye-catching in red and gold, as it slowed to a halt in front of us.

Seated in it, under a fringed, embroidered canopy, were three young women and a boy whom I guessed was about six, maybe seven years old. Pale despite the sunny weather of recent weeks, he gazed out upon the joyous crowd as if barely seeing it.

The woman next to him leaned down and spoke a word in his ear. For a heartbeat a smile brightened his face and he raised his hand to greet the throng. Then he was hidden as Master Guylford stepped forward, bowing and offering his hand to help the occupants alight from the carriage.

I nudged Roger.

'Who's that?'

'Her Grace, the Duchess, of course.'

A slender dark-haired woman clad in dove-grey silk stepped lightly down from the carriage. She stood talking to Master Guylford as the noise of the crowd began to quieten. The boy joined her, having been helped down by Sir William, who turned back to assist the other ladies.

'Not her. The boy.'

'That's her son, Edward.'

'Edward? The Duke's son?' I racked my memory. 'But I thought he was eight or nine years old?'

'So he is. He also is perhaps a little small for his age.'

I shot a glance at Roger, but his face was expressionless.

'Why is he here? Shouldn't he be away in some other household by now?'

'You mean in service as a page, like you and me?'

'Well, like you. Isn't that normal for the sons of lords? If he is to be a knight like his father.'

'Look at him, Matt. Do you think he has the making of a knight?'

I glanced again at the boy standing silent beside his mother. The light I had seen so briefly had vanished.

'He is often ill, Matt, and the Duke and Duchess trust only their own physicians to keep him well. My father says that's why he isn't sent away as a page. They prefer to keep him close.'

'Oh, yes – Old Dick's soft like that.'

I twisted round.

The harsh voice belonged to Hugh Soulsby. It seemed he had elbowed aside the pages behind us – they were glaring at him as he swaggered to a halt among them. At his side was Lionel de Bruyn, one of the other pages I'd often seen him with.

Hugh's face showed some of that spite of our meeting on the weapons ground, but this time it was not directed at me.

Roger rounded on him.

'He's not soft – not in battle, anyway. My father says —'

'My father says —' mimicked Hugh in a high-pitched voice. 'My father the King's man says...'

He swung away, sniggering, before Roger could respond, and with Lionel at his heels like a dog, began to push his way out through the crowd. The cheering had died away now, and the pages and squires stopped chatting to each other, silently parting to let him through.

I watched him go. Beyond the crowd, Master Guylford offered the Duchess his arm and was walking with her towards the steps of the keep. The boy and ladies and gentlemen from the carriages followed. Sir William, facing the crowd, dismissed us with a few words and a clap of his hands.

Roger's eyes were scouring the far side of the courtyard, where the riders had gone to dismount. Some of the horses, still wearing their rich trappings, were being led away towards the outer court.

As Roger started forwards, I grasped his arm.

'Who's "Old Dick"?'

He turned to me, frowning, as though he wasn't sure what I meant. Then his eyes cleared.

'Oh, he means Duke Richard.'

'The Duke?'

'Sometimes among the pages we call His Grace by his given name rather than his title. We mean no disrespect. But that —'

To my surprise he spat on the dusty ground.

'Why doesn't Hugh like him?'

'Hugh dislikes more easily than he likes. It's his way. Give him the smallest of reasons... You, for instance. What have you done to offend him?'

'I don't know. Except maybe be who I am.'

'Exactly. And he doesn't like that. You're not of his sort. Very few are, thank the Lord.'

'But the Duke? Surely he's of his sort? The nobility, I mean. Why doesn't he like him?'

We had started walking across the inner court towards a small group of people outside the chamberlain's office. But now Roger halted and looked me full in the face.

'Do you not know Hugh's story? And didn't you hear what I said about him at dinner?'

'Only that he is the nephew of a lord, and that he is destined for great things. And that his uncle fought for…'

My words trailed off. I realized what I was saying.

'Yes, his uncle – he was a Lancastrian and he fought for the traitor Warwick against King Edward. Duke Richard's brother.'

'But that was so long ago. Almost before I was born. And if his uncle's now at court, the King must have forgiven him.'

'As he did so many nobles. Including some who are now most loyal.'

'So what's the problem now? Hugh can't possibly remember that.'

'But he does just about remember his father. And I don't think Hugh has forgotten – or forgiven – what happened to him.'

'His father?'

'He not only fought for the Earl of Warwick. He also plotted to kill the King a year or two later and was executed for treason.'

'Executed? For treason?'

Roger laughed at the surprise that must have been scrawled across my face.

'Him – and so many others. It was all the rage back then. At least among the Lancastrians. Thank goodness King Edward has brought us so many years of peace since.'

'But – but why? What happened?'

Roger screwed his face into a serious expression, like one of my old masters when he was about to teach a lesson.

'Well, in the beginning there were the families of the Dukes of York and Dukes of Lancaster. And the Lancastrian duke, Henry Bolingbroke, stole the throne from the king, Richard the Second, and became Henry the Fourth.'

'Don't be daft, Roger. I know that. We learnt it all at school. It must be a hundred years ago now, in my grandfather's grandfather's time.'

'Then where do you want me to start?'

My mind went back to my lessons and what I had learnt from my father – about all the plots and battles, over so many years, between the rival claimants for the throne from the houses of York and Lancaster. About how the Yorkists believed they had a better claim than the Lancastrian kings.

I knew our good King Edward of the house of York had now ruled over us for eleven years of peace – the longest such spell for a generation or more. Ten years before that he had won the throne from the third Lancastrian king in a bloody battle just a few miles from my home city, the city of which his father had been Duke. But the crown had rested uneasily on his head while the previous king, Henry, the sixth of that name, was still alive.

Everything flared up again when Edward's cousin and once loyal supporter, the Earl of Warwick, known as the Kingmaker, had decided he could wield greater power through Henry, who many people thought was a weak king. So Warwick had rebelled against Edward to put Henry back on the throne. Then the problem had seemed to be finally solved when King Edward and his loyal younger brother Richard had crushed the Earl and his Lancastrian allies in two battles at places called Barnet and Tewkesbury, somewhere in the south of the country. Poor King Henry had died shortly afterwards in the famous castle known as the Tower in London.

It all seemed ancient history to me. I had barely been born when those battles had raged. And I had never dreamed that I would find myself living in the home of one of the victors – the King's brother Richard, Duke of Gloucester. Or sharing a chamber with the son of one of the defeated.

Not wanting to appear ignorant of this history, I said, 'I mean, surely, if his father committed treason, he would have been attainted. Didn't Hugh lose his right to his lands and any titles? What's he doing here?'

'Of course he did, but he was just a small boy. King Edward forgave him his father's crime and Hugh's uncle took him in to his family. And when he was old enough, he came here to be a page. Don't you know that a good king is a merciful king? Although my father says that perhaps some people forgive too easily.'

Roger had started walking again and as I caught him up, he flashed one of his ready smiles.

'And another thing – Alys told me that the Duke had Hugh beaten just before he went away. She didn't tell me why, but he must have deserved it, and – well, Hugh is not so ready to forgive as the King or Duke Richard. Ah, there she is!'

He broke into a run.

'Alys!'

A slight figure on the edge of the knot of people turned at his call and held her hands out to greet him. It was the girl I had seen on horseback.

Roger flung himself on to one knee in front of her and, taking both her hands, clasped them to his chest, over his heart.

'My lady!'

'Sir knight!'

'It has been too long. Surely you have forgotten me.'

'Nay, how could I forget you?'

'It has been more than a month. Mayhap you have found some other suitor?'

The girl's face, which until then had been mock-dramatic like Roger's own, changed.

'Get up, Roger, you dolt. Don't make fun. You know it's not a matter to laugh about.'

Roger got to his feet. His smile had fled and he stumbled over his words.

'Alys, I'm sorry, I forgot, I…'

'Well, I cannot.'

And with a stamp of her foot, the girl stormed away to the stairs up to the great hall.

The people clustered about stared at us curiously, though some eyed Roger with sympathy. One girl, dark of hair and dark of skin, came across and rested her hand on his arm.

'Don't worry, Roger. She's tired after the journey. She insisted on riding the whole way. Let me try to smooth it over for you.'

Roger's face was pale as he watched her follow Alys towards the keep stairs.

I wanted to ask what he had done wrong, but dared not. So this time I drew his arm through my own and said,

'Come back to the dormitory. The last book my father gave me is a book of courtly poetry. It's in French, but if you like, I can translate for you. Perhaps it will distract you.'

A grateful smile drifted across his face and we set off together back to the pages' chamber. We walked in silence, but my thoughts were full of Roger's 'best friend' and the way she had treated him so shamefully.

3

The Secret

'Master Wansford? Her Grace the Duchess wishes to see you.'

So wrapped up was I in the rhythms of the poem I was reading that the voice caught me by surprise.

I glanced up. Light from the westering sun slanted through the window on to a man clad in the now familiar servants' tunic of blue and dark red – or murrey, as I had heard it called.

'Me? Are you sure?'

'Of course. Her Grace always greets the new pages.'

Roger took the leather-bound book from my hand.

'You'd better hurry. Perhaps we can read again later. We'll still have time before bed.'

My heart thundering within my chest, I followed the servant out of the pages' chamber and across the court to climb the keep stairs. I had been here almost a week and had spoken so far to no one more important than the chaplain who took our lessons. And now I was to stand before the Duchess herself.

I remembered how even my father had been awed, that evening of our arrival, as the outer walls and towers of the great castle cast long shadows towards us in the soft evening sunshine. As our horses' hooves had clattered across the oaken drawbridge beneath that first looming gatehouse, the far-off bulk of the keep blotting out the glory of the sunset. As the huge murrey and blue banner flying on the topmost turret glittered like jewels in the sun's last rays, the white boar stitched upon it almost alive as it rippled in the breeze.

And I remembered how my father had bent his head towards mine and whispered – not in his usual booming council-chamber voice –

'Don't forget, Matt, know your place. You have been offered a great honour in coming here. You must be careful not to misbehave.'

The great hall was empty of people now and the servant's knock at the door in the far wall echoed around its stone corners. A quiet word was spoken within and the man lifted the latch, ushering me through to the chamber beyond.

'Master Matthew Wansford, Your Grace, the new page, as you requested.'

I took a few steps forward, then bowed low as I had been taught. In the moment before I straightened up, I took the chance to glance around this private chamber.

First to catch my eye was a cavernous fireplace, its black iron grate empty on this warm summer's evening. It was perhaps the largest in the castle, although the room was only half the size of the great hall. Tapestries of intricate embroidery and cloth of gold hung to either side, displaying fantastical scenes of knights and maidens, majestic stags and silver unicorns, snow-capped mountain ranges and bronze-leaved forests. Littered around was more furniture than I'd ever seen in a single room, all ornately carved and some well-padded with tasselled cushions.

To my surprise the girl Alys was sitting, sewing, on such a stool in the golden sunset glow flooding in from the nearby windows. She had changed from her dusty riding clothes into a gown of jade-green brocade, and her light red hair was loose across her shoulders in a maze of curls. She looked a different girl from the one who had flared up at Roger that afternoon.

A soft voice broke through my thoughts.

'Welcome, Master Wansford – or shall we call you Matthew? Master Guylford told me of your arrival.'

A second person in the room rose from her seat and stepped towards me, her hand outstretched. It was the lady from the carriage, now also wearing an indoor gown of pale green.

I bent once more, this time to touch my lips to her hand. This was all I had learnt in my one dancing lesson so far.

A warm laugh greeted my nervous attempt.

'Quite the gallant! I'm sure you will be a valuable addition to our household. Now, come sit by me and tell me of yourself.'

The Duchess motioned towards a low stool beside her own chair.

I hesitated, my gaze slipping to where Alys sat, just a few feet away. The Duchess must have seen, for she said,

'Sit and be comfortable, and do not mind Alys here. She is the ward of my sister-in-law the Queen and knows that nothing said in this chamber is to be repeated beyond these walls.'

I perched on the velvet-cushioned stool as I was bid, but could not help glancing again at Alys. Her eyes were lowered as though intent on her embroidery, but a dimple in her cheek suggested she was straining not to smile.

My face was warm at the idea of her listening. Could I avoid telling the Duchess my full story?

'Come now, Matthew. Master Guylford tells me you have been offered a place as a page here at the request of our esteemed friend the mayor of York. Also that our estate steward, Sir Thomas, trades with your father and respects him greatly. How is it that you wish to leave your family and your life in York to join our household?'

Such a direct question. From a Duchess. What could I do other than tell the truth – and hope it didn't get back to the other pages?

'Well, my lady – I mean, Your Grace – it's not that I chose to, not exactly… but… well, I'm afraid I was turned away from the Minster School and my father didn't know what to do with me.'

'Turned away?' A small frown appeared on the Duchess's face. 'You mean you attended lessons there?'

'Yes, Your Grace, for more than five years. I was in the choir at the Minster – that's the great cathedral of our city – and all choristers must attend lessons at the school.'

'So you are a trained singer?'

'Yes, Your Grace.'

'Matthew, you needn't "Your Grace" me all the time.' I didn't dare look at Alys, but I was sure the dimple had deepened. 'Will you sing for me this evening? This chamber may not be so kind to your voice as the lofty heights of our beloved York Minster, but it would please me to hear you.'

'Of course, Your – I mean, of course, I would be pleased to.' Though I could have wished Alys out of the room.

'But first,' the Duchess continued, 'go on with your story. Why were you turned out of the school?' Then, as I hesitated again, she added, 'That is, if it doesn't pain you to tell me.'

I was amazed. That she, a Duchess, had noticed my discomfort – the unhappiness of a mere page. And the concern in her voice made me want to talk. To unburden myself to a sympathetic ear.

My father hadn't understood, had only been angered by the disgrace I had brought on the family. My mother had been too busy with her duties to listen properly. My brothers and sisters – I had been too proud to talk with them about it once my father had spoken. And that had left no one I could trust, as I was no longer allowed to see my old school friends.

But here was a Duchess – someone I didn't know – who wanted to hear about it. And strange to say, I felt I could talk to her.

And once I began, I found the whole sorry tale tumbled out.

'It was the feast day of the Ascension and we had just celebrated High Mass in the Minster. I had had the honour of carrying the great crucifix of our Lord in the procession for the first time.'

I saw the grand parade in my mind's eye once more. Felt again the pride swelling my chest. Then,

'We were just following the choir master across the Minster square back to school when – when John Burton said a bad thing about my new mother. And so I put the crucifix down and – and I punched him. He hit me back, so my friends joined in, then so did his, and in the end most of the choir was fighting each other.'

I didn't mention that the crucifix was knocked over in the brawl, or that the chain of a censer one of my friends had been carrying was broken – or that our surplices had been torn and muddied – and bloodied.

I also didn't tell of how the precentor and choir master had stood on the edge of the fray and shouted at us to stop, and finally waded in to pull us all apart. Or that the choir master himself had received a blackened eye. Or who it was who had thrown that final punch.

But the Duchess didn't seem to need these details. Perhaps she had seen enough choirs in their full finery to imagine the scene.

Her mouth twitched as though she was trying not to smile. And what sounded like a muffled hiccup came from behind me. But as I glanced round, Alys's head was still bent over her embroidery.

Thinking about it now, some weeks later, I supposed it could have been amusing. To an onlooker at least. And there had been many onlookers – including the most important men of the city and all of the congregation.

There we were, maybe a score of boys, big and small, in pure white smocks and collars, slogging it out against the backdrop of our majestic cathedral.

And I had at least paid John Burton back. Not just for what he had said that day, but for all his taunts and jibes over the years. Remembering him being helped away, blood streaming from a smashed nose, made all that had happened afterwards seem almost worthwhile.

For my father had been there too.

'Your new mother?'

The gentle words brought me back to the present.

'Your Grace?'

'You said this boy said a bad thing about your new mother?'

'My —' I swallowed hard, not wanting to carry on. But I forced myself. 'My – my real mother died. A year ago. Not long after my baby sister was born. My father has just married again.'

'I'm sorry to hear it. About your mother, I mean. And do you like this new wife?'

'Well…' I paused. 'She's not my real mother, but, yes, I like her very much. She nursed my mother well during her illness and has been good with the baby. But she's so young – not quite twenty – and my father – my father is quite old.'

'How old?'

'He is over thirty.'

'That's not so old. My husband is almost thirty. If anything were to happen to me I —'

As I watched her, her gaze slipped away and her smile faded, as though her thoughts were drifting. Sympathy for me seemed mixed with some sort of sadness of her own.

'If I died, I would wish that he would marry again. That he might find happiness once more. And then perhaps my Edward would have a brother or sister.'

Then she shook her head as though to rid herself of the notion.

'And so you were turned out of school for standing up for your parents' good name. What happened to this John Burton who said the bad thing?'

'He's still at school. No one else heard what he said. And it was I and my friends who landed the first blows. Two of my friends were expelled with me. Also John's father is one of the wealthiest men in the city.'

'Life is very unfair. And how did your father take it?'

'Not well.'

The angry words had rained down like blows, followed by dark glares and silences, which were even worse.

'He said I had shamed myself and our family, and he called me a rebel. I told him I would have to leave in a year or two anyway, when my voice breaks, but he said I should then have gone to the grammar school like my brothers before me. He wouldn't let me out of the house for a long time afterwards. And even when the mayor suggested I might come here, at first he didn't want to let me. He was worried I would disgrace myself here too.'

'And what do you think?'

I didn't need to think.

'I want to make sure I do well here, to show my father that I'm different from what he thinks. And I want to better myself in the world. And – and I want to serve you and the Duke loyally and as well as I can.'

I slipped off my stool and down on to one knee, bowing my head to her as I had seen Roger do before Alys.

The Duchess's hand rested a moment on my head. Then she took my elbow and raised me to my feet.

'Then I'm sure you shall do well, and go back to him when you have proved yourself.'

'Thank you, Your Grace.'

'Now, let us hear what such loyal service sounds like. Will you sing for us now?'

What could I sing, here, alone? Even when I took a solo part, I always sang alongside the rest of the choir.

But then I recalled a courtly love song I had learned. The choir master had taught us it one day in spring when he'd been in a good mood. Before the feast day of the Ascension.

I straightened my back, lifted my chin, and drew in a deep, deep breath. The romantic French words and the high notes of the tune soared among the oak beams of the chamber's vaulted ceiling. I had never expected to sing them before a Duchess. But neither would the choir master have expected that on the day I gave him his black eye.

It was a sad song about two lovers meeting, then parting for ever. As I sang the final words, tears welled in the Duchess's clear grey eyes. She wiped them away with a tiny lace handkerchief.

'Thank you, Matthew. I can see that the Minster's loss will be our gain. I shall ask Sir William to teach you some of my husband's favourite songs for when he returns. His Grace will not regret Master Guylford's decision to accept you into our household. He is very fond of music and will be pleased to have such a voice sing again at holy offices in our chapel here. Of late we have had only older singers.'

With a few more kind words the Duchess dismissed me. Another low bow to both her and Alys – who nodded without meeting my eye – and I was on my way back to the pages' quarters.

As I walked across the twilit court, it was as though a weight had been lifted from me. Perhaps my crime had not been so dreadful after all. And maybe, now – now it appeared I had won the goodwill of a Duchess – it might change my life for the better.

Roger greeted me with a grin and a pair of dice, and we played until the tapers burnt down. When we could no longer see the dots to tally our scores, we pulled our mattresses close together, ignoring the grumbles of the pages we displaced. We whispered long into the night, about ourselves, our families, our plans for the future. At last, first one, then the other, we drifted into sleep. My rest was more peaceful than it had been for many weeks.

4

Alys

With the Duchess back at the castle, life changed. It was as though while she had been away, everyone had simply been waiting for her return. A new sense of purpose was in the air, and people who had appeared to be enjoying a holiday now busied themselves with myriad tasks and watched to ensure that others were also occupied.

Among the pages and younger squires there was much dark muttering, but I was pleased at the new routine. My years at the Minster School had been ruled by the regularity of services at the high altar. Holy days and feast days for others meant only extra duties for me. Later, after my expulsion, my father had kept me busy studying French and Latin and helping with the accounts at his work place. When, on coming to Middleham, I had the run of a castle, its grounds and village, I had struggled to adapt and find enough to do to fill each day.

Every day still began as it had before. We attended Mass in the chapel next to the keep, before breakfasting on bread and weak ale in the great hall. If the Duchess attended, she would sit in the great chair that Sir William the chaplain had occupied at meal times. The steward sat near to her to help serve her food. The Duke's chair now remained empty.

Then lessons began. They were not the half-hearted affairs Sir William had presided over before handing us on to Master Fleete, or letting us loose for the rest of the day. Now they were proper tutoring by Doctor Frees.

The Doctor had gone away with the Duchess to make sure her son, Edward, continued with his lessons. Now he had returned, all the pages had to endure them. For my part, I enjoyed learning languages from someone who had himself travelled in Europe rather than from the plodding, book-taught tutor I had known at the song school.

The Doctor was a harsh master, and would punish a boy for the slightest fault, as I soon discovered. But I was already ahead of my companions in book learning and Doctor Frees liked the fact that I was keen to learn. He took us for most of our lessons, only passing us over to Sir William for scripture and the dancing master, Master Petyt, for music and other courtly arts.

After our hours in the school room, we moved on to the care of Master Fleete for our daily dose of weapons training. This could be archery, at which I was competent enough having spent many hours learning from my father at the York city butts, or close-weapons. Roger now tried to make sure we were paired together whenever possible. As we were both poor swordsmen, I no longer dreaded these times and gradually began to improve.

The Duke's horse master had also returned to the castle and he encouraged all the boys to ride after dinner – the squires in the tiltyard to practise their jousting skills, the pages simply to roam beyond the castle grounds. Roger made good his promise to find me a horse. She was an old fat mare who had been Sir William's mount before he also had grown stout. A gentle, undemanding ride, with a little persuasion she would break into a canter for a minute or two when Roger and I rode out together, through the meadows along the winding river, or up to the purple heather-clad moor.

I was spending most of my time with Roger now. I was grateful to him for taking me under his wing. I wasn't sure why he had, but the other pages followed his lead and became friendlier.

Only Hugh and his two or three closest friends remained aloof. But I hadn't seen on his face again the hatred of that morning when we fought. It was as though he had been in the grip of some fury unrelated to me. When we met now, he was distant but polite. I was content with that. I hoped he would forget about me, so far below him as I was, in both age and station. That I would be just one among the many pages who were less important than him.

As the days wore on, my suspicion grew that Roger was passing so much of his time with me because he wasn't seeing his 'best friend'. Since the day of her return, Alys had avoided him. She also was tutored by our masters for some lessons, but at other times we hardly saw her. Roger said that, in the past, she had joined him and the other pages on their rides or chatting about poetry or romances, as some girls of the household still did. One such was Elen, the dark girl who had promised to help Roger. I discovered she was Alys's maid-cum-companion. But even she was unable to persuade Alys to join us.

During our first long talk, Roger had told me more about Alys – and the reason for their falling out.

'Alys and I came to Middleham around the same time, when we were about seven. It was the first time I'd been away from my family, and Alys's mother had just died, so we were both unhappy. We just seemed to band together because of that. Then we discovered we both loved riding and hunting and books, especially romances. The Duke lets us read the books in his library. Or at least Alys reads them. Her French is so much better than mine. And sometimes we used to play at being the knights and damsels in the stories.'

'So that's what you were doing in the courtyard?'

'Yes. I thought it would be fun to do it again. Only I'd forgotten the news she'd had not long before she went away.'

'What news?'

'That she's betrothed.'

'Betrothed?' My surprised whisper was more like a squeak. I waited before continuing in case I'd woken the other pages. 'To be married? But she can't be more than twelve or thirteen.'

'It's not unusual at court. They say the Princess Elizabeth was betrothed to the French Dauphin when she was only five.'

'Maybe so, but we're not at court.'

'But Alys is a ward of Queen Elizabeth, even if she's not actually at court. That means the Queen gets to decide what happens to her.'

'How so? You said her mother was dead, but her father…?'

'He was killed soon after she was born, fighting for the King at the battle of Barnet. Her mother was a lady-in-waiting at court, and when she died Alys became a royal ward. And the Queen has decided that she is to marry Ralph Soulsby.'

'Soulsby? Not Hugh's cousin?'

'One and the same. Alys says it's probably to buy Lord Walter's continued loyalty to the King – her mother left her a great deal of land which would make his family even richer if she marries Ralph.'

'I hope Ralph is pleasanter than his cousin.'

Roger was silent for a moment, then whispered, 'All I know is that he's almost nineteen. The wedding won't be for a year or two yet. Perhaps she'll have a chance to get to know him, but it's a horrible idea. And I was thoughtless enough to say what I did about another suitor. I can say such things in jest – she has to face it in real life.'

Appalled though I was about the betrothal, what worried me most was Roger's unhappiness. Was there anything I could do to help him and Alys be friends again? So far nothing had come to mind. I even plucked up the courage to speak to Elen, but she could tell me no more than she told Roger.

'Every time I mention his name to her, she changes the subject or tells me to be quiet. And she refuses to talk about Ralph Soulsby or the betrothal. She just shuts herself up in her chamber when she's not at lessons. Even the Duchess has noticed it. She worries that Alys will start to sicken over it.'

But after a week or two, help came in a form that neither Roger nor I had expected.

As promised, the Duchess had asked the chaplain to teach me some songs ready for when the Duke returned. So each afternoon after our ride, Sir William would call me to the chapel. I didn't mind missing this free time as I loved to sing. Often Master Petyt, the dancing master, was there to accompany me on his lute, which meant that Sir William could choose songs that weren't just church music. As I had studied French and Latin, it was easy for me to learn the words for both types of songs, and Sir William said Doctor Frees might teach me some Italian or Spanish too.

One day when I was practising a *laude* with Sir William, the Duchess entered the chapel. She sat listening until I had finished, then beckoned me to her.

'Well done, Matthew, you sang that beautifully. Sir William is doing an excellent job with you.'

I bowed.

'Thank you, Your Grace.'

'And how are you settling down here? Do you still miss your family and your song school friends?'

'A little, but I'm making friends here.'

'I'm pleased to hear that. And if there is any way I can help you, tell me. Your work here with Sir William is beyond the service we expect from most pages.'

What Roger had said about the Duke's library came to mind and I wondered whether my reading some new French romances to him might cheer him up. That's how, later that day, with the Duchess's permission, I found myself once again in her private apartment.

She was busy in conversation with Master Guylford, but broke off to welcome me and point out the door in the far corner.

'You will have company while you're in there. I hope that doesn't bother you.'

'Of course not, Your Grace.'

But I was disappointed. I had hoped to be alone while I explored this treasure trove of books. Yet I now knew well that in the castle you were lucky to have any privacy anywhere, and the opportunity was too good to pass up. So I pressed the latch and let myself in, as quietly as I could.

It was a small room with a vaulted, white-painted ceiling and two tall, narrow windows. Against each wall was a cabinet filled with books. Except in the Minster library I had never seen so many in one place. But before I could discover what books they were, I saw who was to be my companion.

'Alys!'

The red-haired girl had her back to me, her hand raised to replace a small, leather-bound book in the cabinet at the far side of the room. She swung round, surprise scrawled across her face. Then her features settled into an unreadable mask.

'Oh, it's you, the new page. The singer. What is your name?'

Her tone stirred memories of Hugh – the voice of someone who believed they were more important than you. And yet, she had been so different, those first few moments with Roger.

'Matthew, Matthew Wansford – my lady.'

Those last words slipped out unbidden and I cursed myself inside. Why should I speak to her in that way? She was no older than I was, no better – just because she had been at court and knew the Queen.

'What are you doing here?'

'Her Grace the Duchess said I could look at the books. She's outside with the steward if you want to check.'

Alys's expression didn't change.

'There's no need. You wouldn't have got in here unless she let you. What are you looking for?'

'I just want to see what books there are. Although particularly French romances.'

'You like romances?'

42

'Yes, but –' maybe I could help Roger? – 'but they're especially for a friend.'

She glanced down at the book still in her hand. She sounded different when she spoke again, less haughty.

'I think I saw you riding out with Roger de Kynton yesterday.'

'Yes. We rode through the village and across the water meadows.'

'How is he?'

'He's well. He hopes to be able to fly his falcon on our ride tomorrow. If the weather stays fine.'

Should I have mentioned how much he missed her? Before I could speak again, another voice broke in.

'Lady? Is he so far on with her training? I would like to see that.'

Around the skirt of Alys's gown poked the face of the young boy, Edward. He had been hidden there, perched on a low stool, reading. Now I saw him closer, his face appeared older. Shadows smudged the pale skin beneath blue eyes. But those eyes shone at mention of the hawk.

It struck me that I had no idea how to address him. To be safe, I bowed in his direction.

'Yes, Your Grace. The falconer says he's ready to take her out. He himself has flown her on the moor already and says she's responding well enough to Roger for him to try.'

'Then I shall ask my mother if I can ride out with you tomorrow.'

The boy let his book slip to the floor as he stood and hurried out of the room. Alys bent to slot it back on a shelf. While her back was turned, she said,

'All the pages just call him Edward. The Duke and Duchess encourage that.'

She was so matter-of-fact now – had I mistaken her before? But Edward, rushing back in, prevented my response. He was breathless in his excitement.

'My mother says I may go – as long as you permit me, Master Wansford.'

'Matthew,' I said automatically, 'or Matt if you prefer. I'd be happy for you to come – and I'm sure Roger will be too. Shall we find you when we're ready to go?'

'I'll be here after dinner, or with my mother and Sir Thomas, learning about the estate. Thank you for letting me join you. I haven't often been riding this summer.'

'Why —?' I began, but Alys cut me off, thrusting the book she was still holding into my hands.

'There is a dashing romance for Roger – a new one Her Grace had sent from London while we were away. I doubt he'll have read it yet. Tell him to come to me if he needs help with the French.'

Her abruptness confused me. And was she was mocking Roger – or me?

So, my back stiff, I dipped her the slightest bow, and said, with my best French accent,

'Merci pour vôtre assistance, mademoiselle.' Then to Edward, 'Adieu, à demain dans l'après-midi.'

'À demain, monsieur,' he replied with a smile, unaware of the changed atmosphere. He stretched up to pick out another book as I turned on my heel and left the room.

After offering thanks to the Duchess, I passed out of the private apartment and across the great hall. As I reached the outside staircase, quick steps caught up with me.

It was Alys, her face tinged with pink – from running or something else?

'Matthew, forgive me. I'm sorry for that. I know you speak French well and can help Roger – although I do wish he would try harder himself. It's just that —'

'Just that what?'

'Just – well, I just wanted to stop you asking Edward why he didn't ride.'

'Why?'

'Because – oh, because he hates people to know that he's been ill. The Duchess wants him to ride because she thinks it will be good for him, but he's scared that it will happen again. He had a terrible fever and problems breathing. He was laid up in bed for weeks and it worries him so.' She bit her lip, then carried on in a rush. 'I've told Her Grace that Elen and I will ride out with you to look after him. Will you ask Roger whether he minds me coming?'

At that moment I understood why Roger was so attached to his best friend.

'Of course I will – although I don't think he'll mind at all. À demain, my lady.'

And this time my bow was answered by a perfect curtsey.

5

The Youngest Son

The next day dawned grey and breezy, with the hills across the valley cloaked in low cloud.

Roger's spirits had risen when I'd told him of my meeting with Alys in the evening. But at breakfast his face was as overcast as the sky.

'It looks like it'll rain. Then we won't even be able to ride, let alone fly Lady. The falconer says I can only take her out in good weather. And the Duchess will probably say the same about Edward.'

'Because of his illness?'

He nodded gloomily, slicking more honey on his bread.

'The whole castle was in an uproar when he was sick back in the spring. The Duchess was beside herself. I think she thought he might die. Her physician and the herbalist could do nothing and Sir William says he recommended she tell Duke Richard. But she wouldn't. She knew his duty was raising troops for the Scottish war.'

'Would he have come home?'

'Edward's their only child – what would you do? If need be the Duke could have left the muster to the Earl of Northumberland. Fortunately Edward recovered, but he was too weak to do much for a long time. Elen says he rode a few times when they were at Barnard Castle, but only for a short time and when the weather was fair.'

Roger spent most of our morning lessons gazing out the window in the hope that the weather would improve. But by dinnertime it was clear our plans for the day were dashed. We emerged from the armoury head first into a curtain of squally rain and had to sprint for the shelter of the stairs up to the great hall.

Edward was with us. Today, for the first time, he had joined us at weapons training as well as at tutoring. Even to my untrained eye it was obvious that, although small, he had the makings of a good swordsman. He soon tired, but he was agile and determined in his bouts with the younger pages – amongst whom I was now numbered, with Roger, since my disastrous fight with

Hugh. ('You have a lot to learn,' Master Fleete had muttered darkly.)

Edward overmastered me easily in our skirmish with the wooden swords, but the contrast with Hugh couldn't have been greater. When my footwork let me down and I crashed to the ground at the mercy of his sword point, he put out a hand to help me up and we bowed to each other to end the bout.

Now, as we waited on the steps to be let into the great hall, he was breathing fast, though we had run such a short distance. The clouds gathering on his face mirrored Roger's.

'My mother won't let me go out in this,' he said. 'I was so looking forward to riding with you, Matt, and to seeing Lady fly. I remember when Roger first showed her to me when he brought her home with my father.'

As we filed into the hall, Edward left us to take his place at the high table. I whispered to Roger,

'Couldn't we fly her again in the mews? At least then he can see you handle her – and maybe Alys will come too.'

His face lit up, remembering, as I had, the area kept free of perches to allow space for young birds to be flown indoors.

'Why didn't I think of that? What a fool. I've been so caught up in the idea of taking her out. It won't be the same – she can't fly so high or far – but it will be better than nothing. And hopefully the weather will soon turn.'

Edward was delighted at the idea – as was Roger when Alys also joined us after dinner.

At first she was very cool towards him, despite his careful attentions to both her and Edward. Soon, however, he talked her round. He might not read romances well in the original French, but it was clear he learned a great deal from them. The dimple reappeared in Alys's cheek as she watched Edward, enthralled when Roger helped him entice Lady to his wrist to peck a morsel of meat. And after the third time Roger likened the grace and beauty of a falcon in flight to the grace and beauty of his 'lady fair', Alys gave in and laughed.

'Master Roger, if you live long enough you will make a fine courtier – or perhaps an ambassador at foreign courts. You will flatter the lords and ladies in equal measure.'

'Or maybe a great churchman,' suggested Edward. He proudly held up his leather-gloved fist where the falcon had alighted and was delicately tearing at her reward. 'An abbot or a bishop. They have power enough and time too of their own to hunt and hawk at their pleasure. You might even become archbishop or chancellor of all England.'

'What, like old Rotherham?' said Roger, with scorn. 'Spend all my time in church and grow old and fat with too much good living? Not I!'

'Have you seen the Archbishop?' I asked in surprise.

'I was at court for a time last year. The Duke was kind enough to include me in his company when he went to London to meet with the King.'

'He didn't take me,' said Edward, a pout hovering near his mouth.

'Perhaps you were a little young, Ed,' said Alys. 'It's a long journey and there's nothing much for us to do at court. You wouldn't have liked it. And the air in London is not so fresh and clean as it is here.'

'It's full of smoke,' agreed Roger. 'All those coal fires. I spent half my time there coughing.'

'Is it? Did you?' Edward looked from one to the other, uncertain whether to believe them. 'I've never been to London. I've hardly been further than York.'

'Why would you need to?' I chipped in. 'What's so marvellous about London? I should think you can get everything you could possibly want in York.'

I was proud of my city – and also wanted to cheer Edward up. But even as the words passed my lips, I envied Roger his trip to the capital. My father had been once to London, a year or two before. His tales of its wonders had filled me with a longing to one day visit there myself – to see the multitude of people from every far-flung land, the wide, shining river crowded by boats of all shapes and sizes, the colours and sights and sounds of the rituals and progresses of the royal family and the great guilds and companies of the city.

'Matt's right, Ed,' said Roger. 'London's over-rated. York can match it in every way. Think of the wonderful mystery plays we saw at Corpus Christi last year. Or the Masses in the Minster with the angelic singing of the choristers. St Paul's and the Abbey in Westminster have nothing to beat that.' He shot me a glance. 'You know, Matt, I hadn't realized before – it will have been your voice that helped take us closer to heaven.'

His voice was earnest, but his mouth twitched. I didn't mind him pulling my leg if it helped to perk Edward up.

'I think it would take much more than just Matt's voice to drag you anywhere near heaven,' said Alys, and Roger laughed. But Edward said in all seriousness,

'Yes, my mother told me you were in the Minster choir, Matt. And that you're learning songs for when my father returns. Is that why you came here?'

I felt the colour rise in my cheeks and was grateful for the dim light in the mews. I had whispered my story to Roger that first night, thinking Alys would tell him anyway sooner or later. But I hoped no one else would discover the truth, especially not Edward. We had swiftly become friends, despite our differences in age and rank, and I worried that he would think less of me if he knew.

'In a way. Sir William has been teaching me all sorts of songs, although he tells me your father particularly likes church music.'

'Yes, my father is very religious. If he had his way, I think he would have someone with him at all times to sing such songs.'

'Indeed, the Duke is so pious, he should have become a priest. Then he would have had God's backing to tell us all what to do.'

We all swung round, startled.

Behind us in the gloom stood Hugh. On his wrist was perched a falcon rather larger than Lady, hooded in black velvet as though about to be taken outside. His tone was genial, but discomfort crept on to Edward's face. Alys perhaps spotted it too, as she was quick to retort,

'And so he might have done, as many youngest sons do. But if you remember, his father and older brother were treacherously slain in battle. King Edward needed all the support of his remaining family. Perhaps otherwise Duke Richard might have been meant for a life in the church. What of it? There's no shame in it.'

Hugh flinched at her sharp reply.

'I meant no harm, cousin.'

'I'm not your cousin yet,' Alys flung back, and for the second time since I'd known her, she stalked off. Startled hawks all around flapped and danced on their perches as she passed, buffeted by the tidal wave of anger.

Roger glared at Hugh before following her at a run. Edward and I were left alone with the newcomer. Edward smoothed Lady's feathers to calm her as she bobbed up and down on his wrist.

'A very temperamental girl,' Hugh said, almost to himself, as he watched Alys and her loyal knight leave the mews. 'I will have to tell my cousin.'

Edward, a shadow flitting across his face, returned Lady to her perch and started to tie her jesses to it.

Hugh watched his inexpert fumbling for a moment, then said to me,

'So, Master Wansford, you're trying to gain favour with the son as well as the mother, are you?'

Although he spoke in his earlier affable tone, his attention to me caught me unawares.

'What do you mean?'

'Oh, nothing. Except we've all heard about your singing lessons.'

'What of it?'

'Just a friendly warning. The Duke will see through it, you know. He won't take kindly to someone like you trying to better himself by mixing with his family. He may be both pious and arrogant, but he's no fool.'

My cheeks flushed warm, even as my hands clenched into fists at his words.

Was what he said too close to the truth? It was not my intention. But perhaps the Duke would view my familiarity with his son as blatant ambition. No noble would like that. Had Hugh been right that day when he called me an upstart?

Yet, as the memory stung me again, his next words took me by surprise.

'Do you ride, Master Wansford? Perhaps we should ride out together one day.'

And he turned on his heel and walked away.

6

Windfollower

During the next two days of unrelenting rain, our small riding party grew into a fair-sized expedition. Edward mentioned it to a fellow page, who asked to come and then spoke of it to another. Soon almost a dozen were intending to join us.

Roger was disappointed, but we could hardly stop them from riding with us. All pages were entitled, expected even, to ride often. And Edward was excited at showing off his new-learnt falconry skills.

The last two to say they'd join us were Hugh and his friend, Lionel. We didn't have the courage to refuse, though afterwards I wished that we had.

At dawn on the third day the dale had been shrouded in a thick mist, but by the end of lessons it burnt off to reveal a glowing blue late summer sky. As Roger and I stood in the queue of chattering pages waiting to wash before dinner, Edward rushed up the steps to us. Before he had even caught his breath, he gasped out,

'Mother says I may ride out with you this afternoon. Can we take Lady?'

The pages clustered about us glanced around at his eager words. Hugh was among them, standing two or three places ahead of us. Gazing down on us, he said politely,

'So you do ride, Master Wansford. And as well as Master de Kynton here no doubt.'

I said nothing, and grasped Roger's arm to stop him too, knowing he was still angry after the afternoon in the mews.

Hugh seemed not to notice our silence and carried on, a bland smile on his face.

'If you have no objection, Lionel and I will join you on your ride. Perhaps we can try our falcons against each other.'

When Roger and I arrived at the stables after dinner, with Lady, hooded, upon his gauntleted wrist, our companions were already assembling. Edward was atop a fat grey pony, and Alys and Elen were being assisted to mount their horses – Alys on her spirited chestnut and Elen on… on Sir William's old mare.

Roger's quick eyes caught my grimace.

'Don't worry, Matt,' he muttered. 'I'll find the head groom.'

But before he could move, Hugh emerged from the darkness of the stables, followed by a young under-groom leading two saddled horses. The first, a glossy dark brown, was as big as a knight's war-horse. Hugh took the reins and swung himself easily into the saddle. The other was hardly smaller, a pale grey colt, almost white. It shifted nervously, hooves rattling on the cobbles, as the groom handed me its reins.

My heart sank.

Hugh gazed down at me, pulling on his leather gloves.

'I heard you don't have your own horse, Master Wansford, so I think we've found just the one for you. A fine local-bred colt. Runs like the wind they tell me, and that means something in these parts, believe me. In fact, his name is Windfollower. I'm sure you'll find him an exhilarating ride.'

Once again, his tone was amiable, but this time I was close enough to see something other than friendship in his eyes. But I also felt the rest of the party, including Alys, watching me.

I couldn't back out.

I thanked Hugh, hoping no tremor in my voice would betray my fear, then checked the saddle's girth and gathered the reins ready to mount.

Roger, beside me, said in an undertone, 'Are you sure?'

In reply I simply nodded to the groom, who boosted me up into the saddle.

It was a long way up.

I struggled to inch my right leg over the colt's broad back and down to feel for the stirrup with my toe.

It would also be a long way down.

And it would hurt if I fell.

But —

But I wouldn't fall.

I clicked my tongue and the horse's ears flicked backwards to listen. A little pressure on the reins and its dancing hooves were stilled.

Perhaps a horse so responsive would be easier to handle than I feared.

Hugh, leaning down to accept his hawk from the falconer, shot me a sideways glance, but his face was unreadable.

Once everyone was mounted, we set off. I squeezed the horse's flanks lightly with my legs and was relieved when it walked forward.

The string of riders passed across the courtyard, through the outer gateway and across the drawbridge. Soon the foremost horses were trotting along the cobbled road down towards the village. My colt, again with only the slightest pressure on its sides, followed their lead.

By the time we had steered our way through the village – across the wide marketplace, past the simple stone cross stabbing skywards at its centre, skirting the garden plots and strip-fields towards the river – I had begun to enjoy myself.

Roger, however, riding alongside me, asked,

'How goes it? You seem rather – well, he seems rather large for you.'

'I've never ridden such a magnificent horse. He does exactly as I bid him.'

'All well and good now, but...', a frown furrowed his brow, 'well, I think I recognize this horse. If I'm right, he's the son of Storm, the Duke's favourite stallion. I think he's only just been broken to the saddle. Be very careful.'

I did my best to heed his warning, but it was not easy. Not on this lovely September afternoon, cantering along the water meadows on this beautiful horse, with such well-born companions. What would my father or my old school fellows say if they could see me?

From the riverside meadows, we rode up towards the moor edge and slowed to pick our way through the purple haze of heather. A lapwing broke cover, startled by the leading horses. My eyes followed its wheeling flight, luring my gaze back to the view now spreading out in our wake.

Far below us now snaked the river. Beyond, I could just trace the road that swept down to the valley from the town of Leyburn, nestled among the distant hills, across the old stone bridge, and up into Middleham village. The castle crouched above the sprinkling of houses like a she-wolf defending her cubs.

How different this boundless landscape was from the flat fields and woodlands around my home in York. But, for the first time in weeks, my insides didn't ache with homesickness.

The horses ahead had halted and Hugh was readying his falcon for flight. Roger spurred his horse over to join him.

Soon, by turns, first Hugh's, then Roger's bird was soaring high into the sunlit sky, and swooping low again to chase the lure swung by its master. Edward, the youngest among us, laughed with delight, pointing this way and that as first one bird, then another, hurtled past him.

I watched the spectacle alone, outside the knot of riders. But after a while, Alys guided her horse over to stand alongside mine. A few moments passed before she spoke, her eyes still following the plunging flight of the birds.

'Thank you for letting Edward come with you.'

My surprise at her words mingled with my gladness that she had sought me out.

'Don't thank me. I'm happy to spend time with him. The more I see him, the more he reminds me of my brother Peter. They're a similar age. Besides, Roger arranged everything.'

'Except your mount, I fear. Please take care. I don't trust Hugh and I can't help feeling he chose that horse for you for a reason.'

My first instinct was to reply that she had no reason to worry, that I could handle the horse. But then my dread on first sight of him came back to me, and I glanced down at the bilberry bushes so far beneath me. And reminded myself not to spurn another friend through misplaced pride.

'I hope I shall get back to the castle in one piece. So far I've enjoyed our ride. Though I must admit to feeling more secure on Sir William's old mare.'

Her eyes flicked over to where Elen sat atop the mare, keeping close to Edward.

'Yes, Roger told us when we stopped. I'm sorry for that. If we'd known, Elen would have found some other mount. The under-groom recommended the mare, but Hugh was with him at the time. Perhaps Master Soulsby made some arrangement of his own.'

'Perhaps he did.' I had forgotten his question about riding when we were alone in the mews. Had he planned something? I had checked the girth and bridle before mounting. Neither had been tampered with, and so far the horse had behaved well. Maybe this day luck would be with me.

But I also remembered what else Hugh had said.

'I don't think he likes me much. And he said the Duke wouldn't either.'

'The Duke? How so?'

'Hugh said he would think I wasn't the right sort of person for the castle.'

'Don't listen to him. You are here. Therefore Duke Richard has agreed to it. Nothing happens here without his say-so.'

'But he's been away in Scotland all this time.'

'The Duchess and Sir Thomas send and receive letters by messenger every day. And anyway, what makes you think you're not the right sort?'

'I'm just a merchant's son. Not even a very wealthy one. Although my father is part of the city council.'

'I've often heard the Duke praise our merchants. He trades with them himself. I've also heard the mayor of York applaud him for fairness in all his dealings with local people. Why would he treat you any differently?'

'It's just what Hugh said.'

Alys snorted in a most unladylike way.

'Hugh has his own reasons for saying things against the Duke. You shouldn't listen to them. His Grace got his measure long ago. He treats all the pages equally. They're all beaten when they do wrong, but Hugh – well, Hugh is beaten more often than anyone. I think he holds it against the Duke personally.'

'Roger says he was beaten just before the Duke went away.'

'Yes, and he richly deserved it.'

'What happened?'

'Someone found him throwing stones at a dog – just a poor one-eyed cur from the village. It comes up to beg scraps at the kitchen. He injured it badly. Edward said that when the Duke asked why he'd done it, Hugh just laughed and said it was for target practice. The Duke was so angry that he took a stick and beat Hugh himself, there and then. He always says if you have power over someone or something, you shouldn't misuse it.'

'And yet he would see you married to Hugh's cousin?'

The thought escaped from my mouth before I could bite it back.

Alys drew herself up very straight. From her changed manner, it was as though a curtain of ice had fallen between us.

'I am a ward of the Queen, not the Duke. I must do as I am bid.'

And she tugged on her reins, urging the pony back towards the throng of laughing pages and the plummeting hawks.

I remained where I was, an outsider again. And now, not just worry about Hugh, but my foolish words weighed like a stone in my stomach.

Elen was fussing over Edward as Alys approached them. Even seen at a distance, his face had a distinct pallor. Alys bent to speak to him, then called to the group around the birds,

'Gentlemen, it is getting late. We must return to the castle.'

Hugh's voice was raised in complaint, but Roger immediately drew in his lure and placed the hood over Lady's head. In a few moments, the riding party was once more wending its way down from the moor top, skirting marsh and cotton grass, until we reached the stretch of meadowland behind the castle.

The shadows of trees edging the meadow were lengthening and ahead of us rabbits were emerging from burrows among their roots. Roger was riding with me, chatting about how well Lady had flown, when Hugh spurred his horse alongside us. Upon his broad face was a jovial smile.

'Let the ladies continue homeward, de Kynton. I say we should have some real sport. A silver piece for the first falcon to catch a rabbit.'

Roger couldn't resist. We reined back our horses and he and Hugh dismounted, while I pulled Windfollower round to gain a better view. Alys, passing, glanced across in concern, but she continued on with Elen, leading the tired Edward on his pony.

'Your bird shall fly first as it's the younger,' said Hugh.

Both boys took the hoods from their hawks' heads. Lady began her familiar bobbing routine and the light of the hunt flared in Roger's eyes. He reached skywards with the hawk on his gloved fist and released her. She floated for a moment above him in the air, then shot like a bolt from a crossbow towards the nearest of the rabbits, turning at the last instant, her clawed feet outstretched.

That was the last thing I knew with any clarity.

Out of the corner of my eye I saw Hugh's gauntleted fist point down towards the ground and the lure in his other hand flung towards my horse's hooves. His falcon instantly followed it and the horse, startled, reared up, kicking out with its front feet at the bird.

I grasped desperately at the reins, then felt the great muscles bunch up beneath me, and the horse sprang forward in a panic. Before I could do anything but cling on, he was carrying me at a gallop across the meadow, past the startled faces of Alys and Edward, scattering the grazing sheep, heading for the castle.

Alys cried 'Matt!' in alarm as we passed, then angrily 'Hugh, you —', but anything she called him was lost in the wind whipping past my ears and the thundering of hooves as we sped on.

I tugged on the reins, trying to stop the horse, but it was in no mood to obey. It simply tossed its head as it ran, showing the whites of its eyes.

It told me what I had known all along. I was too small to control it properly. Now, to avoid being dashed to the ground, I had to focus simply on hanging on.

I clutched at the mane with my fingers and at the sides with my legs, feeling the raw strength throughout its powerful body as it galloped on. And I prayed to God, Jesus and the Virgin Mary that I should not be killed.

Up ahead loomed the rear wall of the castle and it struck me with the force of a blow that we were heading straight for the water-filled moat. Its steep sides and dark depths would mean death for us both if I didn't act quickly.

With a strength born of pure fear, I wrenched the horse's head to the left. To my relief it didn't buck or fight it, but veered that way, though without slackening its pace. Now side on to the moat, we were charging down the slope towards the outskirts of the village.

A yell and a pounding of hooves made me look back as best I could.

Alys, crouching low on her chestnut, was galloping headlong across the meadow towards us. Our abrupt change of direction meant she was gaining ground. By the time we reached the dirt road into the village she was only yards behind us.

Another desperate cry from her. I caught only the words 'People… village…'

But it was clear what she meant. As we careered onwards, hooves kicking up mud from the roadway, villagers were scattering before us. Up ahead mothers were rushing to gather up their playing children out of our path. Screams tore at my ears. An old woman crossing slowly, turned, resting on her stick. Her eyes widened at the crazed horse plunging towards her.

Dragging at the horse's reins and mane with what strength I could muster, I steered it to the left again, taking the danger away from the people on the main street. Now instead we were racing across garden plots down the hill towards the river. All the while I could hear the thunder of two sets of hooves as Alys followed, still shouting wordlessly, trying to keep pace, maybe to gain on us.

We passed the last of the houses, flashed across the Leyburn road and on to the water meadows.

As we crossed the road at a flat-out gallop, a group of riders halted on the old stone bridge. Colourful pennons flew above them, the low sun glinted off burnished harness.

A shout went up from them. As I glanced across, two of the foremost riders peeled away and launched themselves towards us, seeking to head us off.

I pulled back on the reins again, but the horse did not respond, bolting still along the river's bank. Flecks of foam were flying backwards now into my face. As I turned to blink them away, I saw one of the unknown riders catch up with Alys, stretch out an arm to grab her horse's bridle and pull her to a stop.

She screamed 'Not me! It's his —', then her voice died away behind me.

The other rider drew level with me, crouched low over the neck of his galloping horse, matching Windfollower's pace stride by stride for a few seconds. A glint of blue eyes, concentrating hard under a dark brow, and he flung out a gloved hand to grasp my reins. With the gentlest of backwards pressure on my horse's bridle, he eased us all to a shuddering halt.

In a trice, he was down from his mount and standing at the head of mine. He stroked its nose gently, speaking calming words to it. It tossed its head once, blowing hard through flared nostrils, then lowered it beneath his touch. Its whole body was shaking beneath me, its great sides heaving with the effort of breathing. And I was quaking too.

I drew my right leg across the saddle and slipped down the great height to the ground. Then my legs buckled beneath me and I found myself in a heap on the floor.

The man laughed, but not unkindly, and then his hand was beneath my arm helping me back to my feet. His other hand kept a firm hold on my horse's bridle.

As I raised my head, I saw he was a slight man, hardly taller than Roger, clad in an ancient leather jerkin and mud-flecked hose. Although young, his face was serious. There were lines around those intense eyes I'd glimpsed earlier, whether of laughter or something else I couldn't tell.

A frown darkened them now.

'Well, lad,' he said, 'explain to me, I pray you, why you were riding a horse that is not yours and that you clearly cannot control.'

7

'A Golden Giant of a Man'

Roger came to my rescue, galloping up to us at the head of a small troop of pages, as though leading a cavalry charge.

Their sudden arrival caused pandemonium.

Windfollower began to buck and kick again in fright. My rescuer struggled to control him, while catching hold of his own horse in an attempt to stop it bolting in its turn. Meanwhile, Alys, still atop her chestnut pony, was being led towards us by the other stranger. She was shouting at him that she had had everything under control until he had interfered.

The two men, the one slight and dark, the newcomer taller and fair, glanced at each other. My rescuer shrugged and laughed again.

'Perhaps it would be better to go into the castle. We can sort the matter out there.'

So saying he swung himself back into his saddle and, gathering the reins of both horses, rode with them to join the company of horsemen waiting on the road. The other man turned his horse about and followed, leading Alys behind him despite her protests. The whole company set off again along the road, and in a minute or two had disappeared into the village.

I was left standing alone, among the pages milling around me on their horses. Hugh and Lionel were not among them.

Roger stuck out his hand. I clasped it and he hauled me up to sit astride his horse behind him.

'Perhaps you are safer riding with me this time.'

Without another word, he pulled his mount's head around and together with the other pages, we rode more sedately back up through the village and into the castle's outer courtyard.

At the stables, all the grooms were busy attending to the two dozen or so horses of the riders who had arrived before us. Windfollower and Alys's chestnut were among them, but there was no sign of her or of the men who had accompanied her in.

As I slid down from Roger's pony, the head-groom called across to us.

'Don't stand there gawping, boys. You can see we're busy here. Take off your horses' tack and rub them down before they chill.'

Roger dismounted and began to unbuckle his saddle. Before I could work out how best to assist, through the outer gate rode Edward and Elen. They had clearly been abandoned during the charge of the pages.

As I hurried to offer them my services instead, I was surprised at the eagerness on Edward's face at the sight of all the horses and banners.

'Is it my father come home already? We heard that he's on his way, but my mother didn't think he'd be here so soon.'

He wheeled his small pony around and pushed it into a canter towards the inner court. The chickens scratching the earth floor scattered before him.

Elen watched him go, then turned her fond smile on me.

'Forgive him, Matthew. It's more than two months since he saw his father and he misses him terribly – though you'd think he'd be used to his absences. I hope it is the Duke this time. Meanwhile, I will gratefully accept your help.'

I held the old mare's head as Elen alighted on to the mounting block. Then she placed her hand in mine to step down to the ground before bidding me farewell and following in Edward's wake.

As I led the mare away, I reflected on how different Elen was from Alys. She always appeared quiet and calm, and I couldn't imagine her shrieking at anyone as Alys had done at the man who had 'interfered'.

Attending to the horses left little time for conversation, but all the same, I was surprised that Roger said nothing – until it dawned on me that he might not have seen anything. Perhaps he assumed Windfollower had been spooked by a rabbit, or even his own shadow. Nor did he react when we returned Lady to the mews and there met Hugh and Lionel.

Hugh hailed Roger from where he was settling his own bird on to her perch.

'De Kynton – a fine attempt at that rabbit. A shame your hawk was distracted. We must fly them again soon.' There was a smirk in his voice. Was it directed at me? But then he added, 'That is, of course, if the Duke gives you that hawk.'

'He promised her to me. Before he went away.'

'Maybe. Now I hear that he's come home. Perhaps he will see how well she flies and want to keep her. He's gone back on promises before.'

'When? The Duke always keeps his word.'

'Is that so? What about those lands in Westmorland he said should be mine?'

'That was the King's decision,' retorted Roger. 'You know it was. His Grace tried his best. But, anyway, you wouldn't have lost those estates if your father hadn't —'

He stopped, biting his lip.

Hugh's face darkened, visible even in the murk of the mews, and his voice lost its light tone.

'If my father hadn't stayed loyal to his cause? Why don't you say it?' He swung round to me. 'You'll soon find out what these people are really like – that is, if you stay here long enough.'

I pulled Roger away.

'Let's get to supper. It must be nearly time.'

I was now sure Roger hadn't seen anything amiss to cause my horse to bolt. I was glad. Perhaps I was mistaken – perhaps it had been an accident rather than deliberate. Whatever the truth, if no one had seen it, no trouble could be made for Hugh. I had no wish to make him any more my enemy.

At supper the talk amongst the pages was all of how the Duke had come home. It seemed that at last the Scottish border castle of Berwick had fallen to his army and he had hurried south as soon as he could. He had been expected to go first to York at the head of loyal soldiers from the city, but his desire to return to Middleham had made him change his plans.

I was pleased for Edward. But my discomfort grew when I realized his father had been among the riders who had witnessed the shame of my rescue from the bolting horse.

Roger still didn't mention the incident. As Sir William said grace, he only remarked that the Duchess and Edward were not at the high table, and that they must be taking supper in their private chamber with the Duke and his knights. There were faces I didn't recognize in the great hall that evening. I kept my head down in case they, by contrast, recognized me.

After the meal, Roger and I took ourselves into the garden to read the romance that Alys had given me. It was there that she found us a little later.

Her cheeks were flushed as she approached and several curls had escaped from the linen coif she wore over her hair.

'Matt, at last I've found you. The Duke wants to see you.'

I started.

'Who, me?'

'Yes, about this afternoon. Don't look so worried. I told him what happened.'

'What do you mean – what happened?' asked Roger. 'Didn't the horse just bolt? It wasn't Matt's fault.'

'Oh, you! I suppose you were too busy with your precious Lady to see. Hugh – I saw him – he flew his hawk straight at Matt's horse. It was bound to bolt. He'll say it was an accident, but—'

'But I shouldn't have taken the horse in the first place,' I said. 'I knew I wouldn't be able to control it. And when Roger told me it belonged to the Duke…'

'That's no matter now. Come on, he's in his office.'

But still I hung back. I had been scared enough when meeting the Duchess, but now it was to be the Duke – and under such circumstances. I'd been given a chance to better myself, and now that would be ruined.

Alys grasped my sleeve.

'Matt, I'm sure he has lots of things to do on his first night home. You mustn't keep him waiting. Don't be afraid. I'll come in with you.'

With reluctance I gave in to her tug at my arm. In a way this was even worse. It might be good to have a friend with you in a time of trial – but to be shamed in front of Alys, perhaps twice in one day…?

As we hurried along back to the inner court, Alys surprised me by squeezing my arm.

'I'm sure it won't be as bad as you think. His badge may be a white boar, but really he's not half so ferocious.'

If her smile was meant to encourage me, it didn't succeed. I was trembling by the time we reached the office in the corner of the courtyard.

Alys knocked. A voice within called 'Come', and we entered the room together, Alys closing the door behind us.

In the golden light of the setting sun flooding through the window were two men with their backs to us, poring over some papers on a table.

As Alys introduced me – 'Matthew Wansford, Your Grace, the new page' – the taller man turned, and I recognized Alys's rescuer from the afternoon.

At that moment I believed I would have recognized the Duke anywhere. The King was famed as being a golden giant of a man, over six feet tall, who blazed like the sun on his royal banner. Clearly his brother the Duke resembled him in every way.

I stepped forward and knelt down on one knee before him, bowing my head for good measure, hoping I could make up somehow for my disastrous afternoon. As I did, Alys hissed something at me and her toe nudged my leg, but I was too busy trying to make an impression to heed her.

'At your service, Your Grace.'

The man stepped forward, his hand outstretched. But rather than raising me to my feet as I expected, he uttered words that mortified me.

'Nay, boy, I am not he. This is His Grace the Duke of Gloucester.'

I raised my head, as the other man turned to face me, and felt my cheeks aflame with embarrassment. Doubly so because I saw now, not a complete stranger, but the man who had seized my horse that afternoon. His worn leather jerkin had been replaced by a velvet doublet of deep emerald green, stitched with bronze thread and seed pearls, and the dust and dirt of his journey had been washed away. But there was no mistaking him.

He regarded me levelly.

'Well, Master Wansford, am I not what you expected? Perhaps you expected someone more like my brother the King, or Sir Francis here, not the runt of the litter?'

The other man laughed and made to protest, but the Duke waved his words away. Through the tears of shame that had begun to smart in my eyes, I saw a wry smile play about his lips.

'I'm sorry, Your Grace, I mistook you.'

'Nay, it's no matter. Why should you know me? We have never met before today.'

I bowed my head again. This could not have begun worse. I might as well pack up my bundle and leave tonight.

'Come, get to your feet. I'll not have you grovel on the ground. Your reputation precedes you and does not suggest you would. After all, our friend the mayor of York has reported you to us as a troublemaker and rebel.'

That stung me, and I sprang up to defend myself. But as I did, I saw that despite his serious tone, he was mocking me gently.

'But perhaps you are not quite so quick-witted as he would have us believe.'

Alys came to stand next to me, bobbing a tiny curtsey.

'Your Grace, this afternoon, Matthew —' but he cut her short.

'Thank you, Alys, I have heard your story. Now I prefer to hear Master Wansford's version of events. Sit down, Matthew, Alys.'

We pulled up and sat on the stools that he indicated. The Duke perched on the edge of the table.

'So, Master Wansford, tell me what happened.'

My head was whirling at this turn of events. But I had to avoid problems with Hugh if I could.

I swallowed before beginning my story.

'Your Grace, I went riding with some of the pages after dinner. I found that the horse I have ridden before was already taken so I accepted the offer of another. I didn't know at the time it was one of your own horses.'

'But you knew it was too big for you and you would have difficulty handling it?'

'Yes, Your Grace, but – but it would have hurt my pride to refuse. I thought the risk was worth it.'

'And what happened on your ride?'

'Some of the pages stopped to hunt rabbits with their falcons. My horse was frightened by something and bolted because I couldn't control it.'

'By something?' His eyes narrowed.

'Yes, Your Grace. By something.'

The Duke continued to gaze at me, twisting a small ruby ring on his finger for a few moments. Then he spoke again.

'I watched you from the road as you guided the horse away from the moat. It might have broken its neck or your own. Then you turned it from the marketplace where villagers, children perhaps, could have been injured or killed by a bolting horse. Somehow you kept your seat and by that you prevented both things. Well done. You may make a good horseman yet – on a suitable mount. We shall have to find you one – better than the old mare Alys tells me you have been riding, but not yet one so young and inexperienced as Windfollower. I will ask my horse master.'

He stood up and, sensing I was about to be dismissed, so did I.

'Her Grace tells me that you also sing well. I would be pleased if you would sing for me soon. Meanwhile,' that half-smile returned – 'meanwhile, Matthew, think twice before trying to protect someone who doesn't deserve it.'

With that he turned again to his desk and in a moment was deep in conversation with his companion.

I followed Alys back out of the office. I didn't know whether to feel elated at the praise I had received or disappointed at my mistakes – and the fact that perhaps, despite my resolve, I might have caused trouble for Hugh.

'Well, that wasn't too bad,' Alys said as we recrossed the court.

'Too bad?' I exclaimed. 'I mistook him for one of his knights. I haven't been so humiliated since...'

Into my memory swam the angry faces of the choir master, with his freshly blackened eye, and the master of the Minster School on the day I was expelled.

I fell silent. Perhaps it hadn't been so long.

'He won't hold that against you. Anyway you should have taken notice of my warning.'

'When I was already on my knees? Why didn't you tell me before?'

'I thought you knew who he was. How was I to know you'd be foolish enough to kneel to the wrong man?'

She had a point. How could I have been so stupid as to assume what someone would look like? No one had described him to me. Why should I suppose a valiant knight to be as large as his reputation? Perhaps there was hope for me if such a man could rise to become the greatest general in the land.

'Anyway, I wish you hadn't told him about Hugh,' I said, voicing my main worry.

'What was I to do?' Alys's green eyes flashed in the last rays of the evening sunshine. 'Let you take the blame for choosing the wrong horse and letting it run away with you?'

'If anything happens to Hugh because of it, if he is beaten for it, I'll be blamed by him instead. He already hates me.'

'Then you'll just have to stand up to him. If nothing else, you'll know that you're in the right.'

66

'I'm not sure that will be any comfort if he and his friends look for revenge.'

8

'Be Thou a Good Knight'

It's safe to say I watched my back over the next few days – as did Roger and Alys – after we saw Hugh come to breakfast late next morning and sit very gingerly on the bench.

Roger nudged me and whispered to me under a pretence of quaffing from his cup of ale.

'Edward told me this morning that his father spoke to the under-groom last night. He said Hugh had paid him money to give the old mare to Elen and saddle the young grey for you. Ed said it was likely Hugh would be beaten this morning.'

Despite our vigilance and the fact that Hugh seemed to be avoiding me, I was still uneasy. What he had said in the mews kept coming back to me.

A day or two after the Duke's return, I asked Roger whether Lady had been given to him yet.

'The falconer told me yesterday that the Duke wants to see her fly. He said perhaps we can ride out and test her soon if this good weather continues.'

From his carefree manner I guessed he had forgotten Hugh's words. And, as the days passed, so did I begin to.

There was no change in routine after the Duke's return as there had been with the Duchess. The only difference was that Edward was happier, and then, after my singing lesson on the Saturday, Sir William told me I would be singing in the chapel for High Mass the following day.

My stomach was fluttering when I rose from my mattress in the half-light of the early morning, and scared dark eyes stared back at me from the watery depths of the pail before I plunged my hands in to wash. But Roger helped me to ready myself, lending me his comb to drag through my unruly brown hair and brushing down my best doublet for me, talking nonsense to me all the while. By the time I met Sir William in the chapel, my nerves had steadied.

As the Mass began, it felt good to be part of a choir again, even if I was the only boy among just seven choristers. I joined in the alleluias as required in the service and sang descant to the men's plainsong. Sir William had even rehearsed some polyphony with us all together that week, although a single boy's voice was almost lost within the intricate tapestry woven by such songs. Then I sang alone the *laude* the chaplain had chosen to welcome the Duke home. My heart swelled with pride as my voice filled the little chapel, while the sun streaming through the windows stained the upturned faces of the congregation all the colours of creation.

After the service, in the vestry below the chapel, Sir William was so delighted he shook my hand up and down until my arm hurt.

'Well done, Matthew, well done. You could not have sung better. I'm sure the Duke will be very pleased.'

Roger and Alys had followed us down. Their praise was not quite so fulsome.

'You'd better be careful, Matt. The Minster School might want you back after that.'

'Don't be daft, Roger. There was far too much spirit in that final song – not enough discipline. I don't think he'd fit in now.'

I wondered about the truth of Alys's words as we made our way to the great hall for breakfast. It had felt different, for the first time singing alone in front of the altar. Perhaps these past few weeks had changed me.

Alys made her way to her own seat, while Roger and I stood waiting for the Duke and Duchess and the little procession of high officials. When they entered, the Duke broke away and came over to our table.

As all the pages bowed, he said,

'That was well sung, Matthew. As fine as anything I have heard in London or Cambridge. If you are willing I should like you to sing every morning at Mass. I will ask Sir William to order vestments for you, smart though your doublet looked. Oh, and I haven't forgotten my promise. Report to the horse master after dinner tomorrow.'

Nodding to us, he followed his family up to the high table. As I watched him go, I caught sight of Hugh staring at me with a scowl. I bowed my head quickly as Sir William began grace.

The next afternoon, Alys, Roger and Edward accompanied me to the stables. Edward had been excited all morning, hinting that he had a secret he couldn't tell. We humoured him, knowing full well what it was about.

Master Reynold, the horse master, was waiting for us. A wiry, bandy-legged man, he was always gruff with the pages, but as gentle with his animals as if they were babies. As the four of us approached, he barked instructions to some under-grooms who took flight like startled birds into different doorways.

'Wait here,' he said to me and ducked into the nearest stable.

Hooves clattered in the darkness and he returned leading a bright bay pony, fully harnessed, with a pair of tall riding boots slung over the saddle.

'His Grace says you're to have the use of this horse while you're at the castle, at least until you grow too big for her. Her name's Bess. And as you have no boots, these are to be yours too.'

I stammered my thanks, but Master Reynold brushed them aside, waiting while I pulled the boots on, then bending to give me a leg up into the saddle.

I patted Bess on her sleek neck, and her ears twitched, but her hooves remained planted on the cobbles. Sitting there felt a world away from when I was astride Windfollower. The ground seemed a sensible distance beneath me and my legs hung comfortably in the stirrups.

Meanwhile the stable lads had brought out the others' horses and soon the four of us were trotting out of the castle, down through the village and towards the water meadows.

I hesitated before leaving the road, embarrassed at the memory of what had happened here only days before, but Roger clapped me on the shoulder as he passed.

'Come on, Matt,' he called, kicking his horse into a canter.

With Alys and Edward following his lead, my Bess pulled at her reins, eager to join in. Another moment's indecision, then I allowed her her head, pursuing the others along the river bank, feeling the thrill of speed, without the fear of destruction.

That was the first of many such afternoons, during which I came to know the local meadows, woodlands, and moors in the company of my now firm friends. The harsh landscape became less alien to me, though I was never quite at ease upon the moor tops. There the heather and bracken stretched for miles all around, and Roger and Alys appeared to navigate by the sun alone rather than any features I could recognize.

One afternoon, when we arrived at the stables, Duke Richard was there talking to Master Reynold. He was clad once more in an old leather jerkin and looped over his arm were the reins of the magnificent grey stallion he'd been riding the day he had rescued me. I now knew this to be his favourite, Storm, Windfollower's sire.

As we bowed and curtsied to him – even Edward – he nodded to us, saying,

'I find I have an afternoon free of other duties. As Edward tells me you ride out most days, I thought I would join you if I may. Your horses are being saddled. Roger, if you feel today would be suitable, you might go and prepare your hawk.'

Roger's smile was broad as he headed to the mews. In a matter of minutes, we four friends were riding towards the riverside meadows with the Duke of Gloucester at our head, Lady perched hooded on his gauntleted fist. Who was happiest among the company, I cannot say: Edward riding his fat little pony at his father's stirrup, chatting busily about anything and nothing, Roger at the prospect of taking possession of the hawk, or me – me, simply being there.

The afternoon was one of the last of that golden summer. The leaves on the trees fringing the river were taking on their autumn shades and in the valley the last fruits of the harvest were being gathered in. But my eyes and ears that afternoon were all for the beauty of that soaring, swooping falcon, for Edward's delighted shouts as his father launched her from atop his galloping horse, for the jewel-hued feathers of the swinging lure, the cry of the plummeting bird, the fire of Alys's curls and in her eyes, Roger's pride as he knelt to accept the promised gift as though being knighted by his liege lord, the Duke's laughter as he hauled him back to his feet by grasping Roger's only free hand, Lady now being perched lightly on the other.

At last we straggled back up to the castle for supper. Edward rode a little ahead with his father, while Alys, Roger and I talked of how much we had learnt from Duke Richard that afternoon about riding and hawking. As the three of us reached the stables, Edward was waiting alone, watching the grooms unsaddling both greys, the Duke's mighty stallion and Ed's little pony. All the happiness had been drained from him.

'What's the matter?' asked Alys, as we dismounted.

'My father's speaking to the horse master,' he told us. 'About preparations for tomorrow morning. He's leaving to go to York. The city's giving him and his soldiers a reception for his victory in Scotland. I asked if I could go too. He said the journey would be too long for me and the day too boring, and then he has to stay for business.'

'You should be grateful that he's saved you, then,' said Roger. But the frown on Alys's face showed she was thinking the same as me. That Edward, having just got his beloved father back, believed he was losing him again.

'We should do something special as well,' I said.

Alys glanced at me as she handed her mount to a stable lad.

'You're right, Matt. Perhaps – perhaps we could ask permission to have a holiday. Maybe miss our lessons and spend the day on the moor? We could take our dinner with us – bread and cheese or cold meat. I'll ask your mother after dinner, Ed.'

Edward brightened at that, and took her hand as we walked back towards the inner court. As they chatted about what to do, my thoughts were on the Duke travelling to my home city, being attended and feted there by my father and his fellow councilmen. In my mind's eye I saw my mother, brothers and sisters among the crowds cheering His Grace for keeping the Scottish raiders away. My stomach churned with homesickness for the first time in many days. But perhaps, another time, if I continued my training at the castle, it might be me riding in with the Duke to such cheers.

After supper, Alys sought out Roger and me to give us the news.

'The Duchess spoke with Duke Richard. They've given us all a holiday tomorrow. She said it was an excellent idea. We can celebrate both his victory and his safe return. She said why should it be just the people of York who do that?'

Next morning in the vestry I slipped on the surplice and collar that had newly arrived for me, and for the first time truly felt the part as I processed into the chapel for Mass. I sang for the Duke that day, aware that later my former fellow choristers would be doing the same in the airy, light-filled space of York Minster, crammed with all the worthies of the city. May the Lord forgive me my pride that he had chosen to hear my voice alone – while those of John Burton and his friends would be swallowed up in the sounds of all the other singers.

After breakfast, the whole household assembled in the outer courtyard to see the Duke and his party off on their journey. As when I had first laid eyes on him, he rode at the head of the company on Storm. But this time he and all his knights were clad in garments of the brightest hues and his standard of a white boar on a murrey and blue background was unfurled above them, fluttering in the early breeze. The Duke leaned down for a final embrace of his wife and son, then the household trumpeter sounded a clarion call and we all cheered as the riders clattered away over the outer drawbridge.

I and my friends rode out the same gateway an hour or two later, with less fanfare, but with the words of the Duchess ringing in our ears – a warning not to ride too far and to rest in the shade when we could. It was another sun-filled day, though there had been an autumnal nip in the air at first wakening.

As usual Alys and Roger led the way and soon we were cantering up the dale in the lea of Pen Hill, the river far down the slope to our right. When we slowed to a walk, I was riding alongside Edward, and before long we were chatting about my father, and about his, and about the countryside through which the Duke would now be riding, until the twin towers of York Minster rose up on the horizon.

From York, our conversation turned to my brothers and sisters and how much I missed them, even the baby.

'She'll be crawling by now, and getting under everyone's feet. My elder brothers will be picking her up and tossing her to each other, like they did when my younger brother was a baby. It used to terrify my mother – but Peter was always giggling with delight.'

'I have no brothers or sisters,' Edward said, his face wistful. What his mother said to me on our first meeting slid into my mind, and I changed the subject quickly.

We halted for our dinner in the shade of some straggly hawthorn bushes on the river bank far upstream. As Alys laid out a rug, and I helped her spread upon it our meagre meal of bread and cheese, Roger pulled from his pouch a folded piece of parchment.

'Look what I received from my mother this morning. She wrote because she's so proud of my uncle. She says he is to be made a knight of the Order of the Bath. It's for his service with the Duke in Scotland.'

'That's one of the greatest honours anyone can have from the King,' said Edward, hewing at the slab of crumbly white cheese with his knife. 'I know because my father told me. He was made a knight of the Order – oh, so many years ago. When he was only a boy.'

'Really?' I asked. I knew a little about the ancient chivalric orders. 'I didn't think they'd allow boys in.'

'He was made a Duke at the same time,' said Edward. 'But I remember more of what he told me about the Order's ceremony. I suppose it was because he was bathed by other grown-up knights rather than his nurse. Then he had to stay awake all night to keep vigil with them in the royal chapel.'

'That doesn't sound much fun,' said Roger.

'He said he could hardly keep his eyes open, but he had to otherwise they wouldn't have thought him worthy. Then in the morning they dressed him in ceremonial clothes and took him to his brother the King. The King buckled a sword around his waist, kissed him, then struck him on the cheek.'

'Wasn't it painful?' I asked.

'Not really. He said it was just to remind him of his vow. The King said "Be thou a good knight" as he did it. He says he has always tried to be.'

We were silent for a few moments. Perhaps, like me, they were all imagining the spectacle. But in my mind also was whether I could ever dare hope for the honour myself.

As if echoing my thoughts, Edward said,

'Do you think my uncle Edward will ever make me a knight of the Bath? Or of the Garter?'

A dimple deepened on Alys's cheek and Roger's mouth twitched, but neither of them laughed.

'I think you may have to wait a few more years, Ed.'

'But my father was younger than I am when he was knighted – only eight.'

'But your father's father had been killed with many of his knights, and his brother had just become King,' soothed Alys. 'I think that counts as a special case. The King needed all the knights he could get.'

'Perhaps,' said Edward, but the corners of his mouth turned down in disappointment.

On impulse I said, 'Why don't we form our own order of chivalry, like the Bath or the Garter?'

Roger laughed.

'You've been reading too many romances!'

But Alys said, 'Yes, why don't we?'

74

Roger opened his mouth again, but Alys nudged him with her foot.

'Come on, Roger. It would be fun for Edward – for all of us. We could have our own rituals and symbols and everything.'

'All right, but perhaps we should keep it secret.'

Was he thinking about Hugh and his cronies?

'Even better,' I said. 'That way it'll be just the four of us, no one else wanting to join and interfering.'

'I'll have to tell my mother,' said Edward.

'Why not?' said Alys. 'We won't do anything she'll disapprove of. But what shall we call ourselves? An order has to have a name.'

We all gazed around and above us, casting about for ideas from things that we could see.

'The Knights of the Thorn?'

'The Order of the Buzzard?'

'The Knights of the Dead Sheep?'

'Roger!' said Alys sharply, and he and Edward sniggered.

All the talk of chivalry and ceremony brought to my mind the sights and sounds of this morning and the enormous standard that had streamed above the Duke as he left with his knights.

'What about the Order of the White Boar?'

They all stared at me.

'In honour of the Duke?'

'What a good idea.'

'I think my mother would like that – and my father.'

'That's settled then,' said Alys.

She picked up Edward's riding crop. Kneeling in front of him, her head bowed, she presented it to him with two hands.

'My lord, if you are willing, you shall knight us here on the battlefield. Well, it almost looks like it with that dead sheep over there. Then we can arrange the rituals and do it again properly later.'

Edward giggled and took the proffered whip.

Roger and I knelt either side of Alys, our heads likewise bowed. He touched us lightly on each shoulder with the tip of the crop, then said, 'I don't have to strike you, do I?'

Alys got to her feet hurriedly, brushing dust from the front of her gown.

'I think we can save that for later – if we feel it's a valid part of the ceremony. I'm not sure the King does it to the Garter

75

knights. They're all nobles I think, and it might cause another civil war if he did.'

'I'm sure we'll remember our duty as knights without it anyway,' said Roger. 'We'll have to swear an oath to uphold the King's law, protect all women and children –' Alys snorted – 'well, those who can't protect themselves – always be loyal to one another, that sort of thing.'

'That's my father's motto,' piped up Edward. 'Loyaulté me lie – loyalty binds me. I'm sure he'd be happy at that.'

'And of course be loyal to him – our liege lord,' continued Roger. 'Maybe it should be the Order's motto too.'

'Maybe,' said Alys. 'Anyway we can talk about it all as we ride home. I think we should head back now – then we'll have time to start drawing up our rules before supper.'

The ride back was taken up entirely with talk of the Order and what our small band of companions would entail. We decided to let only Elen in on our secret. As Alys said, she might be useful for taking messages. Being both a servant and a member of the household, she was able to move everywhere around the castle more freely than either Alys or the pages.

'I don't think she'll want to join herself. She doesn't much enjoy riding or hawking or any of the other things we'll do.'

'Is that what we'll be doing? It doesn't sound so very different from now.'

'Oh, Ed, of course it'll be different. From now on we'll know we're part of a secret order, and that we'll be loyal to each other and our lord until death – like real knights.'

Edward must have run to tell his mother as soon as we returned to the castle. Before supper, the Duchess paused at our table on her way to the dais and said, simply, to Roger and me,

'Thank you for all you're doing for Edward. He's as happy today as if his father had not gone away.'

As she walked on, I made certain not to glance in Hugh's direction, in case there was once more on his face that look of hatred and spite I so well remembered.

9

Autumn

As the days shortened and became cooler, and autumn slowly descended into Wensleydale, my previous life seemed like a dream. My life in the castle was now all that was real for me.

Our brief holiday behind us, we returned to lessons. The schoolroom was chill now in the early mornings, and rain often curtained the open windows.

In a few days, the Duke returned from York. Alys reported to us his surprise at seeing Edward looking so well.

'Usually he mopes around when the Duke's away, and even Roger's clowning can't cheer him up. It was such a good idea of yours, Matt, to start the Order.'

I protested that the idea had been as much hers, but was secretly pleased to have such praise. We had spent several afternoons closeted all together in the empty pages' chamber, discussing the Order's rituals and rules, and I had felt my contributions were as valued as anyone else's. And as it was determined that mine was the neatest handwriting, I was also chosen as our scribe and the keeper of all our secret documents. Everything was folded neatly when complete and stored at the very bottom of my bundle of belongings.

By the time of the Duke's return, we had each sworn our oath of loyalty while dressed in the robe of the Order (Edward's finest blue velvet cloak stitched with gold thread, which barely reached Roger's knees), drunk the draught of friendship (again from Edward's best gold cup), and had our venture blessed by Sir William, whom we also took into our confidence – at least as far as to tell him that we intended to be a band of true friends from this time forth.

Sir William seemed to understand the seriousness of the occasion. He dressed himself in his most festive clerical garments to intone the solemn words, lay his hands reverently on each of our heads and join us in supping the friendship draught.

I spluttered at the strength of the wine.

'Where did you get this, Ed?'

'It's from my father's private store. Only he and Master Guylford have a key to it – but I know where he puts his when he goes away.'

We had reason, a week or two later, to hope that the Duke's and the steward's eyes were not sharp enough to detect that Ed had taken the wine. That store and many others were opened for the festivities for His Grace's thirtieth birthday.

The day began with a special Mass and sermon from Sir William in the village church, giving thanks for preserving the Duke through this his thirtieth year. It was attended by local noble families, the mayor of York, and other dignitaries from the city and surrounding towns.

All at the castle were given another holiday to celebrate along with the villagers. This time it involved sports and competitions, in archery and feats of arms, followed by feasting and entertainments. A dancing bear was brought from York especially for the evening. Then the ladies and gentlemen also danced, and music continued late into the night.

As the torches began to splutter out, but before we were left with just the dark red glow of the fire to cast shadows into the rafters of the great hall, the Duke rose.

After a few words of thanks to those who were still awake, he bowed deeply. Then, taking the hand of his wife, he led her from the hall into their private chambers. Edward, blinking rapidly and almost tripping over his feet in his tiredness, followed them. The dying light of the torches glinted off the brand new cloth-of-gold tunic he had been given by his father to mark the occasion.

Before long the rest of the company also retired. Within seconds of us reaching our mattresses, Roger's gentle snores began to break the darkness and the deep breathing of our fellow pages slowed as one by one they too fell asleep. But I lay awake a little longer, turning over in my fingers the gold coin the Duke had presented to each of us in celebration of his special day. I offered up silent thanks for having been a part of it – and also for our being excused Mass and morning lessons the next day.

After the long warm summer, autumn was all too brief that year. The damp days were dark under low heavy clouds from dawn until dusk, and a day or two of October gales tore the last of the golden leaves from the ancient, stunted oaks and hawthorns that lined the lanes around the castle. By All Souls Day the once-gilt bracken on the moor tops was a sombre dark brown, and everywhere we rode lay pools of brackish water, dark grey beneath the November skies.

But as the dour weather drove us all to spend more time indoors, and Roger became fretful at us not wanting to ride, I didn't mind the change. For me, there was more time to talk with Alys and Edward, and the Duke and Duchess summoned me often into their chamber to sing during the dark evenings after supper.

Once I was there, Ed would ask me to read to him, or share with him simple tunes on the lute. I was still a novice player, having picked up a lute for the first time only here in the castle. But Master Petyt soon declared I was a natural and invited me to take proper lessons. Before long he had found an old instrument for me, battered but serviceable, and I would practise with it on my free afternoons as well as during evenings in the great chamber. I blushed at my mistakes, but the Duke would often break off from whatever business he was conducting, with the steward or the chamberlain, hush his companion and listen too.

Those evenings were a delight to me. Not only did I love to sing, and now to play the lute, and to read aloud the new French romances to Edward. I also had the chance to see how this lordly family spent their leisure time.

The Duke was often at his books or papers, perhaps with Master Guylford or his secretary, Master Kendall, perhaps alone. At other times he would play at chess with the Duchess or his good friend Sir Francis Lovell, the gentleman I had mistaken for him. Sometimes he would simply sit back in his great carved chair and watch his wife as she sewed in the smoky light cast by the torches, or his son playing jacks on the huge hearthstone. At such times I would see a wistfulness in his eyes that was only banished when I brought my final song to a close. Then he would clap his hands two or three times fit to summon an echo from the high vaulted ceiling above, spring to his feet and, catching up a tray set ready by a servant, offer all of us in the room a cup of spiced wine and some small sweetmeats – honey biscuits or marchpane.

Sometimes Alys would be there, undertaking some small task for the Duchess or sitting sewing on a small footstool, as I had seen her that first evening. She would toss her pale gold curls, and accept the wine cup and tidbit. Then, work over for the day, she would tug at my sleeve and draw me over to the hearth to play or read with Ed. My one regret on those evenings was that Roger was not with us.

But Alys was not there either one evening, deep into November, when, cup of wine on a small table at my elbow, I sat trying to bring to mind a tune Master Petyt had started to teach me that afternoon. As I plucked at the strings, I heard the Duchess's voice raised.

'But, Richard, you made him a promise before you went away.'

She was sitting in her usual chair a little behind me, and a moment before her husband had seated himself beside her. He spoke now, more softly, but my ears had been caught.

'Peace, my dear, I would not want the lad to hear.'

Thinking he meant me, I turned my attention to my lute again. But the Duchess's next words told me it was not me they were speaking of, but Ed. Out of loyalty to him – and sheer curiosity – I could not fail to listen.

'He is your son, Richard, and longs always to be at your side. In the spring you promised you would take him hunting this winter. All summer while you were in Scotland he spoke of little else.'

'All summer after he had been so ill?'

'That is months ago now. He has had no attack since April. He has grown stronger day by day since he has been here at home. Particularly since he has been riding out with his friends.'

'But that is not a hunt, Anne.'

'He can remain on his pony all the time. And his friends can look after him. It will do him good. And it's important that we treat him the same as every other page.'

'Although he is our son?'

'You were the brother of the King when you came here all those years ago – but my father treated you no differently from the other pages in his care. We may not choose to send Ed away, but do not let him think he is not as good as the rest.'

There was a pause in their conversation, but I made sure there was no pause in my quiet picking of the strings.

Then the Duke's voice came again.

'You say his friends can look after him?'

'Of course. Roger, Matthew, Alys —'

'Alys!' He sounded surprised, but my surprise was at the mention of my name.

'Why not?'

'A girl – on a boar hunt?'

'Fie to that, Richard. You never questioned when I rode to the hunt.'

'Maybe. But you —'

'But I was my father's daughter?'

'Yes, Anne, indeed you were. Although I think cousin Richard sometimes thought you were a son.'

'Well, Alys is her father's daughter too. You remember Sir Philip Langdown – he was a fine jouster. And you know her, how well she rides.'

Although my back was to them, I had now seen enough of this husband and wife in their private time to imagine how they looked. He with a half-smile now playing around his lips, she with her grey eyes alight at his gentle mockery, but also at the chance of winning her point.

'True, she is another daughter who rides as well as any son. Her father also would no doubt have been proud of her. But as you well know, a boar hunt does not call for skilled riding. It is a time for discipline and strength and staying safe.'

'You say the squires and older pages will take part. Have two or three remain on horseback with the younger ones – let them see the sport but remain at a distance.'

'Perhaps. I will think on it and speak to Master Gygges.'

Master Gygges was the chief huntsman, in charge of all the hounds and huntsmen at the castle, and of supplying the game meat to the kitchens. Over the next few days, I made sure my friends and I wandered often into his domain in case preparations were being made for the hunt the Duke and Duchess had discussed. But all seemed as normal. I had told no one what I had overheard, not wanting to raise Edward's or Alys's – or indeed my own – hopes about the prospect. The Duke had not sounded convinced by his wife's words, and I heard no more about a hunt on those evenings when I sang for them. Not that I tried to eavesdrop on their private conversations – often.

But one afternoon after our ride, Alys and Ed were called to attend the Duchess, and Roger and I again made our way to the kennels. Entering the low building, we breathed in with enjoyment the deep musky scent of the hounds before, as usual, letting ourselves into the pen of Florette, the Duke's favourite.

The tall white hound was strong and fit again, and her pups were well grown, reaching now as high as her flank. All bar one, at least – the small red pup I had noticed on my first visit.

A few days ago, when I had persuaded Roger and the others to visit the kennels with me, this red pup had hung back at our approach. It stuck close to its mother, growling a little, while its larger brothers and sisters bounded forward with tails awag. But I had spent time with it each afternoon and had taught it to trust me. Now it came straight to me on its still-wobbly legs, nudging its warm, soft muzzle into my hand in greeting, while the others fussed around the morsels of meat that Roger had brought.

'It won't be long before they're fully weaned and can leave their mother,' Roger said as he pulled apart two scuffling puppies rolling about in a squabble over a tidbit.

'That'll be a relief to her, I'm sure,' said I. I had felt the sharp teeth of the pups as they snapped at the treats we brought, and even now the red pup was gnawing at the tough leather toe of my riding boot.

The heavy wooden door of the kennels creaked open again and we straightened up to see who had entered. The place was usually quiet at this time, after the final feed of the day.

To our surprise, it was Duke Richard himself, in quiet conversation with Master Gygges. They had walked almost half the length of the building before they spied us there in the murk. Now, seeing us bowing low before them, they broke off their talk.

'Well, boys,' said the Duke as he came up to the pen. 'How is my Florette today?'

'Lusty and strong and at Your Grace's service,' said the huntsman before we could reply.

The Duke leaned on the side of the pen, his quick eyes watching the puppies fighting around our legs. Florette herself came up to him and he fondled her ears.

'Ready for the chase, are you, girl? And how about you, boys?'

He raised his head to look at us, and Roger and I exchanged a glance. There was a sudden light in Roger's eyes.

'Your Grace?'

'I am riding to Pontefract tomorrow for a few days' business and I have a mind to raise a hunt on my return. The monks of Jervaulx Abbey have complained to me that boars have been damaging their orchards and there is a chance of some fine sport. You are rather young to join us —'

'But Your Grace!' protested Roger, but the Duke silenced him with a wave of his hand.

'You are rather young, but you may join us if you wish – if you promise to remain on your horses and away from the fray.'

'Of course, Your Grace – we promise.'

'And – and Edward will ride with us.'

'Edward?'

'Aye. You shall take care of him during the hunt.'

Roger hesitated. Without thinking, I answered for him.

'Of course, Your Grace. You can trust us.'

The Duke regarded me levelly for a few moments. I returned his gaze.

'Yes, I think I can.' He straightened up again. 'Master Gygges will give you your instructions while I am away as you have never hunted boar before. You must obey them to the letter. I will have no accidents that can be avoided.'

He nodded, patted Florette once more, slipped her a tidbit and was gone, the huntsman at his heels.

Roger turned to me, his eyes shining.

'A boar hunt!'

The Duke's words about accidents still sounded in my ears. I swallowed.

'How dangerous are boars?'

10

The Boar Hunt

By the time the Duke arrived home from his business, I had learnt just how dangerous boars could be. Master Gygges took great delight in filling us younger boys in on all the details. I began to regret my eagerness to be helpful.

Roger was far too happy at the chance to go on a hunt to notice my worries, even if we would only be watching. Alys, though, was more observant.

When the three of us met up after an early breakfast on the icy, sunlit morning of the hunt, she laid her hand on my arm. Her breath plumed in the wintry air as she said,

'Keep with Ed and me, Matt. There's no shame in protecting a girl and young lad as the Duke bid you.'

I felt my cheeks redden, though Roger showed no sign of having heard her. He was busy scanning the courtyard for the arrival of the Duke and his entourage. I wanted neither of them to think me a coward, but I had in truth been shaken by all the tales of gorings and slashings by the tusks of boars at bay.

I hadn't foreseen what a major event the hunt would be. All normal activities ground to a halt as the party mustered in the stableyard. It seemed everyone who lived or worked in the castle turned out to watch, despite the bitter weather.

A group of the very youngest pages were marshalled under the eye of Sir William. Their grumbling and complaints reached my ears as we walked past.

'Look, even a girl is going.'

'And the merchant's son. But not us!'

'Ignore them,' said Alys. 'They're just envious. And think of the trust the Duke has placed in us.'

Dozens of horses were gathered outside the stables waiting for their riders, stamping and shifting from hoof to hoof in the frosty air. Once I had mounted Bess, and Roger and Alys were being helped into their saddles by under-grooms, I had a better view of the gathering.

Hugh and Lionel were laughing and joking among the squires and older pages. Both were resplendent in what appeared to be new hunting clothes, trimmed with fur against the morning chill.

Clustered in groups around them were various gentlemen from the castle and beyond. Among them were Sir Francis, Sir Richard Ratcliffe, another of the Duke's household knights, and the burly figure of Lord Scrope, whom I had seen at the Duke's birthday celebrations. Loosely held in his hand were the reins of a superb midnight-black stallion, whose flanks were already steaming in the cold air. I supposed he had ridden over for the sport from his home at nearby Bolton Castle. He had not been at breakfast with the others and now he was tearing wolfishly at a hunk of bread and honey while talking with Sir Francis and Sir Richard. All three of them hailed Master Gygges, just then emerging from the kennels, accompanied by the clamour of the still unseen hounds.

When most of the gathering had mounted, Duke Richard and his family appeared. Edward was already ahorse, but the Duke's mount, smaller than Storm but another grey, was led by a groom. He himself walked alongside his wife.

All muffled in furs, the Duchess took from a serving woman a tray of small silver cups from which steam was rising and offered them to household knights and local gentlemen. The final two she handed to Edward and her husband, who by now had also mounted. Some of Sir William's pages circulated with similar trays until everyone in the company had been served. I cradled my wooden cup to warm my frozen fingers.

The Duke leant down to kiss his wife's hand, then saluted her with his cup, before raising it to the crowd.

'Good fortune to our hunt today,' he cried and drank the contents straight down.

A cheer rose from the throng as everyone followed his lead. Except me. I sipped my drink gingerly at first, remembering my previous taste of the Duke's wine. But this delicious brew was not only hot but spiced, and it crept throughout my body like the warmth of a roaring fire.

The cheer set the hounds baying once more and now at last they were released from the kennels. Most were held on leather leashes, but some, including Florette, were free. I watched as the white hound slipped between the legs of horses and houndsmen and found her master without hesitation. Then the armourer finished passing out boar spears to those who needed them and it was time for the off.

The Duke and his son, clad in matching hunting garb of a rich royal blue, rode at the head of the procession, flanked by Sir Francis and Sir Richard and the other gentlemen. The squires came next, marshalled by Master Fleete, and Alys, Roger and I fell into line behind them, while the grooms and huntsmen with the hounds brought up the rear.

Roger's face was flushed as he urged his horse on. Did my face mirror his? And was the colour caused by excitement or the wine?

We passed the Duchess, standing with Elen and several ladies in waiting. She raised her hand to us.

'Take care of my Edward,' she called.

I doffed my cap and bowed low to her from my saddle.

'We will, Your Grace. Never fear.'

Then Bess carried me on. In a few moments we had passed out of the main gateway and were trotting down to the York road, then on towards Jervaulx.

The pace was fast enough to make it difficult to talk. I didn't mind. Now we were on the road and I had seen the size of the boar spears – and maybe because of the wine – I was feeling less nervous.

Master Gygges had told me about the spears. They were razor sharp, with an iron bar across about an arm's length down from the point. This cross-piece would stop a charging boar in its tracks. Otherwise, Master Gygges said, even with the spear point rammed into its chest, the animal could force its way along the length of the spear to reach the hunter and gore him. I wasn't sure I believed him. But the sight of those cross-pieces was reassuring.

Not that I or the other members of the Order had been given spears. We had been told, very firmly, to stay well outside the circle of hunters and to watch from there. But all the same, it was good to know the boar couldn't escape the ring once it was flushed out of its lair.

Before long we reached the gatehouse of Jervaulx Abbey. Waiting for us was a knot of pale-clad monks, one man at their head more richly dressed in a fur-lined velvet cloak and with a great gilt crucifix nestled on his chest.

Following the Duke's lead, we all swung down from our mounts and knelt on the hard, frost-pointed earth of the roadway. The hounds were hushed by their handlers.

The abbot intoned a blessing before raising the Duke to his feet and bowing low to him in his turn. They spoke for a few minutes with Master Gygges and one of the monks. Then they clasped hands and the Duke and his huntsman returned to their mounts.

Setting off again, we passed an orchard of close-ranked, bare-limbed trees, glimpsing here and there a wizened red apple amidst the dark boughs. Then came the low scrub and whippy stems of a coppiced woodland which, like that near the castle, must supply faggots for the abbey's fires to warm the monks and cook their food. Soon, up ahead reared the giant black trunks of a true forest. Here the Duke raised his gloved hand to halt the company again.

We all dismounted once more, hearing the crackle of frozen fallen leaves beneath our feet.

The grooms made their way forward to take the reins of the gentlemen's horses. Following them came the huntsmen with their leashed charges – a mixture of short-legged thick-set dogs to flush out the boar, tall sight-hounds to chase it if it should run, and powerful-jawed mastiff-like brutes called alaunts to attack it when it was at bay. They were all silent now, their noses questing the air for scent.

Alys, Roger and I waited with our horses as we had been instructed. Master Gygges pushed his way towards us through the crowd of men and beasts, leading Edward, still atop his grey pony. He nodded to us, then gazed around at those of the oldest pages closest to us.

'Master Pynson,' he called, and a senior page I knew only by sight stepped forward leading his mount.

'Master de Bruyn.' I groaned inwardly as Lionel turned with a scowl.

'Master Soulsby.'

Hugh's face was impassive as he swung round.

'You three are to have the care of the youngest here. You will remain on your horses and clear of the hunt circle. Mind you pay close attention to the boys – and my lady Alys. The Duke will be watching.'

With that Master Gygges thrust Ed's lead rein into Hugh's hand and stalked back towards the front of the company. He was swallowed up by the throng of gentlemen in an instant.

Hugh looked at us, curled his lip, then turned his back.

'Well, Lionel, Giles, we must do the Duke's bidding, as always. It's babysitting for us rather than standing in the ring with the hunters. Much pleasure it will bring us, no doubt.'

What came over me I don't know. Perhaps the wine.

'I don't see boar spears in your hands, Master Soulsby, Master de Bruyn. Maybe Master Gygges doesn't trust you in the ring with the real hunters.'

Hugh twisted round, his fist raised.

'You little —'

But Roger slipped quickly between us.

'Now then, Matt. Hugh has no need of a boar spear. He would run the beast through with his piercing wit before anyone else had a chance. Is that not so, Hugh? Edward?'

He appealed to Ed, staring wide-eyed down at us.

Hugh glanced at Ed, then at me, and drew back. Was he remembering his last beating?

He forced a laugh.

'Yes, that's right, of course. I would hate to deprive our fellow hunters of their sport. Come, the hunt is setting off.'

One or two of the hounds were giving tongue again and a horn sounded up ahead. The gentlemen and squires were moving off on foot. Hugh and the two other chosen ones swung up into their saddles to follow.

Roger shot me a puzzled look.

'Why did you provoke him?'

I shrugged and gathered Bess's reins in my hands. Soon the four of us, on horseback again, were trekking after the hunting party as they entered the woods on foot. Behind us their horses were led by the grooms in case they should be wanted.

As we wound our way through the trees, the early sunshine was blotted out by gathering cloud and a biting wind arose, rustling the last shrivelled leaves clinging to the branches. From my vantage point on Bess, I could see the pale ghosts of the hounds as they cast about for scent, sometimes hear one baying as it found a trail.

The hunt was spread out in a great fan, rippling like waves to follow first one hound, then another, as Master Gygges's horn directed. To steer us through the woods, we tracked the rich blue of the Duke's hunting costume, standing out against the black trunks. But all too often it would disappear into dense brush.

After an age of this creeping, a double note floated to us on the rising breeze. Hugh pointed to our right and spurred his horse in that direction, drawing us along with him at a trot.

Roger flashed me a gleeful glance and Alys's face was tinged pink beneath her riding cap. Ed's brow was furrowed, tense with concentration.

We soon caught up with the bulk of the hunt.

Hefting their spears, gentlemen were striding in silence to left or to right, to surround an impenetrable copse. Houndsmen and dogs vanished after them until only a handful remained in view. Faithful Florette as ever was at her master's side.

Spotting us, the Duke waved us further away across a small clearing.

Another double note of the horn. All the men dropped to one knee, each planting the butt of his spear on the frosted ground, lowering the point towards the copse. Then two flushing dogs, straining at their leashes, were let slip into the undergrowth.

The first crashings of the dogs' entry faded, leaving only the whimpering of the alaunts and sight-hounds keen to join them.

Long minutes passed.

No one spoke and the air was as leaden as the sky above.

As the tension mounted, Hugh's horse danced skittishly and he wheeled it in a tight circle to quieten it. Then nothing moved bar Bess's mane lifting in the breeze.

Florette stood alert beside the Duke, stark white against his slender blue outline. To one side loomed the black fur-clad bulk of Lord Scrope, to the other Master Gygges in his usual russet. One hand held fast the leash of a quivering alaunt.

White flakes drifted down from the glowering clouds. As I brushed them away, all around faces turned skyward. Alys held out a hand. In an instant her glove was frosted white. Roger laughed and leaned back with open mouth to catch the snow on his tongue. Hugh checked his horse as it started to shift uneasily again.

Only Ed remained focused on the hunt. And it was from Ed that the cry went up.

''Ware, boar!'

A sudden flurry amid the undergrowth and a huge dark shape burst forth. Pale shadows of dogs were at its heels. It rushed straight at Lord Scrope and for a shattered second the two black forms blended into one. Then with an eerie muffled sound, it tore into two again, and I realized in horror that the man had not had time to swing his spear round. As the beast thundered away, his lordship keeled over on to the gathering snow.

Florette stood her ground, letting out a sharp bark, but Master Gygges launched his alaunt after the speeding boar. Two sight-hounds also joined the chasing pack as it whisked out of the clearing, on into more woodland.

From all around the copse now streamed the huntsmen, attracted by the commotion. More sight-hounds were unleashed and many of the men ran headlong to follow, their boots crunching on the snowy ground. Others stopped and clustered round the fallen mound that was Lord Scrope, their voices raised in concern. Before they closed around him, I glimpsed the Duke on his knees, hands pressed against his lordship's side, where red was flowing out on to the fresh snow.

As I watched, frozen with horror, horses were kicked into movement. Roger and Giles Pynson dashed back the way we had come, calling 'Bring horses, bring horses, man injured'. But Hugh and Lionel whipped their mounts the other way, after the disappearing hunters.

Alys was twisting her chestnut this way and that, unsure of where to go. That was when it struck me that we two were alone.

Ed was nowhere to be seen.

He hadn't followed Roger, he hadn't ridden towards the knot of men around his father.

I grabbed Alys's rein and yelled.

'Ed! He's gone after the boar!'

11

'Witchcraft!'

Fear flashed in Alys's eyes.

'Are you sure?'

I nodded and dragged Bess's head round to send her plunging into the trees after the hunt. With a scrunch of hooves breaking undergrowth Alys came after us.

The snow was falling faster now, almost blinding me to what was ahead, and the noise of the hunt was muffled by it. But from time to time I could just make out the green of Hugh's new hunting coat and I followed it with grim determination. Upon the ground also hoofprints mingled with the bootprints of men who had pursued the boar.

I blinked away the flakes gathering on my eyelashes and shouted back to Alys through what was fast becoming a blizzard.

'We can follow them.' I pointed at the tracks. 'If we lose sight of the others.'

She kicked her horse alongside mine, with difficulty through the dense trees.

'We must stay together,' she yelled, her words all but torn away by the wind. 'I hope Hugh caught up with Ed before the snow got worse.'

We fought on through the driving flakes and the thick undergrowth, parted now and then by a tree-trunk, but always coming together again. Soon there was no sign of Hugh's bright coat and we relied only on the tracks. Perhaps we should have waited and called for help rather than set off on our own. What good would it do Ed if we became lost in his pursuit? But one glance at Alys's face made me go on, pushing all doubts away.

The curtain of swirling snowflakes eased a little. Sounds filtered back to us and figures could be seen between the black trunks, stark now against the settled snow. The hunters seemed fanned out once more, a few dogs among them, and to be hallooing to keep in touch.

Hugh's green-clad form was there, now dismounted and leading his horse through the trees.

But scan as I might, I couldn't see the small figure of Ed on his grey pony.

Before long Alys and I were within hailing distance of Hugh, now the wind had lessened. Alys slipped down from her horse to peer at something on the floor, but I pushed on, shouting to him.

He swung round and even through the tumbling snow I could see him scowl.

'Well?'

The single word was flung back at me on a sudden gust of wind.

'Where's Edward?'

He stared at me for a moment, looked left and right, then very deliberately shrugged and turned away. A new flurry of snow hid him from view in a second.

'Leave him, Matt,' Alys called from behind. 'Come see this.'

She was no longer right behind me, but off to one side, and Bess and I had to fight through the undergrowth to reach her.

Her gloved hand pointed down at the snowy ground. A single trail of small hoofprints led off into the distance, away from where the hunt now pursued the boar.

We exchanged glances.

'Ed?' I asked.

Without a word, she remounted and we set off in single file, following where the hoofprints led.

The way was hard through the dense scrub, our ponies stumbling often on the uneven ground. The snow was cascading again out of a sky we could no longer see. There was only a whirling mass of fat grey-white flakes and soon we were in danger of losing the trail.

I dared say nothing about it to Alys. She rode in front of me, staring intently at the ground. The hunch of her shoulders under her furred mantle told me she was as tense and worried as I. And as we rode on, I dreaded what the Duke would say when we got back.

If we got back...

Would we be able to follow our own tracks back to find the way we'd come? Or were they also vanishing behind us?

A cry from Alys broke into my thoughts and her pointing finger drew my eyes to a change in the trail.

In a scuffled patch of snow and leaf litter, a second set of prints had joined the first. Ed's tiny footprints beside those of his pony. In this part of the forest both we and the horses had to duck to avoid the lowest branches. I guessed that even on his smaller pony, Ed had difficulty in bending so low. The prints were close and often scrambled together.

Alys slipped down from her mount.

'He's tiring,' she said. 'Too tired to stay low in the saddle, and he can barely put a foot in front of the other. Look how he trips. And he's on his own, Matt.' A sob splintered her voice. 'We must hurry.'

Before the snow covers the tracks.

Her unspoken words hung in the air between us, mingling unseen with the still falling flakes.

I joined her on the ground, thankful to be away from the low-hanging branches, and we made better time, leading our mounts.

Alys was surefooted as she led the way, and closer to the ground it was easier to see the footprints. They were no longer going straight onwards, rather meandering through the woods.

After a while she called Ed's name into the swirling fog of snow. The sound was muffled to my ears, but in desperation I shouted too, as loud as I could. Too often the wind whipped my voice back into my face. From time to time Alys would hush me and we would listen for any answering sound. For a long time there was nothing.

Then —

A faint whinny from ahead.

How far I couldn't tell.

But Alys cried, 'We're coming, Ed! Hold on!' and clutched at my hand to pull me on.

Together we pushed our feet faster through the snow clogging our every step. Bess stumbled, limped, nudged me with her muzzle, but I ignored her. We were so nearly there. I could tend to her once we'd found Ed.

Our eyes blinded by stinging snowflakes, neither of us saw the drop before it was too late. The ground gave way beneath us and we tumbled down, arms outflung, into a deep drift. Above us, the ponies snorted in surprise as their reins tugged, torn from our grasp.

I surfaced, dazed and spluttering.

As ever, Alys was quicker. One glance back to check on the ponies, then she was floundering on through the thigh-deep snow. Across the hollow to where Ed lay.

His pony was sprawled in the snow, shivering, showing the whites of its eyes as it lifted its head and whickered at us. Blood from a gashed leg was reddening the snow. But any concern for it was thrust aside at the sight of Ed.

Alys dragged him to sit up, propped against her, and was shrugging off her fur mantle. I helped her, though she would freeze without it, for I knew it would take too much time to unbutton my own doublet – time we didn't have.

Ed's face was ashy-white, his eyes mere shadows beneath the veil of snow. Despite the cold, beads of sweat stood on his forehead. From his open mouth his breath rasped, as loud as the gasps of the blustering wind, and his chest heaved with a fast, unearthly rhythm. As we wrapped Alys's mantle about him, my hand brushed his. Flopped upon the snow, it was clammy to the touch.

Alys flung me a glance, terror in her eyes.

'It's like he was in the spring, Matt. But then the physician was there. We can't get him back in this state – not through the snow. Matt, what should we do?'

For a moment panic surged inside me too.

Then, drawing in one long, slow breath of frosty air – feeling the cool trace of its path down into my chest, ice crystals pricking my lips and nostrils, closing my eyes against the storm – slowly, slowly my head cleared, and slowly so did my inner sight.

As I forced my eyes open and gazed at Ed labouring there before me, it was no longer his face, but that of my younger brother, Peter – tinged with blue, his eyes starting from his head as he too gasped for breath. And the face of my mother, not seen in almost two years, swam into view.

I blinked away the smarting tears, lowering my eyelids again.

Alys's desperate voice called again, 'Matt, what shall we do?'

But above it I heard my mother's soft words, her crooning.

I opened my eyes again, took Ed's face gently in my hands.

'Ed,' I soothed, 'Edward. Look at me, Ed. Open your eyes. Look at me.'

His eyelids fluttered, then parted a little.

Just a crack, but it was a start. Though his breath still rasped, his chest still heaved.

'Look at me, Ed. Listen to me. Open your eyes some more.'

As I gazed at him, the slit of blue widened.

'That's great, Ed. Look at me. Listen to me.'

Now they were fully open, fear was scrawled across his eyes too. He choked, and panted, and clutched at my arm.

I must stay calm, must not let him see the knot of terror in my own chest.

'Well done, Ed. Well done. Now listen to me, listen well. Listen to my voice. Listen to my words. Look into my eyes. Into my eyes.'

My mother's voice was deep inside my head, telling me the words to say. The words she'd said to Peter.

I fought to keep my voice as steady, as gentle as hers.

'Look into my eyes, Ed. What do you see? Do you see a river? A deep, calm, slow-flowing river? Do you see it, Ed?'

His eyes were fixed on mine now. He blinked twice. A strange hiccup slipped out between his gulping breaths.

'Don't speak, Ed, just look, just listen. You see the river, don't you? Deep, calm, slow-flowing? Gently rolling along, slowly rolling along. The sun gleams in its depths, the gentle summer sky, the slow-moving clouds, mirrored in its depths.'

I spoke calmly, slowly, staring deep into his eyes, and they began to relax. I carried on, intoning the words, slowly, calmly, the same words, over and over again, rolling the long, gentle sounds calmly around my mouth, holding his eyes with mine, holding his face with my hands. I continued to murmur, my voice soft, to croon like my mother.

Slowly, but slowly, his wheezing quietened. I could feel his heaving chest soften. Slowly, slowly, gradually, his breathing eased. His eyelids drooped and closed again, slowly, gently this time. As my voice faded away, I saw at last he was sleeping.

My hands released his head, resting it against Alys's shoulder.

I straightened up and stepped back, closing my own eyes once more. I drew in another long deep breath. It was as though I had been fighting for breath inside just like Ed.

In the silence of my head, I thanked my mother – but I could no longer see her face.

I forced my eyes wide, fleeing from the memory, and became aware once more where I was.

Snow flurried around me still, but could not hide the shock dashed across Alys's face.

'Matt! How – how did you…?'

A sharp bark behind us and the sound of someone blundering down through deep snow.

I swung round.

On the far side of the hollow was Duke Richard. His fine blue hunting garb was soaked through, crusted with snow, smeared with blood. His hand was on Florette's collar as she strained forwards.

Surprise was in his eyes too.

'Matthew… Ed?'

He waded through the soft white drifts and knelt beside his son.

Sir Francis Lovell was clambering down the bank after him, while several men, both knights and huntsmen, stayed with our ponies at the top. They stared down at the scene, horror etched on their faces. Someone, somewhere, hissed the single word 'Witchcraft!'

I turned away, my face burning.

The Duke was busy taking off his thick fur cloak and easing it around Alys's quaking shoulders.

He muttered, 'Well done, both of you,' before gathering up his son with a gentleness that brought more stinging tears to my eyes. A corner of Alys's fur mantle slipped away from Ed as he lifted him, and I leaned over to tuck it round him again.

'He needs a physician urgently, Your Grace.'

The Duke nodded at my quiet words, with that ghost of a smile I had seen before. He muttered something to Sir Francis, then stepped forward to face his men, his precious load held before him.

'Gentlemen,' he said, 'there has been no witchcraft here today. My son was taken ill. Master Wansford has calmed him. That is all. I saw everything.'

I didn't understand how this could be true. If he had seen Ed struggling for breath, would he not have thrown himself forward to comfort his son? Not leave him to the care of an

96

inexperienced, hardly known boy? And yet, as I cast my mind back, did I remember a single bark mixed in with the terrifying noise of Ed's gasps?

Whatever the truth, I thanked the Lord that what I had done had worked and that the Duke had spoken for me, otherwise perhaps... But no, no one could have accused me of causing harm to Ed. After all, Alys had been there the whole time, long before the Duke had reached us.

Bundled up in the Duke's furs, Alys stood with me as Sir Francis directed preparations for the return journey. Two saplings were felled to fashion a rough litter to carry Ed and a huntsman bound his pony's leg so it could walk with some encouragement. Within minutes, somehow, we were all ready to leave.

Alys and I gathered our ponies' reins and set off with the others back through the forest. After a few minutes, she said almost under her breath,

'Was it witchcraft?'

'What? Alys, no! How could you think —?'

Her cheeks tinged with pink and she lowered her eyes.

'No, of course not. I'm sorry. It's just that – well, it's just that I've never seen anything like that. What you did. How did you know what to do?'

I moistened my lips before answering. I recalled witches being accused of evil deeds, even in a modern city like York.

'My brother, my youngest brother, Peter. He has an illness, ever since he was little. When it's very cold, when he's been running too hard, when someone's angry at him, sometimes he struggles to breathe just like Ed. And in the winter, if he catches a chill... It's frightening, we've thought that he'll die. Then my mother spoke to a wise woman and she taught my mother what to do, to calm him until he could see the herbalist. I saw her do it many times before... before she died.'

We were silent for most of the journey back. I was exhausted, and Alys perhaps still disturbed by all that had happened.

When we reached the abbey, Ed was carried straight to the monks' infirmary while the rest of us were ushered into the guesthouse. At its crackling fireside we found Roger among a gaggle of other members of the hunting party. The abbey's servants were running to and fro with steaming food and drink for their unexpected guests.

Roger greeted us cheerily, but I'm sorry to say he was soon disappointed in us. He hoped to regale us with his own adventures, but we didn't make a good audience.

'So when Giles and I brought the grooms and horses, and the Duke bound Lord Scrope's wound – lucky for him it wasn't too deep, but, by the Virgin, it was a good hand's span across – are you listening?'

Alys, still enveloped in the Duke's cloak, nodded across the brim of a cup of hot mead.

'Yes, of course. A hand's span.'

I was too busy spooning broth into my mouth to say anything.

'Well, when they'd finished tending to his lordship, everyone who wasn't needed to bring him back here set off to follow the boar. Of course, there was quite a blizzard by then. But Florette and the sight-hounds that were still on their leashes soon found the rest of the hunt. They'd just flushed the boar out of the covert. It was at bay with its back to a fallen tree trunk. It must have been an ancient beast, its muzzle was quite grey – unless that was the snow. Anyway, the alaunts were baiting it. It was a magnificent sight, the hounds darting in and snapping, it brushing them away with its tusks as if they were just flies.'

He waited for a response.

'Mmmm,' said I, chewing on a piece of bread I'd dipped in the soup.

'Just flies,' echoed Alys.

'Well, the Duke realized that Hugh and Lionel were there at the sport, but there was no sign of you two and Ed. I'd never seen him in such a rage before. He pulled them both out of the hunt circle – can you believe, they'd got the huntsmen to give them each a spear? He actually dragged them out with his own hands, shouted that he'd deal with them later, and sent them back through the forest with Master Fleete. Serve them right. Anyway, Hugh was very nearly as green as his new doublet when I told him that I'd been there to see the boar killed.'

'Oh.' I dunked more bread into the broth. Any enthusiasm I'd had for boar hunting had long since fled.

'How did the Duke find us?' asked Alys.

'Oh, while he was shouting at Hugh – away from the circle, of course, he didn't want to distract the dogs – well, he sent Sir Francis with Florette to cast about for Ed's scent. Sir Francis said the snow had mostly covered the tracks, but fortunately Florette has the best nose in the business. It didn't take her long to find the trail and – well, I suppose she led them to you. The Duke wouldn't let me go with them, said it was too dangerous, and... well... I would have missed the kill, so... What happened to you three?'

Alys told him in as few words as possible, only sketching what had happened in the snowy hollow and mentioning witchcraft not at all. I was grateful to her. Roger didn't ask any more about it. He seemed happy enough that we had all survived – and happier still that his first boar hunt had been such a success.

Master Fleete came to check that we had all warmed up and were fit to travel back to the castle. Lord Scrope would stay as the abbot's guest until well enough to return home, but Ed had been given some physic by the monks and would journey back with us.

Shortly before the early winter darkness fell, our procession set off along the road to Middleham, far more subdued than in the morning. Edward slept most of the journey in a covered carriage borrowed from the abbot. He was hot and shivery, but his breath, though a little fast, was no longer a desperate struggle.

The Duke had sent a messenger ahead and when we turned in through the inner gateway, the Duchess was standing at the steps of the keep, once more shrouded in thick furs and attended by serving men with flaming torches. The rest of the party had taken horses and hounds back to the stableyard, but the Duke had allowed Alys and me to ride in the carriage with Ed.

The Duchess flew to open the door and, after checking on her son, directed a servant to lift him from the carriage. Then she rounded on her husband.

Her words were quiet so that Ed and the servant couldn't hear, but my ears caught them. She seemed to have forgotten the talk with her husband that I had overheard those many days before.

'You should not have let him go, Richard, for all his pleading. I knew something like this would happen.'

The Duke handed his horse's reins to a waiting servant and turned back to her with a smile.

'Calm yourself, my love. As you see, he will soon be well.'

'But he could have died out there, all alone in the snow.'

99

'But he did not. And we have our young friends here to thank for that.'

To my surprise, he swept us a deep bow, before offering his hand to Alys to help her step down from the carriage.

'My lady Langdown, Master Wansford. Supper, then bed, I think, after your exertions. You are excused lessons tomorrow – although, Matthew, I would have you sing at a Mass of thanksgiving in the morning if you are up to it.'

'Of course, Your Grace.'

'And then I would see you both in my chamber after breakfast.'

A brief nod to us and he enfolded his wife's arm within his, before following the serving man carrying Edward up the keep steps towards their private chambers. I did not see them again that day.

12

The Runt of the Litter

More snow fell overnight and another bitter morning greeted me as I crept from under my blanket. I had to break ice in the basin to wash, and even before I left the pages' chamber the plumes of my breath unfurled in the pre-dawn air.

A swift trudge across the snowy courtyard and I was soon pulling on my surplice beside the small fire now lit each morning in the vestry. Today Sir William also handed each of us choir members a cup of scalding spiced wine.

'It will warm your voices for the service,' he said in his rich tones, which needed no such medicine. 'And, Master Wansford, His Grace asks that you sing a Te Deum this morning, to thank God for preserving his son.'

Happy to sing the beautiful song of praise, I was also glad when Mass was over. The chapel was freezing despite the fire below.

Duke Richard alone of his family was there. Even he did not appear at breakfast.

I caught Alys as she passed the pages' table before the meal.

'How's Ed?' I asked.

'A little better, I think. I was allowed in to see him for a minute this morning. He recognized me and managed a smile, but his nurse would not let him talk.'

After breakfast, we met again and went together to knock at the door of the Duke's private chamber.

He opened it himself, his great furred mantle and a small wooden box in his hands. Giving us good morning, he swung the cloak about his shoulders and bade us follow him. He strode off across the great hall and down the steps, as usual forcing us almost to run to keep up.

He said not a word more to us as we crossed the outer courtyard. Everywhere the snow, though thick, had been turned into slush by the passage of dozens of feet.

At the door to the kennels, he stood aside to let Alys enter first, then I followed him into the low dark building.

Master Gygges was waiting. After bowing to the Duke, he led us to a large pen where the newly weaned pups lived. I peered over the door. To my surprise, the tumble of young dogs of all shapes and colours – sight-hounds, alaunts, fox harriers, water spaniels – had been joined by Florette's six puppies.

'Matthew,' the Duke began, 'I wish to make you a gift to thank you for your service to my son yesterday. Master Gygges tells me you've been spending a great deal of time with the hounds these past weeks. I thought perhaps you might like to have a pup of your own – although you must tell me if you would prefer a different reward.'

'Th – thank you, Your Grace,' I stammered. 'I would like that very much.'

'You may choose any that you wish from those that have been weaned. Master Gygges is here for advice, if you need it.'

I needed no advice. I had never dreamed I would have a hound of my own, but I already knew which I wanted.

I pointed.

'Your Grace, if I may, that one there.'

'The red one?' said Master Gygges, amazement on his face. 'Florette's runt? Begging your pardon, Your Grace, but even a royal hound can whelp a runt.'

Ignoring his words, the Duke narrowed his eyes.

'Why that one?'

'I don't know,' I said. 'It's just that – well, it may be small, but it seems loyal and brave.'

'Indeed?'

'When we came here first, it stuck close to its mother. As though it wanted to defend her. Then it realized I meant no harm, and it began to trust me. It comes to me even when I have no tidbit.'

'So you have made friends already? Show me.'

I slipped into the pen, crouching low. As usual the pup trotted forward, its liquid brown eyes gazing up at me as I fondled its ears.

The Duke said quietly, 'You've chosen well, for all Master Gygges's talk of runts. You must know, Matt, that its mother is a special dog, the finest I have ever owned. She was given to me by my brother George, his last gift to me before... before he died.'

I glanced up. Who was the brother he spoke of?

For a moment, a distant look clouded his eyes. Then they snapped down to me.

'And what to call it?'

'I don't know,' I said again, racking my brain for an idea.

'Why not name it after me? "Old Dick". Isn't that what you pages call me? Then you will not forget me, even when you are both grown and have left my service.'

Hearing the detestable name said in that casual manner stung me. I threw myself down on one knee before him, scattering the pups.

'Your Grace, I've never called you that. And I swear I'll never leave your service.'

He grasped my shoulder and pulled me to my feet.

'Be not so serious, Master Wansford. I know that I am so called by some – it doesn't bother me. But I thank you for your loyalty – and accept your willing service. Now come – what name, if not Old Dick?'

'My lord,' the huntsman protested, 'it is a she-pup.'

'Indeed, Master Gygges, I was only jesting. Matthew does well to choose a she-pup, don't you agree? They are more loyal than their brothers – and when she is older she will provide you with royal pups, Matt. Her father is one of the King's hounds. But Matthew, don't let her wed too young – it isn't good for them.'

'What about Murrey?' came Alys's voice.

I had almost forgotten she was there, and the Duke also looked surprised.

'Murrey?'

'After the colour of your device, Your Grace. She is a dark red after all.'

'True. Matthew?'

I nodded. It suited her well.

'And now you, Alys. What reward would you have? I have brought jewels.'

He tapped the wooden box sitting on the wall of the pen.

'Your Grace, I would as soon have another of Florette's pups. Perhaps that white one there. She looks just like her mother.'

'As you wish. Matthew, if you please.'

I picked up the pup she'd pointed to, together with my Murrey, and let myself out of the pen.

As I handed the white pup to Alys, the Duke asked, 'And is it for Matthew to name your choice?'

'Oh no, I shall think of a name in my own time. And don't worry, Your Grace, I shall not let her marry too young either.'

She said it merrily enough, but her words reminded me of her betrothal to Hugh's cousin. Perhaps the Duke recalled it too. A shadow darkened his eyes as he bid us farewell and strode away with Master Gygges.

*

In the days that followed I saw nothing of Ed as he recovered from his illness, but rather more of the Duke. He would go away for a day or two at a time on business and before long news came that he was summoned to London to attend Parliament in January. But, despite having much to arrange, it didn't stop him riding out with Roger, Alys and me many afternoons when he was at home.

'It gets me out from under the nurses' feet in the sick room,' he joked.

Alys whispered to us that he often took a turn watching his son all night during his sickness and the Duchess had urged him to go riding for fresh air and exercise. But why he chose to ride with us rather than the gentlemen of his household was at first a mystery.

Then one fine clear day, he rode with us to the top of Pen Hill. There he turned Storm around and, as our chatter died away, gazed back towards the valley. Most of the snow had melted away, just pockets remaining in sheltered hollows. The hills in the distance were blue, like smoke.

His hand shielding his eyes against the low winter sun, the Duke said quietly, 'This was my favourite place when I was a page. I would ride up here with Francis in all weathers and hawk, or chase, or simply watch the folk go about their business in the dale.'

There was no emotion on his face, but was there a tug of wistfulness in his voice?

Roger shattered the stillness of the moment.

'If you had said before, Your Grace, we could have brought Lady and another hawk and seen if we could raise some sport.'

The Duke shook his head, as though scattering his memories.

'Nay, lad, not today. I think I prefer a quiet ride in these days. But perhaps you could bring Edward when he is well again. I would that he could become strong and happy amongst his friends as I did.'

The meaning of his last words escaped me then, and for many weeks after, but we all three promised to do our best for his son.

On those rides, we always brought Murrey and Alys's pup, by now named Shadow as it followed her everywhere. They scampered after our ponies, learning to keep out of the way of their hooves, and were picked up to be carried across the saddle bow or tucked into doublet or mantle when they tired. On this afternoon Murrey, as usual, was the first to flag. She whined plaintively as her spindly legs began to wobble and she dropped behind.

As I swung down to scoop her up, the Duke reined Storm back to wait. Alys and Roger carried on ahead, unaware, Shadow still bounding along at their heels.

Murrey was soon snuggled within my doublet, her tiny head sticking out the unbuttoned top, eyelids drooping with sleep.

As we set off again, riding side by side, the Duke spoke.

'Matthew, as you may know, I must soon ride to London. I will be away for Christmastide as a guest of the King. Then I must stay while Parliament conducts its business.'

'I have heard, Your Grace.'

'Have you ever been to London?'

'No, but my father has. He travelled there once on business. He said it was the most wonderful city in all the world, and he has been as far as Ghent and Antwerp. He said the people wore the finest clothes, the houses were the tallest he had seen, the river the most marvellous —'

Doctor Frees had often drummed into us that pages should speak to Duke Richard only when necessary and when directly spoken to. But my tongue ran away with me as I remembered all that my father had told – until it struck me that my listener had of course seen all of this and more, on many occasions. And that he must think me a fool. A boy who had never left his home town before he came here.

I ground to a halt, with a lame, 'That's what he said anyway.'

But the Duke only smiled.

'Should you like to go to London yourself, then, Matthew?'

'Oh, Your Grace, of all things that would be the best!'

'Then you shall be part of the company if you wish it. I own that when I am away from home I miss your singing at Mass. And for our quiet evenings' entertainment. I keep no singers at my house in London as I am there so rarely, and I do believe my brother's household contains no voices as good as yours. Will you come?'

I was stunned. I'd had no thoughts of visiting London so soon, let alone to be asked to accompany the Duke. It was a golden chance.

But at the same time, what of my friends? How could I leave them so soon after finding them – and when Ed had been so ill?

Yet it would not be for long…

'You need not give me your answer at once. Think about it for a few days. You were apprenticed to the household here, not my personal retinue. If you don't want to miss your lessons, your friends…'

'Edward, Your Grace?'

'Ah, yes. I will regret taking you away from him. It is perhaps selfish of me. But while he is still recovering, you will not see so much of him. Perhaps you can write while you're away – of all those wonders you'll see. And when you return, the weather will have improved and you can all go out riding together again.'

'Improved?'

'Parliament will begin in January, and will last a month, perhaps six weeks. We will leave London by the end of February, unless… well, unless the King hears you sing. He may wish to keep you with him for spiritual guidance.'

'What?'

'Don't stand so aghast, lad. I jest. I'm sure my brother has no need for extra guidance. You'll be back home with your friends before spring.' He paused. 'If you choose to go.'

How could I not? Not only to see London, but maybe also the King himself and the court. I might never have such a chance again.

'Of course I'll go, Your Grace, if you truly wish it. Can I take Murrey?'

*

106

I spilled out my news to Alys and Roger as soon as we were back at the castle.

Alys said they would miss me, that the Christmas festivities would not be as much fun without me.

Roger spoilt it by saying the Duke might have other reasons for taking me.

'Maybe he's worried that you're becoming a bad influence on Ed.'

He said it with a grin, but it sounded too much like Hugh for me to smile too. Had Alys said anything more to him about the hunt? I asked her when we were next alone.

'Of course not,' she said. 'He's just being daft as usual. And he's probably jealous.'

'But he went with the Duke to London before.'

'Yes, but he would dearly love to go again. And the pleasures of Christmas at court… well, we'll have nothing like it here, particularly with the Duke gone. But don't worry about Roger, Matt. Go and enjoy yourself. And don't think too much about your friends stuck up here in the frozen North.'

But, for all her joking, I couldn't banish the guilt I felt. Especially about Edward.

Although I hadn't seen him since our return from Jervaulx, he was often in my thoughts. He reminded me more and more of my brother Pete, especially now I knew he suffered from a similar sickness. Ed would have loved to help me train Murrey, and would no doubt have filched tidbits for her from the Duke's table as he often had for Lady. And I would miss him when I was away, as I did my own brothers and sisters.

So, when I was finally allowed to visit him, I knew it would be hard to tell him that I was going.

Alys said he'd often asked for me during his illness, but his nurse had refused to let any of the 'rough boys' in to see him. But at last the Duchess overruled her and insisted I be admitted, if only for a few minutes.

I took with me a favourite romance in case he wanted me to read, or wasn't well enough to talk. But as I was ushered into the private chamber, I found it wouldn't be needed.

'Matt, at last! I've been so longing to see you. Alys says you have a hound. Mother says you're going to London. And I'm stuck here. Life's so unfair!'

He was half-sitting, half-lying under a mound of rugs and furs on a couch drawn close to the blazing fire. On his lap lay two or three books and a dish of sweetmeats. His face was pale and thin, but he was no longer the ghostly figure I had last seen.

I drew up a footstool alongside him.

'Yes, yes, and yes. But as my father says, we can't always have what we want.'

'But I'm the son of a Duke.'

'Perhaps that can make a difference. But maybe not when you're ill.'

'But I'm not so very ill now.'

'But you were. You quite scared Alys and me, Ed.'

His smile disappeared.

'Yes, I know. My father told me. I don't remember any of it. At least, not after seeing poor Lord Scrope gored and then following the boar. My father says you saved my life – you and Alys. Thank you, Matt.'

I didn't know what to say, but Ed barely gave me time to think.

'He says that's why he gave you the hounds. When can I see Murrey, Matt? I've already seen Shadow. Alys brings her to me sometimes. She says you're training them together.'

I might not need the book, but I had brought something else with me.

I knelt down beside the couch and unbuttoned my doublet. Ed craned forward and his eyes brightened. Murrey was curled up there fast asleep against my chest.

'Oh, Matt, she's beautiful. Can I stroke her? I hope my father will give me a hound of my own soon.'

So the breaking of all my news had been done for me. I was glad – and to see Ed looking and sounding better.

A few minutes later the nurse got up from her chair across the hearth and flapped her hands to shoo me out. Ed made a grab for me, catching the hem of my doublet as I rose to my feet.

'I shall miss you, Matt, when you go,'

'And I you, Ed. And the rest of the Order. But your father says I may write to you while I'm away – he will send the letters with his own.'

'Oh, please do. Tell me all about London, and court, and my uncle if you see him, and my cousin Edward – if he is there with his father. You know, I have never met him. Do write and tell me what he's like.'

I promised, just as the nurse succeeded in unfastening his fingers from my clothing and propelling me out of the room.

His final words as he waved me off left me wondering. He had a cousin he had never met? I had so many cousins at home in York that it was difficult to turn a corner without bumping into one.

I visited Ed twice or three times more before I left for London. Each visit he was stronger than the time before. The nurse allowed Roger to join us too. Perhaps she realized he was a less 'rough' boy than me by far.

Neither Ed nor Roger bothered to hide their envy over my coming journey and they talked endlessly about people and things I would see in London, mentioning names that meant nothing to me.

Not wanting to appear ignorant about Ed's family, I waited until I was alone with Roger to ask him about the unknown cousin.

'Oh, that Edward,' he said. 'You know, the King's oldest son – Prince of Wales.'

'But why hasn't our Ed met him? And why wouldn't he be at court with his father?'

'Matt, haven't you learnt anything here?'

'Oh, is he training to be a page, like us? Even the King's son?'

'Not so much that. He lives out on the Welsh borders somewhere, learning to rule them. It's a bit different I suppose. But otherwise he probably learns much the same as we do – he's about our age or a little younger. He lives in the household of one of his other uncles.'

That reminded me of another question.

'How many uncles does he have? I thought Duke Richard was the King's only brother. But he mentioned another one the other day, George, but said he'd died.'

'No, this one's an uncle from the Queen's family, the Woodvilles. That's probably why Ed's never met him. People say the Duke doesn't like them very much.'

'Why not?'

'Well, there was a scandal when King Edward married the Queen. The Earl of Warwick didn't approve. You know, the Kingmaker? He was the King's cousin of course. He wanted him to marry a foreign princess, not a commoner like Elizabeth Woodville. So the King married her in secret. And then, my father says Duke Richard blames her family for his brother's death.'

'And that's his brother George?'

'Yep, George, Duke of Clarence.'

'So how did he die?'

'He was executed. For treason.'

'Treason? Against the King?'

'It usually is against the King.'

'No, I mean, against his own brother? Why?'

'People say he'd been plotting to seize the throne for years. The King finally lost patience, tried him for treason and had him executed. Duke Richard begged him not to, but apparently the Queen persuaded the King not to listen. She and her family didn't like Duke George.'

'Why not?'

'He didn't like the marriage either, and then he sided with the Kingmaker in his rebellion. The King forgave Duke George then, but something happened years later to change his mind. So the Woodvilles got their way in the end. It's partly why Duke Richard doesn't go to London much now. Though he's not the only one who doesn't like them. Plenty of people seem not to for one reason or another.' He paused, smiling at my puzzlement. 'Tricky things, royal families, aren't they?'

He was right. But family complications were only one of the things on my mind as I prepared for my momentous journey.

I was going to London, to court – and to the court of a king who had executed his own brother.

13

A Long-Awaited Journey

The day of our departure arrived at last. It was not a good day for travelling.

November's snow was a distant memory, replaced by constant drizzle and fog, rolling down from the hills. Roger lent me his second-best riding cloak for the trip, but even so I knew I would be soaked through before we'd ridden half a mile from the castle.

Sir William excused me from singing at Mass that morning. He joked that Duke Richard would be hearing enough of me over the next few weeks, but maybe he noticed how nervous I was. For a day or two, my voice had wavered at the highest notes, echoing the quivering in my stomach at every thought of the journey.

Alys cornered me as I left the chapel.

'Are you sure you want to go? You've been fretting all week.'

'Of course I want to. I'll be fine once we're on the road. I can't let the Duke down.'

But it was also for myself. I couldn't wait to see London. Of all my family, only my father had travelled so far. If I wanted to see the world and have adventures, this was my chance to make a start.

After an early breakfast, it was time for goodbyes.

As always when the Duke was setting out on a long trip, all the castle turned out, and most of the villagers as well.

Despite the rain coursing down my face, I held my head up high as I walked past rows of drenched squires and pages lined up in the inner court. Among them I glimpsed the scowls of Hugh and Lionel. I had hardly seen them since their disgrace on the hunt. As punishment Master Gygges had kept them out of lessons, to do menial jobs around the kennels and stables, and they served the grooms at mealtimes as the lowliest of the low.

I handed my bundle and lute to be packed on the luggage wagon and checked my new saddlebag for the day's essentials. Bidding farewell to Alys and Roger, I swung myself into Bess's saddle. Murrey, snug in my doublet, whimpered at this sudden movement, but was settled with a word and a morsel of meat from my pouch.

Last to arrive was of course Duke Richard. He took his leave of his wife on the keep steps to protect her from the rain before mounting Storm, held there for him by Master Reynold. As the trumpet sounded and the white boar banner was unfurled, he looked up at the keep and raised a hand in salute.

Through the obscure glass of a window I spied the ghostly shape of Edward, waving, safe away from the wet and cold. A shadowy figure stood by him – Elen? I waved too, then urged Bess into a walk.

Those damp murky days on the way to London were among the most miserable of my life. After an hour or two, even the beguiling prospect of that marvellous city was dulled by the endless rain. A few riders tried to boost our spirits early on with marching songs and bawdy ballads, but even they were defeated by the rain. At the head of the company the huge banner slapped wetly against its pole with every stride as we jogged along. Eventually the Duke ordered it furled and we rode along in silence apart from the rattle of hooves and chink of harness.

Each night we lodged at an inn or great house or abbey, and roaring fires would dry out us and our gear. But the next day everyone and everything was again wet through before we had travelled out of sight of our hosts.

I rode mostly alongside an older page called Robert, who might speak to me when there was no better entertainment. But he had the air of thinking he was above a mere merchant's son, even one so favoured by the Duke. Of the Duke himself I saw very little.

One bright memory alone broke up those dreary days on the road.

We had reached a landscape of gently rolling woodlands and fields after the flat fens of the past day or two. Turning off the great road, before long we entered a village of straw-coloured stone houses huddling beneath the motte of an ancient castle.

It was not yet midday. With hours of daylight still ahead, grey and dim though it was, this couldn't be where we would spend the night.

We clattered past the castle gates, whose guards sprang to attention at the sight of our banner – unfurled again that morning.

Beyond rose a large priory church, its elegant stone tower glimmering against the lowering clouds.

It was in the priory precinct that we halted. Once we dismounted, most of the company were welcomed into the guesthouse for dinner. But Duke Richard, along with Sir Francis and his closest companions, entered the church.

Curious, I slipped into the round-columned nave after them. In a chapel to the side of the high altar, the light of many candles flickered on the bars of a cage of stone. Within stood two fine carved tombs, each topped by the effigy of a knight in full armour.

Duke Richard, his own knights about him, knelt before the tombs and the waiting monks began to recite a Mass. With choristers aplenty, I was not needed. As their voices rose in a requiem, I crept back out of the building to join the rest of the company. I asked Robert whose tombs lay within the church, but he had no idea. I was too shy to question the men. Even the Duke's secretary, Master Kendall, who had often been friendly towards me on the journey, was solemn of face as we rode on once more.

At long last we reached London a few days before Christmas, as the bells of its many churches were ringing out for afternoon service.

Robert had been born near the city and had visited it often before joining the household at Middleham. He told me that more than four score churches lay within its walls. I could well believe it from the jangling clamour that greeted us as we trotted through the surrounding fields and farmsteads. But I hardly needed him to point out the towering spire of the Cathedral of Saint Paul. It reached hundreds of feet above everything else, almost touching the overhanging clouds themselves.

Watchmen saluted us as we passed beneath the huge portcullis of Bishopsgate, which would have dwarfed Middleham's gatehouse, and people streamed from houses and shops, curious as to who was making such a clatter on the paving stones. Cheers rose at the sight of the Duke's floating banner. They drowned out the hoofbeats and rippled ahead along the great thoroughfare, as more and more citizens, drawn from their work or firesides, lined our way and added their voices.

Long before we reached our final destination, I discovered that London surpassed all my expectations. It was larger, busier, noisier, filthier, smellier, smokier than anywhere else I had ever been or ever dreamed of.

The houses loomed higher above the streets, the gullies were deeper and more overflowing with rubbish, the roaming pigs, chickens and goats under our feet more numerous, the acrid smoke rising from tavern fires and pottery kilns more suffocating, the racket of smiths, butchers and street hawkers plying their trades more deafening.

Nothing about my home city of York on even the busiest market or feast day had prepared me for this. Yet I was captivated by it all, staring about me at each new wonder until the next came hard upon it.

At one turn, the vast stone frontage of a rich man's townhouse rose from the cobbled highway. Watery sunlight glinted from diamond-paned windows, liveried men stood guard at iron-studded oak doors, fine-worked rugs waved from balconies. At the next, a stinking alley of overhanging buildings and reeking runnels belched forth a flood of downtrodden people – ragged street urchins, crippled beggars, evil-featured men who melted back into the shadows as we passed. Between them, streets lined with black-and-white wood-and-plaster houses, busy taverns with swinging signs, shop stalls with colourful fruit and vegetables, workshops crammed with pottery, ironwork or leather goods, craftsmen carrying their tools, well-fed merchants, aproned goodwives, horse-drawn wagons laden with grain or cloths edged over to the gutters out of our way, gaggles of schoolboys on their way home, staring up wide-mouthed at the splendour of our company. And everywhere the noise of shouting and hammering, and barking, and clanging, and singing, and the crowing of cocks, and the grunting and squealing of pigs, and over it all the clangour of the bells from those four score and more belfries.

Master Kendall, who was riding alongside me, laughed.

'Close your mouth, boy, don't gawp. You mustn't let these Londoners think we northern folk are overawed by their paltry town.'

But overawed I was. And likely it is that my mouth was still hanging open like those of the schoolboys as we turned into a wide courtyard just off the busy thoroughfare. Delicately wrought but stout iron gates clanged shut behind us, cutting off the hustle and bustle of the street.

Before us reared a stone house of size and beauty to rival the palace of my lord the archbishop in York. This was Crosby Place, the Duke's home in the capital.

The procession halted by a flight of steps up to the main doors, the cheering crowds faded away behind us, and before long I was seated by a crackling fire in the main kitchen of the house, clutching a very welcome, warming cup of mulled ale.

That first evening in Crosby Place was the pattern for many others of my stay in London, and in some ways like those I'd come to enjoy at Middleham.

The whole company gathered together with the London household for supper in the great hall – a lofty room, with large square windows and an intricately carved oak ceiling in what Master Kendall told me was the very newest fashion. To my surprise, throughout the meal we were entertained by musicians playing in a gallery high up on one wall. Why had Duke Richard brought me, a novice on the lute, if he already had such accomplished players in the city?

After supper, I settled down in a corner to play dice with two of the local pages, whose outlandish London accents I could just about understand. Before I had time to lose more than a few pennies to them, a serving man came to summon me to the Duke's private chamber. I brushed down my doublet, picked up the leather case of my lute, whistled Murrey to heel, and followed the servant, all the while contentedly aware of the astonishment on the faces of my fellows.

When I entered, the Duke was deep in conversation with his steward. Not Master Guylford, who had remained at Middleham, but the man who looked after the Duke's business affairs in London and had greeted him when we arrived. As ever, Master Kendall was also there to deal with any correspondence, and he waved me to a stool near the carved stone fireplace and bid me play.

I had learned few enough tunes for the lute, and these formal surroundings made me nervous of playing them badly. But I had also started to improvise my own songs, stringing together, as the fancy took me, notes and snatches of French or Spanish poetry that Doctor Frees had taught me. This I did tonight, quietly in the corner, thinking that the London steward couldn't rebuke me, a provincial lad, for getting them wrong.

Before long, the Duke had enough of business and with a few words dismissed both men. As they bowed their way out the door, he dropped into a richly cushioned oak chair before the fire. For many minutes he stared deep into the leaping flames, his face a tired mask, a silver goblet of wine untasted in his hands.

I carried on playing softly, not singing now, not wishing to disturb him, but wondering whether he was aware I was still there. My fingers started to tire and my eyelids to droop, after our long journey and the excitement of our entry into the city. I longed to join Murrey, curled up at my feet on a sheepskin rug before the hearth.

After what seemed an age, the Duke drank deeply from his goblet, then startled me to wakefulness by asking,

'Do you miss your family, Matthew?'

'Your Grace?'

'Your family. I believe you have one. A father at least. You have spoken of him.'

My face grew hot, and not from the fire. I recalled my prattling on the moor.

'I do, yes, Your Grace. Miss them, I mean. It's more than four months now since I last saw them.'

He rose and, going to the table, refilled his cup from a crystal jug standing there. He poured more into another beautifully wrought goblet and handed it to me.

I had to put down my lute to take it. The taste was strong and rich, like the wine my friends and I had drunk to toast the Order.

The Duke had returned to his seat and the reflection of the flames flickered once more in his eyes. Some minutes passed before he spoke again.

'When Parliament is ended, we will return home by way of York. You may spend time with your family then. I know what it's like to miss the ones you love.'

'Thank you, Your Grace.'

'Meanwhile, tomorrow I must go to see my other family, that of my brother the King. Do you wish to join us?'

'I should like that very much.'

'You will see the splendours of his court in Westminster. It puts our little household at Middleham to shame.' He took another mouthful of wine and swirled the goblet gently in his hand. 'It has ever been my brother's desire to have the best of everything around him, whether it be men of learning, the finest horses, wines or beautiful tapestries. He is such a man as will always get what he desires. No one can refuse him anything. It was ever that way.'

He drained the last of his wine and replaced the cup on the table. I sipped again from mine, but dared not drink more for fear I should fall instantly asleep.

As though reading my thoughts, he said,

'Now it is time to retire. It was a long journey and a long day, and there will be another such tomorrow. You shall act the part of my personal page while we are in London, if you will, Matthew. There is none here that I trust so well as you. Ask the servants for your mattress and place it against my door. Sleep well, lad.'

I left the room in a daze, clutching my lute in one hand, in the other Murrey, still caught up in her dreams.

I hadn't expected this. At Middleham, only the most senior pages – Hugh and his friends, perhaps Robert – had the honour to sleep each night, in turn, outside the Duke's private chamber. In times past they would have been the last line of protection for the Duke and his family in case of attack. In these more peaceful days it was just an honorary role, of course. But at the mention of trust, pride welled up in my chest until I felt my heart would overflow.

In a very few minutes, my mattress stretched across the Duke's doorway and Murrey draped across my feet, I settled myself down to do my duty.

14

The Sun in Splendour

The sun in splendour. That was our lord King Edward's symbol. Over the coming days I learnt how it mirrored his glory.

The royal barge was my first taste of it, its murrey and blue banners fluttering, trumpets blaring, oarsmen cheering, and gold-embroidered canopy and cushions glowing as it slid towards the Duke and his party. The palace at Westminster that it ferried us to was the next. It's a wonder that Master Kendall did not continually tell me to close my gawping mouth that day, for I'm sure that once again I looked like a country bumpkin overwhelmed by everything about me.

But before all was the marvel beyond words that was the River Thames. It was all my father had told me and more. The miracle was how I stepped on to the royal barge without falling into the rushing water beneath, so busy was I staring around rather than looking to where I should safely place my feet.

As the barge slipped out into midstream, behind us loomed the great London Bridge. It spanned the enormous width of the river, supported on as many as twenty arches and crammed with shops and houses from one stone-towered end to the other. On either bank huddled wharves and warehouses, in front of them forests of cranes and masts. Then, as we rowed beyond the city wall, frontages of beautiful houses or their gardens swept down to the riverside.

All about us myriad boats glided on the shimmering water, some sporting exotic standards, others simple flags or bannerets. Many were piled high with cargo, others ferried passengers alone. Yet others were all but as glorious as ours, carrying perhaps rich merchants, churchmen or city officials about their business. All gave way at the sight of our regal craft and its score of scarlet-clad oarsmen.

It was a fine day at last, this our first in London, and the distant dazzle of winter sun in river-facing windows announced to us our approach to the royal palace of Westminster. When we arrived at the private landing stage, dozens of red and gold liveried servants scurried to our aid. The Duke and his party were welcomed by numerous gentlemen clad in the most sumptuous velvet and fur-trimmed robes, and by a fanfare of trumpets both on the barge and on shore.

The steward had instructed all squires and pages to wear our livery now we were in London. I was glad. Even in my best doublet I would have been ashamed to have been seen. I lost count of the flunkies in smart crimson who saluted the company as we passed through the myriad palace corridors, and all the servants who ducked out of our way wore spotless white shirts and aprons.

Soon we were following the Duke as he strode through a series of chambers, each more splendid than the last. Then a final pair of immense double doors parted and the heavily armoured guards on either side stamped to attention.

Without doubt opening up there before me was the throne room – the centre of all power in England.

Two huge, carved gilt seats faced us on a high dais at the far end. Above them a canopy of cloth of gold and shining embroidery was crowned by a golden sun. Winter sunlight flooding in from enormous windows in one wall shone on sumptuous tapestries on the other. Chatter and laughter soared up from the assembly of elaborately gowned courtiers into the ceiling of bright-painted timbers far above.

Upon one of the thrones sat a lady clad in blue. I could not make out her face, the room was so vast. From the other sprang a larger figure, as the blare of trumpets announced our entrance.

As I bowed with the rest of our company, this man covered the hall's length in what seemed only a stride or two. The multitude of people fell silent and made way for him, bending their knees. In a second he had grasped the Duke's hand, before enveloping him in a bear-like hug.

The two brothers broke apart again, and the King swung around.

'Gentlemen, ladies,' he thundered, his voice filling the massive room with ease. 'We greet our well-beloved brother, Richard of Gloucester – conqueror of the Scots!'

As deafening cheers and applause rang out, he drew the Duke's arm through his own and led him past the crowding courtiers up to the dais, where another great chair was now set ready.

For the rest of that day there was little for me to do beyond watching and listening to the splendours unfolding around me.

And of all things, the King himself appeared most splendid. All my life I had heard with delight stories of his exploits – at the battles of Towton, Barnet, Tewkesbury – and now at last before me was the man himself.

At first sight, he could not have been more different from Duke Richard, as I had become painfully aware on meeting my new lord in the late summer. The King was a golden giant of a man, magnificent in girth as well as height, and with an immense appetite for life and laughter, who blazed like the sun on his royal banner. But the more I saw them together, the more something about their eyes and gestures marked them as brothers.

A banquet had been prepared to celebrate the Duke's arrival and his victories at Edinburgh and Berwick. As a liveried page welcomed to its lower tables, I enjoyed the best that the royal kitchens had to offer.

We dined on swan, heron and egret, which were rarely seen at Middleham, and never even at the costliest feasts my father attended for the wealthy merchants and aldermen of York. Whole suckling pigs and sturgeon steamed as they were brought to the tables. The gilded crusts of venison pies shone gold in the flare of the sunset, while sweet pastries, marchpane and sugared fruits were silvered by torchlight that came later. Many of the foodstuffs must have been brought in on foreign ships, like those tied up at the London wharves. My first taste of the rich red juice of pomegranates was one I would always remember.

At the banquet Duke Richard sat on one side of the King, while to the other was the fair-haired blue-gowned lady I had glimpsed in the throne room. The Queen was famed as a wondrous beauty, but a cool stillness set her apart amidst the revelry. To either side were several boys and girls, her sons and daughters. A page sitting alongside me pointed some out to me.

'Next to the Queen is Edward, the Prince of Wales. He's to be at Westminster throughout the Christmas season, I hear. His sister Cecily sits next to him. The younger boy to the other side is Prince Richard, and there is the Princess Elizabeth, helping your Duke to the sugared fruits. They say she is betrothed to a prince of France.'

The Princess Elizabeth appeared three or four years older than me, and with fair hair and light eyes was very like her mother. But even at this distance, I saw her catch her father's eye, and she threw back her head and laughed with a similar freedom. On first sight, her brother Edward, our Ed's cousin, showed more reserve, helping serve his mother in a quiet way. But in truth I was too far from the royal party to describe them well.

On the journey back that evening, I planned to compose in my head a letter to my friends at Middleham, describing all I had seen, ready to put quill to parchment on our arrival. But the flickering of torches on the barge, and the glow of lamps on other boats sliding through the midnight water, was so mesmerizing, and I was so full of meat and drink, that Master Kendall had to shake me awake when we reached our landing stage back in the city.

I stayed awake as we rode through the dark streets, with our guards alert to any robbers lurking in the shadows, but once back at Crosby Place I was too sleepy to begin to write. Grateful that the Duke retired at once to his chamber, I was content again to lay my head down on my mattress outside his door and drift back into sleep.

*

As my stay in London lengthened, I was to see more of the court and its inhabitants. Throughout, I attended the Duke and sang at Mass each morning, then was allowed to do as I pleased until he should want me in the evening. Not knowing the city, or trusting myself to stay safe within it, I was at a loss as to what to do. I missed the routine of the Middleham household almost as much as I did my friends.

After a day or two Master Kendall took pity on me and brought me under his wing. Once again my Minster school handwriting proved useful as he set me to copying simple letters and documents for the household. He also lent me writing materials for my letters to my friends. Attached to him, I also became part of the Duke's company when he made visits on business within the city or attended official receptions – none of which, of course, matched our arrival at court. So it was a matter of course that I should accompany the Duke and his entourage when they moved to the palace of Westminster as honoured guests of the King for the Christmas season itself.

At the palace, I wandered its labyrinthine passages as far as my livery allowed.

I was a regular visitor in the cavernous kitchens with their heady aromas of fresh-baked bread and pastries, pig or deer roasting slowly on a spit. The kitchen boys were ever eager to tempt Murrey with morsels of whatever they had to hand. I also found the music room. The tutor, deserted for the holidays by his pupils in the royal family, delighted in teaching me new songs and tunes for my lute. And in the stables I lingered for hours, breathing in the scent of fresh sweet hay and horse sweat. But I never summoned up the courage to ask for a quiet pony suitable for me, Bess not having been brought from London with the lords' horses.

While I lurked there, sometimes Duke Richard would set out for the pleasure of a gallop in the countryside around Westminster. Often he rode with Sir Francis – now made a lord as a reward from the King – or a company of courtiers, only once or twice with the King. I watched them until the last rider was out of sight, and hours later I would watch them ride back again, laughing and calling to each other. Once dismounted, they tossed their reins to stable boys – boys like me.

I was an outsider still – not quite servant, nor one of the palace household. But I was always included with the rest of the guests, no matter how lowly, in the sumptuous Christmas festivities. In the whirl of that time – those days and nights of elaborate feasting, of courtly dancing, of minstrels, of jewelled gowns for the ladies, jewel-coloured velvets for the gentlemen, of gorgeously decorated chambers, draped with swags of greenery and berries, of laughter and jesting and masques – I saw a great deal of the royal family and their courtiers. And as the days passed I also saw a change in Duke Richard.

During Christmastide his morning routine altered hardly at all. I would hear him stir early within his chamber and would rise and hurry to the palace chapel to meet with the other choristers, all of them grown men. The Duke would gather with other devout household members to hear the Mass, the usual polyphony supplemented for this season by *laude* delivered by solo treble – me.

Rarely did the King attend – or any of his close family. Many of the company were still abed long after the service, and even breakfast, ended. The festivities of the night before were responsible for that. At such times the Duke settled himself to conduct business with Master Kendall or simply in the palace's magnificent library to browse the hundreds of volumes there. I would follow him like a shadow in case I could be of service. Day by day the lines deepened on his forehead.

When he spotted me there, watching, his face would clear and he would beckon me forward, showing me some passage or illustration from his book. Sometimes he would ask me to read to him, just as his son often did. In his case, though, from time to time he would correct my French as though he were Doctor Frees. This I didn't mind – the language was often spoken at court and he told me he had travelled much abroad in his youth. Only later did I learn that he had been exiled on the continent for a time a dozen years before, when his brother had briefly lost his kingdom during the Kingmaker's rebellion.

In the evenings I was caught up in all the entertainments, even in the dancing. I silently thanked Master Petyt for teaching me enough that I didn't embarrass myself. I even clasped hands with the younger princesses and their ladies as we wove our way through the elaborate steps.

The Duke and his brother often watched from the edges of the dance, seldom taking part themselves. Once, his eyes on me, the Duke leant to speak close in the King's ear. The King roared with laughter – it reached my ears even above the music – then nodded to me when next I circled round before them. There was nothing unkind about the laugh, warmth even in the King's blue eyes, so like those of his brother. But I did wonder what had passed between them.

After a late supper had been served, and the musicians packed away their instruments, the Queen was always the first to rise and retire to her chamber. These were the times I came closest to her, as she processed the length of the hall, graciously accepting the bows and good wishes of the company, her eldest daughters and son trailing in her wake.

I bent my knee with the others. The torchlight glinted off threads of silver in her golden hair, cast shadows in the lines etched around eyes and lips, limned the puffiness about her jaw, the thickening of her waist. But she was a beauty still.

Prince Edward, a little less than my age, but taller of course, would follow her with a stiff gait, tired but reluctant to leave. His elder sisters, gilt-haired like their mother, dutiful but rebellious, looked as though they would have danced all night. The younger children were not usually seen so late.

As our visit wore on, Duke Richard rarely outstayed the Queen. He might share a final toast with the King, or a brief conversation with his brother's great friend Lord Hastings. But as the drinking and laughter became more raucous, he would take his leave. Few ladies remained by that stage. One who always did was a Mistress Shore, whose husband seemed never to be present. Often the last thing that met my eyes as I followed the Duke away was that lady refilling the King's or Lord Hastings's goblet.

On such evenings, the Duke would ask me to sing before his body servants readied him for bed. A French courtly love song was usually his choice, but sometimes he would enquire what tune the music tutor had taught me that day. My errors brought a smile, not a rebuke. Then he would dismiss me to arrange my mattress. Some nights, after his servants left, I heard him pacing his chamber before sleep overtook me.

By the time Twelfth Night arrived, I sensed the Duke was heartily sick of life at court. He left the revels earlier each night, his eyes shadowed even in the flare of the torchlight, and he spoke more sharply to the servants.

To tell the truth, I was also chafing to leave the confines of the palace. I had little to occupy me beyond being useful to the Duke or Master Kendall. I even missed the broad moors around Middleham and cantering with Alys and Roger across the scrubby heather, Murrey and Shadow scampering at our heels.

On that last day of Christmas I was leaning on Storm's stable door, missing my friends and Bess, when from behind me came the yap of pleasure Murrey would make when tossed a morsel of food. As I swung round, she was rolling on her back, exposing her belly to be tickled by a boy crouching there.

Although his face was hidden, I recognized him, this boy with the richly embroidered riding cloak and shock of fair hair. I knew him, though I had never spoken to him. This was Ed's cousin, also Edward, he who would be king some day after his father.

I watched, saying nothing, while Murrey wriggled on her back in raptures. The boy giggled with delight and reached inside his pouch to fish out another tidbit.

Murrey twisted back on to her feet in an instant and sat upright, alert. As he offered her the treat, she pulled her lips back from her sharp little teeth and delicately took it from his fingers. He fondled her ears and raised his head. His eyes shone despite the dim light.

'Is she yours?'

'Yes, Your Grace.'

'She's a pretty hound. Are you training her yourself?'

'Yes, Your Grace.'

He straightened up. Murrey, seeing there would be no more food, sidled over to lie down at my feet.

'You're not a stable boy, with a hound like that. Who are you?'

'No, Your Grace. I'm here as part of the Duke's party.'

'The Duke? Oh, my uncle Richard.' He gazed at the bustle of the grooms all around us. 'My father said to meet them both here to ride out this morning. It's the last day before my uncle leaves us.'

I tried not to smile too broadly.

'Indeed, Your Grace? I'm sure he'll miss the pleasures of the court when he goes.'

The Prince's eyes flicked back to mine.

'You think so? I fancy my uncle finds less to enjoy here than many another man would. My father tells me he doesn't like life in the city. My mother says —'

But what else the Duke's family said about him was lost in commotion as the King and his brother entered the stables with several gentlemen. The stable men ceased their work and bowed low. I shrank back into the shadows, drawing Murrey with me.

The newcomers stamped their boots on the straw-strewn floor. The Duke's brown hair was starred with fresh snowflakes.

'Come now, Ned,' I heard him say. 'You promised to ride with me today.'

'In this?'

The King sounded surprised, but no more than I felt. Though the clouds had promised snow as I crossed the courtyard earlier, through the doorway I saw that very little had yet fallen. It barely covered the cobbles. It was a poor apology for snow compared with what was usual at home.

'Once you wouldn't have let any weather stop you riding.'

The King laughed and spread his arms wide, lifting his cloak away from his broad frame.

'Once I wasn't so tormented by the effects of good living.'

The Duke turned away from his brother. From my dark corner a twist of emotion was visible on his face, but his voice didn't betray it.

'Perhaps not. But maybe that would be a reason to go.'

'Because I have put on a pound or two since last we met?' The King appealed to his son. 'Edward, do you think me stout? Like an old warhorse who should be put out to grass?'

'Of course not, father.'

The boy laughed along with his father, and for the first time I was struck by a likeness between them. But, as I glanced back at the King, in the harsh glint of the winter daylight stealing in from the open doorway, not soft flattering candlelight, I saw him as perhaps his brother did. And not all the fabulous fashions in the world, the costly brocades and slashed sleeves, the gleaming gems, the thunderous voice and laughter, could disguise the roll of fat peeking above his collar, his broad fleshy face, the redness about his eyes, the puffy fingers of the hand he now placed upon his son's head.

'And yet, as both my son and my brother are soon to leave us, it would be a shame to pass up this chance to ride together. Saddle our horses!'

As the grooms scurried to do his bidding, young Edward hung back.

'But, father…'

'Well?'

'I – I would rather not.'

'Rather not ride? With us? Why so?'

The Prince eyed the assembled company. Lord Hastings was there, his girth and magnificence almost rivalling that of the King, and several other gentlemen I couldn't name. None of the ladies of the court had chosen to ride this morning. The Duke was by some years the youngest there.

'There's no one… there'd be no one I could talk to.'

With another guffaw, the King clapped his son on the shoulder.

'Do you hear that, gentlemen? My son thinks his elders and betters poor company. Or perhaps he misses the pretty ladies in his uncle Rivers's household.'

Edward's face reddened.

'It's not that, father. It's just that —'

'What about that boy? Skulking there in the shadows. Who is he?'

To my horror, the King stepped over and hauled me out of my hiding place. I stood there, all eyes upon me, trembling.

Murrey stuck close to my ankles, a small growling deep in her throat.

'Will he do?'

Edward said nothing, only stared at me.

Duke Richard came up to the King's shoulder.

'He's my boy, Ned. His name's Matthew.'

'The lad who was dancing so properly with Cecily last night?' The King peered down at me, the trace of a smile on his face reminding me of the Duke. 'If he rides and talks as prettily as he dances, young Ned should have no objection. Edward?'

He glanced across to his son. I was grateful that he didn't see my blush.

Prince Edward nodded. He bent down to pat Murrey and sneak her another tidbit, then disappeared after the grooms.

I slipped after the Duke as he led Storm, now saddled, out of the stable.

'Your Grace?'

My voice was hardly above a whisper, but it was enough to catch Duke Richard's ear. The horse's hooves rang as he halted on the frozen cobbles.

'Yes, Matthew?'

'Your Grace, I have no horse.'

He waved a hand back towards the stable building, awash as it was with grooms and their charges.

'There are horses aplenty here.'

'But – but, Your Grace, Bess is back at Crosby Place. And these horses —'

'And these are all king's horses that might dance too prettily?'

I nodded, my cheeks burning once more. But his words were as quiet as my own.

'There's no shame in it, lad. You were not born to this.'

His eyes held mine for a second, then he looped his horse's reins over his arm.

'You shall have Storm.'

'But, Your Grace —'

'Up you go.'

He stooped before me, his hands laced together. Before I could protest again, he boosted me into the saddle. Gazing up at me, he murmured,

'He isn't Windfollower, Matt. He will bear you safely – so long as no falcons are flown at his feet.'

A hint of a smile touched his face as he called,

'Ned, that colt you were telling me of. I will try it, if it can be made ready.'

The King, now astride an enormous bay charger, reined it around to face his brother. One eyebrow rose as he caught sight of me.

'Your horse to a page, Dickon?'

'He's not just a page, Ned. He is my son's friend – and a fine singer. You should come to listen one morning. And he also saved Ed's life. He may take my horse with pleasure.'

The countryside we rode through that day could hardly have been more different to that around Middleham – gently rolling heathland, dotted with small villages, farms, woodlands. But I barely noticed. For here I was, riding, not just with a Duke, and on his highly bred charger, but also with the King of England and his son, the Prince of Wales. What would my father think of that?

If only I had the skill to sketch the scene for him, as Ed did. He sent small drawings in his letters to me of all I was missing at Middleham – Alys training Shadow, Lady on Roger's wrist, Elen sitting reading one of my letters. Yet could anyone capture in mere ink the excitement of riding such a horse as Storm, in the wake of these great men of the kingdom, while chatting with nonchalance to the heir of that kingdom – about hounds, hawking, hunting, my impressions of the court?

The highlight came when the King, who had been riding between Lord Hastings and Duke Richard on his borrowed horse, reined back until Edward and I caught him up.

'Master Wansford,' he said, as I attempted an inelegant bow from atop Storm, 'my brother has told me how you saved my little nephew on the boar hunt. I thank you – and be assured, my family will ever be in your debt.'

I stammered out my thanks and bowed from the waist again, hearing a tiny yelp of complaint from Murrey tucked up in my doublet. The King smiled and touched the tip of his riding whip to his hat before cantering forward once more to the head of the company.

How could I possibly describe my emotions at that moment using dry words scribed on parchment? Perhaps such a tale would best be told in person on our visit to York after Parliament ended. My father would surely change his mind about me then.

On our return to the palace, a party of riders, newly arrived, were churning the snow in the stableyard to grey slush. As I swung down from Storm, one turned and saw me. A handsome fair-haired gentleman about the age of Duke Richard, he threw me the reins of his mount.

'Take my horse, boy, and see you treat him well.'

'But, my lord,' I began, glancing around for a groom or stable lad.

'Come, don't stand there idling. Take my horse, I say. And you will address me as Your Grace – if you address me at all.'

'Yes, Your Grace, of course.'

I bowed low, hurriedly retrieving Murrey as she protested again. The man strode towards King Edward, and bowed in his turn.

'Harry,' the King boomed. 'How are you, my boy? You come too rarely to court. How is your delightful wife, our sister Catherine? Well, I hope.'

Even at this distance, as the newcomer straightened up I could see the grimace on his face, momentarily hidden from the King.

'She is well, I thank you, Your Grace. She would have joined me, but for the fact that I shall be occupied at Parliament and no company for her.'

He bowed also to Edward and Duke Richard, who both returned the gesture, before the King clapped him across the shoulders.

'Go on in, Harry,' he said. 'We'll join you and the Queen when we've finished here.'

Edward wandered over to me as the man stalked off with his companions towards the palace. Ever hopeful of more treats, Murrey sat to attention for him, her wagging tail brushing the thin snow off the cobbles.

He reached into his pouch for a morsel. As he circled it over her head, she stood on her hind legs and performed a perfect pirouette, her nose barely an inch from the tidbit. He flicked it to her and as she snatched it from the air, I asked,

'So who was that?'

He squinted at me.

'Oh, that's Uncle Harry. He's Duke of Buckingham, married to my mother's sister. We don't see him often – he spends most of his time on his estates.'

He held up another treat for Murrey, trying to persuade her to spin again.

It struck me that I'd forgotten to use his title when I spoke to him, but it seemed he wasn't as bothered about it as his uncle. This new uncle.

'I'm not sure my mother likes him much,' he went on. 'Last night I heard her say…'

But he broke off as his father and other uncle came up, just in time to see Murrey perform for him again.

'She'll make a very good dancer,' he said, eagerness bubbling in his voice as she claimed her second reward.

'Just like her owner,' the King said. 'An unusual colour, but she's a fine hound.'

'Of course,' said Duke Richard. 'She's from Florette's latest litter, like to be her last. You remember, your Conqueror is the father.'

'Ah, a royal hound. Then she should have a royal collar.'

The King tossed an order to a serving man who hurried away into a nearby building and in a moment re-emerged, bearing a tray. His master ran a finger across the variety of items on the tray, then selected one, a wide leather strap adorned with brass studs.

He knelt down on one knee beside Murrey and buckled it around her slender neck. I was grateful that my hound, hopeful of another tidbit, had ceased to grumble.

With one large hand on the cobbles, the King pushed himself back to his feet. A narrow shaft of sunlight pinpointed for an instant a gilt fleur-de-lys stitched on to Murrey's new collar.

'A good dog – if perhaps a little small.'

'My huntsman called her a runt,' said Duke Richard mildly. 'Though he did afterwards apologize for the suggestion that a royal couple could bear a runt.'

The King let out a great shout of laughter and slapped his brother on the back.

To my surprise, the Duke staggered forward, more than I would have expected, even with the weight of that great paw behind the slap. A spasm contorted his face.

The King's other hand caught him before he fell.

'Forgive me, brother. I forgot myself,' he said, his face unreadable.

The Duke took in a quick breath, straightening up, then himself laughed, his hands brushing down his doublet.

'It is no matter.'

'But it pains you still.'

'Only after a long day in armour, or when riding an unfamiliar, half-broken horse.'

'Then you will not take the colt?'

'I think not.'

Before I could grasp the meaning of this exchange – was it some private family jest? – the King turned to me.

'And you, Master Wansford. How did you like your new mount?'

'Very well, Your Grace,' I managed to say, startled though I was at being addressed again. 'Though I shall prefer it when I have my own Bess to ride again.'

'Your own horse? That will be soon enough if you are leaving with my brother tomorrow. But perhaps before then you will instead dance with my Bess.' Perhaps he saw the puzzled frown still on my face, for he continued, 'My eldest daughter, Elizabeth. Perhaps this evening it will be her turn to dance with you. Now we know the service you did her cousin.'

I bowed as low as I could.

'Thank you, Your Grace. And for the gift of the collar.'

The King patted my shoulder and walked away back to the palace, his son and brother at his side. I had to hook a finger through Murrey's new finery to stop her trotting after the source of all those treats.

15

Twelfth Night

That night I did indeed dance with the Princess Elizabeth, if it can be so described.

Barely a moment her hand rested in mine each time we circled one another before she passed on to the next male dancer – her brother Edward, standing alongside me. But I was dazzled by her smile, and by the few words she bestowed on me.

'Master Matthew, my father tells me you rescued my cousin Edward in a snowstorm. You have my thanks as well as his.'

That the King had thought to mention me! It was one of many memories from an evening crammed with them.

The last day of Christmastide was marked by the most elaborate festivities. A fabulous banquet with more courses than I could number. Not one or two, but three dancing bears. Then troops of mummers performed for the assembled guests.

It was very different from the Bible stories of our Corpus Christi plays in York, but, may God forgive me, I enjoyed it as much. The jewelled costumes, colourful speeches, ribald songs, fantastical monsters fashioned from sumptuous fabrics stretched over wooden frames, the swordplay agile like dancing, the dances alight with fire-eaters, sword-swallowers, knife-jugglers. And with the dancing that followed under the still-flaring torches, all my senses were sated by the time, long after midnight, when the Queen rose.

She gathered her children around her like her voluminous satin skirts, and prepared to leave. At her throat, the fire of the brands reflected from the liquid depths of the blood-red ruby the King had presented her this Twelfth Night. Each daughter wore a similar jewel, though smaller – blue, green or purple – his sons thick gold chains draped around their necks.

As they each curtsied or bowed to their father, I fingered the soft emerald green cloth of my new doublet. My own gift from him as a household guest. I had found it laid out in the pages' quarters on my return from the ride.

The final deep curtsey was by the Queen to her husband, then the high table almost emptied as she swept from the hall with her family. Only the King and Duke Richard remained standing there together, Lord Hastings now behind them, a hand resting on the shoulder of each.

The Duke of Buckingham reseated himself at the end of the table where he had remained all evening, never rising to join in the dancing. As I straightened up from my bow to the departing Queen, he was nursing a goblet and watching the King and his companions from beneath hooded eyes.

Before long, as usual, Duke Richard took his leave. A bear hug from his brother, clasped hands with Lord Hastings and my lord of Buckingham, both also sporting heavy gold collars, and he was striding towards the door.

I fell in behind him, but a pace or two into the corridor, he swung round.

There were few candle sconces here. After the bright torchlight of the great hall, his face was hardly visible in the shadows.

'Matthew. Stay longer if you wish. It's your last night in the palace. I don't need your services tonight.'

'Your Grace, I would rather not.'

Without another word, he turned on his heel and I followed him through the tortuous twists and turnabouts of passageways to his chamber.

I opened the door for him. Revealed within were his body servants asleep in chairs, one even sprawled before the flickering fire.

I looked to see if the Duke was angry, but he only smiled.

'It's been a long night of waiting for them. Help me wake them, Matthew. If you will attend me, we can send them off to their beds.'

Together we shook them awake.

I smelt wine on one man's breath, and drips of deep red stained the snowy cloth beneath the jug set ready on a table. But I said nothing, and neither did the Duke.

In a few moments, yawning and apologizing, the servants were sent on their way. Murrey alone remained, curled up still fast asleep on the hearth rug, where I had left her at the start of the evening.

I poured a goblet full of wine for the Duke and set it down beside his fireside chair, taking care to replace the jug over the spots on the white cloth. Then, picking up my lute from the corner, I sat upon a stool on the fringes of the firelight and toyed with the strings.

Despite the lateness of the hour, the Duke wasn't disposed to settle. He paced the candle-lit room for a time before pausing at the window. Pushing aside the heavy embroidered curtain, he rested his hands on the stone ledge and stared out at the twinkling lights across the river.

For some minutes the stillness was disturbed only by the sweet notes of the lute and Murrey's soft snores.

'In a month's time – maybe six weeks – we will be home again.'

I started at his voice. Had I been drifting towards sleep?

'Your Grace?'

'Home, Matthew – in a month or so. The good citizens of York have requested that I report matters of Parliament to them. We will stay some days.'

'Yes, Your Grace. And then on to Middleham?'

He glanced round at me.

I ran my fingers over the strings, fearing that he had noticed I'd stopped playing. For the life of me I could not remember the tune.

'Yes, then Middleham. If your father will let you return.'

'Of course he will, Your Grace.'

That he wouldn't had never occurred to me.

If I'd been half asleep before, this thought woke me altogether.

'Being at the castle has been so good for me. I'm sure he will say that. And I've made such good friends there.'

'Ah, yes, your friends. Roger, Alys – Edward. You've been spending a great deal of time with them.'

'Is that wrong, sir? One of the other pages —'

I remembered what Hugh had said, all those weeks ago.

'Well?'

'He said you might not like it. Edward making friends with a merchant's son.'

'Why would I mind that? I myself spend much of my time with merchants – they're the backbone of England in these days. Who – ? No, no matter. I can guess who it was. No, I'm grateful for your befriending Edward. He has been lonely in the past. And angry not to be a page himself. But we couldn't send him away.'

'I have heard him called –' what was it Roger had said? '– delicate?'

'Delicate? I suppose so. He has had bouts of illness ever since he was born. As you saw on the boar hunt. Some say that is what happens when cousins marry.'

'Cousins?'

'Yes, the Duchess is my cousin. Or at least her father was. You have heard of the Earl of Warwick? Though perhaps he died before you were born.'

'The Kingmaker? Just after, Your Grace.' This was even more complicated than Roger had said. 'He was your cousin? But he fought...'

'Against my brother? Yes. Strange, isn't it? That one cousin should fight another – even for such a prize as the crown. I pray that will never happen again. And then our brother George...'

He fell silent again, gazing out at the starlit night.

I recalled what Roger had told me of the Duke's other brother. I gave up trying to pick up the tune again, thinking perhaps I was going to be dismissed.

'Do you have brothers, Matthew?'

His question surprised me. My mind had been so caught up with his family.

'Yes, Your Grace. Three, and two sisters.'

'Older or younger?'

'Two brothers are older, Your Grace, and one sister. And then there is the baby.'

'Oh, yes, the little one.'

I could see his face only in profile, but the glimmer of a nearby candle caught the curve of a smile. Had the Duchess told him my story?

'And do you look up to them?'

'My brother Frederick is apprentice to a bookbinder and getting to be a very fine archer, they say. The other, John, became a cantor when he left the Minster school. And my sister, Agnes, is to be married to a mercer. My father is very proud of them all.'

'And you?'

'I'm proud of them too, my lord. What younger brother wouldn't be?'

He laughed.

'Well said. That should be the way with younger brothers, shouldn't it? Always to love and respect them, but Matthew... never worship them like heroes. One day they may do something that —'

His voice trailed away, his eyes fixed once more on the far distant bank of the Thames.

I wondered at his speech. Was he thinking of his dead brother George? And why today?

I moved to pluck the lute again, but the Duke swung round and leaned back on the window ledge. Beyond his shoulder, the lights across the river mirrored the stars in the velvet midnight sky.

'It's late, Matthew, and I am tired. We must to our beds. If you will first assist me...'

I propped the lute against the stool and was at his side in an instant.

He unclasped the gleaming collar of heavy gold links that had been his brother's gift and handed it to me. I held it, marvelling at its weight, while he unlocked his jewel chest to place it safely within. Tucking the key, on its fine neck chain, once more beneath his white linen undershirt, he began to remove his doublet, while I poured water from a ewer into a basin for him to wash.

There was a stiffness in his movements as he shrugged the doublet from his shoulders and I stepped forward to help him guide the sleeves off his arms.

He nodded at me as he unlaced the neck of his shirt.

'Thank you, Matt. My brother's colt was not a relaxing ride today and I'm a little sore from it. Your help is welcome.'

He sat down on a nearby stool, his back to me, and raised his arms. I gripped the lower hem and pulled the shirt off over his head.

I couldn't stifle my gasp at what I saw then, thrown into shadowy relief by the jumping firelight. Of a sudden I understood what had happened in the stableyard after our ride.

The top of my lord's back was twisted to one side, like the root of a gnarled tree, the curve pushing one shoulder a little higher than the other.

'My lord!' I said, without thinking. I couldn't keep the horror – or the fear – out of my voice.

His reply was calm.

'It's nothing.'

'Nothing, my lord?'

'Well, sometimes it's something. But mostly —'

He stood up and, going to the table, began to wash. As he splashed the water, then briskly dried himself with the towel I handed him, question after question sped through my head. Then he was standing there waiting, and I hurried to gather up his night shirt, laid ready across the bed.

Easing the clean linen over his head, and then gingerly across his shoulders, only one question came spilling past my lips.

'Does it hurt, my lord?'

Duke Richard laughed, a short bark of a laugh.

'At times. Usually only when I've been in full armour all day – or perhaps when I've been softened by too much good living, as at court. Mostly, indeed, I do not notice it.'

'The physicians – can they not...?'

'I've had all the best treatments, Matt – surgeons, poultices, even a wooden rack to stretch me straighter. They didn't do that for long.' Again, a laugh. 'Nothing works. Our Lord gives us each our burden to bear, and we must bear it with fortitude. I live with it.'

He reached for a fur mantle from the foot of the bed and swung it around his shoulders. For the first time I felt the growing chill.

As I grasped a poker to stir the fire back to life, among my still-tangled thoughts, one stood out.

'But in battle, my lord? They say you're a great warrior, the King's most steadfast general. How can you...?'

My words faltered and I fell silent.

How dare I question a royal duke in this way?

But as I turned back to him, no anger touched his face, only thoughtfulness.

He took up the goblet I had filled and folded himself into the carved, padded chair.

'My physician thinks it may have been from too much early weapons training. I was a young boy – younger than you, Matt – when I was first a page in my cousin Warwick's household. I was not always a strong child, small too for many years. Perhaps I tried too hard to overcome that after my father was killed. My brother became King and I knew I had to serve him. And when my back began to... well, I knew I could overcome that too.'

He took a sip of wine.

'Of course, superstitious people might put the blame on witchcraft.'

'Not I, my lord.'

'No, Matthew, I well know your views on such magic. But perhaps your wise woman in York could find some cure or some help for it instead. Indeed, she could do no worse than the learned men I have consulted.'

Perhaps he saw the doubt in my face despite the dim candlelight.

'But as I say, it is no matter. It has never prevented me serving my brother. I learnt well enough how to wield a sword and I gained in strength, if not so much in size.'

'So there is hope for me yet,' I blurted out.

The Duke was mystified, as I sank to my knees in front of him.

'For you?'

'For me to learn enough to serve you well, you and His Grace the King. I may be small now, but... If I work hard at weapons training when we go home. If I can train when you're in Parliament. Perhaps with the other pages at Crosby Place...'

Silence followed my outburst.

The Duke gazed at me for what seemed long minutes. As my blood cooled, I found myself unable to look away.

Then he broke the hold, putting his cup down on the table.

'You're so like my son in some ways – in your eagerness to be a knight. I would that he had your ability with books and figures too.'

'I would give them up, my lord.'

'No, Matthew, never do that. Being a warrior is not the only way to serve. Brain work and book learning are as valuable to the kingdom.'

'But not for a proper man!'

'There are other ways of being a man than fighting. When my father died, I had no choice, but you don't have to take that path. A brave strong heart and determination such as yours are more important for a warrior than mere physical strength, but they can be turned to greater things too. England is at peace now, thanks to my brother. The kingdom has a need for all different kinds of men.'

He rose and stood with his back to the embers of the fire. As I scrambled up too, he stroked Murrey's still-sleeping form with his foot. His eyes were in shadow.

'I think you also have been too idle here at court, Matthew. You need to exercise not just your body but your brain. And I believe I know what to do with you this coming month while I'm occupied in Parliament. But you must promise me —'

'Anything, Your Grace.'

'You must promise me not to become so wrapped up with what you are doing there that you forget to return to sing for me.'

Minutes later I was once more outside the chamber door, my mattress and blanket placed ready, Murrey cradled in my arms, whimpering in her sleep. All that had happened was replaying in my mind.

But before I could gather my tired thoughts into any kind of shape, from around the passageway's dark corner came the bustle of footsteps and the dim glow of candles approaching.

I had time only to lay Murrey down on my bed and straighten up, my hand on my knife hilt, before a small party of men appeared. The first of them carried no lamp, but the flicker of candles held by others cast demonic shadows on the haughty features of the Duke of Buckingham.

He halted, waving one of his companions forward to light my face.

'Ah, the stable boy who was no stable boy. I saw you dancing with the princesses, my nieces – and talking with young Edward. So who are you?'

The colour rose in my face, but I trusted that this mighty lord wouldn't detect it in the gloom.

'Matthew Wansford, Your Grace.'

'And who, pray, is Matthew Wansford?'

I drew myself up as tall as I could – though I still didn't reach to his shoulder.

'Son of Master John Wansford, Your Grace, merchant of York. And now in the employ of His Grace the Duke of Gloucester.'

'A merchant's son? Is that the company a royal duke keeps in these days?'

His companions tittered at the disdain in his voice. He clasped his cloak to him as though afraid I might soil it and stalked away along the dark corridor.

139

As he and his men rounded the next corner and the faint glimmer of candlelight faded from view, I relaxed my tight grip on my dagger pommel. The words of 'my' Duke came back to me: 'The kingdom has a need for all different kinds of men.' They gave me strength as I settled down to my rest.

16

'A Singer for a Singer'

'Master Ashley – this is Master Matthew Wansford.'

I bowed deeply, eager to make a good first impression.

The man before me was of middle age and middle height, richly dressed in the latest fashions from the continent. As he doffed his cap to me, his sandy hair was thinning, but there was a youthful glint in his eyes.

'Master Ashley,' continued Duke Richard, talking now to me, 'deals in fine cloths from Flanders and beyond, but also in books. He supplied many of the volumes you have seen at Middleham and in my brother's library at Westminster. He has agreed that you may spend the next few weeks on his premises, if you will make yourself useful in return.'

'His Grace tells me you have a head for figures and for French and Latin, Master Wansford.'

'Yes, sir,' I said, worried that the Duke had overstated my abilities. 'I will do my best to serve you in any way I can.'

And that was my introduction to my new master and the merchants of London.

It was the first morning after our return from the palace. From Crosby Place the Duke had ridden into the heart of the city with a small group of companions, including me, grateful to be astride Bess once again. He had said little to me of our destination, only that I must treat our host that day with the deference due a master. My employment by Master Ashley was to be a favour, although I could scarce believe that even the proudest merchant would spurn any request made by the King's brother.

We were greeted at the door of a townhouse that rivalled Crosby Place in its splendour, and ushered as most welcome guests to a sumptuous meal of a type that was becoming familiar. The Duke and Master Ashley spoke of many matters as they dined, then retired with their secretaries to a private office. By day's end, a great deal of business had been transacted, not just concerning my entry into this new household.

From that day on, while I was in London, my time was divided between serving and singing for the Duke in one fine townhouse, and busying myself in the offices and library of another.

Master Ashley introduced me to his associates and clerks and I willingly undertook whatever errands or small tasks of accounting or recording they requested. Any spare time I whiled away exploring his marvellous books, either in his own library or waiting to be bound or delivered to his many customers. I even met the renowned Master Caxton, first printer of books on English soil, and visited his shop in the shadow of St Paul's.

After the heady atmosphere of court, being back in the hustle and bustle of a working city was like a refreshing draught of clear, fresh water. In some ways it was far removed from my life in York, in others it brought home to me that merchants were the same the world over. I soon became accustomed to the babble of different languages and the variety of faces, from the fair-haired, sharp-featured Baltic traders to the darker looks of those from the distant south and east. But for all their diversity, their interests were identical: making money, enjoying money, the wonder of travel to far-flung places, the efficient hiring and equipping of ships and pack trains, the joy of hard bargaining, and avoiding the depredations of brigands and princes and city authorities.

Despite the fascinations of my days, I never forgot to return to Crosby Place to sing and play for His Grace. Although Parliament met in Westminster, he preferred to spend the evenings quietly at his city home. He would be closeted for a while after supper with Master Kendall, Sir Francis or his London steward, but sooner or later would summon me from letter writing or games of dice or swordplay. I got along well enough with the other pages, though the younger ones held me in awe for my special service to the Duke.

May the Lord forgive me if I ever flaunted my pride at the favour he showed me in those days. On occasion he would ask his gentlemen to leave him and, cradling a last cup of wine, would listen to me alone in the ruddy glow of the fire's final embers. Sometimes he questioned me about my day and my impressions of London life. In turn he shared snippets of the business conducted by the great lords and gentlemen in Parliament on behalf of the kingdom. I understood very little, but enjoyed his tales of the more colourful characters and their speeches in support of one cause or arguments against another.

One evening well into February, the Duke returned later than usual. He had supped with his brother after a long day of parliamentary business and retired to his private chamber with no other company than me, my lute and Murrey.

'Just a few more days,' he said, as he sat nursing his goblet. 'Then we shall be riding north with most welcome news for your home city, Matthew. Though first we must spend one final evening at the palace.'

'Good news for York?' I asked.

'Aye. Because of its special service to the King in the late Scottish war, Parliament has decreed its citizens need not pay taxes for the next.'

'The next war, Your Grace?'

'The next war, Matthew. Whenever that shall be. Perhaps this coming summer. My brother agrees that now is the time to settle a lasting peace with the Scots. Too long have they brought us trouble on our northern borders. Perhaps your brother the archer will join us at the muster this time.'

Though I continued to pluck the lute strings, I couldn't suppress a pang of envy at the idea that Frederick might march behind the Duke's banner so soon. I knew I was too young to join him, but maybe, in future years…

Within a few days Parliament came to an end. To my surprise, I was called to Master Ashley's courtyard that afternoon. There stood a servant in royal livery leading Bess in full harness, my best clothes in a bundle across her saddle. The merchant himself hurried to bid me farewell, telling me I had been summoned by Duke Richard to attend the King at the palace.

'You have been blessed with royal favour, Matt,' he said, as he helped me fasten my new emerald doublet with his own hands. 'One day that angel's voice the Duke tells me of will desert you, but mind you serve him loyally and your position in life will be secure evermore.'

'Thank you, sir,' I said, 'and for your kindness to me while I've been here.'

'Kindness to you? Nay, you have been useful to us – and your little dog a pleasure!'

Once I was astride Bess, he handed Murrey up to me and I slung her across the front of my saddle. She had now grown too large to snuggle in my doublet, but was still too small to risk down among the thronging hooves and deadly cartwheels of the London streets.

As I took my leave of Master Ashley and urged Bess on to follow the servant out of the courtyard, I thought back across the weeks I had spent here – and of how popular the pup had become. If I had been a willing helper, Murrey had been a quick learner. Everyone in the townhouse now knew that, for a morsel of meat, she would not only dance and pirouette as she had for Prince Edward, but bounce the length of a small chamber high upon her hind paws, or roll over and lie still as though dead until a sharp whistle revived her.

It was a dull ride, all the way upriver to the palace. The servant was a surly fellow who uttered not a word to me, resentful no doubt at escorting a mere boy such a distance. On our arrival, I was ushered into the vestry of the royal chapel. To my amazement, waiting for me there was not Master Banester, who was in charge of the King's adult singers, but the choir master from the Abbey, Master Cornish, with all his choristers.

'This is most irregular,' he muttered as my name was announced by the servant. But he hustled me into line behind his boy singers, thrusting a surplice into my hands and rattling off the titles of songs I was to sing.

Moments later we boys were filing into position in the exquisite chapel. Every seat was already filled – a thing unknown during my stay at Christmas, when sometimes the singers outnumbered the congregation.

The King sat in front, between the Queen and Duke Richard, with several royal children ranged about them. I also spied Sir Francis, the Duke of Buckingham and Lord Hastings among many another richly attired noble gentleman. I recognized several from court, though I tried in vain to recall their names.

Two in the second row were whispering together as we entered. One leant forward to drop some words in the Queen's ear. She shook her head sharply, a frown shadowing her face, and waved him away. Displeasure flitted across Duke Richard's face at the disturbance, but the King appeared unaware. He stood as we singers finished assembling and addressed the gathering. This was to be a special Mass to offer thanks for the success of Parliament.

I took little part in the service beyond the usual responses that were second nature to me after my years at the Minster. As the Abbey choristers' treble voices soared upwards around me in unfamiliar songs, I wondered why I was there, having never practised with them. When I joined in alleluias or descants, I was just one among many – adding little or nothing to the swelling sound.

With the end of the Mass nearing, Master Cornish crooked his finger at me. It was his signal for the first song that I knew – the *laude* with which I had welcomed Duke Richard home all those months before.

As I readied myself, to my horror all the other singers melted away, leaving me alone to face the congregation.

It was to be a solo.

Before the royal family and the foremost men of the realm.

My throat tightened and my chest felt as though a great weight lay within it.

In my terror, my eyes sought out the faces in the front row. The Queen's was impassive and Princess Elizabeth's hidden as she leaned over to chide the younger children, who were squirming from sitting so long. Prince Edward, I remembered, had returned to Ludlow. Their father the King caught my eye, then bent his head to speak to his brother. But the Duke's attention to the service had never wavered. Now he nodded at me, a half-smile, as so often, upon his face.

I swallowed once. I knew I had to sing well and repay his faith in me.

It may be that Sir William would have been rendered speechless by my singing that day, had he been in attendance. The royal chapel, larger than that at Middleham, but far smaller than the cavernous Minster, seemed the perfect place for my voice, as it took wing up to the painted vaulting far above. As it resonated among the gilded carvings adorning every wall. As it hushed the fidgeting listeners and drew even the Queen's gaze in my direction.

By the start of the second song, a *Te Deum*, my fear had fled. At the third, when the other choristers moved forward again to join me, I was disappointed that my time to shine had been so short.

The final notes faded. There was a moment of stillness. Then we choristers were led by Master Cornish back to the vestry. As we passed through the arched doorway, out of the corner of my eye I glimpsed the Queen speaking to her husband, her bejewelled hand pointing towards me.

145

In the vestry, as I struggled out of my surplice, Master Cornish bustled over to me. It ran through my mind that, for all my pride in myself, my performance hadn't pleased him. But his face broke into a smile.

'That was well sung, boy, though your pronunciation could bear some correction. I'm told that you accompanied my lord of Gloucester down from the north country. I think it would be possible to train that out of you if you were to join my choir. How old are you? Eleven? It might be worth the effort for a few more years of that voice.'

The first stab of pleasure at the praise was parried by the pain I felt from his next words. Surely he didn't think me so young? And was my speech so alien?

I bowed my head to him, and to hide my confusion.

'Sir, I'm the Duke's man.' Man! 'I serve him only, and my home is in the north. But I thank you for your kind words.'

Little regret showed in the choir master's face. Maybe he was thankful to be spared so much effort.

'Well spoken, boy. Continue to spread the word of God in that forsaken region. But should you ever be in Westminster again, come to see me. Perhaps we could find a place for you.'

I was saved from thinking of a suitable reply by the entry of a palace servant, who spoke quietly to Master Cornish. The choir master turned back to me.

'It seems I'm not the only one to admire your singing. The King has requested your attendance in his private chambers.'

I had time only to straighten my rumpled doublet and run my fingers through my ever wayward hair before following the servant.

We passed through a maze of passages on the way to a quarter of the palace I had never before visited. Four well-armed liveried men stood guard at the double doors at which we halted. One checked us up and down with a glance, took my name, then instructed two others to push wide the great oak doors.

'Master Matthew Wansford, Your Grace.'

The chamber into which I was waved, though large, was very different to the rooms in which I had seen the King and his family before. It reminded me more of the one to which the Duke retreated in the evenings at Middleham.

Intricate tapestries covered every wall and a bright fire burned on the immense stone hearth. Finely carved chairs piled with plentiful cushions littered the wooden floor, and a long side table was stocked with flagons, long-stemmed wineglasses and bowls of nuts and fruit. Among them were the sun-like oranges that I now knew travelled so far in the ships of Spanish merchants.

But what struck me most, as the hum of conversation of the people gathered there died away, was the brilliant song of birds.

Hanging from hooks in the deep window alcoves, or on wooden stands scattered through the chamber, were scores of tiny wire cages. Each had a single feathered inhabitant. Some wore their drab brown clothes with humility, others sported suits of exotic plumage in red, purple, green, gold. A few I recognized from the city gardens or fields around York. More were as foreign to me as those merchants who must have brought them to English shores. All, it seemed, were striving to out-sing their fellows. But the beauty of their music was tainted for me by sadness that they were so imprisoned.

Duke Richard was one of the small company – a friendly face among the unfamiliar.

As he made his way towards me, I tried to recall to mind the names of these people who were so intimate with the King and Queen.

The Duke of Buckingham was present, speaking with the Princess Elizabeth and Lord Hastings. The two gentlemen who had whispered in the chapel were also there. I now remembered the friendly royal page pointing them out as the Queen's brother, Sir Edward Woodville, and her eldest son, the Marquess of Dorset, who was half-brother to Prince Edward. Others I had less luck with before the Duke took my elbow and propelled me to where the royal couple sat in the centre of the throng.

He bowed low to the Queen and I followed suit.

'Sister, this is Matthew, the boy who sang for us earlier.'

'And who rescued our little nephew in the snowstorm.' The King leaned across from his chair. 'I have not forgotten. And how is your little hound?'

'Not so little now, Your Grace,' I ventured to reply, glancing down to where Murrey wove her slender body between my ankles.

The King laughed and enticed her to him with one scrap, before employing another to draw her on to her hind legs to dance.

Annoyance touched the Queen's face, but it cleared as the Marquess bent his head to speak to her. At her nod, he rose and moved away, while she turned a cool smile on me.

'Most valued service indeed, Matthew. I hope you will accept a gift of thanks from your Queen.'

The Duke breathed a word to me and I knelt before the Queen in obedience to him, Murrey pressing close against my leg. The firelight glanced off the brass adorning the royal gift already around her neck.

The Marquess stepped back to the Queen and handed her something. She held it out towards me.

'A singer for a singer.'

My heart almost stopped at what I saw and heard, but at a nudge from Duke Richard, my hands lifted to accept the gift.

The sweetest, most plaintive trilling imaginable escaped from the exquisite bronze cage. Inside, on a rod of ivory, perched a finch, black and white, a flash of red at its beak, beaten gold across its wing.

Another prod from the Duke and I stuttered my thanks, but the Queen's attention was already elsewhere.

I stumbled to my feet and backed away, glad no longer to have her eyes on me, but still feeling the Duke's gaze. Dragging Murrey after me, I ducked into a corner near the table. There, among the shadows, perhaps we could avoid more scrutiny.

The Duke fell back into conversation with the King and all around the twittering of people rose again to rival that of the birds.

We hid in the corner, helping ourselves to fruit to stave off hunger, until it was time to depart. To my relief it was not long before the Duke pleaded fatigue and took his leave of his brother with a lingering embrace.

We returned to Crosby Place and a quiet supper, after which the Duke had me sing for him, French courtly songs this time. Then he dismissed me with hardly a word.

In the corridor I draped my kerchief across the cage to shield the finch from drafts, and muffle its song. Strange it was to sleep that night with two small creatures in my care.

17

A Homecoming

Within a few days our small party was clattering again beneath the grim portals of Bishopsgate. Only a few citizens scattered along the road cheered us at this early hour as the multitude of belfries rang out joyously for the first service of the day.

My thoughts were jumbled as we left the city. Would I ever hear those four score peals of bells again?

It was a frosty day, a sprinkling of snow once more covering the iron-hard ground. But in the village fields, the first green shoots of winter wheat pierced the earth and narrow buds fringed the twigs of tree and hedge. Spring was waiting beneath the pale grey sky.

But whatever the weather hereabouts, I couldn't delay. My bird was no alien, but a goldfinch. It must surely have been snared close to the city, not in our harsher northern climate. If it were to survive after its luxurious, heated captivity, it would have to be here.

I pulled Bess to the side of the company and halted as though to attend to Murrey. Robert raised his eyebrows to me in a question, but I waved him to ride on.

Lifting the bird's cage from its hook on Bess's harness, I squatted down. I kept the pony between me and the passing riders, although I had my explanation ready if anyone saw or asked after the bird.

For all my caution, as I fiddled with the wire catch of the cage, the shadow of a horse and rider darkened the ground beside me.

Squinting up I saw, of all people, Duke Richard astride Storm.

His eyes took in the scene. The finch, no longer bouncing to the beat of hooves, opened its beak and golden notes tumbled out.

The Duke's quiet voice barely reached me over the sweet sound.

'Releasing the Queen's gift to you?'

I drew my hands away from the cage and stood up.

'Your Grace, the catch, it —'

'Looks strong enough. It's Venetian workmanship. The best.'

A pause, broken only by the bird's song.

The company continued to straggle past, one or two directing curious looks at us. As always I couldn't lie.

'I was going to let it go. To say it had escaped. I meant no disrespect.'

'I know that, Matt. And I suspect none would be taken – by my brother at least. All creatures prefer freedom. He understands that – or he did once. Perhaps there are some at court—'

He broke off and swung down from his horse. Crouching down on the snowy ground, he removed his gauntlets and his strong fingers quickly released the stubborn catch. He handed the cage to me, its wire door swinging loose.

'There. You shall have the honour.'

I grasped the cage in one hand, pinning open the door with my thumb. Reaching in, I enfolded the bright bird in my fingers and drew it out.

It rested for a moment on the palm of my hand, silent now. Then, as I gently thrust it towards the sky, it opened its wings and unsteadily took flight. It fluttered in a circle once, high above our heads, then flew away, along the road that we were following. In a few seconds it disappeared among a stand of trees up ahead.

The Duke's hand was on my shoulder as we watched it together. Then, without another word, he remounted and rode on to catch up the rest of our company.

We stopped that night and each night after at the same houses as on our journey to London. This time, though, we didn't stop at the beautiful church of the tombs. Often now I rode alongside the Duke and after we passed that turning of the road, I found the courage to ask him about it.

'That place is Fotheringhay, Matt. It was my parents' main home and the castle where I was born. When my father was killed in battle, my brother Edmund too, they were buried by their enemies at Pontefract, close to where they fell. But after my brother Edward became King, he had a suitable place made for them here. When it was ready, I followed their coffins all the long road south to their final rest. It's where they would have wanted to be for eternity.'

'Your brother Edmund?' Another one?

'Aye, Edmund. He was only seventeen when he was cut down. Hardly older than you, Matt.'

'But a warrior already.'

'Aye, a very fine one.' He glanced askance at me from atop Storm. 'Of course, he'd been training almost since he was a baby.'

'A baby?'

'Don't stand so amazed, lad. He was a very big baby. At least the size of a two-year-old, our mother said.'

I looked up at him. Of course he wore the half-smile he always did when jesting. I joined in his laughter at my foolishness, but still, I wondered about this other brother – and, as ever, that the Duke spoke to me at all. Me, a lowly page. But, as the days rolled by, his mood became lighter with all the company. As though he, like the goldfinch, had been set free from the stifling atmosphere of London – and perhaps especially the court.

After days of travelling, and when we had left behind those tentative signs of spring, we came to places the names of which were familiar to me. And at long last, one afternoon, when early flurries of snow had given way to weak late-winter sunlight, I spied on the horizon the twin towers of York Minster.

This time it was my turn to point out a landmark to Robert, although his only interest in the city would be the prospect of a fire and hot dinner after a long, cold day's journeying. But for much of the company it was a most welcome sight.

A cheer went up, the Duke's white boar banner was unfurled, and as one the party broke into a fast trot. I had to whistle up Murrey, nosing along in our wake, to make sure she wasn't left behind.

The scenes that greeted our entry into London had been memorable, but they were nothing to our reception here.

A messenger had been sent ahead to alert the council to our arrival and all had been made ready. As we rode beneath the towering bulk of Micklegate Bar, the town band awaited us, dressed in their sky-blue livery. They led the hurrahs of the assembled townsfolk, accompanying them on shawm, sackbut and busine.

I knew these waits from their performances on feast days past – John Swynbourne with his cheeks bulging as he blew his shawm, Walter Kirkeby's brow furrowed in concentration, Edward

151

Skerne joyously free in his interpretations of the ancient tunes. Their eyes widened in wonder at seeing me among this exalted company, before they turned to lead us through the streets lined with cheering people.

The clamour was deafening as we wound our way, at walking pace now, across the Ouse bridge and through the familiar streets towards the Minster. The din of the waits and the crowds was joined by bells ringing out from all the steeples, although there was no service due. The Minster's great bell itself tolled out high above the many-storeyed houses, their windows and doorways colourful with bannerets and streamers.

As we passed from Conynge Street into Stonegate, I scanned eagerly ahead for a first sight of my family home. Before long, there at the window of the overhang I spotted my young mother, standing with my baby sister in her arms. I hardly recognized the baby, so much had she grown since I had last been home, and I'm sure she didn't know me. But her little fists waved in delight at our mother's prompting, and I saw, though did not hear, her giggle at our noisy cavalcade as we rode by. My younger brother and sister Agnes I also glimpsed among the crowds of our neighbours. Peter took off his cap and waved it to grab my attention. Agnes simply beamed at the sight of me.

In time we reached the square before the Minster's huge west door, where the important men of our city were gathered – the aldermen clad in their robes of brightest violet, the councilmen in blue. My eyes searched for the imposing figure of my father. There he was at last, his stern features lit up with pride at the sight of his son riding with the Duke of Gloucester.

I'll not dwell on our welcome by the mayor, or our grand entry into the Minster, or the Duke giving thanks to the assembled throng for their greetings. Or his whispering to me that I should slip away to spend precious time with my family. Or on the kisses and tears and hugs with which they met me, or that first evening sitting round the fire telling of my life in recent months. Or on the warnings from my older brothers not to become high and mighty, or the satisfaction they all felt that my future seemed assured.

Any worries that my parents had had now passed. I was a favourite of the Duke, the Queen had smiled on me (I didn't tell them of the goldfinch), I had danced with princesses, the King had rewarded me – or at least my dog. Murrey was fussed over and fed, and slept contentedly beside yet another fire.

One small incident only marred the joy of my homecoming to York.

On my last afternoon, when I had received word that the Duke's party would start for Middleham early next morning, my brother Frederick took me to practise at the city archery butts. It wasn't a skill I had excelled at since joining the Duke's household, but I had improved since Fred last saw me and he was warm in his praise.

I was nocking another arrow to my string when a voice just behind me said,

'Well, here's someone I didn't expect to set foot in York again.'

I swung round, dropping my arrow, and found myself face to face with John Burton.

Perhaps not face to face. He had grown since our last encounter in the Minster square and now stood almost a head taller than me. Broader too. I might not be so ready to offer him my fist now.

But Frederick, a peaceable type despite his skill with a bow, was at my elbow.

'Matt has as much right to be here as anyone.'

'Even after his disgrace? My father said he should have been ashamed to show his face in the Minster the other day.'

Fred laughed.

'He was there with Duke Richard. I doubt even your father would dispute the matter with him.'

'My father would stand up for himself with the Duke as much as with any man. He's not afraid of him.'

'I didn't say he should be. It's just that Matt is in his favour and the Duke's opinion counts for a great deal in the city.'

'Huh, it would count for more if he did more for us.'

'He's persuaded Parliament to exempt us from war taxes,' I butted in. 'I know that. I was there.'

'What, in Parliament?' sneered John.

'No, of course not. But the Duke himself told me of it afterwards.'

'Well, it's about time,' John shot back. 'My father says the last campaign against the Scots cost us far too much. He says the council shouldn't be so ready to send men and money.'

'It's those men and that money that keep us all safe,' soothed Fred. 'Without Duke Richard, the Scots could easily raid as far as hereabouts, and disrupt our trade. They say his capture of Berwick last summer should help stop the border problems.'

'And he does it all despite the pain he suffers,' I added.

'Pain?' scoffed John.

'From being in armour and on horseback on campaign. His back —' I hesitated.

'What of it?'

'It's twisted – all out of shape.' Should I be speaking of this? 'Since he was a boy. That's what fighting for our safety has done to him.'

John didn't reply. He stared at me, then he picked up my arrow and turned away, nocking it to his own bow. His shot sped far wide of the target.

My fists were balled tight.

Fred pulled me away.

'Leave him. Let's go home. Mother is planning a special supper for your last evening.'

We meandered back through the bustling streets towards Stonegate without speaking.

Several passersby hailed my brother and eyed me in curiosity. Fred was becoming well respected locally now he was growing into a man. He had told me that people were asking him, wondering, at my reappearance in the city with the Duke.

Although I was proud of my new position, my spat with John Burton and the memory of Twelfth Night that it had stirred up had left me choked and uncomfortable. I was glad when we turned into the snickleway that led towards the rear courtyard of our house. But there, away from the busy roadway, my brother halted.

'Is it true? About the Duke?'

I gazed up at him, as tall now as our father. His face was half-hidden from me in the alley's shadows.

'His back?' I had to force the words out. 'Yes. I saw it. One day in Westminster when we'd been riding. And he flinched so when the King slapped him on the shoulder.'

Fred whistled as though surprised.

'You wouldn't think it to look at him. The times I've seen him enter the city in full armour at the head of troops.'

'That's when he says it pains him most. He spoke of it to me.'

'Yet he is as upright as any knight around him. And there is no sign when he is in ceremonial robes either. Old Mother Goodwin at the market – the twist in her back is plain for all to see, no matter what her clothes, winter or summer.'

'Old Mother Goodwin is over eighty,' I retorted. 'Father says her back is arched from carrying baskets and bundles on it all those years. The Duke's is different, the backbone just twisted a little to the side. I only know it because I helped him remove his undershirt to wash, after his servants had retired to bed.'

All those weeks I had tried to shut out what I had seen. My unease must have shown on my face. Fred's expression changed.

'And it hurts him, you say, when he's soldiering? And yet he spends so much of his time at war. Father says he told the council the King may send him to fight the Scots again this summer. Also that Parliament has granted him all the Scottish borderlands from which to do it. And he said York won't be taxed next time to pay for it. The councilmen all cheered when he said that, for all John Burton said.'

'The Duke said it would be good news for the city.'

'But did he also tell you what else it means? That the Earl of Northumberland will have less reason to interfere with our affairs now? Father said the council welcomed that news almost as warmly. No wonder they laid on such a feast for the Duke that night.'

I nodded, although I had no real idea what he meant. City politics had always flown clear over my head when our father railed about them. Perhaps my bewilderment was obvious to Fred, as he said,

'But enough of that, little brother. Whatever the shape of Duke Richard's back, he's done well for us, and especially for you. I know father will wish to toast him for that at supper. Let's get in now – I think I smell roast goose.'

My new mother had indeed prepared a memorable meal to bid me farewell that evening. And tears shed by her and Agnes mingled with the toasts to my good fortune.

Next morning my father accompanied me to the ancient friary where the Duke lodged, and where Bess was waiting for me, saddled and ready, among the assembling company.

He helped me to mount, then, as I adjusted my seat, grasped my sleeve, forcing me to look down at him.

'You have done well, son. We're all proud of you. Carry on serving your master loyally.'

'I will, father – always.'

I took up the reins, thinking to follow the company just setting off, but my father had more to say. His face was sombre.

'But remember, Matt, nobles can be fickle. They can change their minds on a whim, perhaps even one as steadfast as the Duke. If you should find yourself out of favour at the castle, don't forget you always have a home here.'

I smiled. Oblivious to all his years of experience in trade and in the council, like all boys I believed I knew better than my father. And grateful though I was for his reassurance, I was confident I would never need it.

Just hours later, as Hugh Soulsby's nose crunched under my fist, perhaps I should have thought again.

18

A Lucky Escape

The journey back to Middleham was uneventful. At the prospect of seeing my new friends again after so long, may the Lord forgive me, all thoughts of my family left behind in York faded into the distance.

Passing the friary of Jervaulx was my cue to scan the countryside ahead, eager to see the pennon flying from the tallest tower of the castle. Before long, the Duke's huge banner was unfurled above us in reply, and we were clattering up the cobbled street of the village towards the outer gatehouse.

Alys, Roger and Elen were waiting for us, perched on the parapet of the bridge across the moat. As we approached, all three hopped down and waved and called.

A murmur of laughter ran through the company. The Duke, leading the column, turned to say to his companions, 'An advanced guard, gentlemen – we should be honoured.'

He swept off his cap and bowed to my friends, before spurring Storm into a trot and leading the way across the outer courtyard towards the cheering crowds at the far gateway.

Alys led the others as they wound their way among the riders to reach me. They hung on to Bess's harness and stirrup leathers as we followed the Duke, chatting away all together.

'What was it like at court?'

'Did you really dance with the princesses?'

'I want to see Murrey's tricks.'

'Why didn't you write more often?'

'What did you do with the songbird?'

'How were your family in York?'

Delayed by them and laughing too much to answer their questions, I was the last rider to trail into the packed inner court.

We were just in time to see the Duke dismount, kneel momentarily to the Duchess to kiss her hand, before turning to his son and swinging him high into the air. Ed's excited giggles soared above the cheers. Then his father set him back on the ground and took his wife's hand, leading them both towards the steps up to the keep.

The other travel-stained gentlemen from the company threw their horses' reins to waiting grooms and followed.

Master Guylford clapped his hands once to dismiss the assembled household. Soon, once an undergroom had relieved me of Bess, we four were all but alone in the courtyard.

'So,' said Alys, 'how was it?'

She stood before me, hands on hips, fiery curls escaping from her cap as always, green eyes flashing with evident impatience. It struck me then how much I'd missed her.

Roger and Elen exchanged glances.

'Not now,' Elen said. 'He must be tired from the ride. Let him wash and rest, and after supper we can talk.'

Shadow was twining herself around the hem of Alys's jade-green skirt and Murrey stepped forward to touch noses with her bigger sister.

I stooped to caress her head, knowing Elen was right. But before I could respond, a sneering voice came from behind me.

'Well, well, well. Look what's turned up. I didn't expect you to show your face here again.'

As I straightened up, I saw Alys dart a glare past my shoulder, Roger's mouth open and close again in indecision, Elen's fingers pluck at her skirt in discomfort.

My hands clenched into tight fists and I drew in a slow breath before I turned.

Hugh was standing there, his great feet planted squarely on the cobbles, one hand playing with the pommel of the knife he wore at his belt. Lionel as ever was at his side.

Almost three months I'd been away and I hadn't missed them at all.

'I thought the Duke would take the chance to be rid of you when he stopped off in York.'

A hand caught at my sleeve, but I shook it off.

'Why would he do that?'

My voice was somehow calm, unlike my insides, which were churning at his words.

Hugh showed no emotion.

'Because he'd found out what you're like.'

'What do you mean?'

'Why you were sent away in disgrace.'

I waited, saying nothing. But my mind was racing.

How did Hugh know? If he knew. Or was he only guessing? He'd never liked me. Perhaps the favour shown by Duke Richard in taking me to London was simply too much for him.

His face was still unreadable as he spoke again.

'And when you'd spurned the Queen's gift.'

I glanced at the others.

'Her gift?' Roger asked.

'The finch?' Alys raised her eyebrows at me. 'What happened to it?'

'Oh, didn't he tell you?' Hugh said. 'That he let it go? And the Duke saw it and everything.'

'How do you know that?' I shot back.

Hugh smirked.

'But you told me.'

'What?'

'Didn't you? Let me see.'

He reached inside his doublet and drew out a small folded square of parchment.

Making a great play of unfolding it, he squinted down at it, passing the tip of one finger very deliberately along what was written there.

'Oh, yes. There it is. "And it flew due north, as though it too were escaping London."'

I guessed now what he held.

'That's my letter from York!'

'So it is. And a very charming one too. I'm particularly fond of the drawing of all those people on the Minster steps.' He peered at it again. I remembered the sketch I had attempted in response to Ed's pictures. 'Which one is Old Dick? It's a little difficult to tell.'

Hot blood rushed to my head, but still I tried to remain cool.

'How did you get it?'

'Get it? It was given to me.'

'Given? Who by?'

His eyes drifted to my side.

'Why, my Lady Alys's pretty little serving wench. Didn't she say?'

My head snapped round.

There was a pink tinge on Elen's cheeks.

159

'Elen?' Alys's voice was sharp. 'Were you bringing it to me?'

'He – I – he said he'd...'

Elen stammered to a halt.

I turned back to Hugh. He was leering sideways at Lionel, in delight at his triumph over me.

Roger said, 'Don't, Matt. He's just trying to —'

But, without thinking, I seized my chance.

I launched my balled fist towards Hugh's face just as he turned back and it caught him full on the nose. The bone grated as it broke.

Taken unawares, he staggered back, and flailing out with his hands, toppled Lionel over beneath him, into a pile of waving limbs.

They were both back on their feet in an instant, but it gave me time enough to pummel Hugh with each fist before he could lunge towards me. As he reeled back again, Roger and Elen grasped Lionel by his arms and dragged him away.

A snarl disfiguring his bloodied face, Hugh flung a punch towards me. I ducked beneath it, before charging towards him, my head down.

As I drove into his stomach and all the breath whooshed out of his body, I realized I'd been spoiling for a fight since meeting John Burton. But looking up at Hugh now, rocking on his feet before me, I wondered whether I should have picked a different foe.

He regained his balance and his breath. Before I could dance away or duck again, he scythed me down with a great blow to the side of my head.

My teeth rattled as I fell. All went black. Alys's shriek broke through as if from a vast distance.

'Hugh! Matt! Stop it!'

Daylight flooded back as I pushed myself up from the cobbles, swaying slightly like a man in drink.

The huge shadow of Hugh loomed over me, and just in time I flung up my left arm to parry his next punch. Gritting my teeth against the pain, I followed up with my right fist, catching him in the mouth.

Red spurted from a burst lip.

'You runt!' he spat, wiping his sleeve across his mouth, then hurled himself at me.

His weight thrust me back to the ground, where we rolled over and over in the mud and snowy slush. The hardness of the stones, the blows from his fists, the screams and shouts and barking, all whirled and merged together, until we slowed to a halt, Hugh above, me below.

He pushed himself up, cuffing me as he did, until only his knees still pinned me down. As I struggled to throw him off, his other hand reached for his dagger.

A mirthless smile curled his lips as he began to draw it.

But in a flash of green and gold, Alys struck first.

She flung herself at him, lunging at his hand, and the force knocked them both over in a tumble of skirts and mud and hair and legs and yells and two yelping dogs.

Metal rang on stone as the knife was thrown clear across the yard.

Before I could scramble to my feet as the weight was released, several dark figures hove above us.

'Boys!' a harsh, urgent voice shouted. Then, in shock, 'My lady!'

Rough hands dragged me up, and Master Fleete and a number of servants were grasping Alys and Hugh to tear them apart.

Alys's fine gown was muddied and ripped, her hair hanging loose without her cap, a red smear across her bodice.

Hugh's doublet was also drenched with blood, both his and mine I guessed. One eye was already beginning to blacken. The two hounds were leaping around him, yapping, keeping just out of reach of his boots.

A servant bent to retrieve the dagger and handed it to Master Fleete.

The weapons master weighed it in his hand, eyeing up the three of us.

Elen released her hold on Lionel and stepped forward.

'Sir, it was Hugh —'

But he silenced her by raising his hand.

'This is a matter for Master Guylford. Take the boys to his office. Wait with them till he comes. As for you, my lady...'

His words to Alys were lost to me as his servant hauled me away.

As I glanced back over my shoulder, Hugh was being manhandled after me by two servants as he struggled and swore.

He aimed a kick at the dogs, still jumping and barking at him. Roger dived in to scoop Murrey out of the way before she strayed too near his great boot.

'Cur!' Hugh hissed, followed by another loud curse, before he was quietened by a sharp word from one of the men. His face sullen, he allowed himself to be led behind me across the yard to the steward's office.

It seemed an eternity, standing there, a servant between us, waiting for Master Guylford to arrive. An emptiness in the pit of my stomach reminded me it had been almost suppertime when we arrived. Perhaps that's why the steward was long in coming.

But that hollow feeling wasn't caused just by hunger. It was also the fear of what might happen.

Once before I had waited like this, standing next to a boy with blood streaming from his nose, while my own jaw ached with the memory of his fists, and bruises began to blossom across my body.

I circled my shoulders, and winced. This time it wasn't me who had come out of the fight best, for all that I had had the element of surprise at first.

Then I remembered the knife.

It could have been so very much worse for me.

But, knife or not, it was me who had started it. I had landed the first punch – again.

That hadn't been tolerated before, and probably wouldn't be now. And once more my adversary was richer and more powerful than me – not the son of an alderman only, but this time the son of a noble.

By the time Master Guylford arrived, I had persuaded myself that I would be back with my family in York before another day had passed. That I had ruined everything.

I could hardly blink back the tears. Not at the soreness and stiffness creeping through my body thanks to Hugh's fists and the hard cobbles. At my own stupidity.

Hugh got to tell his story first.

All of it was true, if not complete. Until the drawing of the dagger.

The letter wasn't mentioned, only that we had exchanged words. And that I had struck first.

But then he had me on my back on the snowy ground – me, weak and desperate – me lunging for his knife. And Alys entering the fray to stop me murdering him.

When he finished, Master Guylford was thoughtful for a moment. Then he spoke to me.

'Well, Master Wansford, is it true? Did you strike first?'

'Yes, sir.'

'And the rest?'

I remained silent.

There was nothing I could say. I couldn't speak of the letter without revealing how Hugh had come by it and that would be unkind to Elen. And as to the knife – it would be my word against Hugh's – the aggressor's against that of the noble victim.

'Well?'

My breathing raced, my heart thumping in my chest at the injustice, but I wouldn't speak.

Master Guylford waited. Then a shadow passed across his face.

'Very well, then. You shall both be beaten. Report to Master Fleete immediately after Mass tomorrow. Master Wansford, I believe it is your first offence, but you began the fight – and the drawing of a weapon on a fellow page cannot be overlooked. Your punishment shall be most severe. Now you may go – and find what supper you can in the kitchens.'

Hugh flashed me a triumphant smirk as we left the room together and then he strode off across the courtyard towards the kitchens, his head held high.

I – although it seemed I had escaped the worst punishment – I preferred to slink back to the pages' chamber. I only grunted at Roger's questions as he passed Murrey to me, a length of rope now tied to her collar to keep her safe.

Crawling on to my mattress, I hid my head under my blanket in shame. It was an age before I drifted into uneasy sleep.

*

When I woke, I had no idea whether I was expected to sing at Mass, but I readied myself as if it were any other day at the castle.

In the vestry Sir William greeted me in a friendly manner and there was the usual quiet banter among the choir members as we dressed in our robes. It was good to be back in the familiar

163

surroundings of the castle chapel. As I added my voice to the responses and songs of the Mass, I thought perhaps, once my ordeal with Master Fleete was over, my life might return to normal.

But after Mass, as I shrugged off my surplice and heard the empty rumble of my stomach, a messenger arrived.

'Master Wansford is required to attend His Grace in his office.'

I couldn't suppress my groan.

Sir William glanced at me with sympathy, but said nothing, simply waving me to hasten on my way.

In a minute or two, I was knocking on the Duke's office door.

When I entered, he was in conversation with Master Guylford. They both cast a look my way as I bowed and, collecting up some papers, the steward took his leave.

The Duke sat on the edge of the table, as he had on that first day I had seen him. This time he didn't invite me to sit.

'Matthew, Master Guylford tells me that you and Master Soulsby fought yesterday on our return and that you are to be beaten for it. He says you admit to striking the first blow, but you will not say why. Will you tell me?'

I wasn't prepared for this. For all that I had gone over yesterday's events again and again, sifting through my reasons for staying quiet, it hadn't occurred to me that the Duke himself would become involved. Disputes among the pages and minor misdeeds were usually dealt with by the masters.

'I would prefer not to say, Your Grace.'

'I hear there were words between you. That Master Soulsby may have provoked you.'

'Yes, my lord.'

'What did he say?'

The Duke was speaking as though Hugh were responsible. But at the same time I was ashamed of what I'd done and didn't want to involve Elen. So I said nothing.

'Come, Matt. Once before you tried to protect him by not speaking. Don't try again. I would spare you the beating if I can.'

'It's not that, Your Grace. It's just that...'

'Well?'

'It's just – well – it's a matter of honour.'

'Honour?' His eyes narrowed in puzzlement. 'How so?'

'There was a letter. A private letter. And a lady…'

'A lady?'

'Yes, sir, a lady. And I don't wish her to get into any trouble.'

'So you'll tell me nothing more?'

His eyes were still on me. There was silence between us. Then,

'I'm disappointed in you, Matthew. That you should resort to blows rather than words to settle such a dispute. Violence should be a last resort – not the first.'

I hung my head,

'And yet, it is chivalrous, to protect a lady. Especially when, were you to tell the truth, it might spare you a beating. But I have heard that Hugh's story about you drawing the knife is a lie. You could have told me that.'

Raising my head again, I caught the fleeting trace of a smile before he leant across to take a quill and write on a scrap of parchment. He warmed a stick of red wax in the flame of a candle, smeared the end on the parchment and pressed the ring on his smallest finger into the molten wax. When he handed it to me, the scrap held only his signature – R. Gloucestre – and a seal depicting his boar symbol.

'Give that to Master Fleete and tell him I would have you punished for a first offence only. And the lady, no doubt, will thank you for your good deed. Now go.'

I bowed and stammered my thanks, and bowed again.

As I passed out of the door, Master Guylford came back in. I heard him say my name as the door swung to. But I didn't care what they said. All that mattered was that I was still here in the castle. And perhaps my soreness and bruising from the fight would not be made any worse by a beating for a first offence.

So with a lighter step I made my way towards Master Fleete's rooms next to the armoury.

As I crossed the outer court, someone shouted my name.

Alys was hurrying after me.

'Matt, stop! Wait for me.'

Although worried about any delay, I paused. I owed her a great deal, after all – possibly even my life.

She couldn't have looked more different this morning. Her hair was tucked demurely in her morning cap, and a sky-blue gown had replaced the torn and bloodstained one of yesterday.

'Are you going to Master Fleete's for your punishment?'

I nodded. Then a horrible thought struck me.

'You're not too?'

'Me? Of course not.' She shuddered. 'They don't beat girls. They find other ways of punishing us. But I don't understand why you have to be beaten. I told the Duchess what happened about the knife. Surely the Duke has let you off?'

I walked on, not wanting to be late.

'Oh, Matt, you did tell him yourself, didn't you? What Hugh did.'

'I hit him first.'

'But only after he goaded you. You did tell the Duke about him taking my letter?'

'Of course not. Then I would have had to say about —'

'About what?'

'About Elen.'

'Elen? What about her? That she was stupid enough to be sweet-talked into giving it to Hugh?'

'She's not stupid,' I protested. Alys's face hardened.

'She said she was last night. When she was crying at having got you into trouble. She said she should never have listened to Hugh, when he pleaded with her to show him the letter. He said he was just interested in news from court. Then, when she took it from her pouch, he snatched it, and threatened to tell me she'd given it to him freely. She'd have done better to tell me everything straight away. I can deal with Hugh.'

Seeing her eyes flash, I had no doubt she believed that.

'She should have known he was planning something,' she railed on. 'And she knew our letters were private, just for the Order.'

And I remembered how I had never written to Elen in all the time I'd been away. To Alys, to Ed, to Roger – never to Elen.

'So you didn't tell the Duke everything. To protect her. Hugh will think you're weak, not willing to speak up against him.'

'Well, maybe I am. Small and weak. I'm not a noble or a knight, after all. I —'

We had reached the door to Master Fleete's rooms. It was ajar.

Knowing there was an antechamber before the inner office, without thinking I pushed it open. Alys, in her anger, followed me as I stepped over the threshold.

166

My words died away as we saw the scene within.

Master Fleete was standing watching, his arms folded and face grim. One of the apprentice armourers, his sleeves rolled up to reveal his sinewy arms, was bringing down a thick switch hard on the bare buttocks of someone bent over a bench.

It was Hugh, of course. His white backside was streaked with deep red weals from the blows, like the trails of blood on yesterday's snow-covered cobbles.

I raised a hand to push Alys back out of the room, but she had already seen. Her hand flew to her mouth, too late to stifle a gasp.

All three in the room turned towards us. Hugh's face, his eyes bulbous, drained white at the sight of us, then flushed scarlet.

Master Fleete strode across the room and hustled us out, closing the door behind him before we could see any more.

'Wait your turn,' he ordered me, then, to Alys, 'And you, my lady, be off with you. This isn't for your eyes.'

Alys dropped a curtsey, squeezed my hand, whispered 'Good luck', and rushed off back across the courtyard.

Master Fleete grunted once, then let himself back into his anteroom.

I waited outside, fear rising within me. Why on earth had I chosen to be 'chivalrous'?

Though a door was between us, the sound of the switch struck my ears again and again – thwack, thwack, thwack – each time echoed by a muffled groan.

19

'De Cifris'

It was my turn to seat myself with care in the great hall at breakfast, but perhaps I got away lightly. Hugh didn't turn up for meals that day, or to lessons, and I spotted Lionel sneaking food away from the table at dinner.

The last I'd seen of Hugh was when he pushed past me on leaving Master Fleete's rooms. By then I was so terrified I was barely aware of the knifing glare he threw my way, let alone the stiffness of his movements, as the weapons tutor beckoned me inside.

Master Fleete's face was stern as he listened to me and took the Duke's note. He said not a word to me, but as the apprentice bent me over the bench, fully clothed as I was, he uttered a single number. It was fewer than half the strokes I had heard Hugh endure.

For all that, the beating battered both my body and my pride. It would be days before I could ride Bess again without pain.

Roger eyed me with sympathy as I lowered myself beside him.

'A hearty welcome back to the castle,' he said.

I grunted and helped myself to my first food since early the previous day.

Not easily deflected, Roger tried again.

'Alys said you were to be beaten, but that Hugh was to be too. I wonder that he took his revenge in so public a way as to bring a beating on himself as well.'

'What do you mean – revenge?'

His face was all puzzlement.

'Didn't I write of it in one of my letters?'

'Roger, you never wrote a letter to me – not a whole one. At most all you ever did was add a few lines on one from Alys or Ed.'

'Didn't I? Well, perhaps I should have. But then you weren't away so very long. It's just that while you were gone I overheard Hugh say one day that he would get his own back on you and the Duke.'

'The Duke?'

'Yes, at what he said were all the times the Duke had humiliated him. The last and worst was being made to serve the grooms after the hunt. He blamed you for that – I'm not sure why. But I don't see how getting himself yet another beating would help him.'

I shook my head, not understanding it myself.

'It's not even as though there was anything interesting in that letter. Well, not really.' I thought hard. 'Nothing to get beaten for, anyway. Just a description of what happened at York and something about the journey from London. Oh, and about the goldfinch, I suppose. And —'

I stopped.

'Yes?'

'There was a bit of nonsense for Alys. I'd copied it from a book at Master Ashley's – a romance – it made me think of her. A speech made by a knight wooing his lady. It was so exaggerated – all flowery French – I thought she might enjoy it. You don't think Hugh —'

'Took it seriously? I'm not sure his French is good enough for that. Besides, I don't see him as the jealous type. You and Alys – I mean, really!'

He clutched at his heart as though lovesick, and I punched him gently on the shoulder, hissing, 'Stop that! Everyone will hear.'

One or two of the pages had glanced his way, but soon turned back to their meal.

'Well, I want to know how he found out I'd left York in disgrace. That wasn't in the letter.' It was lucky, perhaps, that my meeting with John Burton had been only the day before, after I had sent the letter.

'Perhaps he just guessed,' said Roger airily. 'Or, you know, word gets around.'

'Does it?'

'Maybe Elen told him.'

I searched back through my memory.

'I'm not sure Elen knew. And, anyway, why would she tell him?'

'Why did she give him the letter?' he asked in reply. 'Never mind, what's done is done. You're home again now, and all can go on as before. Spring's almost here, soon the hawking will be good, and surely even Ed will be allowed to ride now.'

Over the next few days everything did seem to return to normal. Normal, that is, as far as life had been during the autumn, before I'd travelled to London. Ed had so far recovered from his illness that the Duchess allowed him to join us in all we did after lessons ended. Before long we were riding up on to the moor tops or along the dale to put Lady through her paces once again. Even the torture of sitting on Bess's saddle passed. Alys was sharp with Elen for some time, but as Elen rarely joined us on our outings, I soon forgot there had been any cause for complaint between us.

Alys, though, did not forget so easily.

One afternoon, as the four of us were wending our way back down to the water meadows, she spoke up.

'We must have some way of keeping our letters private if one of us goes away again.'

Roger, who had been riding slightly ahead, scouting for rabbits for Lady, reined his horse back so we could all catch up.

'We could seal them with wax like the Duke and Master Guylford do.'

'That's no good,' said Alys. 'If it's not an official seal, pressed with their signet ring or stamp, anyone could open the letters.'

'There's a special book in my father's library,' piped up Ed. 'He told me once he uses it to send coded messages to my uncle when he is at war. Perhaps we could get some ideas from that.'

So that evening, after supper, he brought it to us. It was a small volume of handwritten pages bound in dark red leather, the title 'De Cifris' pressed in gold letters on the spine.

'I'll have to take it back before bed,' he said, casting a glance over his shoulder as though he was being followed. 'It's from my father's private shelves.'

'No matter,' said Alys, taking the book from him, her face determined. 'I'm sure we won't need very long. How difficult can it be to make a code?'

Not very, it seemed, once Alys got the hang of it.

She knew Latin better than the rest of us and her number learning equalled my own, even after my years with my father's account books. But while she and I enjoyed ourselves discussing the various forms of ciphers in the book, Roger and Ed were soon playing with Murrey and Shadow.

Seeing this, Alys paused, then said in very rapid French,

'But we must keep it simple. Ed is only young and must not be left out.'

So we went back to the beginning again.

Before long we had a straightforward code in which one letter replaced another in sequence throughout the alphabet. It was the sort that the book called 'Caesar's code' after the great Roman general. But while it was simple, Alys suggested we make it trickier for any enemies to guess by changing the starting letter depending on the day of the week we were writing it. So we started with U replacing A on a Monday, and the start letter moving back three on each day.

I collected my writing things, and by the time Ed had to return the book, we each had a square of parchment bearing the code in my neatest handwriting.

a b c d e f g h i j k l m n o p q r s t u v w x y z
u v w x y z a b c d e f g h i j k l m n o p q r s t Monday
r s t u v w x y z a b c d e f g h i j k l m n o p q Tuesday
o p q r s t u v w x y z a b c d e f g h i j k l m n Wednesday
l m n o p q r s t u v w x y z a b c d e f g h i j k Thursday
i j k l m n o p q r s t u v w x y z a b c d e f g h Friday
f g h i j k l m n o p q r s t u v w x y z a b c d e Saturday
c d e f g h i j k l m n o p q r s t u v w x y z a b Sunday

Ed squinted at his.

'It's Tuesday today, so my name is –' he spelt each letter out laboriously, '*V – u – n – r – i – u.*'

'And mine is *I – f – x – v – i,*' said Roger.

'That's right,' said Alys, after checking.

'It'll take forever to write a letter,' said Roger, unconvinced.

'Not that you ever write letters anyway,' I said.

He smiled.

'Well, it'll take ages to read one, then.'

'Perhaps you can just write certain words or important parts in the code,' Alys suggested. 'Either way, it gives us a chance to keep things secret from Hugh if ever he steals another letter – or from anyone else.'

'Should we start straight away?' asked Ed. 'With any notes we have to send each other?'

I remembered who our main messenger within the castle was.

Maybe Alys had the same thought. Her eyes flicked towards me.

'I suppose we should. Best to get into the habit of using it. We'll soon have learned it off by heart if we practise with it.'

'Shouldn't we give Elen a copy too?' I asked.

'I don't think so. She's not really one of the Order. And if she's caught with one of the letters, she can truthfully say she doesn't know what it's about.'

For me, this wasn't a good reason for excluding Elen, but as Alys still seemed upset with her, I didn't object. So we all began to use the cipher whenever we sent messages.

Not that we often had a need to. While I was away, Roger had been admitted into the Duchess's room from time to time to keep Ed company and that didn't change with the Duke's return. So the four of us had more chances to be together outside of lessons. And with Hugh and Lionel becoming squires, we now had less reason to be wary from day to day.

But for all I was glad to see them less, I envied Hugh and his friend their promotion. I longed to take that next step towards becoming a knight, although I knew it would be at least two years before I would be considered. Yet it spurred me on to work harder in all my lessons, particularly weapons training. I felt I had even more to prove to Master Fleete after my beating.

As the early signs of spring appeared, the Duke was called away again on business. That evening was the first I had spent in the family's private chamber without him there.

No business was done while I sang – courtly songs of the Duchess's choice. She sat sewing with Elen and one of her ladies, often looking across to me and smiling. Alys, Ed and Roger played a game that I didn't know, moving wooden pieces around a board. When, from time to time, they quarrelled over it, the Duchess would hush them, pointing at me.

After half a dozen songs, she laid down her work and, as the Duke always did, handed round cups of wine. Taking mine, I moved to join the others by the hearth, but she placed a hand on my arm.

'Bide a while with me, Matthew. I would speak with you.'

As on my first evening with her, I seated myself on a footstool by her chair and waited while she arranged her grey fur rug about her. It was early April, but the evenings were still chill.

'Well, Matthew, how did you enjoy your visit to London?'

'Very well, Your Grace. The city was all my father said, and so much more.'

'It is a remarkable place. And your time at court? What did you make of that?'

I was silent, unsure what she was asking me. I fear I may have appeared rather stupid, but the Duchess simply smiled.

'It's so long since I was at court, Matthew. My husband remembers only official matters. I thought perhaps you could tell me more than that.'

'Your Grace?'

'About the people there, for instance. Don't stand aghast – I don't mean gossip. We are all family. But we see one another so rarely. Young Elizabeth now. Richard tells me her betrothal to the French prince was called off while you were in London. How did she seem after that?'

I shook my head.

'I'm sorry, Your Grace. I'm afraid I know nothing about that.'

'Richard was full of what it must mean for the King's diplomacy, whether it might lead to war with France. But I wonder how my niece feels about it. After all she must be a young woman now.'

'Yes, she is, and a very fair one.'

In my memory she shone again as she had at the dance on Twelfth Night – lighting up the festivities in her flame-coloured gown.

'She is like her mother then?'

'In some ways, yes, Your Grace. Her hair is long and golden, and she has the grace and face of an angel. But in other ways – well, she seems more like the King.'

'Indeed?'

'The Queen has a cool beauty, while Princess Elizabeth's is warmer, more like the sun than the moon.'

I stopped, hearing myself as though through her ears – a low-born page speaking of the Queen.

But the Duchess only said, 'Do not worry, Matthew. You are not the only one not to have warmed to the Queen. I wonder whether the Princess Elizabeth will not regret losing this chance to get away. And her brother, Edward? I understand he was there too for a while.'

'Yes, until Twelfth Night. We rode out together that day.' The thrill of that ride came back to me now. 'He was a little reserved at first, but Murrey won him round.'

'As she would anyone, of course.'

The Duchess reached down to fondle my hound's ears as she lay curled up at our feet.

'And you spoke together?'

'Then, and at the evening festivities. Though he spent much of his time with his uncle Woodville and the Marquess. He barely spoke to his younger brother, Richard, at least when I saw them. It's as though he hardly knew him.'

'I think perhaps he has few children for company at Ludlow, poor boy. The royal children are rarely all together in one place. You were lucky to see them at the palace. I wish some of them could visit with us here and meet our Edward. But I fear the Queen would not permit it. The King, they say, allows her to rule on family matters. And many of her own family look after Prince Edward at Ludlow.'

'I think I saw several of them at court for Christmas, but... well, there were so many lords and ladies, I didn't find it easy to remember who they all were.'

'No matter, Matthew. I have little enough interest in the doings of the Woodvilles. If the paths of my family and theirs were never to cross again it would be no loss to me. Indeed I would count it a blessing.'

Casting my mind back to what Roger had told me of the Queen's family, I wasn't surprised at her words.

She asked me a few more questions, about what we had eaten at the banquets, the entertainments and the fashions that the ladies had been wearing, especially the Queen and Mistress Shore. I answered as fully as I could, although I knew little enough about fabrics, what certain sleeves or collars were called, or the ingredients of sauces. But she smiled as I described in some detail the gowns that the two older princesses wore on Twelfth Night, and the fabulous gems that each had been given by their father.

The tips of her fingers brushed against a large jewel that hung on a chain round her own neck.

I had not seen it before and without thinking, I leaned forward to peer at it.

Framed in bright gold was a deep blue stone carved with tiny figures.

'That's also a beautiful gem, Your Grace.'

'Isn't it? It was a gift from my husband – for being far from us at Christmastide. His duty to the King and Parliament called him away – but at least he was able to choose from the finest jewels in London. At any rate, from those that had not already been chosen by the King for his daughters. You will have seen them close to, I suppose. Richard told me you danced with both Elizabeth and Cecily.'

'I did, Your Grace.' As ever the blood rose in my cheeks and I bent my head, hoping she wouldn't see it in the candlelight. 'I was shown great favour by the King – as I have been by His Grace the Duke.'

'They both value good service and loyalty, Matthew. Any favour you've received has been well deserved. And I trust your father was pleased with you when you stayed at York. Has he forgiven you your troubles last summer?'

She was pleased to hear how my family had greeted me and been amazed by all that I had seen and done. As I told her of the farewell supper that my new mother had prepared – how she had persuaded my father to break open a cask of good wine to toast his son's success – her smile was warm. Of a sudden my mother's face swam before my eyes again. Or was it my new mother's? The soft eyes and lips of all three blended for that brief moment as tears started to my eyes. Thinking back to the day of my return to the castle, I recalled my fear of losing all this – these people who had welcomed me into their lives, the new respect of my family, my chance to better myself. I vowed never to take that risk again.

Yet, as so often in my life, events – and people – conspired against me.

20

Ill Tidings

The leaf buds were fattening on the trees and the first lambs appearing before the Duke returned from Pontefract.

He brought with him special sweetmeats from the local bakers to help us break our Lenten fast, after weeks of eating little more than fish from the river and castle ponds. Then, after the solemn Good Friday unveiling of the Cross and the Easter vigil, we pages begged eggs from the kitchens' stockpiles, stored since Ash Wednesday. We boiled them hard in onion-skin dyes to roll them down the slopes in the Duchess's pleasure gardens.

The squires looked on, with good humour or disdain, too old now for such childish pastimes. But, to my surprise, and to the laughter of the ladies who gathered to watch us, not only Masters Lovell, Ratcliffe and Kendall, and various other gentlemen, but Duke Richard himself joined us.

Each of the gentlemen had brought his own egg, except it seemed the Duke.

For a moment, there was disappointment on his face. Sir Francis declared, 'Then this year I have a chance of winning.'

But the Duke called Alys forward from where she was waiting with the other ladies.

Her dimples showing, she stepped up to him, bringing from behind her back a small casket. As she lifted the lid, there, nestled in black velvet, was the largest egg I had ever seen. It was intricately painted with swirls of red, blue, green, gold, putting our home-dyed hens' eggs to shame.

'The swans of Pontefract obliged me,' said the Duke, picking it up with a flourish.

He beckoned to his son, who had been fidgeting next to me as the scene played out and now leapt forward with sparkling eyes.

'Come, Ed – help me. It is such a fine egg – we shall roll it together.'

So the Duke and his son swept all before them, not only racing the smaller eggs to the bottom of the slope, but surviving without so much as a hair's crack.

That evening, after a magnificent feast almost rivalling those at court, we gathered as usual in the quiet privacy of the family's chamber.

The Duke had no gentlemen around him, preferring tonight to sit back in his great chair and listen to me sing. His wife and son, Alys and Roger were playing the game with wooden counters at a table drawn up by the fire.

During Lent, Doctor Frees had taught me some new Italian songs, which I sang now in honour of the holiday. The Duke's eyes were upon me throughout, I thought perhaps because they were songs he did not know.

When I finished, he strode as usual across to the cups of wine set ready on the table. After handing one to his wife, he brought the next to me.

'Well sung, Matt. But enough for tonight. Come join the game. Ed will teach you how.'

He placed a hand upon my shoulder and squeezed it. For a moment his expression was unreadable, before he broke into a smile.

'And make sure you try some honey gingerbread. It's the finest I've tasted outside London.'

Days later I recalled that look as I rode out with the Order on the moor.

On my way to the stables I'd been caught by a serving man, who instructed me to attend the Duke in his office before supper. I had no idea what it was about. When I told the others, Alys's sharp eyes flicked my way, but she said nothing.

Ed's mouth twisted with a touch of petulance.

'He's going away again in a few days. To a council meeting. Perhaps he wants to take you with him. I wish he'd take me.'

'What?' asked Roger. 'And be stuck in a dingy castle surrounded by old men arguing all day? When you could be here with us enjoying the sport?'

Ed glanced at Lady, perched ready on Roger's wrist.

'Father says the sport around Sheriff Hutton is excellent. And you know the castle isn't dingy. It's...'

I let their friendly squabble pass over me.

The moor around us was bathed in the glow of early spring sunshine. Trills cascaded down from a skylark silhouetted against the blue vault of the sky far above, and a pair of oystercatchers wheeled across the swathe of heather and bilberry. Their unearthly whooping for a moment drowned out the lark's tumbling notes as they swept past our horses.

I breathed in the sweet scent of spring and wondered when I'd ever been happier.

When I entered the Duke's office later that day, I found him alone, standing at his great oak desk. The surface was strewn with papers. He carefully chose two as he bade me sit down.

He perched on the table's edge opposite me, his face grave.

'Matt, I have received a letter about you from Lord Soulsby.'

'Lord Soulsby, Your Grace?'

'You know of him?'

'Only as Hugh's uncle. And —'

'And as the father of the man Alys Langdown is to marry?'

The Duke was watching me closely.

'Yes, I have heard that.'

I was puzzled. Why should Lord Soulsby be writing about me? Why should he even know of me?

'It has come to his attention that you and Alys have become friends.'

'Of course we are friends, Your Grace.'

'But, Matt – he fears that friendship may endanger the betrothal.'

'Your Grace?'

'Word has reached him of certain letters between you. Letters in which you speak of love.'

And then it struck me – what this was all about.

Hugh. The letter from York. The silly, playful verses I'd copied out for Alys.

'But, Your Grace,' I protested, 'it was nothing. Just one letter. We'd been playing at knights and ladies. I wrote something from a romance I'd found. It meant nothing. But Hugh stole it and—'

I stumbled to a halt.

'Was that the letter for which you were beaten?'

'Yes, Your Grace. Truly it meant nothing. Alys and I – we're just friends.'

'Yes, Matt. You know that and I know that. But Lord Soulsby is a long way away and it's a long time since he was a boy. And I suspect he is not a man who reads – especially not romances.'

The heaviness deep in my stomach began to lift at the sight of his familiar half-smile. I waited for him to continue.

'Clearly he has also been misinformed by... someone who perhaps does not wish you well. He tells me that, as the son of a merchant, you are not a suitable companion for one of the richest heiresses in England, and certainly not for his son's wife.'

'They're not married yet,' I retorted. 'And my father —'

He silenced me by raising his hand.

'Your father has my greatest respect, Matthew, as do all his kind. But some of the nobility... well, some cling to the old ways and do not see that England's strength lies in her merchants and their trade. Peace and commerce – they are what my brother desires. But sometimes such things come only at a price.'

He glanced down at the papers in his hand.

'Lord Soulsby demands that you be sent away from our household.'

It was as though Hugh's great boot had stamped on my chest again.

'My lord!' I beseeched him. In his eyes was that expression I had seen on Easter night.

'Matt, I might perhaps have disregarded him, but... I have also received a letter from the Queen. She is an interested party. Alys is her ward and the Queen may bestow her hand as she sees fit. Lord Soulsby is one of my brother's loyal retainers, and he and the Queen require the loyalty of such men at all times. We must not give Lord Soulsby cause for complaint. In politics one cannot always do what one would wish.'

He fell silent, watching me.

I held my head high, although my eyes were smarting. I dreaded being unable to hold back the tears.

'Then I must leave?'

He nodded.

'I'm afraid so. I know that you are no threat to this marriage, but the Queen and Lord Soulsby will not be told. I shall be sorry that you will no longer be a part of this household. Anne and I will miss your music, and Ed, I know, will miss a friend.'

I could no longer keep my head up. As I blinked and looked down, a drop of water fell and stained my boot tip.

'Must I return to – to York, my lord?'

'If you wish. Or – Matt, I will do all I can for you. You have been a valuable asset here. And I believe that, if you want to go back to London, Master Ashley would take you as apprentice. You were happy, those weeks with him, were you not?'

'Not as happy as —'

There was a sudden commotion outside.

Hooves clattering on the cobbles, the stamp of booted feet, muffled voices, a rap on the door.

'Your Grace!'

A man's voice – Master Guylford's? – urgent.

In two strides, the Duke was past me and at the door, pulling it open.

There stood the steward, his usually tanned face pale. Next to him, breathing heavily, a man in red livery, smeared with mud and dust, clutching a small leather bag.

Beyond, Master Reynold grasped the reins of a tall horse in full harness. It tossed its head, the whites of its eyes showing, lather flecking its neck, its flanks heaving and steaming.

'Your Grace, a message,' said Master Guylford. 'From Lord Hastings.'

'Lord Hastings?'

'Aye, my lord,' stammered the man in red. 'From Lord Hastings. Your Grace, the King —'

'Yes?'

'The King is dead.'

21

'A Sad Day'

A moment of stillness.

I could hear the horse blowing and the jingle of its bridle, smell the sweat of man and beast, see the Duke silhouetted against the scene, the late afternoon sunlight tracing the outline of his dark, motionless form.

Then his hand, still clutching the two letters, clenched the door jamb.

'How?'

The messenger grimaced as he caught his breath.

'Apoplexy, they think, Your Grace. A week – two weeks ago, he caught a chill. He seemed to rally, then —'

The man doubled over with a spasm of coughing, and the Duke raised his hand.

'Bring up a chair. And wine. He must rest before he speaks again.'

The man tried to protest, but the Duke waved his words away.

As Master Guylford, and servants who had now appeared, bustled to do his bidding, he swung round to me.

'Matt, I must attend to this, but I will not forget you. Think on what I have said. If you wish to return to Master Ashley's, I shall arrange it. Now go.'

He turned back to the knot of men clustering around the messenger, now seated near the desk, and I stumbled away, into the light of the courtyard.

Outside, people were running in all directions, and a groom was leading away the exhausted horse. It was easy for me to lose myself in the bustle.

I slunk back to the pages' chamber, empty now as the trumpet sounded for supper. One or two boys passed me on their way to the great hall, but I kept my head down so as not to catch their eyes. I didn't want to speak to anyone now, and the idea of eating was far from my mind.

I sat on the edge of my mattress, elbows resting on my knees, clenched fists forced into my eyes. Murrey, no doubt scenting the salt tears, nuzzled at my hands and whimpered when I didn't move. But I was too wrapped up in my misery to heed her. Soon she curled up on my feet and slept.

Before very long, before I had even begun to think of what to do next or what to say to anyone, a few boys began to drift back into the chamber for their evening pastimes. Roger was one of the first. He flung himself down beside me on the bed, seemingly not noticing my hunched back and my hands shielding my face.

'Matt, why weren't you at supper?'

His too-loud voice jarred me, but he didn't wait for an answer.

'Have you heard the news? The King's dead.'

I grunted, but didn't move. These were momentous tidings, a sad blow for the kingdom. Yet I couldn't think of any news beyond my own.

'Master Guylford announced it before supper. We all had to sit in silence and pray for ever so long before he would let the food be brought in. I even saw tears on Master Fleete's cheeks. They say he rode with King Edward when he was young, and even fought with him at Towton.'

He paused. As I released the pressure on my eyes, I saw his face out of the corner of one. His expression altered as he looked directly at me, perhaps for the first time.

'Matt, what is it? What's up?'

I scrubbed the tears away from my cheeks with the backs of my hands. Murrey, disturbed by the movement, reached up her long red muzzle to lick my face.

Roger's hand, which I'd thought was about to pat me on the shoulder, changed course and moved to caress her ears.

I discovered I didn't want to tell him.

I cleared my throat, afraid my voice might crack.

'And the Duke? How was he…?'

'Oh, he didn't come to supper, nor the Duchess or Ed. I suppose if they'd only just received the message… Matt, weren't you going to see the Duke after our ride? Had the news reached him then?'

I shook my head, glad to think about something else.

'No. Well, yes. The messenger arrived when I was in his office. From Lord Hastings.'

'Lord Hastings? Not the Queen? That's odd.'

'Perhaps she was too grief-stricken.'

'Perhaps. Though I've heard she's a strong woman, not one to stagger under a blow. But what did the messenger say? How did the Duke take it?'

I racked my mind to tease out what I could from my confused memories.

'He was calm. But his face went very pale. It was certainly a blow for him. Yet he attended to the messenger's needs.'

And he had dismissed me gently, guessing how I felt.

'I only heard the messenger say it may have been apoplexy.'

Roger shook his head in turn.

'And yet the King was barely forty.'

He stood up abruptly, causing Murrey to twist away and caper on her hind legs.

'Come on, Matt. Let's go find Alys. Perhaps she'll have more news.'

With some reluctance I followed him out into the courtyard. I would have preferred to keep to my bed with only Murrey for company. But, having missed her supper too, she happily bounded after Roger, knowing he always had a ready supply of table scraps.

At least the search for Alys among the stunned and silent inhabitants of the castle distracted me from my own troubles. As we wandered, Roger pointed to where the great boar standard on the tower had been lowered partway down its pole.

When we finally found Alys, she knew little more than we did, despite having been in the private chamber when the Duke broke the news to his wife and son.

'They were very quiet,' she said. 'I don't think it had really sunk in. The Duchess said something about the Duke telling her the King had put on weight at Christmas. But the Duke said it wasn't enough to cause his death. Then they were silent again until I was called away to supper.'

I recalled my encounters with the King, on Twelfth Night in particular, and wondered that a man so full of life, larger than life even, so strong, so golden, could now be reduced to an empty shell. In my mind's eye I saw him grey and cold and lifeless, lying stretched out like one of the stone effigies upon the tombs I had seen so often at York Minster.

The three of us strolled for some time in near silence through the orchard and kitchen gardens. The buds and shoots of new life and the gentle hum of the first bumble bees were all about us.

As the shadows lengthened in the primrose yellow light, it became clear that Ed wouldn't join us this evening.

How long had it been since he had seen his uncle Edward? He had never met his cousins, I remembered. But I was sure his father's grief would be raw from the way he had spoken to me in London about his brothers. He would want all his family close to him tonight. What must it feel like to have lost yet another brother?

My remembrance drifted back to Fred, John and Peter, their faces laughing in the flickering firelight of my last night in York.

I shivered, aware of the chill evening air now the sun had ducked beneath the far hills. The valley was hushed. Only the doleful note of the church bell in the village broke through the gathering dusk.

Then a scuffling on the gravel path made us swing round.

Elen was hurrying towards us through the trees, her skirts billowing above her quick feet.

'Matt, there you are! You must hurry – you're wanted by the Duke.'

'Me?'

'Is it about your meeting this afternoon?'

'He probably just wants you to sing.'

But Alys's glance was full of curiosity.

I would have to tell them soon that before long I would be leaving for good.

I had to stand back to let Masters Lovell, Ratcliffe and Kendall leave before I could enter the family's chamber.

Master Kendall, clutching a fist full of papers in addition to his usual leather file case and writing tools, squeezed my shoulder as he passed, sorrow darkening his eyes.

'A sad day, boy, a sad day indeed.'

The other gentlemen merely inclined their heads before hurrying away.

I had collected my lute on the way in case it was needed, but now propped it up against the wall outside the door.

As I stepped across the threshold, the scene was very different from all other such times. No business was now being done, and even the Duchess's embroidery lay neglected on a small table.

Ed was curled up next to her on her great chair, his head in her lap. She was absently fingering strands of his hair while gazing up at her husband.

He stood, his back to the great table, staring into the fire, twisting and twisting the red-stoned ring on his smallest finger.

'Richard,' came the Duchess's soft voice. 'Matthew is here.'

The Duke turned to me.

It may have been the effect of the blazing candelabra overhanging the table – only lit when there was much work to be done – but he seemed to have aged many years in the few hours since I'd seen him. Lines had deepened on his forehead and around his eyes, and the pallor of his face was stark in contrast to the dark doublet he wore. But the faintest curve touched his pinched lips as he beckoned me forward to sit upon my customary stool.

'Well, Matt, our talk this afternoon has been overtaken by greater events.'

I bowed my head, uncertain if or what to reply.

'It seems my brother in his will has appointed me Protector of the kingdom. In a few days I must ride south again to escort my nephew Edward to London for his coronation. I will travel by way of York. It is in my mind that you could ride with us. Then you may remain with your family. Or if we have had word from Master Ashley, or if you wish to try your luck as an apprentice in the city, you may continue with us to London.'

I swallowed and nodded, unwilling to trust my voice to speak.

'And, Matt, at the Minster we shall hold a requiem Mass for my brother. I would that you would sing for him again then. One last service for him – and for me.'

I slipped off my stool on to my knees, burying my face in my hands.

'Aye, Your Grace,' was all I could force out.

I felt his touch on my shoulder and raised my head.

There was an unnatural shine in his own eyes.

'I was going to ask you to sing tonight. Perhaps a song to suit the moment. But I see now that would be unfair after the blow that you've received. Go to bed now. Take what sleep you may.'

I bowed my head again. But this time to draw in two or three breaths very slowly.

Then I pushed myself up to my feet, straightening my back, my arms stretching down at my sides.

Seeing his sorrow gave me strength to master my own.

'Thank you, Your Grace, but no. What would you have me sing?'

*

I slept that night more soundly than I would have thought possible. And in the morning, after singing again for His Grace at a special Mass in the chapel, I was strong enough to tell Alys and Roger of my fate.

Lessons had been abandoned for the day as a period of mourning for the King began. We had taken the chance to leave the sombre atmosphere of the castle to walk with the dogs in the water meadows. Sitting now on the banks of the river, legs dangling over the slow-moving water, I related my sorry tale.

Alys was immediately up in arms, her eyes flashing and mouth spitting her anger at Hugh and his uncle, the Queen, even the Duke for not standing up to them.

Roger, though, took a different view.

'But you'll get to live in London.'

'I don't want to live in London. I want to stay here, with – with you all.'

'But think about it, Matt. London's the place to be. You can't do anything stuck here. There you'll be able to do anything you want. I've heard Master Ashley has contacts everywhere in Europe. You can travel, see the world, make your fortune.'

'But – but I want to be a knight. This was my chance and now – now I've ruined it.'

They both fell silent.

I supposed I'd never said it to them before, not like that. Perhaps the only person I had ever truly spoken to about it was the Duke. And I remembered what he had said.

I gazed across the river at the cows quietly cropping grass on the far bank. Would I now have to give up my dream?

Alys was the first to speak again.

'Matt, you'll still be a member of the Order. We all will be. We swore our oath. The loyal knights of Duke Richard of Gloucester – Lord Protector of England. They can't take that away from us. We'll meet whenever we can, in London or – or here.

You can come back when you're able. And we can always write –
now we have the code.'

The Duke had said the same last night – that I could
continue to write to Ed and the others, and he would send the
letters with his official post. Just like when I'd been in London
before.

Except, then, I'd written expecting to return. How could I
this time, knowing that my friends were going on with their lives
without me, lives cut off from mine for ever?

On each of the following evenings, the Duke called me in
to sing to him and his family, and every night was another step
towards my final farewell. Lessons during the day were few and
far between as mourning continued alongside preparations for the
Duke's journey. Even those few lessons I was excused if Sir
William needed to coach me for my part in the requiem planned
for the Minster.

Throughout I did my best not to think too much about
what lay ahead. I astounded the chaplain with my energy in our
rehearsals. He told me he had never been so pleased with my
progress – and that he was sorry to hear I was leaving. As Roger
once said, word did travel at some speed among the castle's
inhabitants.

Hugh's smug delight radiated from the squires' table at
meal times. I was grateful not to come face to face with him in
lessons or weapons training in those days. But as I laboured over
my Latin translation or was bested once again by Ed with his
chestnut sword, I was more bothered about when, if ever, I would
have such chances to study or train like this again.

On the final morning before our departure, wagons arrived
from York laden with mourning clothes. They had been ordered
specially for the party who were to travel on the new Protector's
business.

As I stood outside the Duke's chamber that evening,
waiting for the gentlemen to leave, Elen said how fine and grown-
up I looked in my brand new suit of sombre black.

Alys simply stared, before ushering me in and closing the
door quietly behind us.

The Duke and his wife were alone in the room, he standing
by the fire, his back to us, she in her accustomed seat. As Alys and
I moved towards the pool of flickering candlelight, the Duchess
spoke.

Alys's hand on my arm made me pause.

'Richard, I beg of you, take more men. If what Hastings says is true —'

'That the Queen and her family mean to ignore my brother's wishes? Anne, Edward willed the care of the country to me, and the people and the old Royal Council will respect that. And God will protect me. Whether I take three hundred men or three thousand —'

'Elizabeth will have expected to be regent to her son – and with her family, to control him and the country. You know that. What Hastings says about the fleet in the channel... Such decisions should not have been taken before you and young Edward arrive in London.'

'Hastings will hold the old Council on the right course until our arrival.'

'But if he cannot? If the influence of the Woodvilles is too strong? Oh, Richard, remember... remember what happened to George!'

The Duchess's voice faltered, worry tearing at it like a storm rends a banner.

The Duke swung round, and knelt in front of her, taking her hand.

'Do you think I can ever forget? Anne, you must not fear. The Queen won't prevail this time. The question of a regency is not up to her. My brother has appointed me Protector until his son is crowned.'

'Yes, but what then?'

'Then young Edward will be King in his own right, and if his new Council so decrees, God willing I shall continue to protect the realm. Hastings and the other nobles will have no wish to see the Woodvilles rule through the boy.'

'Poor child,' said the Duchess. 'To have this thrust upon him so young.'

'Aye, a responsibility I would wish upon no one, still less a young lad. He has a deal of growing to do before he can fill his father's shoes.'

Rising to his feet again, the Duke spotted us, hesitating in the shadows. He waved us forward.

I worried that we should be rebuked for overhearing so much. But his face, though stern, looked distracted, as so often in those days.

'You have seen him, Matt, at Yuletide. Young Edward, the new King. We have been speaking of him. He is no older than you.' His eyes narrowed. 'Younger, perhaps.'

'Bigger, my lord?'

At that second, I feared I had taken a mis-step, joking about my size at such a solemn time. But after a heartbeat, Duke Richard laughed, a short bark of a laugh, and the tension that had shrouded the room was torn away.

'Aye, perhaps bigger. Though I fear size is no sign of readiness to rule. Put yourself in his place, Matt – if you can, one of your small stature. Even if you had grown a hand's span already this spring, tell me, would you wish to take on the rule of this realm?'

I shook my head without a word.

'And if you had spent most of your short life far from London and your parents, and the intrigues of court, with only an uncle to teach you? And so soon after your country was racked by civil war?'

It was his turn for a shake of the head. Then his eyes cleared.

'But come,' he clapped his hands and scooped up the tray of cups from the table. 'This is our last night here for... for who knows how long? Though there's been much sadness of late, let us not dwell on what might be, but rather think of when we shall be together again.'

As he said this, he was bowing deeply to his wife and offering her the wine, before turning back to Alys. Then he took two of the cups and, passing one to me, with a faint smile said, 'And of the glorious times that will come to those who are willing and work hard. Here's to those just setting out on their adventures.'

He clinked his cup to mine, half-bowed and drank.

As I returned the gesture, he said, 'And now, Matthew, a song if you will. Make it perhaps a merry one, that my wife can remember to cheer her through the days to come.'

As I sang again for him and his Duchess the songs I had learnt for his first homecoming all those months before, I wondered about all that Alys and I had overheard from the shadows. I had many reasons to think of it again over the weeks and months to come.

*

189

The morning dawned grey and overcast, but in every other way it was unlike the day of my previous departure from the castle. Now there was no tremor of anticipation or excitement, only a weighty dread within me as I walked towards Bess.

Hugh was among the crowd of squires and pages clustered around the horses, but I turned away before I caught more than the briefest glimpse of the triumph spreading across his face – still handsome despite its now crooked nose.

Alys, Roger and Elen were waiting there for me. With barely a word, I hugged each of them before mounting.

Elen, seeing the Duke and his family emerging from the keep, rushed away to attend the Duchess, but not before I spied tears starting in her eyes. Roger busied himself with enticing Murrey to dance for him one last time, but Alys came to stand close to Bess, her hand on my stirrup.

'Farewell, Matt. I'm sorry to have brought this on you.'

I was bewildered.

'You? But I was the one who attacked Hugh, who bloodied his nose. It's me he despises.'

'But if it weren't for his cousin and – Oh!'

She screwed her face up and looked as though she would stamp her foot, as she had at Roger on our first meeting.

'Oh, it's all so unfair! But you will write, won't you? And when the Duchess goes down to London, if I come too, you must visit us. Promise me?'

I nodded, uncertain again, both of my voice, and of whether I could fulfil such a promise.

A muted cheer rose from the gentlemen massing about us. We saw Duke Richard astride Storm, flanked by Sir Francis and Master Ratcliffe, his huge banner unfurling above them all – now with a strip of black cloth stitched along its length.

As the head of the party moved off, I grasped Alys's hand and hissed,

'Don't let them marry you off against your will.'

She glanced back up at me, her eyes widening. For a moment, she seemed too surprised to speak, then came her quick laugh.

'Oh, don't worry about that. If I keep quiet, perhaps they'll forget all about me.'

Bess stepped forward, following the other horses, but Alys didn't immediately pull her hand away. She paced alongside, until

Roger came bounding up with Murrey and Shadow leaping around his legs.

'Take care of her, Matt. See you in London soon.'

He clasped the hand that Alys had just dropped, then leant down to catch Shadow's collar, stopping her following her sister as Murrey sidled into her place at Bess's heels.

I raised my hand to both my friends, but before I could face forward to ride through the inner gateway for the last time, a small figure hurtled towards me through the crowd of pages and servants.

'Don't go without saying goodbye, Matt.'

It was Ed.

I had bade him farewell the previous day, knowing this morning should be his father's time. But now I reined Bess back and leaned down to embrace him again as best I could.

He patted Murrey's head, then thrust up to me a small package wrapped in dark blue velvet.

'It's a gift from my mother, though I know it came from my father's private shelves. She says it tells the story of a perfect knight. Don't forget about the Order, Matt. And come back to see us soon.'

He dropped back. As Bess walked on again, I unfolded the cloth.

Revealed within was a small book, beautifully bound in deep red leather, with a boar device engraved on the front board.

I opened it. The title 'The Death of Arthur' was traced in a fine manuscript handwriting and I knew what a costly present it was.

As we clattered under the jaw of the gatehouse portcullis, I twisted in the saddle and raised my cap to salute my friends. They were standing now all together in a knot at the foot of the keep's stairway. Then I set my eyes to the front, between Bess's pricked ears, whistled to Murrey to keep up, and followed the call of the Duke's standard across the outer courtyard and moat.

The early mist was lifting from the hills and the rising sun glinting off the far, winding river, stitching it like gold thread between the willows spaced along its banks, as we rode down through Middleham towards the road to York and – and were there glorious times to come?

Here ends THE ORDER OF THE WHITE BOAR, the first book in the sequence by the same name. The second, THE KING'S MAN, follows Matthew and his friends' continuing adventures as the momentous Year of the Three Kings unfolds.

The
King's
Man

To

the families of the Hillsborough 96,
who know what it's like to have had history
rewritten in the present day...

and

to my friends of long centuries past,
Angela and Kate –
they know why

1

Broken Rendezvous

The first warning of their approach was the faintest rumble as of distant thunder on a summer's day. The sun shone still, though low in the sky, throwing long shadows across the cobbles of the square. Its last rays touched the tip of the ancient stone market cross to gold.

As the noise reached us, my master raised his head, turning it first one way then another, like a boar at bay hearing the winding of a huntsman's horn. At a word, his companions melted away behind, leaving him standing alone at the very edge of the inn yard. Clad simply in riding gear of deepest mourning, his slight figure moved not a muscle as we waited.

The far-off grumble grew into drumming, then on into hammering – the hubbub funnelling through the narrow street opposite, cannoning off the buildings crouching to either side. I could tell now it was the sound of hooves, of many dozens of horses, galloping along the highroad that cut through this town.

Deep within my chest, my heart beat harder, in echo of those thudding hooves. My breath was racing too. My hands, clammier by the second, gripped my hound's collar and I whispered to her to stay close. Surely even her sharp ears could not hear me above the rising tide of sound, but she lifted her shaggy red head as my grasp tightened, her deep brown eyes gazing imploringly up at me.

No other movement broke the stillness about us, save the flap, flap of my master's dark red and blue banner as it caught the wind, the shining white boar upon it rearing as though brought to life by the sparking tension in the air. The Duke and his gentlemen remained motionless, though each of his companions, I now saw, clasped the hilt of his still-sheathed sword.

The ground underfoot quivered at the coming squall. Murrey's ears pricked, her nose trembled, and perhaps only a minute after its first herald, the storm surge burst from the mouth of the main street out on to the wide market square.

I flinched at the shock of its arrival, but my master, feet firmly planted, did not stir as the company of horsemen flooded towards him across the cobbles. Two or three score, heavily armed, mail glinting, hooves thundering, scarlet and white standard streaming on high in the sharpening breeze. Galloping as though all the devils of hell were at their heels, heedless of the townsfolk who scattered out of their path, clutching at their children and possessions to keep them from harm.

The leading horses checked their headlong rush and clattered to a halt only feet in front of the Duke, blowing hard, their flanks heaving under their costly trappings. The fair-haired man on the foremost stared down for a moment after he reined back his mount, his blue eyes expressionless, before touching the end of his whip to his forehead in salute.

'Greetings, Your Grace,' he began, his breathing rapid after his swift approach. 'I beg you to forgive our late arrival. The King has gone on before to Stony Stratford, and will sleep there tonight. He bid me return to greet you most cordially and await your pleasure.'

This man who spoke so courteously to my master Duke Richard was unknown to me. But a murmur of recognition had rippled through our company as he and his party had swept across the square. Beside me, Master Kendall, the Duke's secretary, breathed the newcomer's name, incredulous.

'Earl Rivers! And he dare show his face here without the King?'

The Earl swung down from his fine-boned mount with the ease of a much younger man, and I recalled that this brother of the Queen was spoken of as once the finest jouster in the land. He bowed now to the Duke, a memory of his sister in his elegant features and light-coloured hair. It was perhaps no more than two months since I had come face to face with Her Grace – yet it seemed a lifetime ago. All was different now.

Duke Richard received the Earl with equal courtesy. But did I detect in his next words a trace of the anger that had surfaced only minutes before, when we had ridden at a leisurely pace through the streets of this evening-quiet town – and found no rendezvous with the new King and his escort as arranged?

'To Stony Stratford? Why so? We were to meet with him here in Northampton.'

The Earl's response was smooth, as though well rehearsed.

196

'So you and I had agreed, Your Grace. But it was in our nephew Edward's mind that there would not be lodgings enough here for all his men and Your Grace's. Therefore he thought it best to move his retinue on to make way for yours. Our manor at Stony Stratford is well provisioned for a large party, and he rests there now with his brother, Lord Grey, and other companions.'

A hiss issued through Master Kendall's teeth at this speech, heard only by those of us nearby. Several paces ahead of us, Duke Richard's expression did not change.

'It is late now for you to rejoin him tonight, my lord. Will you and your gentlemen take lodgings here in the town and dine with us at our inn?'

The Earl bowed once more, and soon grooms and serving men were scurrying this way and that, leading horses and carrying baggage, until only the two noblemen and their closest companions remained beneath the swinging tavern sign. The Duke stood aside with grave civility to allow the Earl to enter first. I brought up the rear, behind Lord Lovell, Master Ratcliffe and the other gentlemen, sticking close to Master Kendall, as had been my habit over recent days.

Since news of the death of old King Edward had reached us, I had dined at his brother Duke Richard's table often in such inns, on our journey south from Middleham to meet and escort the new King to his coronation in London. Now, though, I found a stool in a corner and my hound pup, Murrey, threaded her lithe body between its stubby legs before settling down, her pointed muzzle resting on her outstretched forepaws. From there I watched the tavernmaster and his womenfolk bustling about setting places with their best pewter and platters, and listened while the gentlemen exchanged pleasantries and seated themselves at the richly furnished oak table.

This evening I knew my place, knew that the talk around the high table would not be of a kind for mere boys like me to join in. Yet, as Duke Richard and the Earl raised a toast to the new King in the innkeeper's best wine, I was reminded that young King Edward himself was but a boy, a younger one even than I – and a boy I had once had the pleasure of riding alongside for a whole afternoon last Christmas-tide.

I cannot deny the pang of disappointment that had struck me on finding he was not in the town when we arrived. Had I been wrong to hope we could take up our friendship again as we had left it on Twelfth Night? Yet so much had changed since then. I had been dismissed from my knight's training at Middleham Castle and had to leave behind my friends, Alys, Roger, Elen, and of course, little Ed, the Duke's son. And he – he had lost his father, the old King. Perhaps that day of the ride had been their last together. And now he was about to take on the heavy burden of kingship.

The solemn oath that I had sworn at York Minster came back to me now. Reunited with my old comrades in the choir of that great cathedral of my home city – almost a year after my shameful expulsion – we had sung the requiem Mass for the dead King. The last notes of my solo rose into the heights of that holy space as though accompanying his soul to heaven.

Then the most important men of the city and country of York had knelt as one behind his brother, Duke Richard of Gloucester. Following his lead, all there swore fealty to the new King – the Duke's nephew, Edward, the fifth of that name. The raw emotion of their massed voices, resonant with loyal intent, dashed against me like a storm-wave as I stood near the altar, swamping the sound of my own words. And I had been, oh, so proud of my countrymen.

Another grey morning farewell, to my family and the other townsfolk, then we were journeying again, three hundred strong now with the men who had joined us from my home town.

Always southwards we travelled. To Pontefract's castle with its soaring tower, to Nottingham's crouching on its crag above the River Trent.

Hourly we were met by messengers from every corner of the realm. From Earl Rivers travelling with the new King towards London from his estates in the west. From the Earl of Northumberland with his vow to hold the northern marches. From Henry, Duke of Buckingham, journeying out of Wales to join us. And from Lord Hastings – from Lord Hastings in London, always with a warning.

For in the capital events were moving fast, events I didn't understand. But from the little I heard, and the dark shadows gathering on Duke Richard's face, it was clear the news was not good.

Queen Elizabeth's family, the Woodvilles, were gaining strength, becoming bolder in their claims to take the reins of power now that her husband was dead. And the old King's chamberlain and adviser, Lord Hastings – never the Queen's friend – feared for his position, and perhaps even for his life. The failure of our rendezvous with the young King and the Earl would hardly soothe those fears.

Yet here in this small midlands town, the company of gentlemen passed a pleasant meal. The tavernkeeper himself was busy about them, serving with his own hands the tastiest dishes his kitchen could provide. As the evening wore on, and more wine was poured and more toasts drunk, chatter and laughter spilled from the gentlemen. Duke Richard, however, barely even smiled. Between the toasts, he did not touch his wine, and from my vantage point, I watched him watching the Earl. His lordship's face was soon flushed in the heat of the room, but he also drank little.

No more than an hour after we sat down to our supper, another tumult of horses' hooves and jangling harness and men's voices erupted outside the shuttered windows. A serving man rushed in, bowing, to announce, 'His Grace, the Duke of Buckingham.'

Duke Richard and Earl Rivers were already on their feet as the burly, haughty man I had first encountered on Twelfth Night made his entrance, flanked by several companions, each as weary and mud-flecked as the other.

Duke Richard stepped forward to clasp the newcomer's hand.

'Welcome, Harry,' he said in greeting.

The warmth in his voice surprised me. There had seemed little liking between the two men at his brother's court at Yuletide. But then I remembered young Edward's words to me about his aunt's husband on that winter afternoon: 'I don't think my mother likes him very much.'

Had Duke Richard found an ally against the Queen and her family in these difficult times? One might be needed, if all that Lord Hastings reported was true. Indeed a certain coolness marked the embrace of the Earl and the new arrival, but my lord Buckingham readily joined the party. The inn servants brought in extra chairs and lighted candles, while the innkeeper was tasked with finding ever more plates of delicious food.

Despite the clamour of so many men, soon my head was nodding in the cramped, warm, smoky tavern room and I was wishing for my bed. Murrey had long ago curled up fast asleep beside my feet. Lord Rivers had perhaps also had a long day – how many extra miles had he ridden to Stony Stratford and back? – for less than an hour after the newcomers' arrival, he took his leave to retire. He bid farewell to his host and departed with his companions into the gathering dark.

The two royal Dukes seated themselves again, either side of the long table, and my lord Buckingham waved the tavernkeeper across to splash more wine in their cups. When the man left the room to replenish the jugs, Duke Henry quaffed another mouthful, slammed his cup down, making the candle on the table beside it jump, then asked abruptly,

'What news from London?'

'The same,' said Duke Richard. His voice was quiet, but with a little effort, blinking the sleep away, I could hear well enough. 'Hastings tells me the old Royal Council has reassembled and take decisions under the watchful eye of the Marquess of Dorset.'

'The old Council? That Woodville clique?'

Duke Richard nodded, but said nothing. Duke Henry blustered on, like the guttering flame of the candle by his fist.

'They have no right. Surely Hastings knows that – he should stand against it. No matter that Dorset is also the Queen's son. Only the new King can appoint his Council. And while he is here, with us —'

'I'm afraid the King is not here.'

'Not here?' exploded Buckingham. 'Then where?'

'He rode on with his escort to Stony Stratford this afternoon – fourteen miles hence.'

'Then they intend for him to reach London before us. To crown him before you arrive.' His fist clenched tighter on his cup. 'Why then is Rivers here?'

'To assure me all is well. But also to delay me, I imagine. He gave some poor excuse about too few lodgings here for both parties. How many ride with you?'

Buckingham snorted.

'Three hundred, no more, as you specified. Would now that I had brought four times as many.'

'We are here to escort the King, not as an invading army.'

'Yet Rivers brings two thousand? Hastings told me of it in his letter. That is not a simple escort.'

'He has no more than fifty with him tonight. The rest – if there are so many – are with Richard Grey and the King.'

'Stony Stratford is a Woodville manor. They will have ready access to even more men there. And assuredly there will be ambushes set. The road onwards will not be a safe one to ride in the morning.'

Duke Richard was silent for a moment.

'I doubt they will go so far. Rivers —'

'Is not the leader in this,' cut in Buckingham, his bulky frame leaning forwards over the platters of fruit and cheese still on the table. 'Dorset and the Queen – they sit in Westminster like a spider in her web. They will be directing all from there. And if the Duke of Gloucester suffers an accident in his haste to meet his King – who will question it, once they have the boy crowned and in their power?'

Lord Lovell, by Duke Richard's elbow, spoke softly.

'Lord Rivers showed some surprise when my lord of Buckingham appeared.'

Duke Henry threw a sharp glance at him.

'Maybe he was too focused on your progress to think much on mine. One advantage to so small a party – we were able to press on at speed to join you.'

'But now you are here, and they see our intent to do my brother's bidding with the will of Parliament, they will not obstruct us.'

At Duke Richard's words, Buckingham's features twisted into a scowl, thrown into flickering relief by the light of the many candles.

'With their prize so close to hand? A day's ride, maybe two, and the new King – crowned – is theirs to control. They will not stay their hands now. Do not be naïve, cousin.'

Duke Richard's face and voice remained calm.

'I well know how the Woodvilles scheme. I have no need of your warning. Parliament and the people of London will not allow such manoeuvres. Their loyalty to my brother was steadfast. And if his will is well known...'

Buckingham drank deeply, then placed his cup down on the table, with care this time, and gazed across at Duke Richard. His next words seemed chosen in a more deliberate fashion.

'And if the rumour I hear is true?'

'What rumour?'

'That your brother's death was – suspicious. That maybe – and, as I say, it is only a rumour – that maybe he was... poisoned.'

'Poisoned?

'They say it has become all the rage at the Italian courts.'

Without a second's hesitation, Duke Richard shook his head.

'Nay, cousin, rumours are dangerous beasts and should not be believed lightly. Hastings' messenger said apoplexy.'

Buckingham sat back again, revolving his wine-cup slowly with the fingers of one hand, while watching his fellow Duke.

'Apoplexy can take many forms, so too can poisoning. But how often does a man recover from apoplexy, only to die of it a week later.'

'Hastings did not report that.'

'They say the King fell ill, then rallied. But after several days, and an evening spent in the bosom of his wife's family... The first illness was a failed attempt – seven days later came success.'

A moment of quiet. The gentlemen from Yorkshire exchanged glances, the candlelight catching their eyes.

When Duke Richard remained silent, my lord of Buckingham ploughed on.

'It is perhaps no coincidence that Dorset was made Deputy Constable of the Tower only weeks before. In preparation for seizing power – and the royal treasure. They say Edward Woodville has shipped half of the treasury away to his fleet in the Channel.'

'I have heard that about my brother's treasure also, and perhaps it is true. But I cannot believe the Queen capable of such a crime as murder. She loved my brother... at least, once she did.'

'Yet now her charms have faded. You saw for yourself at Yuletide. Mistress Shore and others had become favourites. And they say Hastings himself has had a part to play in that. Elizabeth's hold over Edward was perhaps broken and her family feared their grip on power ending. When so threatened, it takes little to drive a pack of dogs to turn on the hand that feeds them.'

'But not to kill a king. That is a crime beyond all others. No, even the Woodvilles, for all their scheming, could not turn to that.'

'Careful, cousin.' One forefinger lifted from Duke Henry's grip on his cup, as though in warning. 'Do not forget the fate that has befallen other Protectors at the hands of kings' families. Think of Humphrey of Lancaster – he also a Duke of Gloucester.'

'Those were different days. Times have changed, I thank the Lord.'

'And yet you fear for the lives of your wife and child.'

All this time, sleepily watching the faces of both Dukes in the fluttering of candlelight, I had not taken in the full import of their words. But now I learned – what? That the old King had perhaps been murdered – and that the same fate could befall my little friend Ed and his mother.

The very idea shook me awake. Until that moment I had not grasped how serious the situation was.

Duke Richard's expression did not change, however.

'They will be safe at home in Middleham.'

'And you are willing to stake their lives on that?'

'The Woodvilles can't touch them there.'

'Perhaps not. But we must do our job here well to make sure they remain safe.'

'Not just for them, cousin. For my brother's son and his kingdom.'

'Aye, for the kingdom too,' growled Duke Henry, draining the last of his wine before placing his cup back on the table with deliberation. 'Though, the Lord knows, sometimes I wonder whether it deserves such care.'

Duke Richard rose. All the gentlemen stood with him, my lord of Buckingham last of all, pushing himself up with his ham-like hands flat upon the table. Dog-tired though I was, I had dragged myself to my feet with the rest of the company.

'The care of the kingdom is a sacred trust, cousin. And we neglect it at our peril.' My master's words had a firm finality about them, despite his quiet tones. 'But now is the time for rest. We shall be ready to leave at daybreak.'

My lord Buckingham said quickly, 'And you will send outriders before – to check for ambushes?'

Duke Richard's fingers played with his red-stoned signet ring in that habit I now knew so well, but he didn't speak. After a moment, Buckingham said,

'And Rivers?'

'I will sleep on it.'

'You must deal with him.'

'I said, I will sleep on it.'

'If he manages to get a message to Dorset and the Queen—'

'To say what?'

'That...' Buckingham hesitated, uncertain.

'That I am performing my role as Protector? Perhaps it's a message I would wish them to receive. If the Queen is loyal to my brother's memory, she will act correctly. If not...'

'We will know what action to take.'

'Indeed I will know.'

I caught the slight stress that the Duke laid upon the word 'I', and glancing at my lord Buckingham could tell he had too. His eyes narrowed, but he fought to keep a scowl from darkening his face.

'Then I bid you goodnight, cousin. May the morning bring less trouble than I foresee.'

Duke Richard bowed his head and his fellow Duke swept out of the room past the grovelling innkeeper, his companions close behind.

The sound of their many feet retreated along the street towards the lodgings that had been found for them and I discovered that I had been holding my breath. As I released it, a sigh whispered around the room as though the gentlemen remaining there had done the same.

Lord Lovell was the first to speak.

'He's right, Richard. You should beware Rivers.'

The Duke dropped back into his seat. Taking up his goblet, he at last downed a great draught.

'I'm sure that is wise counsel, Francis. But now I am too weary to think on it. All this talk of murder...'

He swallowed another gulp, then his eyes slid towards me at the moment I was ambushed by a yawn. The ghost of a smile flitted across his face.

'And I see I am not the only one. We must all to bed. It will be an early start, and a long ride to London with our King. I wish you all a good rest, gentlemen.'

He stood and, as his companions stepped back to allow him passage to the stairs, he said quietly aside to Lord Lovell,

'Join me, Francis, we must talk.'

I bowed low as he passed, then scooping up the sleeping Murrey, followed up the steps, a pace behind Lord Lovell. My palliasse had been laid across the Duke's threshold by an inn servant, ready for me to do my page's duty and sleep on guard outside his door. Stepping over it, Duke Richard turned back and placed a hand on my shoulder.

'I have no need of you tonight, Matt. Take as much rest as you can. I saw you fighting sleep – and we'll likely have a long day of it tomorrow.'

I was grateful for his permission to lie down and arrange my blanket. Lord Lovell stifled a laugh as his long legs strode across me, but I was too exhausted to care whether I was the cause. With Murrey a comforting weight upon my chest, my eyelids drooped and I drifted towards sleep. What seemed only a minute or two later there came a muffled apology from his lordship as, stepping back over me, his boot grazed my arm, but then, sinking down, down, into deep, warm darkness, I knew nothing more...

2

Ambush

Until... until... something hard and pointed prodding my ribs. A greyish glimmer from somewhere. The murmur of men and animals at a distance – no, nearer now, just beyond the walls. A whimper from Murrey as I moved. A quiet voice.

'Matt, you've slept long. It is time to rise. Get what food you may before we ride.'

I struggled to my feet, rubbing my eyes.

'But Your Grace, I must help you dress.'

Duke Richard laughed.

'No need, boy, as you see.'

I did indeed. Even the dim half-light could not disguise that he already wore his sober black riding clothes. On his feet were the boots that had nudged me awake, and in one hand a sheaf of papers. Even his sword belt was already buckled on.

'While you lay dreaming, I have already performed half a day's work. Now up with you and run downstairs – you'll find the tavern long awake.'

Ashamed, I gathered my things together and slunk downstairs after him, Murrey stealing along behind. How had I overslept? How had the Duke risen without waking me? What if his enemies had come to attack him during the night?

In the large room below sat Masters Kendall and Ratcliffe among several other gentlemen, all breakfasting already amid a murmur of conversation. Their faces serious, they stood to greet the Duke, who seated himself in their midst and bid them continue their meal.

I found a spare stool at a table alongside Master Kendall, not far from the cheering warmth of the banked fire. The innkeeper's daughter bustled up with a plate of bread and cheese and a cup of ale.

'There you go, sir. Better late than never.'

Was that a wink as she set them before me?

In the pre-dawn flickering of embers and candles I could not be sure – except of the sudden glow of my cheeks. But, taking no notice, the girl turned away to stir up the fire.

As I sat there chewing and dropping morsels down to Murrey, a great clamour of hooves arose in the street outside. As one, the gentlemen jumped up, clapping hands to sword hilts, before Lord Lovell and several others burst through the doorway, their riding gear freshly bespattered with mud and dust.

The Duke sat still at his table as Lord Lovell strode forward. The men nearby made way for the newcomers, resheathing their part-drawn weapons, some seating themselves again, all remaining watchful.

'Well, Francis?'

'We found more after I sent word to you, Richard. No livery again, but undoubtedly Woodville men. We...' he paused, his eyes scanning the gathered faces, 'We questioned the leaders of each band. They all admitted their purpose was to stop you reaching Stony Stratford – by any means. Though none would name who gave their orders.'

Duke Richard rose to his feet. The candlelight played across a strange expression on his face. Sadness I could see. Perhaps also apprehension, determination?

'Thank you, Francis. Sadly it seems my lord of Buckingham was correct – at least in one way. We cannot be sure who is behind these attempted ambushes, but we cannot afford to take any chances. Arrest my lord Rivers!'

The Duke's words were spoken almost in an undertone, but they rang in my ears like a clarion.

Lord Lovell and his men left the inn in an instant, followed by others, until only Duke Richard and a handful of gentlemen remained. To one of these, the Duke turned.

'Go raise my lord of Buckingham, and tell him what has occurred – if he is not already aware. We will leave for Stony Stratford by sun-up.'

To Master Kendall he passed the papers that had lain untouched on the table since we had come down.

'They are signed and sealed, John. See that they are sent. Now that the road towards London is clear, let the messenger also give word to Lord Hastings that we meet with the King this morning.'

Master Kendall nodded and hurried out, but I waited, quiet in the corner, watching.

The Duke stood for a few seconds in complete stillness, no expression now on his face. His eyes were fixed on the fire flaring again on the hearth and one hand rested on the pommel of his sword. I was reminded of when the message had come that his elder brother, the King, was dead – the utter quiet of that moment, the tension in his lean frame, like a bow-string before release. Then he reached out for his cup of ale and drained it, and all was in motion again.

'Come, gentlemen. We must be on our way.'

Outside the inn all the horses – including my pony, Bess – were waiting in the morning twilight, ready saddled by the inn servants. Gathering also from the surrounding dusky streets were the men who had ridden with us from York. The innkeeper himself was directing matters and as we emerged, came over to hold the bridle of the Duke's pale grey stallion, Storm, while his most illustrious guest mounted. He bowed deeply at the Duke's words of thanks for his hospitality and in a few moments the party was on its way.

The hooves rang loud at this early hour, the echoes bouncing off the buildings overhanging the road. Local people who were already up and about their business ducked into the shadows or dragged their beasts or wagons to the side to let us pass.

The Earl's inn was at no great distance. As we approached, rosy-tinged clouds could be seen above the grey road stretching off to the east.

Several dozen horsemen surrounded the inn, silent but for the occasional stamp of a hoof or jingle of bit or buckle. The nearest riders parted to allow the foremost members of the Duke's party through. I urged Bess forwards to ensure I was among them. As we entered the circle, a commotion exploded through the doorway opening on to the inn yard.

Voices raised in anger, a sharp rebuke, scuffling, and men spilling out on to the cobbles. Earl Rivers and Lord Lovell walked calmly side by side, but beyond them, a number of the Earl's companions struggled and cursed in the firm hold of Lord Lovell's men. Their sword belts had been taken from them, carried now by squires in the rear, but the Earl's was still strapped to his waist, the hilt of his weapon gleaming in the mellow early light. His face in shadow, Lord Rivers turned his head to view the ring of silent horsemen.

Duke Richard had reined Storm to a halt just within the encirclement, forcing the Earl to step across the muddy courtyard to reach him. To my surprise, the Duke did not offer him the courtesy of dismounting as he approached, but gazed down at him unspeaking. His face was unreadable, though I sat astride Bess only three or four horses away.

Lord Rivers bowed.

'Your Grace. To what do I owe this early awakening?'

His lordship's manner was calm, but his voice was strained, and made me long to clear my throat. But now that his gentlemen's curses had ceased, the yard was hushed and I dared not.

The Duke lengthened the silence before he spoke.

'Lord Rivers, it has come to our attention that the road towards Stony Stratford is not safe. Bands of men have been waiting to waylay unwary travellers, particularly it seems those who seek to join the King. They admit no allegiance, but they are well drilled and well equipped. I can afford to take no chances on who may have given them their orders. Therefore I require that you and your men remain here for the time being.'

'Lord Lovell informed me I was under arrest.'

The Duke paused again, as though weighing every word.

'I regret using the word, but I must ask you to stay within your lodgings and to send no messages.'

Earl Rivers moved as though to speak again, but he was interrupted by a cacophony of hooves approaching along the narrow main street. A large company of riders cantered around the final bend, then slowed to a walk, only a few of its leaders advancing through the encirclement of the inn.

At their head was my lord of Buckingham. He hauled back on the reins of his enormous jet-black charger as it drew alongside Storm, wrenching its neck into a tight arch and causing it to toss its head against the pain. The first rays of the sun breaking through the clouds on the horizon lit up the sneer upon his face. He also did not dismount, throwing a glance down at the Earl standing before him. Then, with no word of greeting, he turned to Duke Richard.

'Now do you see the truth of what I said last night? Never trust a Woodville.'

Duke Richard's face was impassive.

'I hope you are well rested after yesterday's journey, Harry. As to events overnight, we have no proof of who is responsible. I have requested my Lord Rivers keep to his inn while we ride on to the King.'

'Keep to his inn? Surely it would be best to slap him in chains and drag him to Westminster in a wagon!'

There was now light enough on Lord Rivers' upturned face to show upon it only scorn for the younger man above him. But he remained silent while Duke Richard replied.

'There is no need of that, cousin. If you wish, you may leave a detachment of men here to ensure he keeps his word. For myself, I am in haste to meet my nephew with his escort. I want no more misunderstandings about what is to happen over the coming days.' Now, directing his words more to Lord Rivers, he continued, 'My brother made me Protector of his realm and I intend to fulfil that trust to the best of my ability, come what may.'

Earl Rivers bowed his head and drew back. After leaning down to speak to Lord Lovell, who passed instructions to his own men before hurrying to mount his horse, the Duke turned Storm back towards the road. He raised his voice to ensure that all gathered there could hear.

'And now it is time to be off to Stony Stratford. We must reach the King before he departs.'

And as we all spurred our horses on, the Duke of Buckingham's words from last night came into my mind – about young Edward being soon crowned and in the Woodvilles' power.

3

Stony Stratford

The speed of our progress afforded little chance to enjoy the countryside through which we passed on this fine spring morning. The rolling fields with their bright green shoots and orchards full of apple and pear blossom caressed by the rosy fingers of the early sun were very different from what we had left behind in the north.

Spring had seemed to be racing ahead of us as we rode down from Middleham. Here the hawthorn was already in full flower although it was not yet May. We had left tiny lambs sheltering from the biting wind behind high stone walls, watching their mothers grazing the sparse late winter grass, while here boys and their dogs stood guard over flocks of sheep almost half-grown. All raised their heads at the thunder of so many hooves upon the ancient roadway, wondering perhaps at the fluttering standards of the two Dukes, the glinting harness, the whipping of horses into a lather, and the need for such a cavalcade. Yesterday, had they gazed at the passing of the King, then the later return of Earl Rivers, with similar curiosity?

Stony Stratford, as we entered, appeared no more than a village, its main buildings strung out along the road towards distant London. Glancing around, I understood why Duke Richard had disbelieved the Earl's reason for moving the King's retinue from far-larger Northampton to this place. Men at arms were streaming in from every direction, having no doubt been forced to find what billets they could in the surrounding countryside. Seeing our banners and our hurry, they made way before our party, saluting the two Dukes at its head. Before long we had clattered out of the village and were crossing open pastureland towards an imposing stone manor house, set among barns, fishponds and pleasure grounds. In fields beyond, men were busy collapsing myriad tents, pitched perhaps overnight to house more of the King's numerous escort.

Our swift approach caused a flurry among the scores of men and riders already assembled on the manor's wide cobbled courtyard. Cries of alarm, startled horses dancing around their handlers. One, a gleaming chestnut bearing a rich red saddlecloth, tore its lead rein from the groom's hands and would have dashed away. But Lord Lovell kicked his horse forward and stretched out a hand to grasp its silver-buckled bridle as he had for Alys all those months ago in Middleham. He led it back to where the rest of us had slowed to a halt, just as the huge oaken door of the manor house was flung open.

Through the doorway lunged four or five young men in bright travelling clothes of blue, green, russet, their long cloaks swinging about their striding legs. The face of the leader blanched as he caught sight of us, and his hand flew to draw his sword, which flashed in the sunlight as he brandished it. His fellows likewise unsheathed their weapons and stood with him amidst the general melee, a tight knot of dazzling steel before the manor's threshold.

Duke Richard's nearest companions closed ranks in front of him and the Duke of Buckingham, their mounts' hindquarters bunching together protectively before anyone else could react. I could barely glimpse their adversaries through the thicket of their upraised blades.

But Duke Richard was quick too. Just as I spied another person in the shadows of the doorway, so it seemed did he, for he cried out,

'Put up your swords, gentlemen, in the presence of your King.'

His men instantly obeyed, lowering their weapons, but those about the boy King hesitated, until he himself stepped forward and placed a hand on the shoulder of the man in russet.

'Brother, see, it is my uncle Gloucester. Our uncle Rivers said he was riding to join us. Remember?'

This speech told me that the russet-clad man grasping the costly, jewel-hilted sword was the King's younger half-brother, Richard, Lord Grey. He was still reluctant to obey, and his fellows glanced at him for guidance, their razor-sharp blades poised to strike at a word.

In their moment of indecision, Duke Richard swung down from Storm and slipped through the defensive shield of horses to stand alone before them. As Lord Grey and his men stared at him amazed, their swords still raised, he knelt on one knee on the ground, a small, dark figure against the pale cobbles.

'My liege, I come to bring you my allegiance. Your noble father, my beloved and lamented brother, willed that I should govern the kingdom for you until you are of age. That I will gladly do. And my men and those of our cousin the Duke of Buckingham will here also do you homage.'

All around, our companions dismounted and knelt in their turn. I followed their lead, the cobbles chill and hard through the thin fabric of my hose. As I removed my cap, I watched the unfolding scene out of the corner of my eye.

My lord Buckingham was the last to dismount, swinging his leg stiffly down from the saddle and never taking his eyes away from Grey and his men.

Edward's brother himself appeared confused by the turn of events, transfixed by the sight of Duke Richard kneeling only feet away from him. Tension crackled in the air like a coming thunderstorm, but then, at another word from the new King, he lowered his sword and motioned to his companions to do likewise.

Then Edward stepped past them and I could see him clearly for the first time.

His face was thinner than when I had met him at court, and pale, no longer flushed by our ride through the crisp winter air, or by the music and dancing of the Twelfth Night revels. Though taller than me, of course, to my eyes he also appeared far younger than his twelve years. Duke Richard's question to me at Middleham stole into my mind – it seemed so long ago now: how would I feel to have the job of ruling England thrust upon me at that age?

He stood now in front of his uncle, clad in his sober mourning suit of darkest blue, the colour reflected in his shadowed eyes. Despite these family members nearby, he struck me as very alone. Then he spoke. Though his words were formal, his voice was high and my ears detected a slight tremor in it.

'My thanks, uncle, for your allegiance, and for that of your men. Also to my uncle Buckingham. I know that the loyalty of the foremost nobles of my kingdom is vital to me as it was to my father.'

He put out his hand on which glistened a large-stoned ring and Duke Richard bent his head to kiss it. Then Edward's eyes swept across all those gathered before him.

'But tell me, uncle, where is my uncle Rivers? They tell me he rode back to meet you last evening, yet I do not see him here with you.'

The Duke rose to his feet, and Lord Lovell, who had moved forward to his side, signalled to the rest of us to do the same. Despite the scraping of boots on stone as scores of men obeyed, the Duke's measured reply reached my ears.

'Your Grace – Edward – we have reason to think Earl Rivers attempted to delay us.'

'Delay you?' It was Edward's turn to be confused. 'Why so?'

'To prevent us reaching you before you can enter London. Not only did he miss the rendezvous we arranged at Northampton yesterday, but it seems ambushes were set along the road.'

'Ambushes? I don't understand.' Edward turned to his brother, still standing beside him. 'Richard? Do you know anything of this?'

The young man flushed scarlet and his knuckles whitened on his sword hilt.

'He lies, Edward,' he hissed. 'Do not trust him. Our mother told uncle Rivers that —'

The Duke of Buckingham thrust himself forward at this.

'Your mother, boy? She has nothing to do with this. It is the business of men, not of women, to govern kingdoms. Place not your confidence in anything she says!'

Duke Richard laid a hand on his arm.

'Calm yourself, Harry. Let Lord Grey talk. If he knows anything of the ambushes, I would rather hear him out. And the King asked to know the truth. Although now Earl Rivers is in our custody, he perhaps will explain —'

At these words the blood drained from Lord Grey's face. Before the Duke could finish, the younger man had lunged towards him, his sword arcing through the air. But the Duke's own blade, unsheathed in a flash, parried the blow, and with a twist my eyes barely caught, flicked the sword out of his assailant's hand. His sword point was at Lord Grey's throat and Lord Lovell and his gentlemen had disarmed his companions before they'd even managed to step forward or lift their own weapons.

I was stunned by the speed of what happened. I heard Lord Lovell bark orders at his men. Saw Lord Grey's mouth twist into a soundless snarl as he glared first at Duke Richard, then at Lord Lovell. Then he glanced at his younger brother.

Edward was staring at him, his face white with shock.

Lord Grey's expression changed. His eyes dropped, and a few stuttered words fell from his lips.

'Edward, I'm – I'm sorry – I – we...'

His voice faltered and died away. When Master Ratcliffe stepped up with cord to bind his wrists, he offered them up without a murmur, then followed his companions as all five were led away.

Edward watched until they disappeared into the huge gathering of men and horses in the manor's courtyard. None of the soldiers of the escort had made a move to assist Lord Grey and many now turned away to busy themselves with their mounts or their gear.

Calm restored, the Duke of Buckingham came out from behind Lord Lovell, brushing down his doublet with an air of unconcern.

Duke Richard resheathed his sword and said to the boy King,

'I'm sorry, Edward. I would have spared you that if I could. But now we must talk. Are your chamberlain and tutor within?'

Edward, a look of misery having driven the shock from his face, nodded, then led the two dukes into the manor house. Pausing briefly to speak to his men, Lord Lovell followed them in, closing the oaken door behind him.

Before long I stood almost alone in the courtyard, bar Bess and a few grooms and horses, including the flighty chestnut with its costly harness. I had overheard Lord Lovell's orders to his men, which were to disperse most of the King's escort back to their homes in Wales or the Marches. They would not be needed now Duke Richard had arrived. Despite the scene outside the manor house, or perhaps because of it, the escort didn't need to be told twice. The enormous company that had been assembling melted away again in a matter of minutes.

I was not as sure what to do with myself. So, taking from my saddle bag the precious book that the Duke's son Ed had given me at our parting, I settled down on a mounting block outside a barn, with Murrey at my feet, to read. Yet it was some time before any of the words on the page sank in. My thoughts wandered back unbidden to the scene that had just passed.

I had never before seen the Duke with a weapon in his hand, nor had I ever witnessed anyone wield a sword with such calm precision. Duke Richard was spoken of by everyone as a great knight and a famous general, but I had not placed that alongside the reality of the man I knew best at home – with his family, reading romances or enjoying music, or riding with my friends and me and seemingly few cares across the heather on the moors around Middleham. Here now was another side to him.

Time passed, however, and I ceased to ponder what was happening inside the manor house. My attention was at last captured by the book on my lap, the ominously titled 'Death of Arthur'. So engrossed did I become in that verse tale of an ancient king and his knights that I noticed neither that the Duke's gentlemen were gathering again in the yard nor that anyone had quit the manor house. It was only a shadow falling across the page and Lord Lovell's voice saying, 'Come, Matthew, the Duke wishes to speak with you,' that drove me to my feet again and back into the courtyard, Murrey trotting at my heels.

Duke Richard stood in the doorway of the house, pulling on his riding gauntlets. His face was shadowed, the expression suggesting he was barely aware of the bustle of men and beasts around him. Seeing me, however, he motioned me closer.

'Matt, though you are soon to leave us, it seems I may have a further use for you after all.'

'I'm ever at your service, Your Grace,' I said, bowing.

'So I have found,' he replied. 'And I am grateful for it. But today it is not just me but your new King whom you will serve.'

'I'm honoured, sir.'

He looked down at me and a small smile curved his lips. But he continued in the rather official manner I had seen in him all morning.

'I find that our plans have changed and we must return to Northampton. I would that you would ride with the King.'

'Of course, my lord. It will be a pleasure.'

I truly believed what I said, but his face was darkened by a faint frown.

'I hope so. It will not be like your ride together at Christmas, Matt. It has been a difficult day for the poor lad – one in very many such days since his father died. And it will not be the last for him. Or for us.'

He paused. But before I could think how to respond, he continued quietly,

'He hardly knows me, Matt. I see him shrink from me as though he fears me. He has been shut away with Lord Rivers for so long – and perhaps I have been shut away too long in the north, away from the court. Our paths have hardly crossed, and who knows what he may have been told about me. And now his father...'

A spasm passed across his face and he set off striding across the courtyard towards the pleasure grounds. I had to trot to keep pace, as did Murrey alongside us both.

As we left behind the last of the crowds, finding ourselves amidst the bright-blossoming trees and shrubs, he spoke again.

'If you go to Edward, and speak with him, boy to boy, it may make things easier for him. For all his training to be king one day, now he is just a frightened lad. And my lord Buckingham does not help.'

He halted, causing Murrey and I to skitter to a stop beside him. His frown had deepened.

'Although in one thing Buckingham may be right. Perhaps young Edward has been too softly brought up among his mother's family. When I was his age, his father had set me to work raising troops for his wars. At only a few years older, he had lost his own father and brother and fought to win his crown at St Albans and Towton. I wonder whether this boy would be able to face such troubles as those.'

He fell silent, his shadowed eyes watching the activity back in the courtyard. For some minutes he seemed unwilling to return to his men or to speak again.

Waiting there for him to continue, a question that had been welling up in me since the previous evening at last broke out.

'Your Grace, forgive me asking, but why does the Duke of Buckingham hate the Queen's family so much?'

He stared at me for several moments. Had I perhaps been too impertinent? But then he spoke again.

'Perhaps he has reason enough. He was the Queen's ward as a boy and when he was younger even than you, Matt, she chose to marry him – and his fortune – to her sister Catherine. I fear they have never been happy together. My lord is too mindful of his proud ancestry – and of her family's lowly origins. No matter that he thereby became brother to the Queen, and King... My brother's marriage to Elizabeth has caused much trouble over the years. But perhaps... perhaps now things will change.'

A shout came from among the gentlemen in the courtyard and Lord Lovell raised his arm to signal to us.

The Duke placed his gloved hand on my shoulder.

'Come, Matt, we must be on our way again. And I am relying on you to put young Edward at his ease.'

As we walked back, Edward emerged from the house, flanked by the Duke of Buckingham and several soberly dressed older men, presumably the chamberlain and tutor the Duke had mentioned, and other members of the new King's household. Soon they and we were all mounted – Edward on the fine-boned chestnut Lord Lovell had seized earlier – and back on the main road, travelling away from the morning sun towards Northampton. This time our party, now numbering several hundred men, rode at a more sedate pace, under not just the Dukes' but also the King's colourful banners. Rearing lion, white boar, leopards, silver rose and golden suns fluttered all together in the stiffening breeze.

After a few minutes I pushed Bess into a trot and wound a way through the King's gentlemen until I was riding next to Edward himself. Several of the older men glanced askance at my impudence, but as the King showed no surprise at my approach, and even raised his riding whip to salute me, they voiced no complaint.

'Matthew, isn't it? I remember you from my father's court at Westminster. And your little hound.'

'I'm honoured, Your Grace.'

As ever, I was recollected as much for Murrey, slung across my saddle bow as usual now except on the shortest of journeys.

Edward reached across with his riding crop to tickle her behind her ear. Waking, she lifted her head and gnawed gently at its leather tip.

A smile touched the King's pale lips.

'Does she still dance?'

'Aye, Your Grace. Since you taught her so well at Twelfth Night.'

His expression changed and he pulled his crop away.

'That was the last day I spent with my father,' he said.

I told him I was sad at his loss and we rode together side by side in silence for a mile or two. The Duke had asked me to speak with him, but my training as a page had drilled into me that it was not my place to start a conversation.

It wasn't long, though, before Edward spoke again.

'You were with my uncle Gloucester when I met you at Twelfth Night, were you not, Matthew?'

'Yes, Your Grace.'

'Edward was good enough for you on our ride then, Matthew. I wish that you would call me that again.'

'Aye, Your Gr – I mean, Edward.'

'And you were among his gentlemen this morning. Do you know my uncle well?'

'A little.' Recalling the past day or two – and how different the Duke had been – I could claim no more.

'My uncle Rivers says he is angry at my family. That he hates us because of something that happened long ago – and that he may seek revenge on us.'

'Your family?' How strange that he spoke this way. And did he mean what Roger had told me months before – about the execution of the Duke's brother George, which some blamed on the Queen and her family? 'But Duke Richard is your family – he's your father's brother.'

'Well, yes. I suppose I mean my mother's family. Uncle Rivers is my mother's brother. I know him better than my other uncles. I've lived with him for as long as I can remember. But no one now will tell me where he is, or even – even if he is alive.'

'I saw him this morning and he was safe then,' I said. 'The Duke of Buckingham was angry with him, but he and Duke Richard spoke courteously to one another. I believe the Earl agreed to stay in Northampton while the Duke rode to meet you.'

'And yet he is under arrest? Like my brother Richard?'

'I believe so.' I searched my memory. 'To be honest, I'm not sure I know exactly what happened. It was all so quick, and so early in the morning. But the Earl was well when we left him. And I do know Duke Richard is a good man – and I believe that your father trusted him and wouldn't have made him Lord Protector if he didn't.'

'I suppose you are right.'

We fell into a companionable silence again as we jogged along behind the Dukes and the banners, the great bulk of the soldiers formed up in lines behind us. As my thoughts drifted back over the morning's events, I hoped fervently that I was right.

Within a few more miles, Edward was talking once more. His words spilled out like water from a cracked jug. Was I the first person he had been able to speak to like this since he'd been told of his father's death?

'It scares me, Matt, no matter who is to be Protector. I shall have to be King, I know that. I have trained for it ever since I was small. My uncle Rivers tells me I will be a good King, maybe even a great one. He's been telling me so for months, and I had begun to believe him. But now my uncle Gloucester tells me I still have so much to learn. And my uncle Buckingham says I have been badly taught before now and must have better advisers. He even says that my mother should not help me, even though she is Queen.'

He paused. I had no response ready for him, but he needed no prompting to carry on after a moment.

'I want to be a good King, Matt. I will do all I can to become one. But I had not expected to be King so soon, not for years. Not – not until my father was an old man and I had been in battles like him and uncle Gloucester. And now my father is gone, and perhaps my uncle Rivers and brother too. I'm not sure I know how to go on, or who I should trust.'

He fell quiet once more.

My heart went out to him – this boy who had so much before him, but to whom too much had come so soon. All that Duke Richard and his wife had spoken of that last night at Middleham came back to me – the intrigues among the young King's family, the difficulty and responsibility of kingship, and the horrors of the civil war in our country's so-recent past.

I also thought of my own close-knit family back home in York.

And I knew I would not change places with this King for all his riches, his palaces, his wonderful prospects, his title, his power – not for a single instant.

4

The Road to London

Our entry into the city of London four days later far outshone the Duke's arrival before Christmas. That, though a spectacle in my eyes, had been just the start of a family visit. This by contrast was the first entry of a new King into his loyal capital.

He came flanked by two royal Dukes and accompanied by an escort of five hundred retainers. The procession approaching Aldersgate must have been impressive indeed – so many men clad in ashy black, the only specks of colour being the royal and ducal banners. Duke Richard had even ensured that Edward's gaudy saddlecloth was exchanged for one of midnight blue velvet stitched with silver to match the young King's own outfit.

Townsfolk lined the city walls to watch our coming. A single dolorous note was tolled by the bells in each of those more than four score churches that I knew were in the city, and had thought perhaps I might never see again. Before we reached the vast gatehouse, we were met by the mayor and aldermen resplendent in fur-trimmed scarlet robes, followed by such hordes of important men arrayed in vivid violet that I lost count.

The numbers and finery of the citizens, and the size and clamour of the crowds as we passed under the portcullis, and the din of their cheering, and the sudden outpouring of bell peals from the churches as we wound through the narrow streets, put our reception at York two months before in the shade – though I would never have confessed it out loud.

I fear that Master Kendall, had he not himself been overwhelmed by the display, would have told me to close my gawping mouth as he did on my first entry into London. He and I rode close enough behind the King and his two uncles that the city folk's joy and affection for their new sovereign were clear. Flowers of many hues were strewn before him on the cobbles, swept clean today in his honour, and colourful tapestries and bannerettes draped and fluttered from windows at every turn. On occasion someone would dart forward – a woman carrying an infant, an old man – to beg a favour from the King. To each of these Lord Lovell's men, forming Edward's personal bodyguard, slipped a shiny coin before pressing them back into the throng.

One jarring note alone marred that joyous morning. Far ahead of the river of black-clad soldiers trundled four gigantic wagons piled high with weapons and harness. Seized from the ambushers on the road from Northampton, among the haul was equipment that had been found to bear the emblems of Earl Rivers and his family. My lord of Buckingham claimed this proved they were to blame for the plot. He had wished the weapons to be carried immediately in front of the King, as though the spoils of war of some victorious general on his triumphal entry to the city of Rome. Duke Richard had refused, preferring to send the wagons some way before us. Accompanying them, heralds on every street corner announced the King's approach, bringing the cheering crowds flooding into the streets.

In this way the procession wended its way towards Ludgate Hill and the tall spire of St Paul's Cathedral. In after days, onlookers said it took more than an hour to pass by.

Skirting the massive buttresses of the ancient church, the cavalcade came to a halt at the ornate carved door of the palace of the Bishop of London. Here Edward was to stay and to receive oaths of fealty from all the lords and churchmen and great citizens there gathered. I watched as his small figure, flanked by the dukes, mounted the wide flight of steps to be greeted by the Bishop in his full regalia. Then I turned Bess's head to follow Master Kendall away from the palace, my thoughts full of all that had happened. Would I and the King ever meet again – let alone as friends?

For I believed we had become friends in the days after that tumultuous morning in Stony Stratford. We were often thrown together when he was not needed by his uncles for official business, and he seemed to enjoy the company of someone outside his usual circle. He had asked that I attend him as page, though he already had pages and squires of the body aplenty in his retinue. Duke Richard had agreed, ordering that my mattress be laid outside the King's chamber in the inn that night.

I was proud of my new privilege, but sad no longer to do the same for Duke Richard. For that day a letter had at last reached us from the Duke's friend Master Ashley in London, agreeing to take me as apprentice in his merchant's business, and I knew my brief spell as the Duke's page was over. My unhappiness was doubled when I realized that my last ever night of that service was one when the Duke had had to nudge me awake – knowing that I had failed in my duty on the very night when it might have been most needed.

Much business was undertaken during those days before our entry into London. Master Kendall and several other secretaries were almost constantly employed in sending letters and messages both for Duke Richard and in the King's name. News of the Duke's actions was sent to the capital, and we received word of events there in return.

Everything the Duke had done was approved both by Lord Hastings and by other lords who had been assembling for the coronation. For it was discovered that the Marquess of Dorset had persuaded the Royal Council to set a date to crown his younger brother that was only three days ahead. The Duke of Buckingham insisted this confirmed what he had said – that Dorset and Rivers had planned to rush young Edward ahead of us to the capital – and that it was more proof that the Marquess himself was determined to rule England through the new King.

Master Kendall was my chief informant throughout this time. Not directly, of course. He would often speak of such matters to the other gentlemen over dinner. They were not confidential, he said. But I was not sure how happy my lord of Buckingham would have been knowing his words were overheard by a mere page.

'So, yes, Lord Hastings says Sir Edward Woodville has launched his own fleet and is busy menacing English ships in the Channel. And, yes, it seems he did ransack the royal treasury before he left – half of it went with him on his fleet. And most worrying of all, the Marquess of Dorset did boast in Council that he could rule without Duke Richard.'

Gasps and grumbles rumbled around the supper table as the gentlemen digested these snippets along with their meal.

Master Ratcliffe's wine-cup stopped halfway to his mouth.

'And what of the citizenry? And the lords? How have they taken these outrages?'

Master Kendall stabbed another piece of mutton with his knife and chewed on it for a moment before continuing.

'Well, it seems that separate factions had been forming in the city – those who support Duke Richard and Lord Hastings, and those who openly favoured the Woodvilles.' Several gentlemen hissed in disapproval. 'But Lord Hastings says, now it's widely known that old King Edward appointed the Duke as Protector in his will, and people have heard what he's done here – well, most people believe he's in the right.'

'And the Woodvilles?' asked another gentleman.

'Ah, well, there's a story. And one I wouldn't have believed if it hadn't come from Bishop Russell as well as our esteemed Lord Chamberlain himself.'

Master Kendall laid down his knife and looked around the table at his listeners. When certain he had their full attention, he said,

'When they finally realized that the people weren't with them, and that they wouldn't be able to raise troops to challenge the Duke, the Queen and the Marquess took themselves off to sanctuary at Westminster.'

'Sanctuary?' gasped one gentleman.

'At the Abbey?' asked another.

The rest sat in silence, stunned by the news.

Even to a lowly boy such as myself, listening in with no knowledge of politics, this revelation was shocking. Everyone knew that fleeing to sanctuary was usually only the last resort of someone, criminal or otherwise, who believed they were about to be arrested or even executed. They could throw themselves on the mercy of the church and they would be safe from their enemy – but only for as long as they remained on that church's premises. It was not a route chosen lightly or by those who had nothing to fear.

'Not only that,' resumed Master Kendall, 'but the Queen took all her other children – and what was left in the treasury.'

Master Ratcliffe snorted.

'No more evidence of their guilt is needed if you ask me. If they weren't plotting to seize power, and if they were innocent of those ambushes, why would they flee like that – and take all young Edward's treasure with them?' He shook his head as though struggling to believe what he'd heard. 'If I were His Grace, I'd break down the Abbey walls and drag them out by force. They say King Edward did that to the Duke of Somerset when he claimed sanctuary after the battle at Tewkesbury. But we all know Richard won't.'

The other gentlemen around the table nodded in agreement.

'He's not so like his brother as that,' said Master Kendall. 'He'll probably try to talk them out and offer them a pardon for their crimes. My Lord Buckingham said he should rather leave them there to rot, bricked up like rats in a drain.'

But far from heeding his gentlemen's views or those of the Duke of Buckingham, Duke Richard's calm response had been to write to tell London's mayor and aldermen to expect the new King's entry on the following Sunday, and to request that the great royal seal be kept safe so it did not fall into the hands of the Queen or Marquess.

That night I was woken from my sleep by the noise of men and horses outside the inn.

Squinting out into the darkness, I spied Master Ratcliffe leading a detachment of soldiers setting off away from the London road. In their midst rode the cowed figures of Earl Rivers, Lord Grey and several of Edward's household gentlemen, their hands bound.

The following day we had left the inn at Northampton to travel to St Albans, the final stop before London. Once more I rode alongside Edward. This time he requested that Murrey lie across the front of his fine leather saddle when she wasn't scampering at our horses' hooves. I was happy to say yes, to give him some small pleasure in the midst of all his difficulties. He hadn't talked so openly to me again as he had on the road to Northampton and I could hardly imagine how he felt about what was awaiting him in London – or how his confidence in his mother and her family must have been badly shaken by their actions.

Instead, on our rides, and when he had time to spare from signing documents and letters with his uncles, we chatted on much the same topics as I would with Alys, Roger or Ed – hawking, horses, hounds, archery, romances, music and the foibles of our tutors – subjects favoured by boys our age the world over I imagined. On the morning that we rode to St Albans, he told me of an incident the evening before. Duke Richard had been urging him to practise his new royal signature, and to encourage him, had neatly signed his own name on a scrap of parchment, topping it with his motto.

'*Loyaulté me lie*,' I said promptly. 'Loyalty binds me.'

'I know,' said Edward. 'He wants me to choose a motto too, though I haven't any idea for one yet. He says every nobleman should have one, and especially the King. So he asked my uncle Buckingham to sign too.'

'What's his?'

225

He fished a piece of parchment from his pouch and squinted at it.

'*Souvente me souvene*, I think.'

He handed it to me. Beneath Duke Richard's neat signature and the words 'Edwardus Quintus' in a boyish hand was an unfamiliar ink scrawl.

'Remember me often,' I translated roughly. 'That's rather strange.'

'Not so strange as his translation,' returned Edward. 'He said it was "Often I recall" – but couldn't recall why, or what he meant by it!'

As I laughed along with him, this talk of mottoes brought to mind my very first meeting with Roger and his idea for an emblem for our fellow page, Hugh Soulsby: a dumb ox, or 'vache noir on a muck brun champ'. Roger and I had no love for Hugh – even less now after the part he'd played in my dismissal.

Edward winced as I repeated the tortured French, but laughed again. He reminded me then, not for the first time, of his little cousin Ed. A spark of recognition had also kindled in Duke Richard's eye after supper the evening before when the new King had shaken off his usual melancholy at some quip of Lord Lovell's. Did the Duke see in his new sovereign some likeness to his son too – or was it to his dead brother?

Lord Lovell's men were eyeing us with curiosity. Hastily I tucked the parchment scrap into my pouch. Edward sobered up.

'Don't tell my uncle Buckingham of that. He'd be shocked at someone mocking a member of the nobility.'

I wouldn't dare, I thought, casting my mind back to Duke Henry's haughty words to me at Twelfth Night, when I had encountered him outside Duke Richard's bedchamber in the palace of Westminster. A mere merchant's son, riding with the King, let alone mocking a nobleman? Bricking me up like a rat would be too good for me.

Late that evening, Duke Richard summoned me to his chamber in the Abbey guesthouse at St Albans. Lord Lovell and Master Kendall, passing me, bid me goodnight as I approached the door. The Duke was alone when I entered – the first time I had seen him so since we had left Middleham.

He was sitting staring into the fire that was crackling in the hearth though it had been a warm May day. A flagon of wine and cups were untouched upon a table near his elbow. The guards who were always posted now outside his rooms had announced me, but he did not look up.

'Your Grace?' I said after a moment.

He roused himself and waved me forward. The deep lines and shadows about his eyes, accentuated by the light of the flickering flames, startled me as I straightened up from my bow.

'Your Grace, would you like me to sing? I have brought my lute.'

'Please, Matthew. We have not had enough music in these past days.'

I hadn't sung to him since the night in the castle at Nottingham on our way south. Every evening since he had spent immersed in business which left little time for relaxation. Now, as I sang – the sad French *chanson* that was the first to come to mind – he tipped wine into a cup and sat nursing it for some time, before taking a sip. As the final notes faded away, he poured a second cup and pushed it towards me, with a tiny tray of sweetmeats.

'No more, Matt,' he said, to my surprise. He was rarely content with just one song. Had I made the wrong choice? 'I would rather remember the cheerful songs of our last night at Middleham. For this will be your last evening as part of my household.'

'Yes, Your Grace.'

I needed no reminding. Through all the busy times of the past few days, that thought had never left me – excited though I should be at entering the service of a great London merchant.

I propped my lute against the table and took up the cup he offered, gulping the strong wine. I was glad it burned as it went down, giving a reason for the smarting of my eyes.

'And I wished to speak with you before you leave us.'

He gestured to a stool nearby and I sat, Murrey wrapping herself around my booted feet. As I nibbled on a sweetmeat from the salver, I hoped the Duke would be talking rather than me. Now that I was no longer singing, I wasn't sure I could trust my voice.

'Master Ashley has agreed to take you as apprentice on my recommendation. I know I do not need to tell you this, but serve him well and he will look after you well. It is an opportunity such as few young men have.'

I nodded mutely. I knew full well how lucky I was – even though luck such as this could never make up for what I had lost.

'Though much has changed, Matt, since first I told you that you must leave my service, one thing has not. Though he is my nephew now, no longer my brother, our King will still need the loyalty and support of men such as Lord Soulsby. We must give him no further cause for complaint.'

He paused to toss a tidbit from the salver to Murrey. Leaning forward, he cannot have seen the flame that touched my cheek at mention of the name. At the memory of Hugh's uncle's suspicions about me and Alys – his son Ralph's intended wife, if Alys's guardian Queen Elizabeth had her way.

Sitting back again, the Duke took another sip of his wine, then continued.

'However, it is likely that Alys will accompany my wife to Westminster for the coronation. Your fortunate move to Master Ashley's household in London may allow you to meet with her from time to time while I am Protector. As I said before, you also have my permission still to write.' He broke off, uncertainty upon his face, as though he were about to ask a favour. 'And I hope also that you will continue to write to my son. His health I believe will keep him at home in Middleham.'

'Of course, my lord. And thank you.' I hesitated in my turn before saying more, but knowing it was my last evening drove me on. 'Ed has become almost like a brother to me. I would not want to let him down.'

His features relaxed into a smile.

'I thank you for your loyalty. I know how good a friend you have been to him. To us all. And there is one more thing.'

He took something from a purse lying on the table and handed it to me. It was a small badge, less than the length of my thumb, fashioned from silver in the shape of a boar.

'Here is my token in remembrance of your valued service to us. If ever you have need of me, you may call on me and I will do my best to help.'

Gratitude washed through me, carrying with it fond memories like flotsam on the tide. Before I could stop myself, I replied, 'Thank you, Your Grace. And if you are ever in need, call on me.'

'If I'm in need?'

'Yes, Your Grace. We...'

I almost wished I'd not started, but the amused interest on his face spurred me on.

'We – that is, Ed, Alys, Roger and me – we've founded our own order – the Order of the White Boar – to be loyal to each other and to you. If ever you have need of us...'

Now I said it out loud, to an adult, it sounded foolish to me. But the Duke showed more real pleasure than I had seen for days.

'Then, yes, I thank you, Matthew – I shall call on you and your friends when I am in direst need. In these days, who knows when that shall be?'

And he raised his cup to me, and I to him, and we drank a toast to seal the bargain.

The wine flowed down and into my veins. Warming me throughout, it gave me the courage to ask a question that had been lurking for some time.

'Your Grace, what has happened to Lord Rivers and Lord Grey? The King has asked me and I've been unable to tell him.'

The Duke's hand checked as he lifted his cup to take another draught.

'The King has asked you?'

'Yes, Your Grace. I think he trusts me. That was what you wanted, wasn't it?'

'Yes, Matt, it was.' He was thoughtful for a moment. 'It's a shame you are leaving us. Young Edward might have done better with you as a companion than his tutor, old Alcock. If he ask again, you must tell him the truth. That they have been taken to Sheriff Hutton and Middleham for safekeeping until they can be brought to trial. If they are innocent of any wrongdoing, they will be released. If not, then being uncle and brother to a King will not save them.'

My face must have betrayed me as, with a slight frown, he asked,

'Does that seem harsh to you?'

Not expecting the question, I nodded without thinking.

He laughed, but with little humour.

'Perhaps it is true. Perhaps I seem a different man in these days to the one you've known before? But, Matt, I was bred in war. Before I was eight, my father and brother were killed and I was exiled from my mother and my home. At eighteen I led men and fought in my first battles. Since then I have served my brother in wars in Scotland and France. I would that I had no need for violence and that my life had been peaceful. It may be yet. I hope

229

that my actions – here this week, today, whatever comes tomorrow – will lead to a kingdom where my son, you – and, yes, this boy King – can grow up in peace – where cousin will never fight against cousin again for power. It may be yet.'

He fell silent, cradling his cup and gazing into the fire again. And I knew it was time for me to leave.

I dropped to my knee in front of him and felt his hand on my shoulder one last time.

'Good night, Matthew. May tomorrow bring you all that you desire. And yes, I will remember to call on you if I am in need. It seems that you do indeed have the makings of a fine chivalrous knight.'

I was used to his gentle mockery, but somehow now, although his tone was light, there was a seriousness about his words. Perhaps that was unsurprising after the events of recent days.

All this raced through my brain as I rode with Master Kendall away from the procession in London, together with my last parting from the King earlier that morning.

Edward had clasped my hand warmly, given a last treat to Murrey, and urged me to visit him when he was lodged at the Tower. There I could marvel at his menagerie of wondrous, exotic animals and his fabulous treasure – when it was returned to him. A momentary darkness had crossed his brow at that reminder of his uncle Sir Edward's actions, before being banished by thoughts of the coming joyous celebrations.

Perhaps I believed that I would one day pay such a call on the King about as much as I believed that Duke Richard would ever summon my aid. As I followed Master Kendall through the emptying streets on our way to Master Ashley's townhouse, I told myself I had to put that part of my life – my brushes with nobility and royalty – firmly in my past and look only to the future.

5

'A Bag of Snakes'

The familiarity of Master Ashley's house and many of the people within it were a great help to me over the following weeks as I adjusted to this second immense change in my life. My new master greeted me formally that morning, holding the apprentice papers ready for my signature, but the friendliness with which he and Master Kendall conversed reminded me of the strong links between their households. It gave me hope that I would still be able to see my friends in the Order.

The two men spoke about the late King – 'He was a good man, but would have done better to have spent more time governing than in pleasure' – and of the dangerous times ahead – 'Master Lewis – remember him? – he was talking of Westminster and its cliques as a bag of snakes ready and waiting to be opened – I do not envy the new Protector his task.' And, of course, being Englishmen, of the weather.

'It has been so fine these past weeks that the strawberries are ripening in the more sheltered part of my garden,' Master Ashley said.

Master Kendall shook his head in disbelief.

'It will be another month at least before the Duchess will be eating them at home in Middleham.'

At which my new master called at once for his steward.

Master Lyndsey, whom I remembered well from my time here in the winter, entered carrying a covered basket.

'Master Lyndsey has had some gathered to take back with you. I know how much Duke Richard enjoys them. And there are peaches for him too.'

'Now you are jesting with me!'

'Brought in from France this morning,' Master Lyndsey assured him.

They would have been nestled in straw in shallow crates for the journey as I now knew, having seen the arrival of golden oranges during the winter, shipped in by Spanish merchants from the far-off groves of Seville.

Being reminded of the exotic sights and sounds and smells of Master Ashley's house and store rooms at last rekindled my interest after the shocks of recent days. After all, many good things could come of my change of situation.

Another presented itself almost at once.

'Before I forget,' said Master Kendall, 'the Duke has requested that you arrange for Matthew to continue with his lessons in singing and his instrument. He will gladly pay for them. He believes the boy has a talent that should be encouraged.'

'I will be pleased to,' said Master Ashley, 'at no cost to His Grace. I have no singer in my household at present. Although it may be some weeks before I can find him a suitable tutor. He will be accompanying my party to Flanders in a few days.'

I was astounded that the Duke should have had time to think of music lessons, although I must confess that I would have preferred to keep up my weapons training. But mention of the journey drove all else from my head.

'To Flanders?' I asked without thought.

Master Ashley glanced at me. His smile suggested not anger at the interruption, but rather amusement at my enthusiasm.

'Aye, lad, to Flanders. I have cloth and printing concerns to attend to in Bruges, and you have much to learn about both. Will that suit?'

The next few days were almost as busy as the previous ones as I settled in to my new household.

I shared a small attic room with only one other boy, which was paradise after the cramped pages' quarters at Middleham. He was a fellow apprentice called Simon, a year or two older than me. At first I feared he was avoiding me, but soon discovered that he assumed I would be too big for my boots, having been in the household of a royal duke. We rubbed along well enough after that. For both of us it was to be our first visit over the sea when later that week we packed our few belongings to prepare for the journey to Bruges.

Before we left, mindful of my promise to the Duke, I wrote to Ed about all that had happened since last I had seen him, especially about my renewed acquaintance with his cousin, the King. I made sure to write much of it using the code we had created, so that it could not be understood if it fell into the hands of our enemies. Or at least those of Hugh or Lionel... I had been careful to bring my copy of the cipher away with me, although I had taken the sad decision to leave behind with Alys the sacred list of the Order's rules. I had scribed them in my best handwriting during those glorious days of our early friendship last summer. I had to force my thoughts away before any pangs of homesickness crept up on me.

Master Ashley told me to place any letters with his own.

'They will be taken with mine to His Grace's house, and from there they can be sent on to your friends in the north. And do not fret, lad. We will be back home again in London in time for the young King's coronation. I hear the date has now been set by his new Royal Council.'

Then we were on our way to Flanders.

Though we stayed there four weeks or more, I have few clear memories of that first visit to the majestic trading city of Bruges. Important events were playing out back in London, though I did not know it at the time, and looking back, they colour the little that I do recollect. But remembrance of the churning stomach of my first rough sea voyage will remain with me all my life, the slapping of the white sails of Master Ashley's ship cracking my tender head as I lay retching in my bunk, the salt taste on my lips as, on calmer waters, I stood on deck watching the thicket of ships' masts and the bustling harbourside slide towards us. The ride through endless, flat, poplar-fringed fields that stretched towards every horizon, until I saw piercing the sky the slender finger of a bell tower, its roots at our destination.

The town walls rearing up, the arched barbican over the open gates, traders, farmers, citizens, their beasts and wagons pouring through on to the cobbled streets, mirror-like canals hemmed in by high brick buildings, their gables crazily stepped up towards the clouds, their foundations deep beneath the heavy wooden barges cruising slowly past.

The guttural voices of local stallholders as they hawked goods in their native Flemish tongue, the softer tones of French merchants in their fine robes striding on their way, the clopping of pack asses and mules laden with bales of cloth or sacks of unknown wares, the screeching swifts and twittering martins as they swooped for insects far above our heads, the clang of a single bell in a church on the corner.

The warmth and sweetness of new baking wafting from windows, the earthy stench of dung from below, the reek of sweat amidst the mingling crowds, the smoky smell of meat roasting on a brazier that made the water spring in my mouth, the fruity burst of my first bite of a lattice pastry offered up by a passing trader in exchange for a small unfamiliar coin.

The greetings of my master in that strange local tongue to old friends and acquaintances from atop his slender grey mare, the laughing, waving responses, the immense carpet of paving as we rode into the expanse of the main square, the fine tall buildings jostling for space around its edges, topped always by that towering town hall belfry we had spied from afar.

Master Ashley of course kept a beautiful townhouse close to this central square, though far enough away from the market bustle to be peaceful in the day as well as night. Its main doors opened straight on to the street, but at the rear its walls plunged into the depths of a canal. The window of the tiny room I shared with Simon gazed unseeing down upon the still, dark waters, and across them, into the fruit-tree-filled walled gardens of houses on the far side.

Our days in the city were full of business, learning the ways of clothmakers and merchants, entering strings of numbers in giant ledgers, jotting notes to our master's customers or suppliers, finding our way, hesitantly at first, around the dense maze of streets and waterways to deliver messages or order goods. Once, even, feeding my intense curiosity, having demonstrated to us the working of a printing machine such as Master Caxton now used to make books in his workshop crouched under the walls of St Paul's churchyard.

Tiny metal letters clutched in hands of iron, smeared with ink by apprentices like us, pressed down on immense sheets of paper or parchment, and lifted to reveal neat lines of words on page after page – again and again and again. So far from the painstaking work of copyists I'd watched in the scriptorium at York Minster – labouring all day with goose quill, knife, ink pot, scraper, to produce a single page or less of handwritten Latin text.

This of all that I encountered on my first trip abroad excited me more than any other. With my brother Fred learning his trade as bookbinder at home in York, perhaps, one day, when I had served my apprenticeship too, we might set up in partnership with this wondrous machine. If ever we could gather the funds to afford one...

Finally our weeks in Bruges came to a close and we prepared to retrace our steps back towards the coast and London.

I had had little leisure to think of what might be happening back in England, with all my tasks during the day and singing and playing for Master Ashley in the evenings. Nor had I received a letter from any of my friends, despite sending at least one myself to each of them with Master Ashley's post. I told myself that it would take a very long time for my letters to arrive in London and then be sent far north to Middleham. But still I was disappointed.

The crossing back over the sea to England was calmer than the outward journey and I passed much of the time on deck, marvelling at the sailors' agility in the rigging and gazing at the English coast as it came ever nearer. The sun had set on another day and lights had bloomed in the gathering dusk before we docked. Our party spent that night in a habourside tavern before starting out at first light on the road to London.

After my weeks in foreign parts, the city seemed very strange when we finally arrived, although little of substance had changed in my absence. The river still flowed in its usual course, the main buildings were no different – although they appeared odd to my eyes, now used to the steep roofs and stepped gables of Flemish towns – and the same stench rose from the streets. But as we rode towards Master Ashley's house, I became aware of a whispering in the streets, knots of people talking on corners, a buzz of expectation.

On our arrival, almost before I had passed Bess to a groom to be unsaddled, fed and watered, a servant thrust a small note into my hand. Recognizing the handwriting, I hurried off to my attic room, there slitting open the folded paper, eager to discover its contents.

To my disappointment the letter contained nothing beyond a single sentence in our code:

'Wigy ni myy om un Wlimvs Jfuwx um miih um sio wuh – Ufsm.'

I checked when it had been written – a Monday more than a week before. Then I could translate it using our cipher for that day. Revealed were the words 'Come to see us at Crosby Place as soon as you can – Alys.'

Despite the shortness of her message, seeing Alys's name again, and knowing that she was in London too, drove away my momentary unhappiness. No matter now that she hadn't written before. She had clearly been too busy with preparations for her journey and then settling in to her new lodgings in the city.

It was just supper time and I already knew Master Ashley did not require me to sing that evening. So I resolved to take advantage of the long hours of daylight remaining to visit Alys that day if I could.

The atmosphere at supper was subdued. All the party must have been as tired as I was following our long day's journey, and after more than a month away it was no surprise that our master rose early from the table with his wife, steward and secretary and retired to his private chamber. At that, I also rose, declining Simon's offer of an evening spent playing dice. Soon I was treading the familiar streets towards Duke Richard's townhouse, Murrey sticking close to my heels.

Those streets were busier than I recalled from earlier in the year, but I put that down to the better weather and the lighter evening. It was less easy to explain why the stout iron gates of Crosby Place were barred against me when I arrived, with double the number of men at arms on guard. Given the events of the Duke's journey to London, however, perhaps I should not have been surprised that greater security was required. As I stated my name and business, and showed the guards the Duke's little silver boar badge that I now wore proudly on my doublet at all times, Master Ashley's remark about the 'bag of snakes' at Westminster wormed unprompted into my mind. What had unfolded while I had been away?

I was ushered into the courtyard to wait while a servant went to announce me. Before long Elen, Alys's companion, emerged from a side door. Her dark eyes brightened at the sight of me standing there, Murrey perched neat and upright by my feet, and with a smile she beckoned me forward.

'It's so nice to see you, Matthew,' she said, as she led me through passages and up staircases into the heart of the house that, not long ago, had briefly been my home too. 'We have been stuck so long in London now with so little to do. Your tales of your new life will be a welcome distraction.'

Her words surprised me, not only because it was rare for Elen to speak so openly, but also her complaint about lack of amusements. Surely the capital was full of entertainments for two young girls?

As I murmured something about hoping to be of service, we reached a small door towards the topmost part of the house. Elen opened it, drawing her full skirts aside to let me past, and there, in a small parlour, with her embroidery untouched on her lap, sat Alys.

She rose to greet me, and she at least had not changed. As ever her unruly reddish curls were escaping from her linen cap and, standing with her hands upon her hips, she raised one eyebrow as her sharp green eyes looked me up and down.

'Quite a man about town now, I see,' she said with a curl to her lip.

I had of course swapped the Duke's murrey and blue livery for that of Master Ashley, an altogether more elaborate uniform with a touch of lace at the collar and cuffs. And my boots were of smart black leather, no longer the battered pair of our rides together at Middleham.

Where once perhaps my cheeks would have glowed at her words, now I simply lowered myself on to one knee and pressed my lips to her offered hand.

'But still not fit to woo the lady of my dreams, alas. I must continue to wander the world until I have found my fortune.'

To my relief, she laughed as she pushed me away.

'Fool! But did you not find it in faraway Flanders?'

'Thank you for your letters, Matt,' Elen broke in from where she was now seated on a stool to one side. 'Bruges sounds a beautiful city.'

'It is,' I said, and at her prompting, launched into a description of some of the delights I had met with on my travels. Before long, however, her questions tailed off and my own chatter dwindled away in its turn. Uncertain what to say next, I leaned forward to fondle Murrey's ears.

After some moments of silence, Alys burst out,

'So while we've been kicking our heels here, under siege, you've been out and about enjoying yourself!'

I almost laughed at the drama of her words.

'Under siege? Whatever do you mean?'

Elen's dark hands plucked at her arm, but Alys threw them off.

'Well, it seems like it. We're not allowed to go out unless three or four guards are there to protect us. More than a fortnight we've been here and we've seen almost nothing. With the Queen

237

in sanctuary, there's no court to speak of. And now the coronation's been postponed there are hardly any ladies in the city at all. My first visit to London in six years – it was meant to be glorious. I didn't expect it to be like this!'

What she said stunned me.

'What do you mean, the coronation's been postponed?'

'Don't you know what's happened? Have you heard nothing while you've been away?'

'I – we were so busy. And – and I had no letters.'

It wasn't meant as a rebuke, but her face was suddenly aflame.

'Oh, Matt, I'm so sorry. Everything was in an uproar after we received the Duke's news from Northampton – then we were travelling – then more uproar when we arrived here. Your letters did reach us – but we didn't know when you would be returning...'

Her voice trailed away, before rallying again.

'Not that I should make excuses. Ed managed to write to you.'

'Ed?' I asked, casting my eyes around the chamber. Was my little friend hiding in some dark corner as when I had first met him in his father's library? 'Where is he?'

'He stayed behind at home. The Duchess was worried he might become ill in the heat and smoke of London. At least that's what she told him. Although with everything that's happened to the Duke... He wasn't happy. We kept his letters for you, as we weren't sure where to send them. I suppose he'll have told you himself.'

Elen was on her feet, searching in a small trunk on a side table. Turning back, she passed me four or five folded and sealed papers.

I broke with a snap the wax seal on the uppermost, into which was cut a primitive 'E'. Within was a densely packed page of Ed's childish writing.

'He's written it in code, hasn't he?' said Alys, pale once more, her lips curved in a faint smile.

'Every word.'

'I knew it. He always uses the code now, whenever he can. Even just for the briefest notes. He says, "What would Matt say if I didn't use it?"'

'And tells us how much he misses you,' Elen put in.

And I him. But I didn't say the words. That was a different life. When I had been the friend of a Duke's son.

Folding the letter up again to save for later, when I had my cipher to hand, I dragged my thoughts back to the present.

'But what were you saying about the coronation? And the Queen – she's still in sanctuary? Why?'

'I can't believe you don't know anything. Surely Master Ashley did?'

On several days my new master had been agitated when he received his letters and had taken himself off with his secretary Master Hardyng to his study overlooking the quiet canal. But he had never shared news with us lowly boys.

'Perhaps. But don't forget, I'm just an apprentice now – not party to great events.'

'All of London knows it,' she cried in exasperation. 'Lord Hastings has been executed!'

6

St Paul's Cross

I was too shocked to speak at first.

The old King's closest friend, Lord Chamberlain of England, the huge bear-like man I had seen laughing and riding and drinking with the King and Duke at Christmas? Executed?

'How?' I stammered. Then thought – stupid question. I knew. A sharp axe to the neck, of course. Rather – 'I mean, why?'

'They say he'd been plotting with the Queen and the Marquess of Dorset,' said Alys, her eyes alight, though agitated, at the story she had to tell. 'That they were aiming to seize back power along with the King. That he didn't like Duke Richard being Protector and favouring the Duke of Buckingham when he – Lord Hastings – thought he should be in charge of the Council. The Bishop of Ely too, and the old Chancellor, Rotherham – oh, and Lord Thomas Stanley – they've all been arrested as well.'

'Arrested? But you said executed?'

'Well, Lord Hastings – they say that when he was accused – at a Council meeting in the Tower – they found a hidden weapon on him. Master Kendall says his lordship called for the men at arms to support him, but they overpowered him instead. So he was tried at once and executed almost straight away. Master Kendall thinks the Duke acted on the spur of the moment – decided that removing Lord Hastings would take away the main focus for the plot.'

'And has it?'

'Maybe. A couple of days later the Queen allowed the King's little brother, Richard, to leave sanctuary. He's joined Edward in his apartment in the Tower to prepare for the coronation. Perhaps that means she thinks the game's up.'

Edward's last words to me before his glorious entry into London came back to me – about my visiting the menagerie of exotic beasts near his lodgings at the Tower. How close had the boy King been to the place of execution? Had he heard the commotion or the dread sound as the axe fell?

Alys was watching me, as though awaiting my reaction. As I pondered, her earlier words came back to me.

'But you said the coronation's been postponed.'

'Well, yes. There had been a rumour that it would be before all this happened. I think something else is afoot.'

'Why do you say that?'

'Well, Master Kendall knows something, but he's keeping tight-lipped about it for once. The Duchess looks worried all the time – at least whenever we see her, which isn't often. She and the Duke are staying at Baynard's Castle with his mother as often as here. And anyway, I daren't ask her. When all's said and done, we're just children.'

'So's the King,' I said, 'even younger than us. Do you think he knows what's happening?'

She shrugged.

My mind went back to my talks with Edward on the road to and from Northampton, his confusion and questions about his family, his uncertainty about Duke Richard, his worry about being a good king. I recalled also the Duke kneeling to him, unprotected, on the cobbled yard of the manor house, his kiss of the ring, the oath he had led in York Minster, his words to me about being brought up in violent times. His smile when I had pledged him my loyalty. The flash of his sword when threatened by Lord Grey.

'I'm sure the Duke's doing right by him – by us all. He's an important man. He has to make big decisions, he's always had to. And the old King trusted him to make the right ones or he wouldn't have made him Lord Protector.'

'But it's all so far away from our life at Middleham. And I wonder what will happen next. Sometimes it seems as though everyone is holding their breath, waiting to see. It's all so frustrating. And we have no distractions from it here.'

She bit her lip.

'I suppose that sounds terrible, to complain about being bored when a man has just lost his life. But I truly wish there was more for us to do. It might take our minds off all this. Even if we could just ride more often.'

I was glad to think about something other than the bewildering news.

'Perhaps we could ride out together. I have no duties on Sunday.'

Alys clapped her hands together at my words. Elen's eyes were shining too as she said quietly,

'Are you sure, Matthew – that you wish to give up your holiday?'

I bowed to both of them.

'It will be my pleasure. Duke Richard let me take Bess to Master Ashley's, but I've hardly have a chance to ride her since, except for the journey to the coast. And he gave permission for me to see you if you came to London.'

Alys screwed her mouth into a pout.

'Despite Lord Soulsby?'

The reason for my being sent away from Middleham swam back into my head.

'The Duke said we must give his lordship no cause for complaint. But what suspicions can we attract just riding out in the city – two girls and a boy in full view of the whole populace? Nothing, surely, to upset the marriage plans for his son.'

A shadow seeped into Alys's eyes, like a cloud shielding the sun from view. Aware of my mistake in reminding her of her betrothal, I gabbled on.

'We could see some of the most famous sights hereabouts – the Guildhall, maybe, the great bridge, St Paul's. It really is a most wondrous church – almost as fine as the Minster.'

Elen helped me out in my discomfort. She stood and gave me her hand, saying with her gentle humour,

'That's very kind of you, Matthew, to think of us and our entertainment. And if you're escorting us, perhaps we'll need only three men at arms this time.'

Indeed, when I called again at Crosby Place on Sunday morning, the girls were attended by no more than two of the Duke's soldiers, already astride their horses, halberds hefted in their gauntleted fists. Perhaps, as the city had remained calm in the days since Lord Hastings's death, there was little risk in ladies venturing forth. For me, the shock was still fresh – that this man I had met and who had seemed Duke Richard's ally should have met such a brutal end. And on the Duke's orders.

Like Alys I suspected there must be more to the story. Everywhere in Master Ashley's household and throughout the streets of the city, people appeared to be waiting, watching, whispering in shadows.

Bess's coat had been brushed until it shone and Murrey's royal collar also polished for the occasion. Alys was once more atop her pretty chestnut pony and Elen had borrowed an old palfrey from the household steward. He said that, though large, it was sweet-tempered and would be ideal for carrying a lady safely about the bustling streets. As we set off for St Paul's, we soon appreciated the value of horses not readily disturbed by crowds.

Sunday was of course a holiday for all the citizens of London, whether master, journeyman or apprentice, and the streets were always thronged after morning service. But today, as we approached the great cathedral, it was more difficult than usual to force a path through the seething hordes of people. The soldiers had at first trailed in our wake, chatting and little resembling the bodyguard Alys had lamented. But now they pushed their way to the front. At sight of their dark red and blue livery, the townsfolk melted away to either side.

I thought nothing of it and was just telling Alys and Elen something of the first of Ed's letters that I had painstakingly deciphered, when we rode out on to the square about St Paul's Cross.

This roofed stone pulpit I knew to be a place for meetings and preaching to the populace. So it was scarcely surprising to glimpse a tall man clad in a brown habit standing upon it, the morning sun glinting off the dome of his tonsured head. Around him clustered an enormous crowd, as though half the population of the city had collected there.

What I did not expect was a sizeable gathering of horsemen on the far side of the square, ranged before the soaring walls of the cathedral itself. The swathes of velvets, silks, lace and fur trimmings they displayed, and the rich trappings of their horses, marked those at the front as among the wealthiest men in the land. All lords had been summoned to a special sitting of Parliament due to begin in a few days, but I wondered to see so many here.

Beside me, Alys murmured, 'Look. Duke Richard.'

Running my eyes along their ranks a second time, in their midst I spied my old master's slight form upon Storm. Both man and horse were arrayed in deepest purple cloth. In previous weeks I had become so accustomed to seeing the Duke in his sombre black mourning clothes that I had not observed him before.

'And as ever at his side nowadays, my lord of Buckingham,' Alys went on. 'I wonder what we shall see or hear if we remain?'

The Duke of Buckingham had reined his midnight stallion to a halt a little in front of the other lords. Seeing him, attired in vibrant purple shot through with gold thread, a stranger might have imagined him to be the leading man in the government of the realm. But now the friar at the cross started to speak and what he said soon drove away all thought of Duke Henry.

First of all the man raised his hands as though to silence the crowd. This was a gesture so unnecessary it made me want to laugh. Here as elsewhere, it was as though everyone was holding their breath, waiting. The silence was broken only by the shifting of horses and the faint cry of a child, hushed as soon as it began.

He cleared his throat.

'I take as my text this morning a verse from Solomon, chapter 4 verse 3: Bastard slips shall not take root.'

His voice was strong and distinct and it caught the attention of everyone there.

Following a brief discussion of the meaning of his biblical text, to my surprise he spoke in glowing terms of the old Duke of York, Duke Richard's father, of how he had been a great nobleman of England, heir to the true kings of old, before his betrayal and brutal murder by the usurping Lancastrians. And of all his sons, the friar said, only one, Richard, Duke of Gloucester, had been born in our great realm, in England itself. He was therefore the most truly English, as well as a man of firm moral standing and authority.

I glanced at Alys. What did she make of this?

But like the crowd hemming us in, she was transfixed. Whether she was staring at the friar or at the multitude of lords beyond, I could not tell.

'As for legitimate authority, it seems he alone possesses it,' the man's voice rang out. 'For it has come to the attention of the highest lords of our kingdom that our late King, Edward, the fourth of that name, was intemperate in his ways. Before he married the lady Elizabeth Grey, known as Queen, he had been wed to another, one Eleanor Talbot. And it was while that lady was still living, that he took as his wife also that said Dame Elizabeth Grey who bore him his two sons and numbers of daughters. Therefore in the sight of God and our holy mother church, those children are not fit heirs to the throne of England.'

He paused and the faintest whisper or a sigh ran through the assembled people. Then the friar spoke once more.

'The late Duke of York's second son, Edmund of Rutland, died without issue. His third, George of Clarence, having been attainted for his treason to our late King Edward, his offspring are also unable to inherit. So it comes to the final son, Richard of Gloucester, who alone is fit to rule.'

He continued to speak, praising Duke Richard for his nobility, his honour, his steadfastness to his royal brother, his valour in battle, his love for the church, and again, his father's descent from kings all the way back to the Conqueror.

But I couldn't take it all in.

I turned to Alys in bewilderment.

'Alys, what does it all mean?'

She remained staring straight ahead, her face unreadable, as she said softly,

'It means that Duke Richard will be King.'

I looked across to where the Duke sat unmoving on Storm, but he was too far away for me to make out his expression.

7

To be a King

Over the next few days the full story filtered down even to me, a lowly apprentice.

All London was agog with the news, although many who had been in the city these past weeks had had some inkling of what might happen.

'I knew it, as soon as the coronation was delayed again.' A woman's voice had floated up to our ears as we pushed our way through the crowd out of the square. The friar had finished his speech and the lords had turned their mounts' heads to follow the two Dukes away from the cathedral. 'I knew something was amiss.'

And, 'I had my suspicions after old Hastings lost his head,' said one groom to another as I left Bess to be unsaddled on my return to Master Ashley's. 'They say he'd been keeping secrets for the old King for years. Maybe this was one of them. It was bound to catch up with them in the end.'

News had travelled through the city faster than summer lightning on that day.

I accompanied Alys and Elen straight back to Crosby Place, the soldiers preferring to usher them back to the safety of its walls and barred gates after the friar's pronouncement. Yet the crowd remained calm and drifted away alongside us, barely glancing at us or our escort's livery as we passed wordless through the bustling streets.

Alys's thanks were muted as we parted at the townhouse entryway and, each wrapped in our own thoughts, we did not speak about what had happened or of meeting again. But a day or two later another note in code arrived, again summoning me to her side.

'*Qcas og gccb og dcggwpzs - Ozmg.*'*

By then the talk of my master's journeymen and servants was all of my lord Buckingham having spoken to certain collections of lords and great men of the city about Duke Richard's right to the throne. And it was said that on this day the matter would be discussed by a meeting of Lords and Commons in Westminster that would be a Parliament in all but name.

As before, I walked to Crosby Place after supper.

Elen met me in the courtyard, this time with nothing more than a simple greeting, and retired with her sewing to a stool by the hearth after showing me in to the parlour.

Alys was standing staring out of a window, but swung round as we entered.

'Well, is it true?'

I was taken aback by her abruptness.

'Is what true?'

'What they are saying. What everyone apart from us in his own household knows about. That Parliament will ask the Duke to be King.'

I sat down, even though she hadn't invited me to.

'That's what I've heard. Master Lyndsey, my master's steward, he says all this is why Parliament wasn't postponed when the coronation was.' He had been speaking of it to Master Hardyng, the secretary, in the dining hall. Not that I'd been eavesdropping... 'He says the Bishop of Bath and Wells told the Duke and the Council that the old King had been married before he met the Queen. That he had himself performed the ceremony in secret. So when King Edward married the Queen, he was already married – to someone who was still alive.'

'So poor Edward and the others are...'

She couldn't bring herself to say the word, dropping into a chair next to mine with a mixture of emotions chasing across her face. I carried on to save her.

'The King's second marriage was bigamous, so it wasn't legal, yes. So Edward can't become King because he's not the legal heir.'

Silence reigned for some minutes, before Alys spoke again.

'So who was she? His first wife.'

'Lady Eleanor? Master Lyndsey says she was the widow of a Lancastrian knight. Her first husband died some time before King Edward took the throne.'

'A widow? Just like Queen Elizabeth was when she met the King. And her first husband was a Lancastrian too.'

'Was he?' I asked. As usual, the intricacies of the royal family were a mystery to me. 'How odd. According to Master

247

Lyndsey, both ladies were older than the King too – by five or six years.'

Alys's green eyes narrowed in thought.

'And both marriages happened in secret, didn't they? When the King and Queen married, they didn't tell anyone for months. Until the Earl of Warwick said he was arranging a marriage for the King with a foreign princess. Then it all came out. It was quite a scandal. The King should have asked the Lords for permission, of course. And the Earl was especially angry. All his plans went for nothing.'

Another silence. Were we all thinking about how similar the stories were?

Elen said quietly, 'There was a rumour too that the Queen had used sorcery to bewitch the King.'

Alys rounded on her.

'Sorcery – pah! Beautiful women don't need to use sorcery to bewitch men. And everyone says the Queen was very beautiful when she was younger.'

She still is. The words teetered on my lips, as my memories of Christmas surfaced in my mind, but they didn't spill out. Instead, smiling at Elen, who had shrunk back at the sharp words, I said,

'Master Lyndsey says there were lots of rumours about the King. That he promised to marry several beautiful ladies before the Queen, but he didn't honour his promises.'

Alys nodded, as ever taking no more notice of Elen.

'I heard that when he married the Queen, it was because he wanted to show that he could make his own decisions – that he didn't need the Earl to do it for him.'

'And meanwhile poor Lady Eleanor was in a convent.'

'Why do you think she never said anything?'

I shrugged.

'Who knows? Though they say she died not long after. But I wonder whether the Queen knew.'

'Well, it might explain a lot if she did.' Alys sat back again in her chair, her long pale fingers playing absently with a red-gold curl that hung down loose from her linen cap. 'Why the Woodvilles wanted to keep the Duke away from London. Why the Queen went into sanctuary so quickly. Perhaps they feared it would all come out once the old King was dead.'

248

'And maybe that's why they were so keen to get Edward crowned as quickly as possible,' I added, thinking back to those days before we reached London.

Then I remembered with a start what else had been spoken of at Northampton. Should I mention it? Perhaps not.

But Alys's sharp eyes had somehow caught my thought, even as I bit it back, and she stared at me now, expectant.

'And what?'

'And – well, the Duke of Buckingham said then that there was a rumour the King had been poisoned.'

'Poisoned?'

'I know he'd blame the Queen's family for anything,' I hurried on, 'but he said it wasn't a coincidence that the Marquess had just taken charge of the Tower and treasury.'

'Really?' Alys didn't appear shocked by the notion. Her calm face recalled that of Duke Richard as he had listened to my lord of Buckingham bluster on. She said thoughtfully, 'Well, whether or not he was poisoned, perhaps they believed that everything was in place for a smooth, fast takeover if they hurried Prince Edward on to London. That he was young enough to be controlled while they hung on to power. No one would have dared to question his right to the throne once he'd been crowned.'

'But surely they must have known Duke Richard wouldn't be happy about it all – particularly if he was to be in charge as Protector. And isn't it well known that he doesn't like the Woodvilles? I remember Roger mentioning it – something to do with the death of another brother.'

'The Duke of Clarence?'

'I think that was it.'

'He rebelled with Warwick against King Edward, but it was only years later that he was executed for treason. Some people think the Queen persuaded King Edward not to pardon him, because he'd spoken up against their marriage – and that was when the marriage was believed to be legal. And they also say that Duke Richard stayed so much in the north later to avoid her.'

'Did she and her family hope he'd stay in Middleham out of the way?'

'I suppose it's possible. Maybe they didn't know he'd be named Protector and would have to come down to London.'

I cast my thoughts back to the days after news of the King's death had reached us.

'Didn't the Duchess say the Queen would have expected to be regent? When we heard her and the Duke speaking about it. They sounded surprised at the Duke becoming Protector instead.'

'I do remember Master Kendall saying after we arrived in London that the King changed his will just before he died. Perhaps that was when he appointed the Duke as Protector.'

'So it might have come as a surprise to the Queen and her family as well, if they thought she'd be ruling the country through her son,' I said. 'But – but, really, do you think it's possible? That anyone would kill a King? Especially his own wife.'

It was Alys's turn to shrug.

'I don't know, Matt. But they do say power and wealth do strange things to people.'

'I don't suppose I'll ever find that out,' I tried to joke. Our talk had become serious – treasonous even, with mention of killing a king.

But Alys didn't laugh.

'The Queen's family had all their power and rich appointments direct from the King too. Perhaps they feared losing them.'

'Would Lord Hastings have been worried about that too? I heard someone say that maybe he knew about the first marriage, that he'd helped keep it secret. Did he think that if Duke Richard discovered he knew all about Lady Eleanor...'

'That the Duke might not want him on the Royal Council?' Again Alys read the notion that was only just half-forming in my mind. 'That's possible. He'd never been the Queen's friend, but maybe that pushed him to plot with her and her family – the fear that they'd all lose everything because of the Duke.'

We sat in silence once again, but from a tightening of her lips and the fingers twining in the lock of hair it was obvious something more was gnawing at Alys. It wasn't long before she spoke up.

'And then there's my lord Buckingham. Master Kendall says he's been acting like another Kingmaker this past week or two – pushing the Duke to take the crown if it's offered to him.' A shadow passed across her face, like a stray cloud veiling the moon. 'But I can tell you – each time I've seen the Duke since we've been here, he's looked very unhappy. Not as though he's in any hurry to get any more power. Money, now – Master Kendall says he could certainly do with more of that.'

'Why? Surely the Duke is not short of it.'

'It's because the royal treasure has disappeared. Duke Richard's been paying for everything out of his own purse – and that includes arranging the coronation – until it was postponed of course... Though they'll be arranging another one soon, if all they say is true.'

In the quiet that followed, Murrey, curled up as normal on my feet, whimpered as she twitched in her sleep. Was she chasing rabbits in her dream, or being chased herself?

Nudging her with my toe to rouse her, it occurred to me that something was missing.

'Where's Shadow? I haven't seen her.'

'Have you only just noticed?' Alys replied with some scorn. 'She's back home in Middleham. The Duchess said she wasn't a suitable dog for a lady at court. I don't see why. But at least she's company for Ed. He's desperate for a hound of his own, especially since you left with Murrey.'

'The Duke said he probably wouldn't come for the coronation.'

'He wasn't pleased. I heard him shouting at his mother when she told him, then sobbing. But she promised she and the Duke would be back before summer's end.' She hesitated. 'Though that may not be likely now.'

Yet more of Duke Henry's words at Northampton came back to me.

'Perhaps they thought he'd be safer at home. My lord Buckingham hinted...'

'Yes?'

'Well, he hinted that not only Duke Richard, but Ed and the Duchess might be at risk from the Woodvilles' plotting.'

'Then it's just as well that the Duke and other lords in the Council and Parliament have taken charge and removed them from power. I hear that Lord Rivers and Lord Grey are to be tried for treason. If they're found guilty, they'll be executed like Lord Hastings.'

The Earl's handsome, courteous face forced its way before my mind's eye, and Lord Grey's, contorted by hatred as he tried to strike Duke Richard. As I rose to take my leave, aware from the creeping twilight that the evening was growing late, my thoughts were in turmoil. How complicated were the lives of great men and women – and how dangerous could be the roads that they chose.

*

The next day Master Ashley did not appear at dinner, having left the house during the morning formally dressed in scarlet robes. When he returned to supper, it was to a house abuzz with talk and rumour of events that day in Westminster.

We apprentices were waiting in line to wash our hands before entering the dining hall when Mistress Ashley bustled out to greet her husband.

'So, is it done?' she asked without ceremony, as a servant helped him off with his mantle.

His face grave, he nodded.

'Aye, wife, it is. And done well. His Grace is no longer Protector, but King.'

And after he sluiced the city dust from his face and hands in the bowl held up for him, he spoke to all of us now thronging about him, apprentices, journeymen and servants.

'This morning Parliament called on His Grace the Duke of Gloucester to ascend the throne. In front of a large gathering of lords and citizens, he agreed and at once was hailed as King Richard the Third.'

A murmur arose from the assembled household and Simon, standing next to me, whispered something in my ear. But I had attention for no one but my new master as he continued his tale.

'Then His Grace, followed by all the nobles and men there present, rode to Westminster Hall, to the King's Bench, to take the royal oath. He was a sight to behold – seated in that great marble chair surrounded by all the justices and great men of the kingdom, with the cheers of all of us gathered there ringing in the very rafters. He spoke those words so solemnly, and called for all persons, rich or poor, lord or commoner, to be treated equally in the law. Then he summoned Sir John Fogge, the Queen's cousin, from sanctuary and clasped him by the hand, swearing to be his friend.'

Master Ashley paused, running his eyes around all the eager, listening faces, then nodded as though answering a silent, but important question.

'To me, wife, boys, that is the mark of the man who is now to be our king. And let us hope that Queen Elizabeth hears and herself comes out of sanctuary before long.'

With that, he strode into the dining hall. In a few moments we were all seated at the tables, our heads bowed as grace was said, followed by a prayer for this special day. Though my mind still raked over the confusing events of recent weeks, my voice joined with fervour in the call for our Lord to protect our new sovereign.

8

Men from the North

Over the following days the tension in the city relaxed. Even the arrival of troops from the north was met with good humour rather than the Londoners' usual suspicion.

Master Lyndsey had overheard Master Ashley speaking with friends who had witnessed their reception. And as ever I overheard Master Lyndsey discussing it with Master Hardyng the secretary as I laboured over a tally of numbers in a ledger.

'The talk among the city folk was all of hordes of northerners being on their way,' said the secretary. 'Three or four thousand, they reckoned. And of what it meant. What the King might intend by summoning them.'

'And afraid that London's rights and freedoms might be threatened, I'll be bound,' scoffed Master Lyndsey. He was a man from the Midlands, who had travelled much with Master Ashley before settling down in the capital as his steward. 'That's always the way in this city. Ever worrying about its own affairs, never those of the kingdom at large, let alone the person of the King.'

'Well, the people have a right to be concerned, here as anywhere else.' Master Hardyng of course was a Londoner. 'These have been difficult times – not knowing from one day to the next what will happen. Who will be in charge.'

'Aye, perhaps. But Duke Richard knew who he could trust when things were uncertain. No doubt that's why he summoned men from the north when he was protector. When he didn't know what the Woodvilles meant to do, or how much support they would have.'

'But now things are settled. Parliament has made him King. Why are they here?'

'They're still camped outside the city walls at the moment. Nothing to worry about. And Master Ashley's guests say they'll be dismissed back home once they've patrolled the streets during the coronation. You know how ruffians and vagabonds delight in thieving amongst crowds of people. But they also said how much the local people laughed and mocked at them.'

'Why so?'

'Because of their ancient gear. Tatty and worn, apparently. They said these northern troops weren't fit to clean the boots of their own city guard.'

What Master Kendall had once told me about Londoners' sense of their own superiority sprang into my mind and I was thankful that my brother Fred was not among the troops this time.

A day or two later I was running an errand for Master Ashley when the sound of many men and horses tramping resounded through the streets. People from all around hurried to discover what was afoot.

I followed, pushing my way to the front of the growing crowd lining Thames Street.

Trumpets blared, and on all sides cheers rose and kerchiefs were waved.

Behind the lines of scarlet-clad trumpeters, and at the head of marching columns of soldiers and horsemen, rode two men. One was a nobleman I did not know, atop a bay charger, a blue lion rearing on the yellow shield slung at his saddle. Beside him rode Duke Richard – or rather, King Richard. The sunshine glinted off the gold thread of the royal standard fluttering above.

Storm bore him on towards where I stood hemmed in by the cheering crowds. The stallion's hooves stepped high across the cobbles, the crest of his neck curving proudly beneath his murrey and blue trappings.

My old master raised his hand in response to the acclamation, and smiled up at a baby held out at an upper-storey window, waving its pudgy little arms at him. But his eyes were shadowed with tiredness, dark lines etched beneath them as on the day he'd learnt of his brother's death.

What he had said of the burdens of kingship flashed across my mind, and with it also the haunted face of his nephew Edward when he had spoken about becoming king so soon.

Before I gave thought to my action, I stepped forward and called, 'Your Grace!'

One of his companions spurred his horse towards me, no doubt concerned at any threat such a sudden movement might pose. But somehow my cry reached the King's ears above the tumult, and he recognized me despite my new livery.

'Matthew?'

He reined Storm back and the whole column of troops behind came to a halt.

'Hold your hand, Richard. It is Master Wansford, my late page.'

It was Master Ratcliffe who had driven his mount forward, and who now swung away to face the still cheering crowd.

Beyond him rank upon rank of soldiers stood to attention, alert to all around them. From their liveries and banners of yellow and blue, alongside men in the Yorkist colours of murrey and blue, I took the other nobleman to be the Earl of Northumberland who had led the troops down from the north. He was, I knew, little liked in my home city. He watched in curiosity as the King leaned towards me, resting his forearm on Storm's crest, and spoke again.

'Well, Matt, are you proud of your northern countrymen? They rallied promptly to my call in case aid was needed in these past weeks' upheavals. You know of the great changes that have occurred? Though I hear Master Ashley has been in Flanders.'

'Aye, Your Grace. We returned some days ago. I was with Alys and heard the friar's sermon at the Cross.'

He gazed down at me, the expression on his face difficult to read.

'Great changes, indeed,' he repeated. 'But Alys – she is still the late Queen's ward, though she will remain part of the royal household until Elizabeth should decide to leave sanctuary. Then – then Elizabeth can do with her as she wishes. But in the meantime... I see you still wear my badge.'

I seized the fabric of my doublet where the silver boar was pinned and thrust it towards him as though in proof.

He nodded.

'You may use it to enter the Abbey for the coronation – if your new master allows a holiday. It may be that you will see Alys there.'

'Thank you, Your Grace.'

Behind him, the Earl edged his mount forward as though in impatience.

'Sire?'

As the King straightened up at his voice, the face of the boy king Edward swam before my eyes again.

Perhaps fearing to lose this one chance, I blurted out, without thinking,

'And Edward, Your Grace? He who was to be —'

I stopped, knowing I was impertinent.

King Richard's expression didn't change.

'You mean my brother's son? He and his brother lodge still at the royal apartments in the Tower. They will be safe there until their mother comes to her senses and can take them again into her charge. I doubt he will be at the coronation. His change of circumstances will be hard enough for him to bear. Too often children must deal with the consequences of their parents' mistakes. But he is young and will adapt.'

Master Ratcliffe turned his horse back towards us.

'Your Grace. We are expected at Baynard's Castle. The lady Cecily...'

'You are right, Richard. We must not keep my mother waiting, though I am now King.' His familiar wry smile. 'God speed you on your life's path, Matt. Offer prayers if you will for your new King and his Queen.'

'I – I will, my lord,' I stammered.

I stood back as he urged Storm into motion once again. With a barked word from their commander, the whole body of troops streamed after him, their vibrant banners whipping into life above the tide of leather and steel.

As Master Ratcliffe passed, he leant down and slipped something into my hand. Murmuring the words 'From the King's bounty', he then kicked his horse on to follow the retreating backs of the King, the Earl and their companions.

I opened my hand.

A bright coin lay on my palm, crisp and new, a head with a crown adorning one side, a tiny boar stamped nearby.

It could have been the head of any king, such was the crudeness of the features. But the name 'Edward' was scribed around the edge.

I shoved the coin into the pouch at my belt. Then, though I should not have delayed my errand further, I watched the rest of the procession as it passed.

Among the hundreds of men marching beneath banners of Gloucester, Northumberland and York, I recognized here and there neighbours from my home town. I drew a grin or a nod if they spotted me.

One face, however, I did not expect.

In the last cohort of riders, resplendent in the murrey and blue of the King's livery, I glimpsed my old adversary.

Hugh Soulsby.

I had not seen him since I had left Middleham. Since his revenge had led to my dismissal.

His eyes were fixed resolutely ahead as he was carried forward by the dark brown colt I remembered from the castle, his harness gleaming in the spring sunshine.

At first he did not see me. But then something – what was it? – made him glance to the side. And his eyes caught mine.

A moment, a hesitation.

Then he recognized me. His eyes narrowed. And his lips parted, mouthing words I could not hear above the tramp, tramp, tramp of the marching feet and clattering hooves.

But I guessed his meaning, as those lips curved into a smirk. Triumphant in his victory over me.

As always.

And then his hand stole towards the pommel of his knife.

Emotion rushed within me. Not hatred, perhaps, but raw resentment. That he, rather than I, should be serving the new King as his loyal supporter.

I pushed through the crowds to get away. Surprise showed on the faces of people around me. That surge in my chest must be reflected in a vicious twist to my features.

I hurried on, eager to leave those ugly thoughts behind me.

*

The day of the coronation was duly declared a holiday by Master Ashley, but though I hastened to the great Abbey at Westminster as soon as breakfast was over, I was too late to gain entry. Guards stood with their halberds crossed to keep back the crowds and only laughed at my attempt to pass on to the expanse of crimson carpet leading from Westminster Hall to the huge door of the Abbey's west front.

'I wish I had a groat for every one of those I've seen today,' grumbled one as I showed my boar badge and tried to explain. 'I'd be the richest man in London.'

'The church is full to overflowing,' said another. 'Only nobles or churchmen allowed through now. Take your place out here with the other little people.'

I bristled at his last words, but I could do no more. So I stayed where I was, hoping no one taller would push in front. But when the proceedings began not long after, I had as good a view as anyone not within the buildings themselves.

First to emerge from the Hall, to the blast of trumpets and cries of heralds, was a procession of churchmen, clothed in the finest regalia. A tremendous gilt and jewelled crucifix the size of a man was carried aloft before them.

Next came a line of noblemen, sumptuously dressed, each bearing a symbol of kingship – swords, a mace, a sceptre, the golden crown itself. Among them were the Earl of Northumberland and, striding just behind, the King's great friend, Lord Lovell, his features solemn.

A further fanfare burst forth.

And from the shadows of the tall doorway, flanked by several bishops and clad in purple velvet trimmed with ermine, stepped King Richard himself.

The crowds around me shouted and applauded and hurrahed as one.

But I found I had not the voice to join in. Now, only now, at last, I grasped the full truth of what had happened. The Duke – my Duke – had become King of all England and would today be confirmed such.

He walked forward beneath a richly embroidered canopy held high above his head on golden poles. His slow pace allowed all those present the time to behold him. Thunderous cheers crashed against the towering buildings, echoing about the square.

A few steps behind, bearing the hem of the train that cascaded from the King's shoulders, paced the Duke of Buckingham, almost outshining his sovereign in a gown of blue stitched with gold cartwheels. Beyond him flowed a stream of other lords, the last carrying another gem-studded crown.

The Duchess came next. More than two months since I had bid farewell to her at Middleham, her face above her silver gown was no less pale than it had been then. Her train of cloth of gold was held by an older lady with pinched cheeks and eyes shrewd as a weasel.

And then, in the cluster of ladies following, I espied Alys, her reddish curls for once demurely caught up in a netted cap of silver thread dotted with seed pearls. She spotted me and the serious look upon her face fell away. But her joyous wave was shushed away by the more mature ladies around her. In moments she was swept on past me and into the Abbey's cavernous depths.

Though I was not within the great church itself, the torrents of music and song that washed forth and what Master Ashley had told us of the ceremony meant all unfolded before my mind's eye. The swelling song of the choir as the King and Queen entered St Edward's shrine to take their seats of estate. The Latin service intoned before their approach to the high altar. Their anointing with the holy oil. The Mass celebrated in front of the enormous sword of state. The solemn oath sworn by all the nobles. The King kneeling as the Archbishop held the crown above his head...

I waited with the restless crowd on the cobbles of the Abbey precinct. Then a fanfare of trumpets blared, a deafening cheer went up within, the bells in the tower pealed, birds, startled from their perches on the roofs and stone sills of the ancient building, flew up into the glowing blue of the sky, and Duke Richard I knew now was King.

9

Rebellion

'Well, boy, you've settled in here with your new master and no mistake.'

My father's hand was heavy on my back as we strolled together around the garden of Master Ashley's townhouse, aflame now with early autumn colour. Pride radiated from him and from his voice like warmth from the October sun.

'The mayor asked after you when he heard I would be visiting. It's been the talk of the council chamber, your having fallen on your feet again. First with the Duke – though I suppose I should say King – and now here. I trust you know how fortunate you have been.'

'Yes, father.'

Did I sound convinced?

'It's not every boy who could be disgraced at the Minster one minute, and the next be apprenticed to one of the richest merchants in London.'

'No, father.'

The memory of that disgrace – the choir master's black eye and his anger at the riot I had caused – surfaced in my mind for the first time in many months, but I thrust it away. That was a different life, I was a different boy.

My father was on only his second ever trip to London in the course of his own merchant business. This was mostly in woollen and other cloths, but he also branched out into various luxuries, such as the books that Master Ashley had recently begun to print in the capital. The two men had met for the first time this morning and my father had been greeted as a welcome guest before they conducted a little business. I had waited outside my master's study door, wondering if I had been forgotten, despite my father's insistence in his letters that he was eager to see me in my new life.

The weight of his hand lifted from my shoulder as he paused to admire a cluster of blushing grapes hanging from a vine that clung to the sunniest wall of the garden. He plucked one of the smallest and popped it into his mouth, chewing once or twice before speaking again.

'And of course we all had a glimpse of your old master last month. It's been many years since York was honoured by a visit from a king, let alone one so newly crowned. I'm sure ours is the most loyal city on his progress around the kingdom.'

As I was constantly being reminded by town criers and household gossip and letters from Alys, only weeks after their coronation King Richard and his wife had set off on a regal tour around England. They had wended their way up to my home city by way of Oxford, Gloucester, Worcester, Warwick and other like towns, meeting the most important men of the kingdom and showing themselves to their people.

'He cannot have been entertained half so royally anywhere else,' continued my father. 'And his entry was a far grander sight than any I've clapped eyes on – ten times the spectacle we laid on for him last spring when he was still Duke. No doubt that's why he chose to make his son Prince of Wales in the Minster.'

His hand, holding another grape, stopped halfway to his lips as he gazed down at me, his eyes quizzical.

'How strange to think that the little lad was once your friend, Matt.'

Not 'once', I wanted to say as his hand carried on its way and the grape burst between his teeth in a shower of juice. Ed was still my friend, though he was so far distant. He had told me all about his special day at York in a letter I had received only a week or two before, decorated as always with his tiny drawings. He had not given up on our friendship, even if my father had, for all that he was now a prince.

'It was certainly a sight to behold, his investiture,' said my father, walking on again between trees laden with fruit and leaves of brilliant red and gold. 'More splendid than the coronation itself, some say. And the gifts that were given to the King and Queen – dishes piled high with gold – and the feast afterwards at the Archbishop's palace! Hundreds were seated there that night!'

Ed – too excited by the events to translate everything into our code – had written of his new gown of cloth of gold sent specially from London, and of the golden wreath with which he had been crowned by the Archbishop, and of walking back along the aisle of the Minster at the side of his mother and father, also wearing their crowns. And of the cheers and shouts of the gathered crowds as they showed their love and affection for their new King and Queen and their small prince.

Alys's most recent letter, nestled in my pouch alongside Ed's, had also likened the day to that of the coronation, but said that these celebrations had been more joyous. In York the King and Queen acted as though they were among friends, she wrote, not touched by the intrigues and gossip and rivalries of the court at Westminster. As the royal party had travelled further north from the capital, though he was always busy with work and petitions the King had at last relaxed. He had even laughed when councils of towns he visited tried to give him presents of money to help with his expenses. Alys said he always refused them, declaring he would rather have his people's hearts than their money.

These letters from Alys and Ed, a few from Elen – none at all from Roger, of course, just odd lines scribbled at the end of others' messages – were the most precious things in my life now, together with Murrey – my only remaining links with that part of my life that had gone and now, looking back, seemed so brief. I kept them safe always, hidden in my bundle in my attic room or, the most recent, tucked in my pouch with other of my treasures, to be read and reread in any moments of leisure. My fingers itched to retrieve them now as my father spoke more of my old master and his family.

'It's said the King plans a great council to rule in the north – to show that he will not neglect us now he must live here in the capital. His sister's son, the Earl of Lincoln, will be a great man thereabouts in his place, no doubt to keep my lord of Northumberland in check. And little Prince Edward will stay on in northern parts and learn to govern alongside him.'

Ed's howl of disappointment on being told this news tore through my head as though I had been there with him. His last letter to me had been full of the dread of being left behind when his beloved mother and father made their way back to London, as had happened in the spring. Now his fears were shown to be well founded. He would see it as a further cruelty, although my father obviously approved.

Our conversation turned then to our family matters – the coming marriage of my eldest brother, John, how my baby sister was growing, that my new mother was praying for a baby of her own – and soon it was time for my father to say his farewells. Once he had embraced me, Mistress Ashley arrived in a rustle of silk skirts to relay her husband's apologies at having been called away on business. She pressed into my father's grateful hands a basket of grapes and violet plums from the beautiful gardens, and then he was gone.

All that was left was his familiar smell of lanolin, leather and ink lingering in the air, the warm memory of his pride in me and loyalty to our King – and his usual reassurance that York would ever be my home if I should need it.

My mood was mixed as I returned to my work in the printing house – happiness at my father's praise, longing to see the rest of my family again, sadness at not witnessing the festivities in York with my friends, sorrow for Ed. But I had little time to rake through such thoughts as there came a hollering and a hammering at the main door – loud enough to reach us above the clacking and groaning of the printing press at work.

Master de Vries, the new print master lately arrived from Flanders together with the mint-new printing press, told Simon and me to keep working as he hurried off to investigate. But of course, intrigued, we followed him out and through the connecting passageways, to find in the entrance hall half the household staff clustered, chattering like an excited flock of starlings.

In their midst was Master Lyndsey, clapping his hands and raising his voice, calling for calm. Beside him Mistress Ashley was speaking in an undertone with a stranger clad in dusty leather armour, who clutched a sealed letter in one hand.

As Simon and I lurked in a doorway watching, Mistress Ashley led the man away towards her husband's study. The hubbub quietened and at last Master Lyndsey's words could be heard above the uproar.

'Our master has already been called away to the city council, so no doubt we shall soon know more. But this messenger says the call has gone out for men to rally to the city's defence. The militia will be gathering at the usual muster points. All men of fighting age are free to attend.'

With that he followed his mistress and the soldier into the study and the crowd splintered off in all directions.

Master de Vries caught sight of us hovering in the background and flapped his hands at us.

'Away you go, boys,' he said in his heavily accented English. 'Work is over for the day. But you must keep to the house. It may not be safe on the streets.'

264

'But what has happened, Master?' Simon asked, as the print master took us each by the elbow and steered us back towards his workshop.

'Nothing is quite clear yet, boys, but they say that there have been rumblings of discontent in some areas since the summer. Since King Richard stood against the old King's family and then became King himself. Now rebels have declared themselves and are marching on London.'

'On London!'

Simon was a local boy and terror was splashed across his face.

'Aye, lad. But fear not – it will take several days for them to march in from their lairs in Kent.'

'Kent? But that isn't so very far,' I protested, remembering the country I had ridden through with Master Ashley's party on the way to the port on the coast.

'They will be trying to gather supporters on their way – that will take time, if they manage it at all.'

Fear was still in Simon's eyes, despite Master de Vries's calming words.

'But what will happen when they get here? My family —'

He fell silent as the print master raised his hands.

'Master Lyndsey says the Duke of Norfolk has been making preparations for some time. He has already called up his men to take the field against any rebels. And once London's own defenders are gathered, there will be nothing to fear. Master Hardyng tells me that Londoners are most valiant in their city's defence.'

'But why? Who are they – the rebels?' I asked.

'The word is that they are Lancastrians – and supporters of the old Queen's family.'

'The Woodvilles?' said Simon. 'Why?'

'They'll no doubt be men who fear they may lose their jobs and preferments under King Richard,' Master de Vries replied, searing scorn in his voice. 'And maybe they would if they carry on their corrupt lives and don't adjust to the new King's ways. It is said they plan to place the old Queen's son, young Edward, on the throne, despite the boy's bastardy.'

My thoughts snapped back to the events of early summer. And to the old Queen, Elizabeth Woodville, who was still living in sanctuary after more than five months.

'But how would they do that? And would Parliament allow it?'

Master de Vries's face was grim.

'They've timed it well, I'll allow them that. With the King away in the north of the country, with few men about him, and most of the great lords out of London... If the rebels are able to capture the city and the Tower, and prevent the King from returning... If they can raise enough men to face him...'

He shook his head, then shrugged.

'But I am sure the city will stand firm against them. And my lord of Norfolk has rallied many men to him already, with more to come. It seems there were warning signs... I doubt the old Queen and her family will win out and get the chance to put their case to Parliament – whatever case they believe they have.'

By now we had cleared away our work tools and with the dark bulk of the printing press brooding still and silent as at the end of a normal day, Master de Vries dismissed us. His last words were a reminder not to leave the house.

But of course I could not heed him, not today, not with rebellion brewing against my old master.

Saying nothing to Simon, or any of the household, I slipped out of a back door and into the bustle of the city, uncertain at first where to direct my feet. But it wasn't long before I was aware of small groups of men, in twos and threes, some clutching bundles, hurrying away from the river. I guessed they were on their way to join the defence.

With Murrey sticking close, I chose two men to follow, winding my way behind them through the crowds of people thronging the streets – peaceful still, carrying on with their usual business. Had they, perhaps, not heard of the threat on its way?

Unlike Simon I had no worry for my own family. My father had said he would be leaving London the next day to return to York, and if Master de Vries was right, it would be some time before the city would be facing any real danger.

The two men I was trailing had the appearance of young craft journeymen, around the age of my elder brother, perhaps leatherworkers or cobblers from their clothes and the calluses on their hands. They joked and laughed together as they jostled their way through the townsfolk, heading always north through the maze of alleys and courtyards in this part of the city. They seemed not to observe they had two shadows on their heels – one human and one hound. All around us other men, most older, a few younger, some grim-faced, more of them lighter-hearted like my guides, strode purposefully in the same direction. Soon we all merged with a stream of men flowing along a wider street, lined by a mixture of fine merchants' houses and craft workshops. Far ahead of us loomed one of the massive gates through the city wall.

In all my months' apprenticeship and, before that, my time in London during the winter, I had never ventured into this area. But as the stone gatehouse rose above us and I passed with the others through its dark archway out into sunlight-flooded open fields, I guessed where we were. This must be Moorfields, the marshy land where the men of York had camped before the coronation and before their triumphal entry to the city behind the King and Earl of Northumberland. Where Master Lyndsey had said Londoners had turned out to mock them and their ancient gear. Now Londoners themselves were collecting together here to repel a real threat.

Hundreds were there already as I trudged out on to the tussocky ground. Within moments I had lost my two guides amidst the hustle and bustle, as busy as a summer fair back in York. My eyes were drawn this way and that by men shouting to each other, greeting friends and clapping them across the back, leading horses, mules, asses, pushing and shoving every which way to find a path through the gathering. Two or three times I had to skip smartly out of the way before a boot or a hoof stomped down on my foot. Murrey's sharp barked warnings reached my ears above the clamour as her warm flank pressed comfortingly against my leg.

After a while a pattern emerged in the chaos. Here and there huddles formed around soldiers clad in leather armour like the messenger at Master Ashley's. These officers clasped wood-bound wax tablets such as I had used in lessons at the Minster school and were busy jotting on them as they spoke to the men clustering about them.

Attaching myself to the nearest knot of men, I hovered on the fringes, straining to hear what was being said over the racket all around. I stood there only a minute or two before the officer spotted me and beckoned. The men to either side pressed back to let me pass.

My steps forward were slow, despite my earlier eagerness to join the city's defenders, aware as I was of all those eyes upon me. The officer waved me to him once more.

'Hurry up, boy.'

His eyes narrowed, his stylus poised above his writing tablet.

'Have you brought me a message from your master? Will he or his journeymen be joining us later? Just give me his name and I will write it down.'

I swallowed, my face warm under his stare.

'No, sir, not my master, but me. I've come to offer my service.'

My voice sounded high and hesitant to my ears, a boy's voice only still, and all about me laughter flared. I wished then that I had not come. But I was heartened both by Murrey's growl and that the officer himself did not laugh.

Instead he squinted at me again, looking me up and down.

'Nay, lad, you're rather small to join the muster. The city's not so desperate yet. Nor likely to be, from what I've heard of these paltry rebels.'

The laughter changed to cheers and the officer allowed himself a smile.

'So, be off with you. Or your master will be missing you. Next?'

I stood my ground, stopping those around me from stepping up.

'But, sir, is there no way I can be of use? I want to serve my King. Look!'

Remembering my boar badge – for all it had been no help at the coronation – I pointed to where it was still fastened to my doublet.

His face altered. Was it suspicion or –?

His next words confirmed it.

'So you wear the King's badge? Who did you steal that from, hey?'

I was shocked at the idea.

'No one!' My fierce response prompted another rumble from Murrey as I protested, 'He gave it to me with his own hands. When he was still Duke. I was his page.'

'Any thief could say that.'

'You can ask my new master. He'll vouch for me.'

To my surprise, the officer roared with laughter.

'Don't fret, lad. It's just my little joke. You're not the only one here today who wants to serve the King – nor who has a badge

268

to show. Though,' he leaned in close, peering at my chest, 'not all perhaps such a pretty one. Most I've seen have been hessian ones, given to all and sundry at the coronation. Maybe we can find you a job after all. Have you keen sight?'

'Aye, sir,' I said, drawing a breath in relief.

'Perhaps the watch will have a use for you. If your new master can spare you.'

He laid a heavy stress on the word 'new' as though he hadn't believed my earlier words. But I didn't care.

And that was how I came to be atop the great wall of London at midnight.

10

The Watch

It was a fine clear night, the faintest nip of early frost in the air as I paced along the walkway on the top of the city wall.

Above me, a dusting of stars, no moon; behind me, any lanterns still burning in the city blotted out by the ancient fortress known as the Tower.

People said a castle had stood here since the Conquest, guarding the crossing of the river. That it had never fallen, even during the cousins' war more than three centuries ago, when Queen Mathilda and King Stephen had fought each other for the crown. I prayed tonight that its venerable stones would prove invincible once again if the rebels should attack.

The elegant square building called the White Tower dominated the castle complex, overshadowing every other structure in the several acres enclosed on three sides by the deep moat, on the fourth by the river. This night few lights shone through its arrow slits. Its defenders were not on high alert.

Master de Vries had been right. More than seven nights now I had paced for hours along the wall top, before handing over the watch to my replacement and tracing my way back through the pitch-dark streets to throw myself, bone-weary, on my narrow attic bed. And still there was no sign of the Kentish rebels.

This morning, on an errand for Master Ashley, I had watched as a hundred horsemen or more and several companies of footsoldiers had filed through the city streets, despatched across the river to seek the rebels. At their head, beneath a banner of a silver lion rampant, rode the Duke of Norfolk, newly honoured with that title by King Richard before his coronation. Watchful eyes in a face lined by many summers scanned the cheering crowds even as he raised his mailed hand to salute them. I had seen him once or twice before on visits to the watch or city guard, speaking to officers and men as if he were one of them. They touched their caps or doffed their helmets, but soon they were joking with him with no mind to his noble status.

A shiver ambushed me as I gazed across the country beyond the wall. A keen breeze carried with it the scent of burnt stubble from the autumn fields, mingled with the salt smell of the tide as it raced up the river towards the bridge. Not a glimmer of light in that direction, save one on the mast of a merchant ship I had marked before sundown, tethered downstream of the city, no doubt awaiting the ebbing of the tide. No movement or sound either. Nothing that could herald the approach of the rebels.

The darkness and silence were split by a shattering, drawn-out roar, answered at once by Murrey, starting up, snarling in her turn.

I grabbed at her collar before she flung herself off the wall to find the source of the challenge. I knew it well enough now, though my little hound still could not understand. For there within the Tower precinct was the famous royal menagerie of exotic beasts.

I had never seen them, but my fellow watchmen had told me of the graceful long-necked creatures which reached far above a man's head, colossal grey thick-skinned animals with snakes for noses, sandy-coloured horses with splayed feet and hills upon their backs, ferocious giant cats with shaggy manes upon their heads and roaring voices that split the night. Lions. The noble beasts of kings and emperors.

How I longed to see them! And had thought several times to take myself to the great gateway into the Tower and ask to be admitted.

I recalled how young Edward – then King – had invited me to visit him there and view his wondrous exhibit. But also to mind came the reception of my boar badge by the officer at Moorfields – how it was a two-a-penny thing, perhaps no more to be considered a key to the Tower than it was a key to the good graces of the militia.

I fingered it now as I relaxed my grip on Murrey, her snarl having subsided to a grumble deep within her throat. I knew it was not a tuppenny-ha'penny thing, not really. Forged of choice silver, not cut from drab cloth, and handed to me alone by a royal duke, soon to be King. But by that token, not to be employed for tawdry purposes, such as fulfilment of a base desire to spy on strange, savage beasts.

For just that reason I had refrained from attempting entry to the Tower to find Edward himself – lodged there still as far as I knew, with his brother Richard, in the luxurious royal apartments of the Garden Tower. Its dark bulk, close to the menagerie, was visible from my vantage point, its wide windows facing the river black squares now, only one or two still outlined with flickering firelight.

I had thought often of Edward these past nights, as I had during the summer. Of what he did, how he spent his time – and how he bore the thought that he was now never to be king. Perhaps he had been relieved. His words to me on our long rides together had suggested as much. Yet what was in his mind now, if he knew of the rebellion in his name? Did he hope that the Kentish rebels, and those also recently reported south of the city in Surrey, would prevail, seize him from his lodgings, defeat his uncle Richard, and put him back upon the throne? Did he even still believe that was his place after the revelations about his parents' marriage – or lack of it – and his declared illegitimacy?

I bent down and stroked Murrey's tufted head, my touch rewarded by her raising her eyes to mine. Reflected in their velvet depths, stars glowed like the dying embers of a fire.

'Matt!'

The voice hailing me was Simon's.

He had caught me leaving Master Ashley's on the evening of my first watch and had insisted on coming with me so he also could serve King Richard. The officer in charge had shrugged and told him to relieve me for the second watch of the night.

The stretch of wall that we patrolled was only short – maybe half the length of that guarded by adults of the watch. Perhaps the officer was merely humouring us young boys in our zeal to be of use. But I was glad even just to do this. And, having found among our master's many books a volume on the basics of swordplay, Simon and I had pledged that once this danger was past, we would join together in training. We had already lodged an order for two hardened chestnut swords with a local woodturner.

'Is all quiet?' he asked now.

'All quiet,' I agreed. 'Save the lions.'

He flashed a smile, just perceptible in the darkness.

'Maybe they're hoping to greet the rebels with a warm welcome.'

'I could do with one of those. It's a chilly night.'

'The brazier's still lit in the guard house. Captain says there will be spiced ale if you don't dawdle.'

We clasped hands and, whistling to Murrey, I picked my way down the nearest flight of narrow steps clinging to the inside of the wall. A little way along, snug against the ancient stonework, crouched a small building. A warm, wavering orange glow spilled from its open doorway, illuminating to one side two seated men, casting dice and talking quietly. At my approach, one rose, while the other reached for an axe lying upon the ground next to him.

I stood still and cleared my throat.

'Matthew Wansford of the watch, sir.'

The standing man nodded, his face hidden in the gloom.

'Aye, lad, I knew from that shadow by your side. Rest easy, Dan.' He waved his hand to his companion, who replaced the axe upon the cobbles. ''Tis only the lad who takes the first watch and his little hound. There's nothing to worry about – you'll have time aplenty to win back your pennies from me.' Then again to me, 'All's quiet, lad? Neither hide nor hair of the traitors?'

'Nothing, sir.'

'Long may that continue. Take yourself off to your bed, lad. Or if you prefer, warm yourself at the fire and sup what mulled ale the guard have left.'

My nostrils twitched at the enticing scent of clove and cinnamon wafting in the night air and, with a bow to the captain and his friend, I stepped into the outer chamber of the guard house.

A scatter of stools, a small table or two, an earthenware cauldron suspended above the iron latticework of the brazier in the middle of the room, crammed with glowing coals, tiny flames licking at their edges. Snores penetrated the stout door from the inner chamber, where the company of guards rested while awaiting any alarm.

I ladled out some steaming ale and took myself off to a stool against the far wall. Murrey settled herself at my feet as I took a first sip. The liquid scalded my tongue, leaving behind grittiness from the spices.

Setting the cup upon a table to cool, I fished in my pouch, drawing out the small leather-bound volume of 'The Death of Arthur' given to me by the Duchess – now Queen, I corrected myself. Safe within it were folded the most recent letters from my friends, so far away. I opened the book now, and with it the letters. I couldn't read them in the poor light thrown by the brazier, but I didn't need to. As my fingertips brushed the smooth papers and the faint spider-scrawls of ink, I recalled them almost word for word, I had read them so often.

My glimpse of the Duke of Norfolk in the morning brought to mind Alys's lively tales from the court, and how his wife had been slighted on the day of the coronation. Though a great friend, she had been robbed of the chance to hold the new Queen's train for the ceremony by Lady Stanley, wife of a Royal Council member, who claimed seniority. Alys had been scathing in her letter:

> *She claims her first husband was an Earl, but even a newly made Duchess is senior to a Countess – in everything, except perhaps age. The Queen and Duchess laughed about it later, but Lady Tyrell – who has quite befriended me since I've been here – said the Duke of Norfolk had words with Lord Stanley about it.*

And indeed this morning my lord of Norfolk had appeared the sort of steadfast gentleman who would display such loyalty to both his wife and his King.

Voices broke through my musing, above even the cacophony of snoring from the sleeping guards. Outside, the captain was speaking, not quietly to his friend as before, but challenging a newcomer.

The new voice stirred something deep inside me, unnerving me before I could even distinguish any words, although the captain's tones had become friendlier. Murrey uncurled her lithe body and pushed her head up against my hand. I felt rather than heard the rumble in her throat, then the fur bristled on her head. Was she sensing my strange disquiet, or had the voice itself provoked her?

Among the snores, now, snatches of the conversation became audible – single words, odd phrases. 'Rebels – West Country – His Grace – royal seal – Grantham – Duke of Buckingham – foul traitor – ready to take up arms – Tudor – the south coast – string 'em up.' As I struggled to make out what was afoot, the familiarity of the second voice grew, until at the captain's final words, 'at the fire', it at last struck me with the force of a blow who stood outside, reporting.

I sprang to my feet, my hand flying unbidden to the knife at my belt as a broad shadow cut across the doorway. It stepped forward, the firelight grasping at its face, and my fear was confirmed.

It was Hugh Soulsby.

His eyes met mine, but for a second he didn't recognize me. Then his features twisted, and the brazier's flickering flames and their pitch-black shadows transformed him into all the red-painted demons from hell I'd ever seen daubed on church walls.

The moment passed. Moving to one side, he revealed the captain's companion, Dan, following in his wake.

Hugh dropped the helmet he was carrying on to a nearby table and shrugged his thick travelling cloak from his shoulders. Beneath was the iron-studded leather armour now worn by so many men around the city.

Dan scooped out a cup of spiced ale and handed it to him, turning back to the cauldron to fill another. Seeing me there, he gestured with the ladle as though offering to replenish mine, but I shook my head in silence.

'Sit you down, lad,' he said to Hugh as he poured ale for himself. Then to me, 'And you, lad, if you want to hear this squire's report. He's brought word of the rebels. It seems the treachery is spreading.'

Inside, a part of me was screaming at me to leave, to get far away from this boy who had been such an evil influence on my life. But he and Dan stood between me and the doorway. And, for all my loathing of Hugh, I dearly wanted news of the rebellion.

Hugh didn't glance at me again as he drew up a stool close to the brazier. He seated himself and rubbed his hands, stretching them towards the fireglow, before picking up his cup again, rolling it in his hands to warm them some more. Dan also sat and I lowered myself back on to my stool, tucking my book and letters away in my pouch. Murrey rested her head upon my knee, letting out a faint whine as I caressed her silky ears.

'Come, lad,' Dan was saying, 'you were in full flow to the captain when I came back from relieving myself. Can you start your report again, briefer this time, if it suits you?'

'Aye, sir.'

Hugh took a taste of his ale and his shadowed eyes peered at me a moment above the rim of his cup. As he lowered it again, a hint of his usual smirk fleeted across his face, before he turned again to his questioner.

'As I told your captain, sir, I've been sent by order of the Royal Council to report to all the guards along this stretch of the defences. Your company is the last. The Council reports that the rebellion is swelling. There has been word from the King that rebels are marching also in Wales and the west country. His Grace has ordered the Great Seal to be sent to him at Grantham.'

The little I knew of how the kingdom was governed told me that mention of this royal seal was important, but what Hugh said next drove all thought of it from my head.

'And he has proclaimed the Duke of Buckingham a traitor.'

'Buckingham? A traitor?' Dan's amazement was no greater than my own.

'Aye, sir. It seems he is leading the rebels in the west, marching out from his stronghold at Brecon. The rebels in Kent and Surrey have already declared him their leader.'

'Is it possible?' Dan's question echoed that careering round my own head. 'Can he be so rash? I heard the King had granted him all the lands and titles he coveted. What can he seek to gain?' His shook his head in disbelief. 'They say few men have rallied to the rebels so far. And with the King mustering a great army in the midlands, the north steadfast in its support – and London holding firm for him – what hope can my lord of Buckingham have of taking the city and putting the boy Edward back on the throne?'

'They say that is not his aim.'

'Not his aim?' Dan spluttered. 'Not the aim of these Woodville lackeys who dare to take up arms against their rightful King? What then can be Buckingham's plan? And why has he thrown in his lot with them?'

Hugh gulped again at his drink, lengthening the expectant moment as though to increase its drama.

'They say, sir, that he has taken the cause of Henry Tudor.'

Dan was shocked into silence. His mouth hung open, a dark void in the firelit oval of his face.

A coal fell with a clatter within the brazier, breaking the stillness, before I dared to speak.

'Henry Tudor? Who is he?'

Hugh shot me a glance, but said nothing.

Dan shook himself and closed his mouth, before opening it again to spit out the words,

'A traitor from the line of Lancaster. He calls himself the Earl of Richmond, but that title was taken away from his family for their treachery. He claims he has more right to the crown than any Yorkist – and he fled to exile in Brittany years ago rather than bow down to King Edward. And Buckingham's family were of course Lancastrians in the past.'

Hugh's face showed no expression as Dan turned to him again.

'And is there news of Tudor's movements in all this?'

Hugh shrugged.

'None that I have heard. Though there have been rumours that the Duke of Brittany has been equipping ships and soldiers for him.'

Dan spat into the brazier. It sizzled and flared.

'Pah! Rumours. There are always rumours. And Brittany, France – always keen to stir up trouble for us. Old King Edward should have dealt properly with them years ago. But, no – he preferred their gifts and promises of friendship and weasel words.'

'But we have had peace with them.'

'Peace? At what cost? Their constant manoeuvrings, helping our enemies behind our backs, harbouring them as they plot against us, allowing pirates to plunder our ships and disrupt our trade – maybe encouraging them. That's not a peace worth the name. And now this. Lady Stanley should have been told to deal with her son long ago.'

The familiar name prompted me to ask, 'Lady Stanley, sir?'

'She's wife now to Lord Thomas Stanley, who is close advisor to the King and Council. But she is mother to this Tudor by her first husband. And they say she has some influence.' Dan was thoughtful for a moment. 'Though it must be said, Lord Stanley and his family's loyalty to King Richard and King Edward has been questionable at best.'

'Sir!' Hugh protested. 'My uncle, Lord Soulsby, is Lord Thomas's man. Who questions his loyalty questions the honour of my family too.'

At this, the man stood quickly and bowed to him.

'Then I beg pardon, lad. I repeat only what I have heard. Take no offence, I pray you. We are all here united in our loyalty to the King.'

'Indeed, sir, we are.'

Hugh buried his face in his cup once more and I could not read his expression.

'Yet still I cannot understand why Buckingham would throw in his lot with this pretender,' continued Dan. 'If anything, he himself has as good a claim to the throne as Tudor does. Better, even. And word was that the rebellion sought only to restore old King Edward's son to the crown.'

Hugh placed his cup back upon the table and raised his hands again towards the brazier, as though still cold. He looked at neither me nor Dan as he said,

'Perhaps other news can explain it, sir. My uncle tells me that word has come from France that King Edward's sons are...' he paused, '... are dead.'

The word plunged like a stone into the room.

Dan's mouth fell open again.

'Dead?' I choked the word out.

Hugh stabbed me with a look.

'Aye. Dead.'

'How so?'

'Murdered.'

I could not speak again. It was as though hands were upon my throat, squeezing it, stopping my words, my breath.

Dan picked up where I left off.

'It cannot be. They are safe within the Tower.'

'And who has charge of the Tower?'

'King Richard, of course. And the Constable.'

'The Constable. Aye. Since the summer, the Duke of Buckingham. And the Deputy Constable, Brackenbury. Both loyal to the King. Yet now... As you say – and my uncle too – what cause should my lord of Buckingham have to turn rebel against the King?'

Thought after thought could be seen chasing across Dan's face, mirroring the turmoil in my own mind. What was Hugh suggesting?

'You cannot be serious, boy. That our King... that King Richard...'

'Why not?'

'But King Richard...'

'God's teeth, sir! He has already taken their crown. Placed himself on the throne in their stead. My uncle says this would be the next sensible step. He says he would do it himself if he were in the King's place.'

'What next step?'

278

'To rid himself of the boys. Once and for all.'

His eyes wide, Dan looked about him and back through the dark entranceway, as though afraid of who might be watching or listening in the shadows. Hugh took another mouthful of his ale.

'Have a care, lad. What you are saying is treason. And for what reason would King Richard commit such a crime? Parliament set the boys aside. King Richard is the rightful King. There's no need for – for murder.'

'Maybe so. But it's the talk of Brittany, they say.'

'Who says?' I found my voice again. Hugh glanced my way.

'My uncle. He has contacts. People who hear things. Who know things.'

'More rumours, you mean?' I remembered what King Richard had said to the Duke of Buckingham of rumours – when he was himself still Duke, all those months ago in Northampton. 'They're dangerous things. You should not believe them lightly. And these people who've said this. They don't know him. And they're miles away. How could they know anything?'

'Word gets around.'

'Or it's sent around,' Dan put in. 'Brittany, you said? Maybe by Tudor, then. He wants to be King himself, if the rebels defeat King Richard and are spurred on by this. And the boys would stand in his way too.'

'But they're not in King Richard's way,' I insisted. 'Their father's bigamy ensured that.'

'Aye,' said Dan. ''Tis true. Though what he was thinking of... But he was ever reckless, they say, old King Edward – especially when it came to women...'

I turned to Hugh.

'And how could you repeat such evil about him. You know him.'

Hugh glared at me.

'Know who?'

'King Richard, of course. You know what he's like.'

'Aye, I do.'

'Then you know he could never do such a thing.'

Hugh's face betrayed no emotion. But he raised one eyebrow.

'Do I?'

My hands curled into fists as I leapt to my feet.

Murrey, dislodged, sprang up too, her lips drawn back in a snarl, baring her white dagger-like teeth.

I grasped hold of her collar before she lunged towards Hugh.

Restraining her gave me time to think – about what, on impulse, I had been about to do. About the mistake it would have been. And what my then master had said when I had resorted to violence against Hugh once before.

With King Richard's words circling in my brain, I brought my breathing back under control, though my heart still thumped against my ribs, the torrents of blood rushing in my ears.

I drew myself up to what height I possessed.

'I'll listen to no more of this... of this treasonous talk,' I said with all the dignity I could muster. And, dragging a wriggling Murrey along with me, I stalked out of the chamber.

Behind me, Hugh's laughter pealed out, pursuing me as I headed off into the night. And as I strode across the cobbled yard towards the street, his shout assaulted my ears:

'What are you so upset about? By the devil, I've heard the boys are both brats – just like their good-for-nothing milksop cousin.'

11

Return of the King

I slept little for the rest of that night and showed up to work on the morrow bleary-eyed and yawning.

Simon, whose watch ended long after mine, wondered at my shortness of temper as we laboured together over the printing press, helping Master de Vries sort the tiny letters in their cases, positioning the vast sheets of paper, raising and lowering the weighty platen. When we ceased work for dinner, he took me aside before we entered the dining hall.

'What ails you today? You're as irritable as Murrey when she snapped at that wasp in the summer.'

Poor Murrey had had a terrible time after the wasp had stung inside her mouth. She had pawed and pawed at her swollen cheek until it bled, and I had been forced to bind all four of her feet in cloth to stop her clawing her face to ribbons. I wished now that I could scratch in the same way the sore, raw spot left by Hugh's words.

I told Simon as briefly as I could what had passed the night before. He too was horrified and dismissed the rumours as lies and slanders that should never see the light of day. But I overheard him later telling the journeyman printer as we returned to work – and I regretted mentioning it to him at all.

But, as Hugh had said, word got around – even without my help. By the time of Alys's next letter, the rumours had reached even Middleham, where she and Roger had remained with Ed and the Queen when King Richard had ridden south at the first stirrings of the revolt. Her horror at them and scorn for those who could spread such lies dripped like caustic lime from her words as she told of how the rebellion was viewed from far away in the north.

The Londoners are no fools. They clearly don't believe the King could be so wicked if they have rallied to his defence as you say. And the same in all other parts of the kingdom. Very few people seem to be supporting the Duke of Buckingham, or this Tudor. But now I understand a conversation I

281

overheard weeks ago between the Duchess of Norfolk and Lady Tyrell.

She had switched to our code, as she always did when writing about gossip or anything that might be confidential.

Qb eia ijwcb epmbpmz bpm jwga apwctl jm uwdml nzwu bpm Bwemz· Q bpwcopb qb eia bw abwx bpmu jmqvo i nwkca nwz zmjmttqwv, tqsm bpmg pidm jmmv – jcb uigjm qb eia ijwcb bpmqz ainmbg· Ivl eqbp bpm Lcsm wn Jcksqvopiu ia Kwvabijtm wn bpm Bwemz...*

She had broken off, as though she could not bear to think any more on the subject, and had turned to telling of how the Queen was sick with worry and had had to be stopped from following the King.

Master Fleete said King Richard had enough to worry about without her safety too. Best for her to remain in Middleham, in the midst of their most loyal subjects. Although Master Fleete himself immediately took horse with other men from the castle and rode to join the army.

Real news of the course of the uprising was hard to come by over the following days. But in time came the word that we had all been waiting for.

Master Ashley had been summoned again to attend the city council, and I was on an errand for Master de Vries to collect supplies from a shop in St Paul's churchyard, when a gathering crowd attracted my attention. I joined its very fringes, clutching to me the various bundles and packages to keep them safe from cutpurses.

A crier had mounted the steps of St Paul's Cross and was holding aloft a proclamation. Damp stains were spreading on the pale paper in the heavy drizzle. The crisp golden days of early autumn had descended into a dreary, wet November.

'God be praised,' the crier bellowed, as the whispering and mutterings of the crowd died away. 'Let us offer thanks to the Virgin for our deliverance. For the rebellion is over.'

Cheers rose into the air as though pigeons taking flight, but many of the people hushed their neighbours, eager to hear more without hindrance. The crier obliged as the uproar settled back into expectant silence.

'By the Grace of God and with the aid of his loyal subjects, our lord King Richard has defeated the rebels. No battle was needed. On the approach of the King and his army, men fled in terror before his righteous cause, deserting the great rebel and traitor the Duke of Buckingham and his allies in malice. The said Duke, like a base coward, in turn fled in disguise, but was captured and taken to Salisbury to be tried for treason. On Sunday last he was beheaded in the market square as a condemned traitor.'

A shiver rippled through the crowd at these words, like a chill breeze lifting fallen leaves on a winter's day. The crier waited for a moment before speaking again.

'His Grace the King declares that no yeoman or commoner who took arms with the said rebels shall suffer his wrath. But all are urged to deliver up to his commissioners those well-born rebels and traitors still at large. By name these are: the bishops of Ely and Salisbury,' a gasp rose from the gathering, 'the Marquess of Dorset,' knowing nods were exchanged between two men in front of me, 'Sir John Fogge,' the man embraced by the King on the day of his oath-taking, 'Sir John Cheney, Sir William Stonor, Sir George Brown, Sir Giles Dawbeney...'

The list continued – names unknown to me – of knights who had taken up arms against their King in Wales and the west country, and in counties south of the Thames. There a last stand had been made at Bodiam Castle in Kent – taken finally by the Duke of Norfolk. Along with the names were the sums of money to be paid as rewards for their capture – a thousand marks for the Marquess and bishops, five hundred for each knight.

As I listened I wondered that such men could break their oath of loyalty to their King, that churchmen could involve themselves in such affairs (though I later learnt that one bishop was himself a Woodville, the other a close friend of Lady Stanley) – and how the Marquess had escaped from sanctuary at Westminster, where his mother, the old Queen, was still holed up. I marvelled less now at her decision to remain there.

On finishing his litany, the crier rolled up the proclamation and stepped down from the cross. The crowd were left to chatter among themselves and potter away to their business.

Over the days to come, more word arrived of events in the west country as the King travelled through Dorset and Devon to restore order there and reward men who had remained loyal. More executions were reported, but fewer by far than the names read out by the crier. Later I heard that some men had fled with the Marquess to Brittany, but still others had been pardoned – and often even allowed to keep their lands and wealth. Later still, even the Marquess himself was offered a pardon – but I get ahead of myself...

Among other familiar names mentioned was that of Lady Stanley – and of her son, Henry Tudor. For once a rumour had had some truth in it. Around the time of Duke Henry's execution, Tudor was sighted along the Dorset coast, then off Plymouth, in command of two ships crewed by men in the pay of the Duke of Brittany. On receiving the news of King Richard's victory, he had turned tail and was presumed to have slunk back to his foreign lair.

Alys's next letter wrote of the disappointment of his mother, Lady Stanley, and how she had been at the heart of the rebellion – the centre of a web of intrigue between Buckingham, the bishops, Tudor and others of her Lancastrian family exiled on the continent.

Nyrk r nzkty!* She showed her true colours during the coronation. Yet the King has chosen to be merciful to her. Her lands are to be confiscated – but just given to her husband, who stayed loyal despite her plotting. So it's not much of a punishment. But as the Queen says, the King needs to keep such men as Lord Stanley happy – though she didn't look too happy about it herself.

Mind you, Lord Stanley and his brother William were not always loyal to King Edward, though they were later forgiven. Did you know? How difficult it must be to be King, when everyone is after power and wealth. Why can't they all just live in peace and enjoy the quiet life and prosperity it brings?

Hugh's words about his uncle being Lord Stanley's man nudged into my mind as I read the letter – and the story Roger had told me all those months ago in Middleham, about the execution of Hugh's father for treason. And I too wondered at this endless desire for power – at any cost.

Two or three weeks later, just at the start of Advent, news tore through the city that the King was to return from his progress back through the southern counties.

Crowds flocked to see him as he was led into the city across the great bridge by an escort of mayor, aldermen and chief citizens, my new master among them. All clothed in rich robes of crimson and violet, they offered a splash of colour on this drear day. Above, against the pale blue winter sky, fluttered the royal standard and the familiar banner of white boar upon its field of murrey and blue. The silver lion of the Duke of Norfolk shone alongside. Behind the high-stepping horses of the standard bearers rode the King, astride Storm as usual, and the older Duke, with Lord Lovell and Master Ratcliffe heading the host of gentlemen bringing up the rear.

I had stolen away from my duties to snatch a glimpse of my old master, back in his capital city after an absence of more than four months. Unable to push my way through the throng, I had only a distant view. But even from so many yards away, the change since I had last seen him was unmistakable. He and the Duke laughed with one another, raised their hats to the cheers of the people, touched their breastplates over their hearts, bowed and waved to those who called to them from the overhanging house-fronts, and reached into their own purses to scatter coins to those at the front who begged for alms. Lord Lovell and their other gentlemen, though, were watchful, eyes scanning the crowd as though they feared there might still be trouble, even here in this loyal city.

As I straggled behind the procession of soldiers who marched in their wake, the mayor reached the steps of St Magnus's church and stood with his fellow councilmen awaiting their honoured guests. The King strode up to him, the Duke a step or two behind. They accepted bows, gifts and a speech of welcome, then embraced the mayor and several of his companions. Turning, the King spoke some words himself to the gathered multitude.

Though too far away to catch his speech, my head soon rang with the roars of the people, rolling back to me in waves, until everywhere around me was awash with noise. As I thrust my hands to my ears to deaden the sound, King Richard threw up his arm in salute, and then was gone, swallowed up in the church by the following flow of purple and red of the principal men of London. Master Ashley told us later of the service of thanksgiving and

285

immense feast laid on by the council to celebrate the King's triumphal return.

It was the start of a joyous run-up to the Christmas season, though, for me, one very different to that of the previous year, when I had been guest at the court of the old King. All the solemnities of religious services were interlaced with the customary feasting and gifts, but the highlight for me was the practice of 'topsy-turvy' on Twelfth Night.

I had heard tell of it at the York Minster song school, but, living always at home and not as a boarder at the school, I had never been a part of it, or seen the Dean serve the choristers and canons at table, or any other of the customs involved. So to witness Master Ashley don rough clothes and place an apprentice cap upon his head, and Mistress Ashley tie a housewife's apron about her oldest gown, and both carry trays of meat and drink to tables, and bow to us boys and journeymen as they served us and poured our ale – and even sing for us during the meal, poke the huge Yule log in the hearth and clear away the empty dishes – it was all remarkable to me. It was a tradition in such households across the city and beyond – although it never reached as far as my father's house in York's Stonegate.

Ed enjoyed a memorable Christmas-tide too, though upset that his mother had travelled to London to join his father without him. In his many welcome letters, he also sorrowed over the loss of Alys who had headed south with the Queen, but he revelled in riding out each day with Roger and the other pages, despite the snow and warnings about his health. Once again, little snow fell in London – though in Middleham Ed said there were icicles as long as his arm hanging from the stable roof in celebration of Jesus' birth.

But one letter in particular almost bubbled over with his delight.

But my big news – can you believe it? – I have a hound puppy of my very own! Roger says my father feels guilty that he was not with me at Christmas – again – so he decided I should have one. I don't care what the reason is. Sir James Tyrell, the new master of the pages and squires, surprised me with her on Twelfth Night. It almost made up for my mother and father not being here.

She's beautiful, Matt – pure white like Florette and Shadow. I've called her 'Belle', because that means 'beautiful' in French. When we went out, I had to carry her in my doublet just like you did with Murrey, otherwise I would have lost her in all the snow! These past few days she's snuggled up with me since I've been unwell – it's nothing much, just a chill caught on one of our rides. (Fqq'v vgnn Oqvjgt.*)

I'm sure I'll be better soon and perhaps in the spring I'll be able to travel to London – I can't wait for Belle to meet Murrey. Or maybe you can come with my mother and father when they return here after Parliament is finished in the spring? Oh, why are you not still part of their household?

But, despite Ed's lament, I was no longer part of his family's close circle, and must accept it, cheerfully if I could, no matter how much I missed the company of all my friends.

Time passed. All was quiet in the realm. And so, 1483 – the tumultuous year of the three kings and the great rebellion – turned to 1484.

12

The Visitor

'Master Wansford, you are wanted in our master's study.'

One of the household servants stood before me in the print house.

I paused, the roller in my hand slick with ink, poised to run it across the frame full of type. Simon glanced at me, his eyebrows raised.

'Me? Are you sure?'

Bemused at the summons, I handed the roller to Simon and removed my heavy apron, folding it and placing it carefully on a nearby table.

Master Ashley I knew to be away from London on business in East Anglia. Mistress Ashley, though kindly to all the apprentices, had little to do with us unless we were ill or otherwise out of sorts. Master Lyndsey? I searched my memory for any reason he could wish to see me and I could discover none. While perhaps not the perfect apprentice, I had committed no misdemeanours of late that would prompt the mistress to charge the steward to punish me.

With Murrey as ever at my heels, I made my way through the entrance hall to the narrow door tucked away towards the rear. I knocked once, and the door was opened straight away by Mistress Ashley herself. One hand clutched a spray of spring flowers – sky-blue forget-me-knots, pink gillyflowers – and a small pair of iron shears, as though she had been interrupted in gathering her usual posies from her garden.

An oddly familiar expression shadowed her eyes for an instant and her free hand stretched out to squeeze my shoulder.

'Matthew, lad, come in, come in. Here is a friend come to see you.'

She drew me into the room, where the fresh sunlight slanted in through diamond-paned windows overlooking the garden. As I passed her, she patted my back again.

'I shall leave you alone to talk.'

And she glided out, pulling the door to behind her.

To my astonishment, there before me – strangely small against the magnificent carved stone fireplace of my master's private chamber – was –

'Roger!'

I had not met him for more than a year – in person or in letters. Though I wrote to him often enough, it was seldom any response came my way. As he had insisted on our first encounter, he was made for dancing and sport, not classroom learning – or, so it seemed, letter-writing. I had resigned myself to that long ago, though the loss of our fellowship and his unfailing cheerfulness had left a gaping void in my life.

As I stepped forward to greet him, I thought at first that he had not changed at all. Except perhaps he had gained a few more inches on me. But was there something else too? For a moment, I struggled to pinpoint it. But, when I shook his hand before heartily embracing him, it dawned on me. The usual laughing light had vanished from his eyes.

He drew away from my hug at once and shifted from one foot to another, his fingers fiddling with the strap of his pouch, before he leaned down to stroke Murrey.

Puzzled that he would not meet my eyes – what had I done wrong? – I forced myself to break our silence.

'I did not think to see you here in London, Roger. How are you? And your family?' His father's estate was not far from London, I knew, and that he had a townhouse in the city. 'There is no trouble at home, I hope?'

'No, not at all, though I am on my way to see them.'

'I thought you were to stay in the north and help Ed rule this new council of his.'

Roger's gaze slid sideways towards me and, as he straightened up, his mouth twisted as though in unhappiness.

'Do not joke, Matt. It is hardly a time for jests.'

His words and uneasiness worried me not a little.

'It's no joke, Roger. I would not dare. I leave that sort of thing to you. Yet today... Why so serious? Why are you here? Is Alys well? Elen?'

'The Queen has sent me to visit my parents. She thought it might make me feel better. But she said perhaps I should see you on the way.'

'Why? Have you been ill? Ed has not told me of it in his letters. Nor Alys. Though maybe she had not reached Middleham before you left. Although you said the Queen... Alys was travelling with her and the King...'

Roger stared at me.

'What? Haven't you heard?'

'Heard what?'

'But I wrote you a letter. At least, I thought I did.'

I laughed, a hollow, strained sound to my ears.

What hadn't I heard?

'You? A letter? I've received only one from you since I left Middleham. And that was just four lines asking what I knew about the rebellion. But perhaps there were others and they've all gone astray? Though Ed's and Alys's always arrive.'

I was gabbling, I realized, wondering at his seriousness, my alarm growing. My final words emerged in a stutter.

'This letter, what – what was it about?'

'About – it was about Ed.'

'Ed? What about him?'

There had been rumours. There were always rumours. About this or that. Master Ashley said they were sent around to confuse people, demoralize them, stir them up against the King, as in the late rebellion, or against this noble or that alderman, to thwart his ambition, or –

But this – about Ed – this –

'Matt,' Roger swallowed, forced himself to go on. 'Ed – Ed's dead.'

It was as though my heart, my very core, had been torn from my chest.

'Dead? But... but he can't be. I had a letter from him, only last —'

When was it? Last week? Last month?

This spring had been so busy. A trip to Friesland early in the year, the return delayed by storms in the channel, the need to catch up on work. The letter had been waiting for me on our return. Before I heard tell of any rumour...

In it he had written of... of longing to see his father and mother when they rode north again in the spring... of training his new pup with Roger, and... of having caught a chill, when out riding.

But it was nothing, he'd said. And he'd begged me not to tell his mother – as he always did if he'd done something amiss. As if I would now have the chance! She was worried about his

290

health, he said, had given instructions that he was not to ride in the wintry weather.

And yet he had. Behind his tutor's back. And delighted in it. In cantering through the snowy water meadows, up on to the moor, overlooking the patchwork of strip fields in the valley, edged with drifts of snow and dark stone walls and the skeletons of thorn trees.

'He had been ill,' Roger said, his voice cracking. 'Not so serious. A chill. But it lingered.'

Yes, I knew.

'But then he would go riding again. Too soon. Although Doctor Frees had told him he shouldn't. And his mother in her letters. Though we all told him...'

Yes, yes, of course. That was Ed. Impatient to be well, to do what everyone else did.

'It was a cold day. And when we were on the moor, he... We didn't know what to do... Perhaps if you had been there...'

Haltingly, Roger told me all that had happened. And as he told it, I could see, hear, feel, as though I had been there.

A cold, sharp spring day. The knifing of the breeze in the nostrils. Plumes of breath rising from boys, ponies, grooms as they hurried about making all ready.

The clang of shod hooves on cobbles, the dull thud across the water meadows. The musty smell of last year's heather brushed by horses' legs up on the moor tops.

Black points of mud. Leaden sky above.

Boys laughing gaily, the snorting of their mounts, the sounds carrying across the still moor.

Then a gasp. And another.

Ed's breath rasping in his throat.

Boys clustering in concern. Leaden grey of his skin, bluish lips, eyes wide.

The rising scent of panic in the chill air.

A page remounts, dashes for the castle, the physician. A cloak, another, bundling Ed. Somehow, somehow, get him back to safety.

The thunder of hooves across the water meadows, up on to the moor. Adults' cries.

Master Fleete passing the small bundle, racked with coughs, struggling breaths, up to Master Gygges. Gentle hands, holding, supporting, before him on his mount.

The straggle of pages watching, the riders picking their way down and across the final fields. Following more slowly, dread weighing heavy inside them.

Back within the cold stone walls. Gloom cast by drawn curtains, paling only in the smokiness of lighted tallow.

Hushed, whispering.

Waiting on the steps, outside Ed's tower room.

The tang of herbs burning, warding off bad humours.

Nurse bustling, in, out, fetching, carrying. Bowls of steaming liquid, trays of this and that.

Master physician... closing the door behind him. Head shaking, eyes moist.

Small white pup whimpering, scratching at the wood.

Tap, tap, tap.

Then – silence.

Darkness.

Candles quenched.

The pungent fumes of incense, drifting.

Muttered words in Latin. The wails of women.

Men with trails of tears upon their cheeks.

The sad tolling of a single bell at the parish church.

Wetness upon my cheeks too. I buried my face in Murrey's fur. Her warm tongue licked the hand that clutched her.

'It was so quick.'

Roger's voice seeped into my sorrow.

'Too quick to summon the King and Queen. They were far away, still journeying north. Nothing could be done. It was days before they came. Alys was distraught. And Belle...'

The shivering white pup. Curled up against the cold, grey, still little boy.

Gently lifted away, crying to go back. Whimpering, scratching at the door.

'We nearly lost Belle too. She didn't want to leave him, wouldn't eat for days. Shadow had to care for her, almost like a mother. But she kept going back to Ed's chamber, trying to get in.'

Tap, tap, tap.

Roger's words faltered to a halt. He had no more to say.

His face glum, he stared out of the window as I wiped away my tears with my cuff.

Silence.

Save for the birds trilling their lilting spring songs among the fruit trees beyond the splintered glass.

A soft knock.

Mistress Ashley's lace-framed face peered around the door.

Roger started. He swung back to me, his eyes not meeting mine.

'I must go. My mother...'

I nodded, unable to trust my own voice.

'I will write,' he said. 'I promise. When I – when I go back. I'm to join the household at Sheriff Hutton, with the Earl of Lincoln. Now Ed – now there will be no household at Middleham.'

And he was gone. No farewell, not a backward glance.

Mistress Ashley guided me to a chair, sat me down, patted my shoulder again.

'Stay as long as you wish. I have told Master de Vries. If you need anything, just send the servant for me.'

Her tone was pitying. As she left the room, her last words to herself reached me.

'Poor little lad. And the Queen's only child...'

And I recollected that she herself had no children of her own, despite long years of prayers to the Virgin and St Anne.

I heard no more from Roger – I did not expect to, in truth, though all year I had hoped – but in a day or two a letter arrived from Alys. In it she told of the moment when the King and Queen had received the news of their son.

I've never seen such grief before. The Queen was overcome. The King could do nothing to comfort her, though they clung to one another as though they would never let go.

The royal party had journeyed sadly up to Middleham instead of the joyous spring progress it was to have been. A quiet funeral for Ed, then it was back to business for the King. For word had reached him that Henry Tudor had not given up his ambition, despite his flight after the failed revolt. In a ceremony in Brittany on Christmas day he had sworn an oath to marry Princess Elizabeth – old King Edward's eldest daughter.

He says it is to unite the houses of York and Lancaster, to stop the rivalry once and for all – though most Lancastrian supporters gave that up long ago, under King Edward. But it's said that the French King is helping him plan for an invasion of England, to challenge King Richard for the throne. I don't think he'd dare to land here in the north – no one would give him their support, their loyalty to the King and Queen is too strong. But there is talk of the King travelling round the north country to check the defences anyway. I think perhaps he doesn't want to go far from Ed too soon – or at least the place where he now lies.

I'm not sure whether the Queen will return to Westminster as planned – maybe she won't want to be apart from the King. She has been so distracted with grief. After the funeral, she walked for hours alone on the moor – she wouldn't let any ladies join her. The King was so worried when he heard – he had been in important meetings all day. And when she returned her gown was all torn and muddy, and she had lost her favourite jewel – do you remember, the beautiful necklace the King gave her after you returned from Christmas in London? The servants searched everywhere, but the Queen couldn't recall where she'd wandered and they never found it.

I did remember it – the vivid blue stone clasped in gold that I'd seen about the Queen's neck in happier days, when she was still Duchess. And when I had still been servant to her and her husband – and friend to their only son.

13

Paths Cross

Spring turned into summer, and summer passed slowly.

My grief remained raw, and now I had only one regular correspondent whose letters lit up the ordinary days of my apprenticeship. And even that source of enjoyment appeared under threat following a long-awaited event.

After almost a year, the old Queen – now to be called Dame Grey after her first, legitimate husband – had finally emerged from sanctuary, together with her daughters. And on her return to Westminster from the north, Alys was warned that her fate might soon be decided.

She tried to look on the bright side in her letters, despite her lingering sadness at Edward's death. As she told me straight away, this change didn't mean she was to marry Ralph Soulsby just yet. Nor was she to be made to join the household of Dame Grey, who had taken up residence in the countryside. Instead she was to attend her guardian's daughter, the Lady Elizabeth, who had remained at court.

Elizabeth has been very friendly to me since she came out of sanctuary. She's only a few years older than me, but she says she remembers well when my mother was lady-in-waiting to her mother. She's even said I may keep Shadow with me now I've brought her back from Middleham. She loves hunting and hounds too – she used to hunt with her father as often as she was allowed. I'm sure I'll be very happy with her.

And who knows where I might end up? Lady Tyrell says the King must surely find Elizabeth a husband soon – if only to ruin Henry Tudor's plan to marry her himself. But the Queen pointed out that the King promised good husbands for Elizabeth and each of her sisters before their mother agreed to leave sanctuary, and he says there's no hurry. He wants to find the right match for her – a royal husband, if he can, though she is no longer seen as a true

daughter of a King of England – and Tudor's threats don't
worry him. So maybe I will get to travel abroad as you have!

Yet, for all Alys's cheerfulness and hope for the future, her
regret at leaving the Queen and King after so many years was
clear. And especially only months after their loss of Ed.

'They send their respects to you,' she wrote, 'and their
thanks for your prayers when Ed died. They're still grieving,
despite the show they must put on for courtiers and diplomats. I
see the sadness in their faces at quiet moments.'

Although the King had said Alys could continue to write
to me, as Dame Elizabeth had not forbidden it, perhaps the
pleasures of a young princess's household distracted her, as her
letters became less frequent. Then, as my second summer in the
city drew to a close, they ceased altogether.

I continued to write – how could I not? Alys, and Elen
who had accompanied her to Elizabeth's new house, were my last
link to the chapter of my life that meant so much to me, the last
link in a chain that was falling to pieces. Yet our lives had drifted
so far apart now that I did not wonder at the change. I was after all
only a merchant's son, and now a lowly apprentice. Our paths had
brushed against one another for a brief time, like the closing of a
butterfly's wings as it alights on a beautiful flower, then fluttered
apart, perhaps to touch again no more. I dutifully wrote of the
humdrum events of my existence, of the bright interlude of our
late-summer visit to Bruges. But though I had on my return
enclosed a kerchief of web-like lace as a gift for each of them from
my travels, I no longer expected any reply.

Yet reply, of a sort, I did receive, unlooked-for though it
was.

Autumn was gathering pace, and the early evening mists
were rolling off the river into the embrace of the smoke rising from
the city's coal fires, when one evening I was returning through the
dusk from an errand. I was almost safe back at my master's house,
when rounding a corner out of an alley, I all but bumped into a
couple strolling together, as it seemed, along the street outside his
gates.

The lady uttered a cry. The gentleman took a step
backwards with a curse, lifting up the lantern he carried.

I bowed my apology swiftly. As I straightened up, a
familiar voice spoke my name.

'Matthew? Is it you?' A gentle laugh. 'I see it is, for here also is Murrey. I hope she has not forgotten me.'

The lady was in fact a girl. It was Elen.

The light cast by the lantern slanted through the strands of mist on to her dark cheek as she leant to pet my hound. Beyond her, a mounted groom led two horses, one the palfrey I remembered from Crosby Place, the other a dark brown colt, tricked out in the murrey and blue of the royal household.

Her companion laughed too.

'Ah! So it is. Well, perhaps it is not unexpected. One must be ready to meet the rat if one ventures near its lair.'

The words were spoken lightly, but with a mocking undertone. For Elen's companion was also known to me. Hugh Soulsby.

My delight at Elen's appearance after so long was matched by my distaste at seeing him. I returned his slight bow of greeting, hooking a finger through Murrey's collar in case I needed to restrain her.

'So, Master Wansford, this is where you've been hiding from us all this time.' He threw a glance about him, holding his lantern aloft though the darkness was not yet pressing in upon us. 'I can understand why Mistress Elen has not ventured here herself before today.'

Elen stared at him, her lips parting, then closing as though she was uncertain what to say. But I brushed his words aside, not even looking at him. Master Ashley's townhouse was one of many fine merchants' residences hereabouts, for all they were hedged around by workaday artisans' dwellings and shops.

'I'm very pleased to see you, Elen. Do you wish to come and meet my master? I'm sure he will welcome you warmly.'

'No doubt,' said Hugh, before Elen could utter a word. 'I'm sure he'd welcome anything that brings him closer to a royal household.'

I could not ignore that – not after his many insinuations against myself in the past.

I turned to face him.

'Why do you say that, Master Soulsby? Do you not know my master has long been a friend of the King?' For Master Lyndsey often spoke of their lengthy friendship, as well as of the many deals they had conducted together.

Had Hugh grown even taller since our last meeting? He stared at me as though scrutinizing an insect on the ground before him.

'Of the King, indeed? Oh, of course, the *King*. From when he was just a *Duke*, I suppose. His royal brother's *dog* of all *works*.'

My skin crawled at these words and the stress he laid upon them, and Elen plucked at her skirts as though in discomfort. Murrey's ears pricked up and her snout lifted, alive to the rising emotions. My hand tightened on her collar.

Hugh carried on regardless, his all-too-familiar sneer now unfurling across his handsome face.

'And these jumped-up merchants – of course, they'll do *anything*, with *anyone* – so long as they gain a *profit* by it.'

That was more than I could bear. Not only a slur on the King and Master Ashley, but also on my father.

But as I let go of Murrey's collar and thrust myself at Hugh with my fists upraised, Elen threw herself between us, both hands flung up to grasp mine.

'No, Matt, no!' she gasped out, clutching at my balled fists.

Behind her, the lantern light flared on Hugh's face. A spasm clenched his jaws together, before they relaxed in a smirk and he tossed back his head with a bellow of laughter.

'Ha! And you – a jumped-up merchant's son yourself – having to be defended by a girl!'

Her sudden release and the sudden movements and the sudden noise were too much now for Murrey. She wriggled free from between Elen's skirts and my legs and exploded in a fury of barking and snarling and snapping.

His guffaw cut short, Hugh backed away abruptly, swinging the lantern down like a scythe in front of his legs to ward her off, while he groped for his knife. Murrey in turn shied away, but then lunged forward again, still barking ferociously at him as he tried to draw the dagger. As I made a grab for her collar, and missed, Hugh swiped at her again with the heavy iron lantern, this time catching her a glancing blow on the shoulder that sent her tumbling over across the cobbles, yelping. But she twisted back up and leapt forward once more, throwing herself back towards him, while I flung myself at her and Elen snatched at the flailing lantern, shouting at Hugh to stop.

In all the commotion I hardly noticed the click and creak of the opening gate, before a voice thundered above the tumult,

'What is all this? Why this uproar?'

At last I managed to catch Murrey by the scruff of her neck and drag her away, but not before Hugh, unable to use his other weapons, lashed out with his boot, clouting her in the ribs as she wriggled helpless in my grasp. Murrey squealed, then squirmed around and snarled as I hauled her with me towards the courtyard wall. A moment later, realizing she was in my grip, she calmed down and stood quivering while I ran my hands over her back and side, checking for any wounds. Though she winced and grumbled in her throat, I was soon satisfied she was no more than bruised.

Stroking her still-bristling head, I looked back to see Hugh resheathing his knife and lowering his lantern, while Elen smoothed down her skirts and tucked away the wisps of hair that had been dislodged from her cap.

Before them stood Master Ashley and a companion, a tall man clad in a travelling cloak and hood, both their backs towards me.

Hugh bowed with something of his usual swagger, though his face was pale at the shock of the attack. His mouth opened, but before he could speak, my master cut in.

'No, say nothing more. I heard what you said about the King. Have you no respect?'

'But, sir —'

'Don't try to explain. Be off with you, boy!'

Hugh was now easily a finger or two taller than Master Ashley and far broader, and he stood his ground a moment, staring at him, his chest still heaving beneath his royal livery. His lips moved as though he would speak again. But my master's companion took a step towards him and Hugh thought better of it, proffered the slightest of bows and turned to Elen. His voice was icily polite as he said,

'My lady, it has been a pleasure. We must ride out together again another time. Pray remember me to your esteemed friend, Lady Alys.'

And, seizing her hand before she could snatch it away, he pressed it to his lips. Then he strode to the brown colt, whisked its rein from the groom's hands, passed him the lantern, mounted and, spurring the horse's sides, was gone.

Elen wiped the back of one hand on the other, a deep red tingeing her cheek, just visible in the twilight.

Master Ashley took her hand and, patting it once, drew it courteously through his arm.

'My dear, you are trembling. You must come in and my wife shall give you a restorative. Matthew – follow us.'

Murmuring a word to his companion, he led Elen through the gates into the courtyard. The other gentleman walked at her other side as though supporting her, and the groom, now dismounted, led the palfrey and his own horse towards the stables.

I trailed behind my master, still clinging on to Murrey's collar so she stuck close to my side, and wondering for the first time why Elen was here at all – and why Hugh had been with her.

A servant had hurried ahead and Mistress Ashley met us at the top of the main entrance steps, her concerned face lit up by torches newly flaring to either side. Master Ashley relinquished Elen's arm to her as she said,

'Come in, come in, my dear. What has happened?'

The mistress urged Elen into the dining hall, waving away her quiet protest that all was well, and I was left in the entrance hallway with my master and his companion, uncertain what to do next. They gazed after the ladies through the still-open door, then spoke together in an undertone. Their speech was not clear to me as I lingered near the main door, but its rhythms betrayed that it was not English.

His hood now thrown back, in the glimmer of candles ranged in sconces around the hallway the other man was revealed to be not only tall and lean, but also the possessor of skin and hair as dark as Elen's, perhaps darker even. He was attired beneath his fur-trimmed cloak in outlandish robes of vivid silks, and, with black eyes that glinted like the eyes of a hawk, he had the air of one used to being obeyed. It was no wonder that Hugh had had second thoughts about confronting my master when he stood beside such a man.

He took his leave a moment later, and I watched with my master as he strode to the stables. There another man in similar robes held the bridle of a dapple grey stallion with a proud, curving neck, alongside his own, similarly noble horse. A groom helped the gentleman to mount and soon the gates clanged behind the two strangers as they rode away.

Master Ashley placed his hand on my shoulder, driving out of my mind all thoughts of who they might be.

'Shall we see how your young friend is? She is Lady Alys Langdown's companion unless I am mistaken.'

Given the closeness between his household and that of the King, I was unsurprised that he knew of Elen. I was perhaps more surprised at his next words, and the mild manner in which they were spoken.

'And the squire? Is he perhaps Lord Soulsby's nephew, Master Hugh?'

'Aye, sir, he is.' Though I did my best, my voice was not so calm.

'I heard that you two had a disagreement while you were at Middleham. I see that it has not been forgotten. You would do well perhaps to avoid him while in London if you can. His family were ever ones to bear a grudge.'

This also was no surprise to me, and no doubt excellent advice – if I could avoid all accidental meetings too.

I followed him into the dining hall. Within, Mistress was fussing over Elen, now resting upon a bench, sipping deep-red wine from a crystal goblet.

'Ah, husband, let Matthew come in. Elen here says she was on her way to visit him when this unpleasantness occurred. She has quite recovered herself now.'

With smiles and reassurances, Mistress Ashley retreated with her husband and I was left alone with Elen. A single candle on the nearby table cast a corona of light around her.

'Are you well now, Elen?' I asked.

'Yes, I thank you, Matthew,' she replied, her colour rising again. 'It was nothing, indeed. Just Hugh...'

A pause, before she continued.

'I did not wish him to accompany me. He was outside Lady Elizabeth's stables as I left, chatting with the stable lads. When he saw me, he offered to ride with me. He said the way might not be safe.'

'Although you had your groom?'

'He was just being polite.'

Another pause.

To distract her from her discomfort, I pulled up a small stool for myself and then changed the subject. I had no wish to speak more of Master Soulsby.

'And how is Alys?'

'She is well, thank you.' Elen brightened at the words. 'She is the reason for my visit. Though she did not want me to come.'

'Not?'

My disappointment must have been obvious to her, for she went on hurriedly,

'Only because she would rather have come herself. Or have written.'

'But she has not?'

The weeks without letters had bothered me more than I had known, for all that I had justified them to myself. The words cut as they came out, and Elen's eyes flinched as at a wound.

'She would have written if she could. Believe me, Matthew. It is not her intent to neglect you. She is as frustrated as you can be, but she would not let me write to you in her stead.'

I regretted my words now. My tone softened.

'Why? What has happened?'

'She was thrown from her pony.'

'What? But you said she was well.'

'Don't worry – she is not badly hurt. But the bones in her wrist were broken and so she cannot write. Her arm is all swathed in bandages. She says it does not pain her greatly, but it may be some weeks still before it is strong enough to hold a quill.'

'I hope she may recover more quickly than that. But she was thrown, you say. Yet she's such a good rider, and knows her pony so well.'

Elen smiled her quiet smile.

'Yes, Matthew, we all know she's a fine rider. But – and she would tell me off for saying this – she was riding recklessly. She had just heard she was not to travel to Gipping, and she was annoyed. I believe she took it out on her poor pony and spurred him more than he was used to. He jibbed and threw her.'

'Gipping?' I racked my memory for a trace of the name.

'To visit Lady Tyrell. It is her husband's estate in Suffolk. Alys has not seen Lady Tyrell since she left the Queen's household and they had become such friends at court. Sir James Tyrell is now master of the King's henchmen. I'm sure Roger will have told you. He is his master now, and of all the pages.'

I shook my head. Despite his promise, Roger had written hardly a letter to me since his return to the north.

'I don't often hear from Roger. And I have not seen him since the spring. Since he brought me news of...' I swallowed, pushing away the memory. 'Since he came to visit his parents.'

Elen bowed her head and reached a hand down to stroke Murrey's ears, but the tear growing on her long black lashes sparkled in the candlelight like a star on the darkest night. She blinked once or twice and after a moment, lifted her head again. Her emotion left no trace upon her face as she continued her tale.

'Lady Elizabeth was to visit Lady Tyrell with her mother, Dame Grey. Naturally Alys was to join them. But Dame Grey sent word at the last moment that Elizabeth was not to go with her.' She glanced about her, as though the shadows in the dining hall teemed with listeners, then went on. 'The older ladies in the household say it's because there is a rumour that a Portuguese Duke wishes to marry Lady Elizabeth. They say he has sent an ambassador to London just to see her.'

I remembered Alys's letter about the King's marriage plans for his brother's daughter – and her words about perhaps travelling abroad with Elizabeth herself.

'Is the rumour true?'

'I don't know,' Elen replied. 'There are always rumours swirling about at court – about this and that. Always gossip and intrigues, lords and ladies plotting and vying against one another for royal favour and attention. Alys says it's one of the reasons why the King and Queen stayed away from court so much when old King Edward was alive. They do all they can to prevent it now, but Lady Tyrell said it's impossible to go against centuries of tradition.'

'Then maybe there is nothing in it, just talk among idle folk.'

How would I feel if it were true? If Princess Elizabeth were to marry and take Alys with her to Portugal or any such foreign land – and perhaps Elen too? And with Roger so far away in Sheriff Hutton. And Ed... Even after more than a year I had not made such good friends in London, for all that Simon and I worked together, trained together, lived and laughed together. Yet, I should not grudge Alys her chance to travel and see exotic lands if it should come. But how would it affect her future marriage too?

Perhaps Elen read some of my thoughts scribed on my face, despite the dimness of the light cast by the single candle in its silver holder.

'It may not happen. We must wait to see how the King's diplomacy fares. Yet I for one hope Lady Elizabeth marries this Duke, or someone similar, soon.'

'Why do you say that?'

'Because other rumours say that the King offered her hand in marriage to Henry Tudor, in hope that in return he would come back to England, pledge his allegiance and give up his claim to the throne.'

'What? King Richard?'

Elen nodded.

'Do not look so shocked. They say King Edward, her father, did the same when the French prince ended his betrothal to her – though he was no more successful than King Richard has been so far. If the rumour is true.'

'But Tudor is an enemy. Why would they do that?'

Elen's lips twitched, though whether in a smile or a grimace I could not tell.

'Because there are many ways of turning an enemy into a friend, Matthew. To offer them a young lady – and the land and wealth and titles that come with her – is one of them. Perhaps the best one if you are a king.'

In the silence that followed my mind flitted to another such case. Almost without thought I asked,

'Is that why Alys was promised in marriage to Ralph Soulsby?'

Elen stiffened as though offended by the question, but maybe it was pain rather. Her dark eyes glistened like molten glass in the candle's gleam.

'In a way, perhaps. Though Lord Soulsby has long been an ally, not an enemy, of the King, and King Edward before him, for all that his brother was a traitor.' She hesitated. 'Yet perhaps that is another reason to hope Lady Elizabeth will marry someone other than Henry Tudor. Alys might go to Portugal or another royal household with her, if the Soulsbys would give up their claim to her. We can but hope it will happen.'

Even though it would take her far from me too...

'And,' added Elen, casting a glance about her again with a small conspiratorial smile, 'for Lady Elizabeth's sake. She told Alys she would refuse to marry Tudor if she could. Not only has she never met him, but she says she knows his mother, Lady Stanley, too well to want her for a mother-in-law.'

I joined her in her smile, Alys's words about that lady's actions at the coronation and after coming unbidden to my memory. Yet still the effect of such a change for myself pricked at my mind.

'If it should happen, I wonder whether we can remain friends. Portugal is so very far away.'

Indeed I had only a vague idea of where it was. I had not often encountered its merchants in London – never in York – although I knew them to be dark of skin like those of the Spanish kingdoms – and to be courageous seafarers who had for generations traded with distant lands.

Elen's eyelashes fluttered down again, hiding her eyes from my sight, as she said, her voice a little husky,

'I'm sure we can. Whatever distance should separate us all. And we do not know what will happen yet.'

Silence reigned. The candle guttered, throwing flickering shadows across the walls and making the fantastic beasts leap and gambol on my master's fine silk tapestries.

Then Elen stood, her abrupt movement dislodging Murrey, who had been lying asleep across her small booted feet.

'I must go, before it grows too late.'

'I'm sure my master will send a serving man with you to guard you.'

'There is no need. My groom —'

'Was no defence against Hugh.'

She waited while I called a household servant to send in search of the mistress. As he scurried away, she laid a hand upon my arm.

'Thank you, Matthew. It has been good to see you after all this time. I – I know Alys has missed your company, and she – we both welcome your letters, and all your news. Your life is so much more interesting than our own.'

Her words surprised me. For me the life of a simple apprentice could never match that lived by fine ladies and gentlemen at court.

'But,' she went on, 'Alys says it would be safer to use the code more often now. She says we can never know what spies there may be in Elizabeth's household – or at court. I think she is being perhaps a little dramatic. But all these rumours and intrigues have to start somewhere.'

305

Master Lyndsey the steward himself came to escort Elen to the stables. There her palfrey and groom stood waiting, along with one of Master Ashley's own stable lads, hefting a halberd in case there should be cutpurses or footpads lying in wait on the journey back to Westminster. Affixed to the groom's saddle was a covered basket, no doubt a gift of fruit and autumn blooms picked from the garden for Lady Elizabeth's household.

Once mounted, Elen leaned down to offer me her gloved hand. As I pressed my lips to it in farewell, she said softly,

'Stay in touch, Matthew. And be sure to tell us of your mother's happy event when it comes. I so long to hear news of your new baby brother or sister.'

I watched her ride away into the darkness flanked by both grooms, until the twinkling of their lanterns turned a distant corner and could be seen no more. And as I retraced my steps to the light and warmth of my master's house, I marvelled for the first time at all she had said. In the many months I had known Elen, she had not uttered half so much before. Yet in all that evening, only once, perhaps twice, had she spoken of herself.

Elen's prospects, her future, were at least as uncertain as those of Alys, or the Lady Elizabeth, yet her thoughts and words were only for them. What were her own dreams and desires?

But then she, like myself, was but a small person, entangled in the lives and affairs of those greater than ourselves. We had little say or sway over events, or even, sometimes, choice in the paths that we had to follow.

14

The Light Fades

Another autumn. Another Advent. Another Christmas-time.
Another chill, grey London winter.

Alys was as good as her word – or as Elen's, at least. Once
the physician pronounced her wrist healed, she took up her quill
again and penned more of her usual lively letters – even if they
were shorter and not so frequent as they had once been. Perhaps
her duties were more onerous now she was a young lady at court,
or perhaps it was the tedium of always writing in code. But, still,
they were full of the colour and finery of the royal festivities of
which she and Elizabeth were a part.

And her words about the King and Queen heartened me,
filling me with the good cheer suitable to the Christmas season –
although amongst her happy news was the faintest of shadows on
the horizon.

*During Christmas they have looked happier than I had seen
them for months, at least since that terrible time in the
spring. The Queen and Elizabeth and all the ladies have
been wearing the most sumptuous gowns of cream and gold,
while the gentlemen have dressed mostly in blues and greys.
But on Twelfth Night – what a spectacle! We were all clad in
red or gold, like flames in the great fireplaces of the palace.
The Queen had made a gift to Elizabeth of a gown exactly
like her own, and the King had presented them both with the
most beautiful jewels. He then led both of them out to dance
while everyone cheered and clapped.*

*We learned later that earlier in the day the King had
been brought reports that Henry Tudor is again planning an
invasion in the summer. Lady Tyrell told us that the King
was pleased, saying he wished to deal with that problem
once and for all.*

*I do hope you have enjoyed Christmas too. Did
Master Ashley and his family wait on you apprentices topsy-
turvy fashion like last year? I meant to suggest that to the
King and Queen this Christmas season. I hope your new*

*baby brother is still well. The Queen laughed with delight
when I told her your father had named him Richard in
thanks for all that the King has done for you. She said that
on her next trip to York, she will visit your mother to thank
her, though that will not be before springtime at the earliest.
Do you think that will be time enough for your mother to
prepare?!*

In friendship,
Alys

And so 1484 had turned into 1485.

Then, with no warning, came shattering news, as
heartbreaking in its way as the news of Ed's death almost a year
before.

A glorious morning in early spring. I was at work with
Simon and Master Ashley in the counting house. A huge leather-
bound ledger lay upon the table before me and I was busy tallying
up the figures neatly written in long columns on the open page. But
gradually the numbers grew dim and the sunlight streaming into
the room faded.

A quizzical look touched Master Ashley's face and he
went to open the door.

Cries of alarm filtered in from the distant streets. But my
master, glancing upwards, only laughed.

'Come, boys,' he said, beckoning to us.

Bemused, I laid down my quill and, with Simon, followed
him out of the doorway.

As we walked down the narrow alley, no clouds darkened
the ribbon of sky above us, and few enough floated in the expanse
that opened up when we emerged on to the tiny riverside wharf.
But all colour was bleeding from the heavens, the world around us
turning grey as though night were falling.

On all sides wharvesmen were muttering prayers, dropping
to their knees, crossing themselves. Out on the water boats drifted
with the current as sailors and steersmen likewise abandoned their
tasks.

But Master Ashley remained standing, pointing towards
the far bank.

'There, boys, look at that. Do you see?'

A single ray of sunlight glinted off the blue stone of the
ring on his index finger, but I looked beyond it, past the tower of

Southwark Priory across the river, darkest black now against the grey sky. And I saw.

It was as though the sun were a lantern partly shuttered, its light now coming only from a thin crescent like a fiery new moon, its horns pointing earthwards. A dark, dense disc blotted out its radiance, moving slowly, oh so slowly, across it. Then my eyes hurt and I had to look away.

'Mother of God!' Simon's voice, beside me, was muffled.

'Do not be afraid,' said Master Ashley. 'It has been foretold by learned men and is not a portent of evil things. It is just the dance of the spheres in the heavens, as the ancients explained. The moon travels across the sun and hides his light from our sight. Soon she will move on and day will return.'

And so it did. But not before long minutes had passed, as that dark shadow crawled further across the failing orb, and dread had gripped my heart also.

In the eerie twilight, the birds ceased their song, but the men's quiet pleas to God and the Virgin Mary murmured on, vying with the slap of water against the wharf timbers. On the river, lamps were raised on masts, casting strange glimmers across the black oily waters. And from far to the west, a vast distance behind us, a single bell tolled. Its sad note crept through the darkness, giving a rhythm to the mumbled prayers, as slowly, so slowly, the light seeped back into the world.

Only later did we discover why the great bell of Westminster Abbey had rung. Master Ashley, it seemed, had been wrong about the bad omen. As the light of the sun had drained away, so too had the light of the King's life. Queen Anne was dead.

A letter arrived from Alys a few days later. It could hardly contain her sadness. Sorrow flowed from every word she wrote.

She told of her visit to the Queen the day before her death, of how that lady lay pale and thin and exhausted after her long struggle with illness, her hand cold to the touch beneath the furs and rich coverlets of her sickbed. Of how her voice rose scarce above a whisper as she told Alys to be good and obedient and to live her life well. As she joined her in a simple prayer and then bid her farewell.

I recognized the stain of tears on the letter and could barely hold back my own, though it had been long since last I had seen Her Grace.

Murrey pressed her wet nose against the hand that held the letter and whined, her brown eyes wide gazing up at me. I caressed her head, but read on. She leaned her flank against my leg as though to warm it. As so often she was a much-needed comfort.

What makes it even sadder – if that's possible – is that one of Elizabeth's ladies says the Queen may have been with child. That may have made things worse, or even have been why she was ill. If that were true, and not just another rumour, it might explain the King and Queen's happiness at Christmas-tide, especially after losing poor Ed. But if it were that that led to Her Grace's death...

I asked Elizabeth if she was not afraid of what might happen in her own marriage when it came. She just laughed and said her mother and grandmothers had had lots of babies, without problems, and it's well known that that is what's important for girls. I think she can't wait to marry – though no plans have been spoken of recently – not since the Queen became ill...

As I read the final expressions of friendship in Alys's letter, my thoughts were only of her words about the Queen, and then the Lady Elizabeth. Was Alys afraid for herself? She had never struck me as someone who thought that having lots of babies was important for girls. But perhaps the knowledge that she herself was destined to marry Ralph Soulsby – and presumably bear his children – was becoming all too real.

A week later, I slipped away from my duties in the city to stand with my cap in my hand and head bowed as Her Grace, the late Queen, was carried in her richly carved oak coffin the short distance from the Palace to Westminster Abbey. Many in the dense crowd around me, both men and women, wept openly, mourning this beloved daughter of the Kingmaker, as the great bell of the Abbey tolled for her final journey.

I learnt afterwards that, in keeping with age-old tradition, her husband was not seen to attend the solemn requiem Mass or witness her body being lowered into her grave near the high altar as the choir sang the Te Deum. But I recalled our evenings together in the private chamber of the castle at Middleham, the lady's careful training of a boy to sing her husband's favourite songs, a toast with a silver cup before a hunt, the kiss of a hand, a man staring into a fire as he thought of his family far away, his grief on the day he learned of his brother's death, the swinging of a small son into the air in the joy of a return. And my heart ached for the loneliness of a king.

15

'Still the Chivalrous Knight'

I stood waiting at the panelled oak doors. My heart thumped fast inside my chest and below it bubbled up an unsettling sensation like a pit of serpents coiling and uncoiling within me.

I had not thought ever to stand here again, and now that I did... would my nervousness overmaster me?

The guards to either side, resplendent in their murrey and blue livery, were motionless, but their eyes watched my every movement. I had already straightened my doublet, dragged my hand through my unruly hair, ordered Murrey to sit close against my boot. Now, as a murmur of voices trickled from beyond the doors, I forced myself to study the beautiful grain of the wood, casting my thoughts back over why I was here, in hopes that it would steady me.

The message had arrived a few days before. At first I had not known what to do. Surely I could not be so bold as to do what it asked? Then, my mind at last made up, I had come as soon as I could, before my fears got the better of me. For what it would be worth. I had little expectation of success.

As I waited, my restless fingers brushed the corner of the letter folded up in my pouch.

Dear Matthew
Forgive me for writing, but I know that Alys won't – her pride won't let her. She thinks because she is now a lady of wealth and position, she must suffer in silence. But I don't see why she should – not while there is still one person left who might help her.

We've tried everyone else, all her friends at court or elsewhere, but they all say the same thing – that her marriage has been arranged and she must go through with it.

But I remember you saying that the King – when he was still the Duke – and his brother King Edward before him, after you saved little Edward on the boar hunt – they said that if they could ever help you, you need only ask. Alys

was with you on that day in the snowstorm. If you can get to
see King Richard, surely he'll not refuse your request?

    Dame Grey always said Alys should marry once she
turns fifteen, but Lady Elizabeth persuaded her mother to
wait until after the summer. She wants Alys to attend her as
long as possible, perhaps until her own wedding – though
we still don't know when that will be. But now we hear Lord
Soulsby is becoming impatient.

    They say the King is planning to leave Westminster
for Windsor and then the north in the middle of this month,
so there isn't much time.

    Please, Matthew, try to see the King and do what
you can. Alys will ever thank you.

    Your good friend,
    Elen

So, begging from Master de Vries an early end to my
day's work, I had ridden on Bess out towards Westminster, and
made my way from the streets into the royal stables. Once there,
enough stable boys and household servants recognized me – or, if
the truth is told, Murrey and her dancing – for me soon to be
ushered into the chamber of the King's secretary.

Master Kendall had welcomed me with a smile, almost
soothing my worries at my impudence, and he agreed to take my
boar badge to the King on my behalf. But it was a full hour or
more after he left, when the hollow deep in my stomach was
roiling again, that a servant had finally come to guide me through
the maze of passageways to these doors.

At last one of them opened, and the servant waved me
through.

'Master Matthew Wansford, Your Grace,' he announced,
before bowing and backing out of the room, leaving me standing
there alone. On the hard stone floor of the private chamber of the
King of England.

The room had changed little from the late winter's day
more than two years ago when I had been ushered into it before.
As then, a fire was even blazing in the cavernous fireplace, this
May-time being unseasonably cold. All that was missing was the
colourful swarm of noble lords and ladies – and, to my relief, the
many cages and their imprisoned songbirds. The only sounds as I

straightened up from my deepest bow were the hiss of the flaming logs and a voice I did not know, fussing.

'If Your Grace would please be still, just a little longer, I can perhaps finish this evening, and then I need bother you no more.'

In one of the wide bays of the chamber were two figures, flooded by the late afternoon sun streaming in through the windows.

Closest to me was the man who had spoken. His back towards me, he was standing at an easel, dabbing with a fine-tipped brush at a painting upon it.

Forgetting my fears for a moment, I stepped forward to gain a better view. It was plainly intended as a portrait of King Richard, but in truth it was very different to the man seated in a carved and gilded chair beyond.

There was an unnatural stillness to the painted, unfurrowed brow and the distant, haunted gaze of the blue eyes below it. A gem-encrusted chain was draped across shoulders arrayed in a sumptuous embroidered gown of crimson and gold. In the one suggestion of movement, the long thin fingers of one hand played with a unadorned ring on the third finger of the other.

But the man who sat deep within the window recess was clad all in unornamented black. And far from unlined, his face was pale and drawn, dark shadows beneath his eyes, his lips pinched. In looks he had aged more than just the year or two that had passed since my last glimpse of him – from afar on his triumphant return after the rebellion.

Yet, as I recalled the events of those brief years, particularly the sorrows of recent months, it was a marvel to me that he – king of all this great land – should catch sight of me and smile in recognition of a mere page. He beckoned to me, and a light and life shone in his eyes that were not captured on the canvas.

'Matthew. It has been a long time since last we saw you. Come forward.'

My insides lurched again, but I did his bidding, kneeling before him and kissing the great jewelled ring on his hand, as I had seen him do to his nephew Edward – as seemed so very long ago. His hand rested an instant on the top of my head before the painter tutted.

'Your Grace, please. How am I to capture your likeness if you will keep moving?'

'Will you wait awhile, lad?' the King murmured, and I withdrew a little to one side. Finding a footstool nearby, I sat with Murrey curling round my ankles, grateful to watch the scene and allow my nerves time to settle.

Also in the room, at the end distant from the artist's tableau, several gentlemen were talking in hushed tones, gathered about a table upon which was strewn a mess of papers. Master Kendall winked at me and Lord Lovell nodded in recognition, but the unknown faces of the others expressed surprise, as though unused to seeing a boy such as me in the King's private chamber. But they continued their discussion, one from time to time carrying a document to the King to sign. He would take each paper and read it through, before flourishing the quill handed to him, perhaps turning to comment or ask a question. In between times his black-shod foot tapped as though in impatience, or he twisted his red-stoned signet ring as I had seen many times before.

A frown like gathering thunderclouds grew on the painter's face and he moistened his lips with his tongue as though about to speak again. Perhaps King Richard also noticed, for, before a word was uttered, he sprang to his feet and clapped his hands.

'Enough! No more today,' he cried. 'We shall finish another time – if more time is really needed.'

'But, Your Grace,' the man protested.

'No more, I say. Get out, get out!' And the King flapped his hands towards him as if he were actually going to shoo him out of the room.

Flustered, the painter collected his things together and bowed his way from the chamber. Soon only the easel, the painting upon it and the faint echo of his retreating footsteps remained.

Lord Lovell laughed.

'Dickon, you terrify that man. You have done it so often now. If you are not careful, he will depict you as a tyrant.'

'Me? It is he who is the tyrant. With his "Pray be still, Your Grace," "Just one more sitting, Your Grace," "Perhaps another hour in the morning when the light will be better, Your Grace." How many hours does it take to paint one man's face? Does he not understand I have work to do in the mornings?'

'And in the afternoons and evenings, Your Grace,' said Master Kendall, advancing with another document for the King's signature.

Sighing, the King took up his quill again.

'Yes, indeed, John. But let this be the last today. There may be other more pressing matters needing my attention.'

As he bent his head to read the paper, his glance flicked towards me, and curving his lips was that half-smile I well remembered. Heat rose in my face and my stomach churned again at the thought of why I was here – in contrast with the important royal business he had no doubt been conducting.

Within a few minutes all the gentlemen filed from the chamber. I stood out of respect. Lord Lovell inclined his head once more as he passed and Master Kendall patted me on the shoulder, murmuring words of encouragement. Then the King and I were alone.

Going to the table, he poured ruby-red wine into two long-stemmed glasses. He handed one to me and took the other over to the easel. His expression was unreadable as he inspected the painting. Then he glanced across to me, where I stood waiting for him to speak.

'Well, Matthew. It has indeed been a long time. It seems that you have grown.'

I bowed low. 'But not so very much, Your Grace. No more than you might expect.'

King Richard laughed that short laugh of his.

'No, perhaps not. But you are yet young, and have time ahead of you. Does Master Ashley feed you well?'

'Aye, Your Grace – meat or fish every day, save on fast days. He is a good master – I thank you for that.'

'You are most welcome.'

He eyed me a moment, then, stepping back towards the crackling fire, waved me to a seat. It was an ornate, high-backed, cushioned chair this time, not a footstool, and he settled himself into its twin across the hearth. In one hand he cradled his wine-glass and, now, in the other was my silver boar badge. His fingers turned it over and over, his eyes following the lights it caught and scattered from the flames.

My training as a page had taught me that I must not speak before he did. Yet several minutes passed in silence. Perhaps unwisely, I took refuge in swallows of the rich, smooth wine, seeking to quell the nerves rising again within me. I had drained almost half the glass before the King spoke.

'They told me you wished to see me, but couldn't tell me why.'

'That's because I didn't – I – couldn't tell them.'

'Couldn't?' Looking up, he raised one eyebrow. 'Why? Is it a matter of honour again? About a lady?'

My memory was sharp of that morning at Middleham more than two years before – the day of my beating. When I had told him of my letter to Alys, but refused to say how it had fallen into Hugh's hands – that he had snatched it from Elen. Did the King remember that too? Had he ever known who the 'lady' had been?

'In a way, yes, Your Grace.'

'You have not changed your tune then? Still the chivalrous knight?'

That stung a little. But he could not know of all the hours I had trained since leaving his service, mostly alone, learning to wield my chestnut sword. And I knew it was not meant unkindly.

I bowed my head.

'It's about Alys, Your Grace.'

'Alys Langdown? Then you are still friends?'

'Aye... At least, I think so. I haven't seen her for almost two years. Since your coronation. And then only from a distance.'

The King sat back a little in his chair.

'Ah, that was a day to remember. And yet... it was a difficult time, that summer —' He frowned, then his eyes cleared, snapping back to me. 'But what is this about Alys? She is well, is she not? I understand she attends my niece.'

'Yes, Your Grace. I believe she is well. It's just that she...'

'Yes?'

'She is to be married. This summer. To Ralph Soulsby.' I hesitated. The King continued to watch me.

'And?'

'She doesn't wish it, my lord.'

'Why not?'

'Because... because she has not chosen her husband herself.'

'That is usual for a young lady of noble birth.'

'But she doesn't even know him. Not really. She's met him only once – years ago.' I searched my memory for Alys's tale about Ralph long ago at Middleham. 'She was just a little girl, no more than eight or nine, and he was spiteful to her. She says he had just been made squire when he came across her reading in the Duchess's garden. He took away her books and threw them down the well because he said girls should not be taught to read and write.'

'That was a long time ago, Matt. People can change – they often do.'

'But if he was a bully then... Your Grace, please can you stop this marriage?'

King Richard was quiet for a moment, as though considering. But then –

'I'm afraid I cannot. Alys is a ward of Dame Grey herself, not the crown. Alys's mother was one of her ladies. When... when Elizabeth was Queen, she arranged the marriage to secure the loyalty of Ralph's family for the King, my brother. She has not chosen to break the betrothal since.'

'But now you are King, Your Grace. Surely you could step in and prevent it?'

'But, Matthew, as King I also need the loyalty of the Soulsbys and their allies. That has not changed. Nor, to my knowledge, has Elizabeth's mind on the matter. And you may not have cause to worry – love can grow after marriage, even when that is arranged. I saw it with my parents.'

His gaze drifted towards the fire's glow as he took a sip from his wine-glass.

I knew I should leave it there, that I shouldn't argue with a king – no matter how much familiarity he had allowed, both this evening and in times past. But for Alys's sake – and maybe the wine I'd drunk was half to blame – I carried on, not thinking at first what I was saying.

'But, Your Grace, you married for love, didn't you?'

His glance swung back to me, and I realized what I had done – barely more than a month after he had buried his beloved wife.

But in his face was no anger at my words, if that was what I feared. Far worse was the deep sorrow inscribed there, in the shadow darkening his eyes and the twisting of his mouth.

It was a moment before he mastered his emotion and said in a soft voice,

'So I did, Matt, so I did. But a king must look on these matters differently – as I have learnt. Marriages are not just about two people. They're about families, dynasties, countries even.' He swallowed another mouthful of wine, before placing the glass on a small table at his elbow. 'My brother also married for love – twice. And see the outcome of that.'

He chose a sweetmeat from a dish on the table and leaned down to entice Murrey away from my feet. As always when food was offered, she deserted me to go and beg for the tidbit. The firelight glinted in the King's eyes as the hound danced her pirouette for him.

'It may be that you and Alys can remain friends after her marriage.'

'I don't think that will be possible, my lord. I cannot think Lord Soulsby would allow it. He objected to my letters before.'

My words, the tone – their impudence struck me to shame, but it was too late to bite them back. Yet the King remained calm, as Murrey sat to attention, awaiting another treat.

'I was sorry to send you away, Matt. But I could not jeopardize Lord Soulsby's loyalty to my brother. His family had turned traitor before and Edward had worked hard to win them back to his cause. It is difficult always to keep noble men happy, as I have found too. Had it been up to me, I would have laughed off Hugh's tale-telling and kept you with us.' He coaxed Murrey to dance again, slipping her another morsel and smoothing the dark red tufts of her fur. 'My wife especially was sad to see you leave.'

'She was very kind to me. From my first days at the castle.'

Silence enshrouded us.

The King's hand rested still on Murrey's poll, his own head bowed.

Was he caught up in memories, as was I? Of that first time I had seen the Queen – Duchess as she was then – step down from her carriage to the cheers of the household. When she spoke to me that evening of all my troubles and asked me to sing. Her tears as she listened to the French lovers' lament.

Perhaps, again, I should not have spoken. Perhaps my shame and regret goaded me, making me think I could make amend. Once more the words spilled out before I could check them.

'Her Grace told me then – the first time I saw her – that if she were to die, she wished that you would marry again.'

Another silence.

Then he said softly, 'All those weeks of her illness, we did not speak of it – I – I could not speak of it.'

'She said – she said, it was so that you might be happy again, and because she hoped Ed would have a brother or sister.'

He raised his head and the pain in his eyes was raw. And as he spoke again it was as though I, a boy only, were not there.

'My wife dearly wanted more children. But after Ed was born, the physicians counselled her against it – warned us it might kill her. And then, when Ed died —'

He broke off. Reaching for his wine-glass, he sat back again and took another gulp. Twisting the glass about in his hands, he watched the swirl of the crimson liquid for a moment or two.

'My advisors also urge me to marry again, that I must have an heir. But – it is too soon, much too soon. And not, of course, my niece. That poisonous rumour...'

I knew, of course, what he meant.

It had been all round London, not long after Queen Anne's death. The whisper that the King planned to marry his brother's daughter, Elizabeth – to gain an heir, to appease the Woodvilles – to thwart Henry Tudor's plans. So far had the rumour spread – it even reached the ears of my family in faraway York – that the King had been forced to deny it publicly in front of the mayor and citizens of London.

Alys had been most indignant, both for the King and for Elizabeth. She abandoned the code and her handwriting became spiky and ragged, the quill point almost tearing through the paper at her angry underlinings.

How ridiculous it is! She's his <u>niece</u>, and he's so much <u>older</u> than her, and she's... well, if her brother could not be king, what advantage could King Richard gain from marrying <u>her</u>? Why do people not <u>think</u> before they repeat these things?

Elizabeth is mortified. She says that she has grown to <u>like</u> her uncle, now that she knows him better, but she could never <u>love</u> him like <u>that</u>! She'd much rather marry 'her' Duke Manuel. He's nearly the same age as her, and her friend Lady Brampton has told her so much about the *beauties of Portugal. She so longs to marry. She can't understand why it's taking so long to arrange...*

Watching King Richard now, perhaps that delay was no mystery. He had been quick to dismiss his gentlemen, as though he had no heart to continue his business. A tiredness hung about him, a heaviness, that brought to mind the tail-end of our Christmas-time at his brother's court.

And also into my mind nudged the image of my own father in the weeks after my mother's death – when he was not seen at his workplace for days on end. It had been as though he could not bear to think that his own life would go on as normal. Only a visit from his great friend the mayor persuaded him that he must pick himself up and carry on – otherwise his business would fail and his children starve. And then, later, came the gentle smiles and soft words of the nursemaid who became my new mother.

Again, unbidden – except perhaps by the wine – I spoke up.

'My father married again. Some months after my mother died. For weeks, though, I think he wished he could join her. But now he is very happy. And I have another brother.'

This time, perhaps, I did not need to worry that I had spoken out of turn. A faint smile played around the King's lips – hard to discern in the fading daylight and the flickering fireglow, but it was there.

He raised his wine-glass as though to toast me.

'All my advisors say the same, Matt – all have a similar story to tell me. Yours, at least, I know to be true. And I thank you for it.'

Placing the glass down again... was that a sigh as he did?

'Were my life to end tomorrow – yes, sometimes I wish I could join my wife and son. But life goes on... Your father is a fortunate man. To have found happiness twice in his life. And to have such a son as you.'

I thanked the saints for the failing light. Colour was rising in my cheeks and a boy of my age was too old to be seen blushing like a child.

The King perhaps didn't notice.

'Well, I shall make a bargain with you. I shall consider your advice on remarriage if – ' I waited for what I should have to do – 'if you continue to wear my badge loyally and come to me again when I am in need.'

'But, Your Grace...'

Now I was confused, as his hand stretched out towards me, the silver boar on the palm gleaming in the firelight. The words of our last conversation at Northampton, when he had first handed it to me, tumbled through my brain.

'Your Grace, it was I who came to you with my request.'

His half-smile became a half-laugh.

'Aye, so it was. And yet it seems to have been you who has helped me. At my present time of need. So I shall make an addition to our bargain. I will ask Dame Grey to reconsider Alys's marriage. I can promise nothing, mind – legally I have no right to ask, so do not raise your hopes or hers too high. Do we have a deal?'

'Of course, Your Grace. Thank you.'

I took the badge and pinned it to my doublet in its usual place, over my heart. I sensed his eyes following the practised movement.

'You still wear it proudly, I see.'

'Aye, sir, and always shall. And... and loyalty will always bind me.'

Those words of his motto had not crossed my lips in two long years since riding with... with another King on the road to St Albans – Edward, the boy King as was... When he had passed me the fragment of parchment with this King's signature on it. That scrap remained in my bundle with other treasures I had collected, safe alongside all the letters from my friends in the Order, Ed's drawings, the book his mother had given me and the shiny coin Master Ratcliffe had handed me at our last brief meeting.

King Richard thrust out his hand, but to my surprise, not for me to kiss his great ring of state, rather to shake my own.

'I thank you for that, Matt. Loyalty freely given is beyond any price. I have not forgotten that you were ever a true friend to my son.'

'And he – and you – were ever friends to me.'

Then all my sadness from the past year welled up in me.

I bowed low to hide the tears that were shining in my eyes, and, as the King bid me farewell, I backed out of the room, still bowing, as I had seen the servant do earlier. Minutes later, as I passed through the towering gatehouse of the palace, it struck me that, for the first time ever, I had not sung for my lord, the King. Would I ever have another chance?

That night I begged a rushlight from Master Lyndsey and sat up late composing, for once, a letter to Elen. It saddened me that I could not write with better news, but I hoped that such a promise from the King would be welcome. But I received no reply. Only some time later did I learn that the Lady Elizabeth and her household had already travelled north to join Ed's cousins, the young earls of Warwick and Lincoln, at Sheriff Hutton.

Alys's letters also ceased. Did she no longer want to write to me as I had failed in my task? Or had she been warned off because of her coming marriage?

The lack of letters from Roger – also of course at Sheriff Hutton – was nothing strange. Perhaps the Order was truly at an end, despite our solemn oaths, and I would have to seek for new friends in my future life. But I resolved that I would ever be true to my own pledges.

And so spring turned towards summer.

16

Dangerous Days

The month of May drew on and the King left the capital as Elen had written, wending his way north to his castle at Nottingham, crouched on its crag at the very centre of his kingdom. There he seemed to be waiting.

For rumours were being blown about London like the blossom of fruit trees in my master's garden, scattered by every early summer squall. Henry Tudor would invade. Henry Tudor was on his way. Henry Tudor would land in the south, the east, the west. Never the north, of course. Troops were gathering at all compass points, ready to march to the defence of the King and his kingdom wherever they were needed.

One letter I did receive that summer was from my brother Fred, telling me that he was joining a company of archers. His words brimmed with his excitement.

We are to be ready at half a day's notice, with all our gear to hand, to march wheresoever needed to serve the King.

Our father speaks with pride of his grandfather, who told his tales of the great battle at Agincourt, where he fought with the fifth King Henry. He says, if Tudor lands in England, I too will be fighting the French, as it is only they who support him in his claim to the English throne. Or perhaps King Richard will take the fight to France. Then I will travel to foreign lands like you and our great-grandsire.

My brother, an archer fighting for the King.

Hugh Soulsby – last seen wearing the King's livery.

Troops of soldiers in the colours of great lords daily marching through the London streets.

Enormous cannons, barrels of gunpowder, piles of armour and weapons, hauled on wagons from the Tower out towards the city gates, or shipped on barges across the river.

Everyone was ready to fight for our good King Richard.

Except me – an apprentice only, fingers stained with ink, not calloused by the bowstring, neither donning armour nor gathering equipment ready to rally to the royal banner. And yet I wore his badge. How could I serve my two masters loyally?

I redoubled my efforts with my wooden sword, ashamed though I was that it was all I had, that and Master Ashley's book on swordplay. Simon, whose ardour for weapons training had cooled after the great rebellion, now joined me when he could, fired by my tales of glorious battles and hard-won victories, half-remembered from my time with Master Fleete.

We hid away from the other apprentices, in whatever secluded corner of our master's garden we could find. There, for the first time, I bested another boy with my sword. But I had learned much from Ed too, and helped Simon to his feet, returning his chestnut weapon and praising him on his first attempts.

My footwork was already better than before, after almost two years of lone study, and Simon and I trained hard in our free hours, together exploring how we might improve. During the working day, I also took on more of the strenuous jobs, lifting, carrying, bales, barrels, the heavy bolts of cloth, the weighty platen of the printing press. I could feel myself growing fitter, stronger, as the summer wore on.

Then in the middle days of August came the news for which all appeared to have been waiting.

Henry Tudor had landed – in Wales. Almost as far away from the capital as he could.

With so much distance to cross between there and the centre of government – and with King Richard awaiting him already in the middle of the country – his must be an impossible task. As the King summoned to his side men from every part of his kingdom, east, west, south and north, surely the might of his army would prove too much for Tudor to challenge.

And yet, and yet... rumours again swirled about the streets of London, whisperings that all might not be well, that not all the lords would rally to the King's cause.

'They say some have not forgotten their Lancastrian allegiances,' Master Lyndsey told Master de Vries one morning as Simon and I laboured over the press, printing pages for a small religious book destined to be sold in country fairs. Though great matters were afoot, life and work continued as normal.

'What, despite the King's efforts to unify the country, and those of his brother before him?'

Master de Vries still did not understand English politics despite almost two years in London.

'No, indeed,' snorted the steward. 'Or perhaps that is just an excuse. Perhaps King Richard simply has not done enough for them personally.'

'Do you think that is so?'

'Well, he doesn't always hand out plum jobs and lands and costly gifts to buy men's loyalty as was done before. Nor does he uphold their claims against the common folk just because they are wealthy landowners. For him, justice is justice, no matter whether you are rich or poor.'

'And so he is resented by them?' Master de Vries shook his head in sadness. 'That in these days it should come to that!'

'Such men want to cling to the old ways,' said Master Lyndsey, taking up a close-printed page to check while he spoke. 'They complain that it is no longer enough to be of the right family, to have been born to power and wealth – they can no longer expect to keep them always. Nor to rule in courts of law as was their habit.'

'But the ordinary folk. They must be contented with this new order of things?'

Master Lyndsey laughed.

'There's little I know about such folk beyond the city walls. Perhaps it means little to them what King Richard does for their sakes – even making his laws in English so they can understand. But the merchants and artisans of London, now – they are well pleased with King Richard. His laws protect them and their trade – in England and abroad. To be sure, Matthew,' he turned to me, as I snatched a break from the heavy work to listen in, 'your father in York must feel the same? Merchants are merchants, wherever they may be.'

Indeed my father did – that I could confirm. In his letters he told of how his business was thriving, and how the new Council of the North was governing well, allowing the towns to prosper under the peace with the Scots. And he proclaimed, like Fred before him, that the free men of York and its surroundings would answer the King's summons at a moment's notice.

And yet the rumours continued to swirl. Ordinary men might be ready and willing to fight and die for their King, but perhaps not all the powerful nobles who commanded them.

Before another day passed, my mind was made up. I might be a boy only, just an apprentice, no knight or seasoned warrior, but I would travel to my King's side, to serve him in whatever way I could.

But first I had to gain my other master's permission.

I found him alone in his office after breakfast.

'Go to Nottingham, Master Wansford? You?'

Master Ashley's eyes narrowed as though I had asked him something he did not quite understand.

'Aye, master. To aid King Richard in his fight against Henry Tudor.'

'But, Matthew, the King will have an army of trained soldiers.'

'I have been training, sir, ever since I entered your service.'

'I know, lad, and you have done well to. But such troops train together under experienced captains. They know their commanders and how to obey in the heat of battle.'

My fear had been that Master Ashley would view my efforts as mere play, but he had not simply laughed at me. I was heartened by that, and resolved not to be put off.

'But, sir, men say that not all those commanders will prove loyal to His Grace. The Welsh chieftains have not yet moved to challenge Tudor on his march. They say perhaps even Lord Stanley —' I hesitated, remembering what the King himself had said about rumours – and this rumour was about one of his closest advisors – 'they say even Lord Stanley may play him false. Perhaps I can't make much of a difference, but he may need all the men he can gather.'

'That may be. These are dangerous days, Master Wansford, dangerous days.'

'Then let me go, sir, I beg you. I swear I will return once the King is victorious.'

A few seconds of silence. Master Ashley pursed his lips while he considered. Then,

'Very well, Matthew. You may attend the King. It may be that you will somehow be of service. But you must promise to keep yourself out of harm's way as much as you are able. You may take a note from me to Master Kendall. He will know how best you can serve His Grace – and you must follow any instructions he gives you to the letter.'

I stammered my thanks, not thinking too much on his words and only grateful for his leave to travel. In a few minutes he had, with his own hand, written a short message, imprinting the wax seal with his signet. He gave it to me, along with a handful of coins.

'Go to the armourer on Cheapside and buy yourself jack and sallet for your protection. Ask our cooks for provisions for the journey. And take the pony you brought with you from the north. I understand the King is mustering his army at the town of Leicester. Set off today and you may be able to ride there with men at arms from our city.'

He watched as I placed the money and note in my pouch, then added, his face sombre,

'Fare thee well on your journey and in your service, Matthew. And mind you obey Master Kendall in all he says.'

I swept off my cap and bowed, then hurried up to my attic room to collect some things for the journey. I was sorry not to speak to Simon before I left, but knew I should hasten on my way, and somehow felt this journey was one I must take alone. But I spared some moments to write a few lines of explanation to Alys at Sheriff Hutton where I assumed her to be.

It was only as I wrote the final words of code that the seriousness of what I was undertaking truly came home to me.

If I should not return, think kindly of me. I will have remained true to the Order's oath of loyalty and to the King.
    Qtdfqyd gnsix rj!*
    Your friend always,
    Matthew Wansford

Before my thoughts could dwell further on the dangers I might face, I sealed up my note and dropped it with Master Ashley's letters before making my way down to the kitchens. Half an hour later, I was astride Bess, riding to the heart of the working quarter of the city, a bag of food in my saddle bag, faithful Murrey at my heel.

17

The Camp

London had been busy in its preparations for war. As I waited impatiently at the armourers while men for the levies were kitted out before me. As some strapped on their padded jacks, tried sturdy sallets on for size on recently shorn heads, hefted new-made weapons. As their friends and colleagues, veterans of other battles, jeered and catcalled, arrayed already in their own gear, worn, but buffed and burnished for this coming campaign.

As I followed the long column of troops out under the dark stone arch of Newgate, their baggage wagons rumbling across the cobbles behind. As the gathered crowds, faces darkened with anger, cheered or shouted encouragement.

'Long live King Richard!'
'Death to the traitor!'
'Tear those French dogs to shreds!'
'A York!'

Yet it was all as nothing to the bustle and tumult as I rode Bess into the town of Leicester. The company of soldiers I had journeyed with halted in fields outside, awaiting further orders, but I pushed on, past outlying houses, towards the squat gateway through the town walls.

All around us streamed men in leather armour and bold liveries, hollering to soldiers coming out of the town and bumping against us.

'Out of the way, boy!'
'Move that scrawny animal off the road!'

Nervous, Bess shifted beneath me as we passed beneath the iron teeth of the portcullis. Once out of the darkness of the archway, I slipped down from her back and led her into the empty courtyard of a nearby church, its grey spire rising tall into the cloudless blue sky. With one hand stroking her velvet nose to calm her, I surveyed the scene before us.

The main street leading into the heart of the town was lined with shops, but today their store-fronts were battened up out of the way of a seething crush of men and beasts. It was amazing that any were managing to move at all, so pressed were they within that narrow lane. But as I watched some made minute headway in one or other direction.

Everywhere pennants fluttered aloft alongside the sharp steel of pikes, harness jingled, men shouted and laughed, oxen lowed as they towed creaking carts. Women and children leaned out of overhanging windows, their mouths agape at the sights. Some waved kerchiefs and hallooed like the crowds in London. Other faces were clouded with worry or fear. Over everything lay the reek of sweat mingled with the choking dust kicked up by all those feet and hooves and wheels on this warm August afternoon.

How would I find my way to Master Kendall through this strange and busy place?

As I hesitated, a more enticing scent wafted into my nostrils.

A girl about my own age was walking towards me, a tray loaded with rich brown pastries suspended by thick cords from her neck. The air above them shimmered. They must have come straight from the oven.

'Mutton pasty, master?' she asked. 'Only a penny each.'

My mouth watered. I still had bread and cheese in my pack from Master Ashley's kitchen, but it was a long time since I had tasted hot foot.

As I reached in my pouch for the coin, she wrapped a pastry in a clean cloth. I took it and thanked her. And here was a chance to discover what I needed to know.

'The King?' she replied, as I sank my teeth into the juicy pie. Warm gravy trickled from the corner of my mouth. 'I watched him ride out over Bow Bridge with his army this morning. A very beautiful sight it was – with crowds cheering and the sun shining on his golden crown and all the knights' armour.'

I wiped my chin with the cloth.

'He's already left? Then who are all these men?'

'Oh, they're just the stragglers, I suppose. I heard his lordship of Northumberland arrived only late yesterday, and some men from the south today.'

'The army must be very large.'

'Many thousands strong, I think. The King should easily beat the traitor. They say most of Tudor's men are in the pay of the French King or else are Welsh rebels.'

She spat on the dusty ground.

Heartened, I asked another question that had often been in my mind during my long ride north.

'Have the men of York joined the King already? They would wear livery bearing the white rose and sound like me when they spoke.' I now knew from long experience that my accent still marked me, and the northern speech of Fred and his fellows might be even more obvious.

She was quiet for a moment, as though counting back through all the soldiers she had come across over the past few days.

'I don't remember any such. But perhaps they were camped in the fields outside town. My father told me not to venture beyond the walls to sell my pasties.'

I thanked her again. After asking for directions, I finished the last crumbs of the tasty pie and moved off to find the road the King had taken hours before. Leading Bess and with Murrey sticking close, I pushed once more into the stream of men and animals that flowed through the streets of this small town.

As we skirted the high wall of a priory, its bells tolled the hour of vespers. I would have to hurry if I wished to find the King before darkness fell. Minutes later I was astride Bess once again, the west gate of Leicester receding behind us as we clattered up and over a hump-backed stone bridge spanning a rushing river.

Soon, as the narrow streets opened up into wide fields, the bustle lessened, but always there were soldiers to all sides. Men in the livery of the Earl of Northumberland were still breaking their camp and loading equipment on wagons and horses, and at my questions they waved me on in the way they would soon be going. I urged Bess into a trot as we passed into the rolling, thinly wooded countryside.

The red orb of the sun was resting on the horizon ahead when I finally came upon the royal army. Two guards wielding pikes blocked my path, but stood aside at the sight of my silver boar.

As I rode on, to either side the golden evening light lapped row after row of tents spreading across fields as far as I could see. It gleamed on the steel points of stacks of pikes and spears planted on the ground between them, and sparked on the helmets of men hurrying every which way, their calls ringing through the growing dusk. As the sun started its descent below the distant hills, camp fires flared all around and wood smoke was sharp in my nostrils.

Bess tossed her head in alarm as a strident clanging rang out to one side. A burly man was hammering at a dented breastplate, which caught and reflected beams of light from the sinking sun.

I swung down from the saddle and placed my hand on Murrey's head. Her fur bristled against my palm. As the clamour ceased, her low growl crept up to my ears. So, also, to those of the armourer.

Turning, he ran his eyes down me, then up again to my face, before saying,

'And whose company are you in, sir?'

Was that a hint of scorn in his voice? Yet, in the dying light his face appeared friendly enough.

'No man's company yet,' I said. 'But I seek Master John Kendall, the King's secretary.'

Again I tapped the badge pinned to my doublet.

He peered at it, then pointed to a ridge some distance away. Atop its crest stood a tent larger than the rest. Its sides glowed in vibrant reds and blues, and the last rays of sunlight touched to flame the sunburst and rose stitched on the banners flying from its crown. Upon one standard I spied also the proud, pure white boar of my old master, before a breath of wind folded it out of sight. Then the sun set and the camp was in darkness.

I touched my cap to the man in thanks and wound my way through the endless tents, fires, carts, piles of weapons and harness, groups of men and horses, keeping my eye always on the outline of the royal tent, black now against the deepening blue of the evening sky.

As I drew nearer, monstrous shadows loomed between lines of horses and into my nose, mixed with the mouth-watering aroma of soldiers' stews, wafted a peculiar acrid smell. Then the flicker of a cooking fire lit up a gaping bronze mouth and slanting barrel, and I knew these were the King's precious cannon, drawn all the way from the Tower of London. The evil stink hanging in the air was the stench of gunpowder.

More guards sprang up at my approach and this time two seized my arms. Their leader took my badge from me as I tried to explain. He frowned as he listened, the deep incised lines of the boar thrown into relief by the blazing brand in his hand.

'Seeking Master Kendall, and in the King's service? Are you a spy, boy?'

'No, sir,' I protested, but did not struggle. I had dropped Bess's rein, but kept hold of Murrey's collar, hearing the rumbling in her throat again. The men, though their grasp on me was tight, stood clear of her. 'I have a message from my master in London and seek only to serve His Grace.'

The man laughed.

'Be not so afraid, boy. One can be a spy and still serve His Grace. Several have come these past days with news of the traitor and his movements. Give me your message, then. We shall see it gets to Master Kendall.'

He held out his hand, but I shook my head.

'Sir, it is for Master Kendall alone. My master said I must hand it to him myself.'

The man raised an eyebrow in surprise, though his surprise could not be as great as my own as these words that spilled out unplanned. Yet he did not argue. He simply nodded and, turning, strode off up the ridge, his fellows marching me along behind him. Bess remained with the other guards, but Murrey trotted along beside me, my fingers still hooked through her collar. The firelight glinted in her eyes as her muzzle swept from side to side, as though questing for a scent.

Within yards of the royal tent crouched one far smaller, its sloping sides glimmering pale in the glow of nearby fires. We halted before it as the chief guard cleared his throat and called, 'Master Secretary?'

The tent flap was thrust aside and a familiar figure emerged, at first dark against the flickering light within. But then the guards' torches lit up the astonishment on Master Kendall's face.

'Matthew! For the love of God, what are you doing here? You should be safe back home in London.'

'You know this boy, sir? He says he has a message.'

'Yes, yes. I know him. You may leave him with me.'

He eyed me curiously as the guards released their grip and saluted him before marching back the way we had come. As their footsteps died away, he lifted the tent flap as though to usher me through.

I stood my ground.

'If you have a message for me, come in, Matthew – I will need light to read it by.'

But still I did not move. What prompted me, I don't know, but I heard myself say,

'Master, my message is for the King.'

'The King?'

'Aye, master. For him alone.'

He studied me a moment and I was thankful the nearest camp fires lay behind me – for I was blushing at this second lie. With my face in shadow, this tell-tale sign did not give me away, as he asked,

'Is it from Master Ashley?'

I nodded without speaking, fearing a tremor in my voice would reveal my untruth.

'Come, then.'

Amazed that my little subterfuge had again worked, I followed him the few paces up to the larger tent. Its now-unseen banners slapped against their poles far above. The canvas flaps were tied back, but a pale curtain was drawn across the entrance to keep out the night air. A warm glow and murmurs of voices and laughter seeped around its edges and the guards to either side snapped to attention as we approached.

'His Grace is within?' asked Master Kendall and, without waiting for an answer, he pulled aside the curtain and led the way inside.

Having seen the royal tent only from a distance before darkness had fallen, I was taken aback now at its size.

More than a man's height above my head, its canopied ceiling was supported by a complex skeleton of poles, and the space beneath almost equalled the great hall in Master Ashley's grand townhouse. In a far corner was an elaborate campbed swathed in luxurious red fabric, beside it a waist-high wooden chest on which stood a tall crucifix, several books and a variety of silver plate. To every side the canvas walls were hung with exquisitely embroidered tapestries, the vivid reds, golds, blues, greens shimmering in the gleam of the many torches lodged in iron brackets all around.

In the centre of it all, a stout oak table laden with platters, bowls, goblets and myriad papers was surrounded by standing men, the faces of several of whom I recognized as they turned towards us, Lord Lovell, Sir Richard Ratcliffe, the Earl of Northumberland among them. King Richard himself was seated in an intricately carved chair behind it.

He rose to his feet as Master Kendall and I bowed.

'Master Wansford, Your Grace. He brings you a message.'

The King strode round the table to stand in front of us before we even straightened up.

'Matthew?' His eyes were wide with surprise as I raised my head. 'Master Ashley has sent you to me?'

'Aye, Your Grace.'

I prayed that my rising colour wouldn't betray me now that my goal was so close. But even my small successes so far didn't prepare me for what happened next.

The King swung round to his gentlemen.

'Go about your business, sirs. Allow me some minutes with this boy.'

'But Richard —' protested Lord Lovell, but the King clapped him on the shoulder.

'Leave us, Francis. All may become clear in time. But now he and I must be alone.'

Lord Lovell nodded, some kind of understanding dawning on his face. He and the other gentlemen bowed low and withdrew, the entrance curtain falling gently into place behind them. Only Master Kendall remained.

The King turned to him.

'You too, John.' Master Kendall opened his mouth as if to object, but the King raised a hand to silence him. 'Though I would trust you with my life, John, that is not the issue here as you well know. And I have no more need of my secretary this night. Leave us.'

Master Kendall made again as though to speak, then, perhaps thinking better of it, bowed in his turn and followed the other gentlemen from the tent.

And I was alone with King Richard.

18

The Eve of Battle

He stood before me, his hand out-thrust.

I fumbled in my pouch for Master Ashley's letter. As I drew it out, a sudden pang of guilt griped at me. How dare I, a mere apprentice, lie and cheat my way into the presence of my King?

I dropped to my knees, passing the small square of parchment to him with my head lowered.

He murmured his thanks and moved away to the table. The tiny crack of the wax seal breaking reached my ears, then the crackle of unfolding parchment.

A short silence. Then,

'But this is to Master Kendall. Why are you wasting my time, boy?'

His voice was sharp.

I hung my head still, waiting for his rebuke. Why had I been so stupid?

But then came his familiar bark of a laugh.

'And just asking that you be found a job here.' Relief washed through me at his change of tone. 'Away from any danger, of course.'

My cheeks burned again and my fists curled into balls. Despite my earlier self-reproach, I leapt to my feet, ready to protest.

The King was leaning back against the table, watching me levelly, a half-smile on his lips.

'Nay, boy, do not be so quick to anger. Your master asks John to find you a job wherever you may be useful to me – as you are so keen to serve and so full of youthful foolishness. But, for himself, Master Ashley asks that you be kept from harm as he has many uses for you.'

I was not so used to his gentle mocking ways as I had once been and I jibbed at the words.

'Do not heed him, Your Grace. I want to serve you in the battle – I know it is coming.'

'Yes, it's coming. Tomorrow – did you know that?'

'Tomorrow?'

I swallowed, but found my throat dry. I had seen the camp, the soldiers, the weapons, but had no idea the battle would be so soon.

The King, however, appeared untroubled.

'Aye. Tudor and his forces are just a few miles from here, at Merevale my scouts tell me. Tomorrow we shall meet face to face with our armies at our backs.'

'Your Grace, I – I wish also to fight at your side.'

'I thank you for your brave loyalty, Matt, but you cannot fight. You have no armour.'

'I have my sallet and my jack, like many of your men. Master Ashley gave me money for them – he must have meant for me to wear them in the fight.'

'Or perhaps to protect you from the jibes and buffets of the older men. They may not take seriously your attempt to join them.'

I had no reply to that after my reception at Leicester. But the King considered me a moment, and his tone softened as he said,

'Yet, Master Wansford, you seem to have grown since last I saw you, though that was so short a time ago. Or is it just your sallet that makes you appear taller?'

I still wore my helmet, though in the presence of the King. Hastily I slipped it from my head and, to cover my embarrassment, said,

'My mother used to say that spring and summer are the time for growing, my lord. And I have been training hard to serve you.'

'Training?'

'Yes, my lord, as best I can. When Master Ashley can spare me from my duties.'

'That is commendable, Matthew. Every man should be prepared for war in case the call should come.' I smiled inside at his use of the word 'man', but then he added, 'Yet I have army enough, as you see. Brackenbury came with his London troops, and the Earl of Northumberland at last with his men from the north. Even Master Kendall will strap on armour tomorrow, though he is a man of words, not of the sword. How could one boy...?'

The rumours that had been circling in London sprang into my mind.

'But they say, Your Grace, that some great lords may not rally to your banner.'

'Is that what you have heard? And you feel that you can make up for the failures of such men?'

'They say the Welsh chieftains are marching with Henry Tudor. Even perhaps Lord Stanley...'

A shadow flitted across the King's face, then was gone.

'Lord Stanley? Aye, his family have betrayed my family before. In the past they have waited to see which way the wind will blow. But this time he will stand firm. He and his brother William... They will see that my army numbers several thousand more than Tudor's rabble of French mercenaries. They will see that the wind blows for the rightful King of England, not that half-Welsh traitor, no matter that he has the ear and money of the King of France. They will stand firm.'

'Yet Lady Stanley, Your Grace – is she not Tudor's mother? Did she not plot against you before?'

'Aye, lad, she did. But I spared her then and let her lands remain in her family. Her husband now speaks for her loyalty. And his son who is in my camp speaks for his.'

'My lord?'

'His son, Lord Strange, Tudor's stepbrother, is here at my pleasure. He is my guest,' a wry smile, 'or my hostage if you prefer. My brother Edward and I – we have forgiven the Stanleys often in the past. Now it does no harm to have a little insurance for their honour. He can remind his father and his uncle who has been the source of their prosperity, and who will reward them richly in the future. Sadly it seems that is the language such men understand.'

He pushed himself up from the table's edge and went to sit again in the great chair.

'But, Matthew, it is your fate we must attend to now. I have thought of the way you can best serve me. Are you ready to do my bidding?'

'Of course, Your Grace.'

'You shall help me by returning to London with an important message to your master.'

'But, my lord —' I protested.

'Matthew, I would not have you fight tomorrow, for all your training and your keenness and your leather armour. You are only a boy —' he raised his hand to stall my further objections,

338

'and I may have other uses for you once we have won our victory here. You have proved yourself valuable in my service before, and as King, I think perhaps I can make further use of you – if Master Ashley agrees to release you. I imagine Lord Soulsby will have forgotten your youthful misdemeanours by now, and surely can have no reason against my employing you again.'

What did his last words mean?

'Does Alys not have to marry Ralph now?'

'Dame Grey agreed to consider the matter. I have not yet had word of how it shall turn out. But Ralph and his father ride with Sir William Stanley. If all goes well tomorrow, they may look to be rewarded with more lands and wealth than even Alys Langdown can bring to them – and as King perhaps I can find another, greater heiress to satisfy them.'

Was he serious? His expression made me uncertain. And did Alys herself – far away as I believed in Sheriff Hutton – know anything of the matter? Yet I was sad for that other, unknown heiress – if she existed.

Whatever the case, though, I had to take the King at his word.

'Thank you, Your Grace. I will be for ever in your debt.'

'It is the privilege of a king to be able to reward all his followers, whether big or small, and one that I enjoy. But in the meantime, you can serve me best by delivering my message.'

This time I didn't protest. I would do my duty as my sovereign saw fit to order. Even if it were just a ploy to keep me safe from the fighting...

King Richard selected a quill and parchment from among the mess of writing equipment on the table and set to work writing with his own hand. This was a thing unseen by me before, as it had been with Master Ashley in London. At normal times both my masters relied on their secretaries. He took his time, consulting a book that lay among the papers, and it was several minutes before he folded the small sheet and dripped molten wax upon it to seal it. Then he walked around the desk and handed the note to me, together with a small leather purse.

'There, Matthew, my message, with expenses for your journey.' The purse clinked as my fingers closed around it. 'You must deliver the message into Master Ashley's own hands. Into no one else's. Do not use it to find your way into the presence of the

Archbishop of Canterbury – or of the Emperor or the Pope in Rome. No more deceptions please.'

I laughed and stowed the parchment square and purse in my pouch.

'No, Your Grace. I'm sorry.'

'Do not worry. It was but a small deception – and I'm grateful that it brought me such a messenger as you. You may perhaps travel more easily than one of my men, should tomorrow—'

He broke off, and perched once more on the edge of the table, fiddling with his signet ring.

''Do you still sing, Matthew?'

'Aye, my lord. Though —' Heat rushed to my face again. Once or twice in recent weeks my voice had faltered at the higher notes.

'Though you find that you are growing up? It comes to us all in time.'

'I can sing as well at the moment – I think. Would you like me to tonight?'

'Why not? For old time's sake. It may be the last time before...'

He swung away and poured deep red wine from a flagon into a pair of engraved silver goblets on the table. Handing one to me, he sat again in the oaken chair and raised his goblet.

'To old times. And old friends.'

We both drank. As the warmth of the wine coursed down my throat, I remembered other toasts he had made – at the boar hunt, the night before we had left Middleham, that evening in St Albans. Old times, indeed, and friends who were no longer with us.

I took another sip, then returned the goblet to the table.

'What would you have me sing, Your Grace? I have no lute with me.'

'You are still learning it?' I nodded. 'Master Ashley as ever keeps his promises. Something perhaps in English, Matt – our own fair tongue. And nothing sad on this eve, in case my soldiers shall think me melancholy.'

As he settled more comfortably in the chair, I reflected that such a song would be suitable for such a man – a King who was the first to write his laws in English, not in French, so ordinary people could understand them. And some in his kingdom found fault with that?

The first song I chose, in praise of our Holy Father, I had learnt at the Minster, one of very few the choir master had taught us that were not in Latin. But the second Master Petyt, the dancing master at Middleham, had himself composed, in memory, he had said, of his own youth spent touring from one castle to another, teaching lords' children to dance. The jauntiness of the melody set the King's foot tapping, and to my relief my voice soared to its heights without failing.

As the last notes died away, a rustling arose behind me.

Murrey, stretched out at my feet throughout, shot up and sprang towards the sound, snarling, her sharp white teeth bared, her lithe red body aquiver. The King also rose, a hand on his sword hilt, and I swung round to face whoever, whatever, had made the noise.

It was Lord Lovell, frozen halfway through the entrance, the pale curtain raised in one hand. Amazement was sketched across his face as he eyed the hound, standing bristling in his path.

Before I could call Murrey back and scold her for her ill manners, the King laughed.

'Let that be a warning to you, Francis. How should she know you are not a spy of Tudor's come to murder me?'

'If I were, Richard, would I come through the front door?'

'Then perhaps you must station guards all around my tent tonight. Or should my safety be left to one small hound alone? A brave little thing, is she not? And to think she was one of Florette's "runts".'

Lord Lovell edged forward, letting the curtain fall behind him, all the while keeping a wary eye on Murrey.

I whistled to her and she padded back to me. The whites of her eyes no longer showed and the fur on her back was smooth once again, the faintest rumble only in her throat. The King threw her a morsel of something from a platter on the table and she caught it and devoured it hungrily.

'Runt she may be,' said his lordship, 'but perhaps she should lie across your threshold tonight. You could do worse. Your young squire has asked to be allowed to join his uncle.'

'Young Hugh?' asked King Richard. I started at the name. 'And have you given him leave?'

'I thought it unwise to. After all, if Lord Stanley...'

341

His mouth clammed shut as his gaze slid towards me.

'We have one guest already, Francis,' the King replied, unperturbed. 'We will have no need of more. Let him go – if he can find his way to Stanley's camp through the darkness.'

'If you are sure, Richard?'

The King nodded.

With a final glance at Murrey, settled again at my feet, her head on her paws, Lord Lovell ducked out through the curtain back into the night.

The King sat back in his chair and swallowed a mouthful of wine, his face thoughtful.

I found my voice, heedless of whether I should speak.

'Hugh Soulsby is here?'

'As you heard – at least for the present.'

He watched me as I struggled to keep my feelings from showing on my face. But the light cast by the torches and the candles on the table was enough for his sharp eyes.

'You have not forgiven him?'

'Should I have?'

My question in reply was impertinent, but as so often, he did not notice – or chose not to.

'Perhaps. It is a long time ago. And maybe it was for the best.'

'That I should be sent away?'

'You have made a good life for yourself in London. You will learn a great deal with Master Ashley, have many opportunities other young men would give much to have.'

'If you say so, Your Grace.' Thinking back over all that I had missed these past two years – time with my friends, training as a squire like Roger – and Hugh – a touch of insolence crept into my voice. 'But perhaps not everyone forgives as easily as you.'

'It is not always easy to forgive, Matt. But sometimes it is necessary and repays the effort.'

'Will you forgive any who betray you tomorrow? Will you pardon Henry Tudor? Lord Stanley, if he should prove traitor?'

'Lord Stanley will stand firm. And there will be time enough after the battle to think of forgiveness – if it is needed.'

Did he truly believe his own words? I could not tell. But his calm half-smile made me ashamed of my outburst.

'But in the meantime, Matthew, you must be on your way. Your badge will take you safely back through my army. Find your way south to the old road that is Watling Street – that will take you directly to London. And mind you go straight to Master Ashley – that is most important.'

Once again it occurred to me that this supposedly vital message was no more than a ruse to send me away from the coming battle.

Before I knew what I was doing, I threw myself down on my knees.

'Not tonight, my lord. Let me take Hugh's place – let me be your page again and sleep at your threshold. Murrey and me – as Lord Lovell said. You know you can count on our loyalty.'

At first my plea was met only with silence. Perhaps my earlier words had angered the King? But then he spoke again.

'Very well, Matt. You may act as my page one more time. You and your brave little hound. But you must be away early, at first light – before the camp is fully awake.'

His amused tone reassured me he didn't hold my speech against me. But was he remembering, as I did now, the last time I had been his page? That morning at Northampton, when he had had to nudge me awake. When his life could have been in danger from the Woodville plotters.

Surely he didn't recall it. But I told myself I must not sleep at all this night, despite my long journey.

'Thank you, Your Grace, I won't fail you.'

The rest of that evening was a blur of busyness. Lord Lovell soon returned, along with Master Ratcliffe and other gentlemen I did not know. Before Murrey could do more than growl, I hauled her over to sit alongside me on a stool beside the campbed. There I shared with her the last of the food I had carried from London, while the King and his men discussed the morrow.

I understood little of what they said in their quiet deliberations. After a while I took up a leather-bound book of hours from the oaken chest and sat turning the pages, until the King should be ready to retire. I marvelled long at an exquisite picture of Our Lady within, kneeling by a golden-haired, gilt-winged angel, a prayerbook open upon her desk, even as this book lay open before me.

But then my eye was caught by one text towards the end, headed by a fabulous capital letter scrolled in the brilliant murrey and blue of the King's colours. The beautiful handwritten Latin beseeched merciful Lord Jesus to free his servant, King Richard, from every sorrow and trouble and from all the plots of his enemies, and to defend him from all evil and all peril, past, present and to come.

I read the prayer over again and again. How much would my lord need such help in just a few hours' time?

From time to time the guards outside snapped to attention, and a soldier bearing a message, or some sly man, sidled through the curtain into the tent. At first I strained to hear the reports, but before long the effort was beyond me. The past days' fatigues took their toll. Despite my resolve to remain awake to protect my King, I must have drifted into sleep, my back leaning against a costly tapestry, my hand still resting on Murrey's head, close against my thigh.

'Matt.' King Richard's voice seeped into my brain as though through fog or from far distant. 'Matthew?'

I stumbled to my feet. Murrey grumbled as my movement disturbed her.

The King stood before me. The tent was empty of his gentlemen, and shadows danced within it as the torches guttered and burned down.

I rubbed my eyes.

'Your Grace?'

'It is time to sleep, Matthew. A mattress has been placed ready for you.' The brand behind me had long ago died, and his face was in darkness. 'Take what rest you may. It will be a long day tomorrow – for both of us.'

His hand was upon my elbow, leading me towards the doorway. There, just within the curtain, lay a palliasse, covered over with the blanket I had carried with me from London. As I lowered myself on to it gratefully and my eyelids likewise drooped, I was too sleepy to protest as I heard the King say,

'Sleep well, Matt. I shall wake you in good time, never fear.'

19

Blood Moon

Tap, tap, tap.

I shake my head. But the sound is still there.

Tap, tap, tap.

In my head.

I turn.

A grey veil of mist parts before me. Tatters drift off to either side, to left, to right. I put up my hand to push them away. Clammy, cold air.

A dark, vaulted space. Ceiling high above. So high. So dark. Mist vanishing like incense into the void. I look back down.

Before me now a great grey slab of stone. A figure hunched over it.

Tap, tap, tap.

I step forward.

The man twists to stare at me, then turns back. Hammer, chisel in his hands.

Tap, tap, tap.

Upon the slab, a boy. Yet not – Cold, grey stone.

Dark shadowed eyes. Sad shadowed eyes.

I know his face.

Tap, tap, tap.

Biting at the stone. Scarring it. Scribing a name.

I step closer to read it.

E – D – W – A – R – D.

Across the cold, stone boy, two faces. Two boys.

Hollow eyed. Kneeling. Dark shadowed eyes.

I know their faces.

Who? Where?

Tap, tap, tap.

Cold, damp, upon my hand. A push. A whimper.

Tap, tap, tap.

I opened my eyes.

Darkness.

Murrey's nose moist against my palm. Whining. Shoving me to wakefulness.

I drew a deep breath, murmured a prayer to drive away the dream. A sad dream, I remembered. But it was vanishing fast. Like mist touched by the sun's early rays.

I stretched out my limbs to waken them.

Tap, tap, tap.

I froze, my body rigid.

But, no, not the chipping of cold stone this time. The faraway clang, clang, clang of hammer on hot metal. The armourer of last night? Or another. Closer this. But still distant.

A man's cough. Nearer. Outside the tent.

The whinny of a horse, a crunch as hoof scraped on dry ground.

Little noises. Night-time noises.

I knelt up, pushed my blanket away. Drawing the curtain aside revealed more darkness. But greyer now.

My eyes adjusting, I dragged myself to my feet and went outside. Two guards shuffled to attention, then relaxed, nodding at me, the mere boy.

Different men now. How often had the guard changed while I had lain there, oblivious?

The moon was setting.

Almost full, it rested a moment on a far-off hill. But it wasn't the great gold coin of other nights. Its gleam was tinged red.

'Blood moon,' muttered one of the guards as it slid down behind the dark bulk of the hill and soon was lost from sight.

I shivered.

He spat on the ground.

'Bad tidings for the traitor.'

A camp fire flared before a nearby tent, then another further off.

'Not long till sunrise, I reckon,' said the second guard.

He grasped my shoulder, turning me around and pointing. A thick grey line sketched the outline of trees on the other horizon. The tentative call of a bird broke the silence, another chirruping in answer. 'Time to wake His Grace?'

Slipping back through the flap, I rolled up my mattress and blanket, then felt my way across the pitch-dark tent. At the table, I

346

fumbled in my pouch for my tinderbox, and struck a light on a candle in its gilded holder.

I shielded the flickering flame with my hand and, with Murrey a lithe shadow at my heel, approached the King's fabric-shrouded bed.

He was sleeping still, his head upon an embroidered linen pillow, an arm outflung across the fine cloth of his coverlet. In the pool of candlelight his face was younger than I had ever seen before, the lines smoothed away by sleep.

For the briefest moment the face of his son, poor Ed – not glimpsed for two years – swam before my eyes. Then my dream came back to me.

My hand shook and the candle flame quivered.

Murrey whined, her dark eyes liquid in the candlelight as they gazed up at me. The fingers of my free hand twined themselves in the tufted fur of her head.

The King's eyes opened, then narrowed at me, bending over him.

'Matthew?'

'My lord, it is time to rise.'

I drew back, pulling Murrey with me.

He eased himself off the bed, then reaching for a thick fur mantle upon a nearby chair, swung it around his shoulders and strode towards the tent's entrance. As he tugged the flap aside, the guards stamped to attention. He bid them a quiet good morning as he passed.

I trailed after him, still clutching Murrey's collar. The metal fleur-de-lys stitched there was cold against my hand. I recalled old King Edward buckling the leather strap around her neck as I stepped forward to stand beside his brother.

We gazed out at the camp as it began to stir.

Before us, grey ranks of tents marched down the dark hillside, swallowed up by the pool of mist gathered on its lower slopes. In the distance only the tips, their pennons limp in the windless air, poked above the milky depths.

Among the nearer tents, ghostly figures glided, their calls, laughs, greetings to their fellows floating to us above the wreathing mist. Here and there the comforting glow of camp fires. I could see cooking pots hung over the hot coals of the closest.

Far to our right, men were busy among rows of horses, feeding and watering. Again the clang, clang, clang of hammer on metal, but this time I did not heed it. Instead I watched King Richard as his gaze swept across the awakening camp.

A chill still cut the air. As the King gathered his fur cloak about him, I longed for my blanket but did not move to retrieve it.

A serving man scurried up and knelt before the King.

'Your Grace? Do you wish me to waken your chaplains?'

'Aye, and my lords Norfolk and Lovell, if they are still abed. Also Lord Strange. We shall take Mass together this morning.'

The man hurried off and we were silent once more.

Rooks cawed in distant trees. Above our heads, the last sparks of the stars were fading as the greyish light grew in the east.

Then the King spoke.

'Well, Matt, what do you think of your first battle camp?'

And without waiting for an answer, he walked towards the horse lines. To left and right men stopped what they were doing to bow and hail him.

''Morning Your Grace.'

'A fine day for a battle – once that mist clears.'

'The traitor will be quaking in his boots at sight of that moon last night!'

How could they be so bold? To speak first to the King before he had spoken to them?

But perhaps it was a privilege of soldiers. King Richard evidently found no fault with them, for he only smiled and greeted them in return.

But when we reached the first of the horses, the man who hastened up to us took no such liberties. As he knelt before King Richard, I recognized him as the horse master from Middleham.

'I bid you a fair morning, Master Reynold,' said the King. 'How are you and your charges today?'

Master Reynold rose to his feet.

'Well enough, Your Grace, though it was an unquiet night. As ever, they sense what is to come.'

The horses, mostly dark shadows, were quiet now, busy with their nosebags while grooms scuttled among them checking legs and hooves. In the first line, a pearly grey stood out in the lingering darkness. Storm, the King's favourite. Last seen by me carrying the King in his triumph.

His Grace ran a hand along his neck, pulled out strands of forelock trapped beneath his halter.

348

'Well, boy,' he murmured, 'you have served me well in the past, but today your son shall do me the honour.'

As he slapped the stallion's neck, he glanced past him towards the second row of beasts. And there, tossing his head while a groom brushed his gleaming moonlight coat, stood Windfollower.

Almost three years had passed since my eyes had beheld him, but I knew him. His power and the terror of being on his back as he bolted headlong across the water meadows at Middleham rushed back to me now.

The King looked down at me. Whatever he saw in my face caused him to say,

'He has changed since your little adventure, Matt. He's now well trained and a fitting mount for a king about to ride into battle.'

He gave Storm a final pat and turned towards the throng of tents again. As the light in the sky grew, their outlines were becoming more distinct against the veil of mist. To the east a low bank of cloud on the far hills was edged with pink where the sun would soon rise.

The King's face was calm as he surveyed the landscape.

'One last battle, perhaps,' he said quietly. 'With Tudor dead, there will be no more false claims. I shall push the French to a treaty, like the Scots. And Portugal –'

He glanced at me. Though the light was dim, I caught the trace of a smile.

'You will be pleased to know I have followed your advice, Matt – and that of my advisors, of course. About remarriage, I mean. It has helped to hear that Anne – Her Grace the late Queen – had spoken of it. Though I know not why she spoke of it to you...'

'I had been telling her my story, Your Grace. Of my stepmother and my father.'

'Of course. A happy man. And why should I not find happiness again? I have sent ambassadors into Portugal to offer myself in marriage to the Infanta Joana.'

'Infanta, Your Grace?'

'Princess, Matthew. The King's sister. And though she is Portuguese, she is descended from our third King Edward, and so is the senior Lancastrian heir to the English throne. If we marry, it will unite the houses of York and Lancaster for all time. Would that not be a fine thing? To make an end to the reason for all these years of fighting over the crown of England.'

'Aye, my lord. Truly it would.'

'And she is a most beautiful and religious woman – so her ambassadors tell me. I expect to receive a portrait of her soon. I wonder what she will think of mine.'

The flicker of a nearby fire danced in his eyes as they ranged across the now stirring scene.

I remembered that day in Westminster when I had entered the palace to find him fidgeting while the painter took his likeness. How sad his eyes had been then, so soon after his wife's death. Was that the portrait that would be sent – or would another of him in this more buoyant mood be preferred?

Mention of that far-flung land spurred another memory.

'I had heard tell that your niece, the Lady Elizabeth, is perhaps also to marry into Portugal.'

'How do you know this?'

'Is it no more than a rumour, Your Grace? I'm sorry if I've spoken out of turn.'

'Do not worry, Matt. It is one rumour that I hope may have some basis in the truth.'

'Alys Langdown told me of it in a letter.' Or had it been Elen? 'That a Portuguese duke was seeking her hand.'

'Manuel, yes. He is Joana's cousin. And is Elizabeth happy with the arrangement?'

'Alys says she can't wait.'

As the words tripped out, I feared that I had again blundered, but the King only laughed.

'That is good – that she is keen to wed. It is a pity that Alys herself is not.'

'I'm sure she will do your bidding in all things, Your Grace. But... but she would perhaps do it more cheerfully if her husband were not to be Ralph Soulsby.'

'Alys always was a headstrong creature. But we will await the outcome of the battle – and Dame Elizabeth's decision.' He turned to face me. 'Or, tell me, Matt, do you have some other husband in mind for her?'

'No, indeed, my lord. Not I.'

His back was towards the lightening east, his face cast in shadow, and I could not tell whether he was in jest. Flustered, I sought to divert him and reached in my pouch for a morsel with which to entice Murrey to dance.

My hand brushed against cold metal.

Closing my fingers around it, I drew it out. It was the coin that Master Ratcliffe had handed me in London. The crowned head and tiny boar stamp were as fresh as when newly minted more than two years ago.

As I lifted my eyes, they were caught by the ghostly tendrils of mist still drifting before us.

'I dreamed last night of your son, my lord.'

'My son? Edward? You saw him?'

A tug in the King's voice made me regret my words.

'I saw a stone cutter. He was carving his name.'

Tap, tap, tap.

'And I saw two other boys. They weren't Ed, but – but they looked like him.'

I glanced up at the King.

He was staring ahead once more, but his eyes didn't see the newly bustling camp.

'Like Ed – but not Ed.'

'I think they were his cousins, Your Grace, your nephews. The princes that were. I rode with Edward, the elder. I knew his face.'

He was silent.

Perhaps I should have said no more, but...

'Your Grace – those rumours...?'

'Rumours?'

'About your nephews, Your Grace. That were whispered during the rebellion.'

'Ah, yes, those rumours.'

He gazed ahead still.

A pause.

'You believed them?'

'No, Your Grace,' I protested.

'But you remember them.'

'It was just my dream, Your Grace.'

'I had hoped they would be forgotten. Out of sight, out of mind, they say. And they have, haven't they?'

I said nothing. Did he mean the rumours – or the boys?

'The men at Merevale will not be fighting for my brother's sons today. No, rather they will fight for a French-backed pretender who they say has already proclaimed himself king. A traitor who has little more claim to the English throne than many here – or others still abed far from here.'

'My lord?'

'They say he plans to marry my niece Elizabeth. A Yorkist bride, to make his claim more secure. No mention of her brothers. And Tudor could not let them live if he were to become king. There, that is their death warrant – unless those rumours are true and I signed it myself long ago.'

He fell silent.

I cursed myself inside. I should not have mentioned the boys, stirred him to such thoughts. Not on this morning.

Did he sigh before he spoke again?

'But, in any case, the deed is done. Two years ago I accepted the crown – and today I must fight for it. If God grants me victory here, I will know I did the right thing. If I should be defeated —'

Before I dared challenge his words, a serving man bustled up to us and bowed.

'Yes?'

'Your Grace, all is ready for Mass. The gentlemen are gathered in your tent.'

The King nodded, then turned back to me.

'Pay no heed to rumours, Matt – and perhaps even less to dreams. My brother Edward once told me of a terrible dream he had – full of demons and the shades of executed traitors come back to haunt him. Later that day, he won a glorious victory. Have you heard of the battle of Barnet? Myself – I had slept hardly at all that night. I was just eighteen. It was my first battle...'

He placed his hand on my shoulder.

'But this will not be yours, Matthew. You must soon be on your way. Attend Mass, then be off.'

'But, Your Grace, I —'

'Do not be mutinous. You must not await the outcome of this battle – your message is too important. Your master should already know what he must do, but it will do no harm to remind him. Come.'

He swung round. At last the sun broke free above the hill and its crowning bank of cloud, and King Richard's face was flooded with a wash of morning light like liquid gold.

He squinted and raised a hand to shield against its suddenness, then laughed.

'The sun in splendour indeed. It shines upon this day's endeavour.'

And he strode towards the royal tent, the servant in his wake.

But I hung back.

I was angry at myself for revealing my dream, ashamed at provoking the King to speak of – of a matter I had not even thought of for almost two years. Who was I – a mere subject – to question a king – whatever he might have done?

Murrey nuzzled my hand as I watched the sun rise above a copse of trees atop the far ridge. Among them, the spire of a distant church was stark black against the golden sky. As I set off slowly after the King, an idea nudged at my mind.

Inside the tent priests in full vestments were preparing for the Mass. The towering crucifix I had seen the night before stood ready on a cloth-of-gold-covered altar, a silver chalice and a salver for the bread alongside.

Several gentlemen, known and unknown to me, came to greet the King as we entered. Lord Lovell, his fair face solemn as he bowed, then embraced his old friend. Sir Richard Ratcliffe, Master Kendall. Three or four others. One, a young man with a thatch of whitish-blond hair and the palest of brows, hung back until nudged forward into a bow by Master Ratcliffe. Then came His Grace the Duke of Norfolk whom I recalled from my glimpses of him long ago in London.

Tall and lean, his face tanned and lined by long years of soldiering, he inclined his head, then clasped the King's hand in a firm grip.

'Dickon. I trust you've slept soundly.'

'Aye, Jack. Well enough.'

'My lords Stanley and Northumberland are not attending Mass?'

'I did not summon them, though Lord Strange here stands for his father.' The fair young man bent his head towards the King again, his face expressionless. 'Their lordships will have enough to do this morning without trailing here from their camps. Each must take care of his own soul today.'

The King's companions joined him in his smile, but as he stepped across to the campbed to throw off his mantle, their smiles dropped away.

I hastened to pour water into a basin for the King to wash, then helped him on with a loose morning robe. As I fastened it about him, I asked quietly,

'Do you wish me to sing at the Mass, Your Grace?'

No candles lit this corner of the tent and his face was shadowed as he answered,

'Nay, lad, not this morning, though I believe my lord of Norfolk there would like to hear you. Perhaps I will send for you for our thanksgiving Mass on our return to London. But not today. Save your strength – and your voice.'

It was with relief that for once I took no more part in the Mass than the other worshippers. Not only had I been afraid my voice would let me down, but my dream still weighed heavily on me, despite the King's words. The prickling in my eyes came as no surprise as the priest intoned the familiar words of the prayer from last night: 'most gentle Lord Jesus Christ, keep thy servant King Richard, and defend him from all evil and from all peril past, present and to come...'

Before long, we had tasted the bread and the wine, and had risen from our knees, and the candles on the altar were snuffed, and the gilded crucifix was being lifted and affixed to a long pole of beechwood. The priests held it aloft and led the way out into the noise and bustle of the sunlit camp.

A trestle table had been set up outside, loaded with sweet-smelling fresh bread and cheeses and jugs of wine. Beyond it squires stood ready with a suit of magnificent armour, every piece shining like polished silver in the early sunlight.

I swallowed hard. Of a sudden, the coming battle was very close.

As if sensing my fear, King Richard came over to me. He had shed his morning robe and begun to don the garments he would wear beneath his armour.

'Now it is time for you to leave, Matt. There is food for your journey. John tells me you will find your pony in the horse lines. Remember, go straight to Master Ashley and deliver my message.'

'Of course, Your Grace. No – no deceptions. And... Your Grace...'

354

'Yes?'

'I hope you find your happiness, Your Grace. God be with you.'

He smiled.

'And you, Matt. Now, go. And don't fail me in this small service.'

I knelt and kissed the great ring upon his hand, my eyes stinging once more. His other hand was heavy upon my head as I said,

'Never, my lord.'

Then I rose and walked away without another glance, not trusting my face not to betray me as I gathered my bundle, whistled to Murrey and hurried towards the strings of horses.

It took me little time to find Bess, the smallest by far among the mounts assembled there, and in a matter of minutes we were trotting past the last rows of tents and wagons and straggling soldiers, and heading away from the camp.

But I did not make my way towards the great highway of Watling Street as I had been told. Instead I circled round to the north, staying upon high ground when I could, always keeping the army's camp in view.

So I saw when it broke up – as companies of soldiers marched towards the south-west, as teams of huge horses were set to hauling black cannon, as parties of horsemen wheeled away after them, their armour catching fire in the sunlight.

And I followed.

May the Lord forgive me, I betrayed my King, and followed as his army marched towards battle.

.

20

View from a Tower

'There's no more room!'

The man's face loomed dark against the square of daylight far above.

'He's only a little 'un.'

'And he's wearing the King's badge.'

'Why's he not fighting then?'

Laughter erupted around me as the question was dropped down on us like a stone. I was thankful we were in darkness as I knew my face was aglow. Why wasn't I fighting? Why was that the only one of King Richard's orders that I had obeyed that day?

Another head joined the first staring down.

'Is he a deserter?'

'No!' I cried.

'He's only a boy – twelve or thirteen,' offered a motherly voice. For once I took no offence at being thought younger than I was – perhaps it could work in my favour. But another of the villagers clustered around me was not so sympathetic.

'Wearing a sallet?'

I slipped my helmet off and thrust it into my bundle.

'He'll have picked it up after some deserter threw it down,' the second head called down. 'Fleeing from the traitor's camp, no doubt, when he caught sight of the King's army.'

'Spoils of war.' The first face laughed. 'We've all done that. Send him up. There's room enough for a little 'un – if he promises not to breathe.'

'Go on, lad. Leave your bundle and hound down here with us. You don't want to miss the fun.'

Hands shoved me from behind and I hauled myself up the steep ladder, past a great bell hanging silent, up to the wide-open trapdoor high above. The two men there reached down to pull me through and I emerged, blinking, into the dazzling sunlight.

More than a dozen men were gathered on the small platform atop the tower, two or three deep against the parapet at the southern side.

The first man who had spoken, stocky, grey-haired and little taller than me, eyed me up and down. A livid scar adorned his cheek, scything it from eye to jaw.

'Small enough, and not from these parts, I reckon, from the making of your jack.'

He took hold of my elbow and forced his way through the small crowd.

'Make way, make way. The lad's come a long way to see the sights.'

Some grumbling greeted his words, but it was good-natured, and the men parted to let us through to the waist-high parapet beyond. My companion rested his hands upon the stout carved stone blocks.

'There, boy. Is the view all you thought it would be?'

I leant forward beside him and my heart jolted within me.

Spread out before us was the rolling countryside I had travelled through that morning. For as long as I could I had kept the royal army in sight, but at last I had had to turn away, seeking this distant vantage point. I had not been sure the ancient church would provide what I wanted. But I could not have wished for better – unless it had been riding on the wings of the hawk I espied hovering in the heavens high above us.

Perhaps a mile or more from us, at the end of a long ridge of land, was a vast gathering. I could barely make out individual figures at this distance, but it was plain what I was seeing.

Huge hosts of men, armies; sunlight glistening on armour, weapons, battle standards. Many, many thousands there must be. Ants against the green landscape.

'Mary, mother of God.'

The words slipped out before I could stop them.

My grizzled companion grunted.

'The King's army has found its position, but Tudor's is still advancing, I think. And what of the others?'

I turned to him. His shrewd dark eyes were watching me.

'My eyesight is not what it was, lad. Not since I took this blow at Barnet.' He pointed to the scar and grinned. 'And age is catching up with me too. I didn't let you up here just out of the goodness of my heart.'

'You fought at Barnet?' I cast my mind back to the stories told of that battle a year or so after I was born.

'Aye, lad. And barely escaped with my life. My lord picked the wrong side. I only survived by playing dead after the Earl of Oxford's array was broken. That was due to the Duke of Gloucester, of course. His Grace the King, now, that is.'

'You fought for the Lancastrians!'

'Don't be so worried, boy. It was a long time ago. And footsoldiers like us don't get a choice who we fight for. Save if we choose to desert, of course.' With his elbow he nudged his neighbour, who laughed along with him. 'But if we were called, we'd be for the King today. We don't want the French meddling in our affairs. Now tell us what you see. You've the youngest eyes here.'

A glance about me showed he told the truth. Most there were older than he. Yet all had the light of excitement in their eyes.

So I turned back to the scene laid out before me like a map unrolled upon a table. My voice sounding strangely distant to my ears, I did my best to report all I saw.

'The largest army – closest to us – near the end of that ridge – that must be the King's. I see a crowd of horses behind, and great banners flying there. I think one is King Richard's white boar, another the royal standard. That must show where the King himself is. In the distance dust is still rising, but that army seems to have halted. At its head is a banner with a great star and a blue... another boar, I think. Is that possible?'

'The blue boar? Aye. Then Tudor's vanguard is led by the Earl of Oxford. Perhaps he's come to make amends for Barnet, eh, lads?' More laughter among the men. 'What else do you see?'

'Far off to the left – that other great band of men. As large as an army – but away from both the King's and Tudor's. Many knights on horseback – I see the sun flash upon their armour. But who —'

I fell silent as King Richard's words came back to me: 'Lord Stanley will stand firm.' And I thought of the 'guest' in the King's camp.

'Who is it, lad? Can you see his standard?'

'Lord Stanley. I cannot see so far, but it will be Lord Stanley and his brother.'

The man turned and spat behind him, away from the crowd of onlookers.

'Of course. The Stanleys ever bide their time. It may be that the King will have to do without them today, but surely he has men enough – so long as Stanley doesn't throw in his lot with Tudor at the start. How are the King's men arrayed?'

I tore my gaze away from the motionless Stanleys.

'The King's banner is in the centre. Ahead are row on row of men, a standard with a rearing lion stitched in silver in their middle.'

'Jack of Norfolk.' The man nodded in approval. 'The best choice for the forward line. The King could have no one better. Then it must be my lord of Northumberland in the rear?'

Some way behind where the King's standards streamed proudly in what breeze there was, stood yet another formation of troops – more thousands of men and horses. The largest of their banners was clear and bright to my eyes – a blue lion on a yellow background. Such a one as had been carried aloft behind the Earl of Northumberland on the streets of London, in happier times more than two years ago. Yet, try as I might, I could not spot among his troops the white rose on blue of my fellow men of York. Had my brother Fred yet arrived to serve his King on the battlefield?

As I described the banners to my avid listeners, upon the wind came the blare of trumpets from the King's army, tinny to my ears at this distance. A tremendous shout went up from the ranks of men, then my senses were assaulted by the most monstrous sound. A deep boom, deeper than ever John Swynbourne had played upon his shawm, closer perhaps to a thunderclap resounding through the narrow streets of York.

I staggered backwards under the force of it, clutching at my fellow watchers.

'In the name of —'

'Rest easy, son,' my companion said, though his face too was drained of colour. ''Tis only —'

Another hellish crack, then its echo, struck us.

''Tis only the cannon. See where they're arrayed. To the left of His Grace's flank – where those clouds of smoke are rising.'

Flame spat, brilliant red, more smoke rose, and again the powerful retort punched my chest.

Another flash, another crash, and dark figures could be spied, scurrying around as if in dense fog. Then an answering thunderclap sounded from far beyond Tudor's army, and another, and soon I could see little beyond the mist drifting across the distant landscape and hear nothing but the booming of the cannon and the ringing within my own head.

'And so the battle begins.' My grizzled friend raised his voice above the uproar. 'See the forward lines closing upon one another?'

My eyes followed where he pointed.

'The archers will be doing their worst as well as the cannon. Just thank the Lord you're not down there among the first rows. The sky above you is black with the arrows, the smoke eats into your eyes and throat. Men, comrades, fall alongside you, in front, clutching at shafts plunged deep into their chests – their heads, faces, torn away by cannon balls.'

His eyes were haunted by shadows from his past as I gaped at him and then back at what was unfolding far ahead of me.

'Still you have to move on, clambering over bodies, slipping in the blood and broken flesh. Until the great crash and clamour as the armies meet – pikes, maces, swords – hacking, cutting, stabbing, slicing. The clang and clash of steel on armour, the thud of mace on mail, the crunch of axe on bone. Men's groans, the terrified cries of horses, the stamping of boots on earth as you all try to gain purchase, to push, push back at your foes.'

A catch in his voice, then he forced himself on.

'The smell of sweat and iron sparking, the warm splash of blood, the taste of fear. Seeing the faces and eyes of your enemies in the shadows of their helmets, knowing the horror you see there they also see on your face.'

The cannons paused, and so did he.

Then, quieter –

'Can you imagine it, boy?'

I could. I did.

From my eyrie in the church tower, I watched and saw and heard all that he said.

Though distant from the battle, I could hear the screams, the clarions, horses whinnying, the far clashing of steel. See the surging movement like eddies in floodwaters, the sunlight flashing on weapons upraised and striking down, the weaving patterns of vivid liveries and standards as the battle rippled to left and right along the forward lines – for what seemed hours.

Time passed, oh so slowly.

'And still Stanley waits.'

'And Northumberland,' said the second man. 'For what?'

'For want of a backbone?' asked a third. His words were met by grim laughter.

'Or loyalty,' the veteran of Barnet growled.

'He and the King were ever rivals in the north country,' agreed his neighbour. 'Perhaps he thinks Tudor more likely to leave him be to have his way up there.'

'Look, now!' The veteran grabbed my arm, squinting along the line of his outflung finger. 'The King's vanguard is being turned back by Oxford – there to the far right. Do you see it, boy? It looks like Tudor has put most of his men there – he has few enough now in the rear. The weight of them is pushing Norfolk's troops back.'

His scar stood out sharp in the harsh sunlight as his head swung from side to side, scouring the scene.

'There – look! The King has already committed more men to the centre. Now Northumberland must come in – to help shore up that flank.'

But though, in the time we had been there, horsemen had galloped from the King's party back to the Earl's – messenger after urgent messenger – the rearguard did not move.

More waves of soldiers surged forward from the centre into the front line and rippled out to the right edge, but still the line was being pushed back, slowly, slowly, like the tide.

The standard of the Duke of Norfolk was always at the forefront, in the fiercest of the fighting. The silver lion reared proudly above it all. But then, of a sudden, it disappeared from view as though sucked down by a riptide below the surf of battle. It resurfaced for an instant, then was swallowed up once more.

'The banner – the silver lion - where's it gone?' I asked.

'Norfolk's? Is he down? That will be a grievous loss to the King. Why doesn't Northumberland come?'

I willed the Earl to march forward to support his King. Surely he would prove his loyalty by advancing his men into the attack? Twice, thrice, more, I had seen the great white boar banner thrust into different areas of the forward line, held aloft by one of the King's bravest knights as my soldier companion said – and I knew by that sign that King Richard himself had joined his men in their deadly struggle with the enemy.

In my mind's eye I saw him, urging them to greater efforts, leading them by his example, standing four-square alongside them swinging an immense war axe or his bright sword. Once only had I witnessed him brandish that sword, on that fateful day in Stony Stratford, disarming Lord Grey. After my companion's word pictures, I imagined him now, wielding it with deadly intent, striking left, right, at Tudor's footsoldiers, or at any of his knights who ventured so far.

Was Henry Tudor showing such valour on this battlefield?

Now, again, the boar banner pressed into the thick of the fighting, this time to the right near where the Duke of Norfolk's standard had been seen no more.

And another horseman rode back to seek the Earl.

Yet still Northumberland held back.

My fellow watchers were free with their curses on the Earl's head, and more on top for Lord Stanley, whose forces remained unmoving off to the left.

I described for them again the King's withdrawal from the line, as his banner returned to the higher ground. There, they told me, among soldiers kept in reserve and horses waiting to be used, he would have a matchless view of the course of the battle, and be well placed to decide what best to do.

From our vantage point, we saw the fighting spilling further to the right.

'Perhaps Oxford senses a weakness there now Norfolk is gone,' said one man, concern rising in his voice.

'Do you think he's dead?' The image of the man who had greeted the King so warmly this morning sprang up in my mind. Though I knew not why my thoughts should turn on him more than many another man killing and dying on the field before me.

The grizzled man shot me a glance full of pity.

'Aye, lad, no doubt about it – dead or at least badly wounded, with many of his men. Otherwise, another of his knights would have caught up the standard – his men would rally to it in an instant. Now, instead, Oxford is piling his troops there as if he believes the line will break. See them stream along from the centre, and from his reserve far behind?'

My eyes scanned the heaving mass of men as more trumpets sounded. The thin reedy notes hardly rose above the buzz and grumble of all the other battle sounds merging into one.

Then, my gaze raking to the left, I spied something to the rear of Oxford's forward line.

'What banner is that?'

'Where?'

'Among that small knot of men behind the fighting. Its background green and white – upon it a red... a red dragon?'

And in that instant I was no longer on a church tower. It was as though I was once again at my King's side.

'The red dragon? Where do you see it?' I heard him say.

I pointed without speaking.

'The Dragon of Cadwallader! Tudor's symbol. Well done, lad. Francis? We have Tudor in our sight. There to the left – behind the main force.'

'But, Dickon,' Lord Lovell's voice was weary, 'it is the fourth time today.'

'Aye, but those before were just decoys. Surely this must be him. Out there, he is not aiming to draw us into the forward line.'

'But what good is that to us? The thickest press is on the right flank. And without Northumberland we have few men to spare.'

'Then that is what he will least expect – that we should aim at him direct. See – he has few men himself. Oxford has thrown everything into the forward line and left him scarcely protected and stranded in the rear now the weight of the battle is moving to the right. One swift stroke and the day will be ours. And with it, an end to all this bloodshed.'

'A swift stroke? You would lead cavalry there? But the way runs past the Stanleys!'

'What of it? Lord Stanley has not chosen to strike yet himself, for either side, though he must see that Oxford has the advantage of us on that far flank. And he knows we still have Lord Strange. He may yet be gambling on my forgiveness for himself and his son – think it better perhaps to do nothing and watch our victory, than risk all and throw in his lot with Tudor.'

'It is too great a risk, Dickon.'

'Then what would you have me do? With Norfolk dead and without Northumberland we cannot now hope to break Oxford's line.'

'Perhaps... perhaps withdraw. Regroup in front of London. Live to fight another day. As your brother once did.'

'My brother Edward? The forces against us that day were overwhelming. Cousin Warwick at their head and half the country behind the old King. Not like this. Not a Welsh rebel with a rabble of French mercenaries. We cannot cede him the battle.'

'Yet it would buy more time. Time for more men to rally to your standard. The men of York, for instance. Your agents say

Northumberland delayed mustering them so they have not yet arrived. In how many other towns has that happened?'

'Perhaps too few to chance it, Francis. No, we have our opportunity now to deal Tudor a fatal blow – if we do not debate too long. But, Francis, you –' a heartbeat's silence, then, softly – 'you need not ride with me.'

'You wrong me, Richard, if you think I will desert you now.'

'Nay, old friend, I know you would never do that, whatever the odds.' Then, his voice firm once again, 'To horse, then. And bring me those men who will follow me to finish this battle now.'

King Richard stood staring out across the smoke and screams and stench of the battlefield as Lord Lovell strode off. Alone once more, motionless, his slight figure cased in plates of steel and surcoat of murrey and blue, muddied and bloodied, fleurs-de-lys, sunbursts, lions – once golden, royal symbols – hardly recognizable beneath the grime. A gauntleted hand resting on his sword hilt. A moment of stillness against the deadly backdrop of the battle.

Then, shattering the seeming calm, a squire led up a light grey horse in full shining armour – Windfollower, dancing skittishly upon his hooves at the bustle and noise pressing in again all around. But King Richard stepped up to him, and at a word and a gentle stroke of his nose beneath the faceplate he quietened, remaining like a statue as the King, iron-clad himself, was boosted into the saddle.

Soon the company of household knights was gathered, a sea of glittering armour, bristling lances, dark red and blue livery, snorting stallions sporting toughened steel as fine as that of their masters.

At their head rode Lord Lovell. To one side was the King's standard bearer, his armour and surcoat already befouled with dirt and blood, like his master's, his strong fist grasping the staff of the great white boar banner. To the other were the shadowed faces of Master Kendall and Master Ratcliffe. Then they flipped their visors closed.

Another squire ran up to the King, a circlet of gold encrusted with jewels in his hands. The King reached down for it, then thrust it skywards. The gems sparkled in the brilliant sunlight.

'Gentlemen, this is what Henry Tudor seeks today. The crown of England. But he shall not have it. Not while I live and have breath within me. Are you with me?'

As one, the knights roared, 'Aye! For Richard!' and clashed their lances against their shields.

The King jammed the circlet down upon his helmet, then snapped shut his visor and wheeled Windfollower about. The other horses bunched up behind him in their eagerness to be off as he raised his own lance, then pointed it forward.

'Á York!' he cried.

'For Richard and England!'

Their horses began to pace down the slope, slowly at first, then gathering speed, faster, faster, until they reached full gallop. The sound of their hooves was as loud as cannonfire as they charged across the battlefield. The silver of the armour and colours of the livery blurred to the sight with the speed that swept them past the battle line and ate up the ground towards Tudor. Above it all, the white boar standard flew as I had seen it long ago upon the highest tower at Middleham.

On and on they thundered, King Richard and Windfollower at the very front, until with a nightmare crash the charge broke like a storm-wave on the wall of Tudor's defenders. Those men had barely time to cluster round him in defence before the impact. Surprise was still mingled with growing fear on the faces of those who died first.

The King and his companions flung away the shattered butts of their lances and set about them with mace or battle axe. Unmounted men had little chance against them and they soon cut a swathe through the ring of defenders around the red dragon banner.

Screams of men and horses rent the air, with the ringing of metal on metal, and the sickening crunch of blade on bone. Blood churned the earth to mud under foot and hoof, but sure of foot and hoof, the King and his men were gaining ground.

A lone man in the richest armour could be seen by the dragon standard, thrust now deep into the ground, defended by a giant of a knight with battle axe seeming as tall as he. The goal of the charge was within their grasp. The King spurred Windfollower forward towards the gigantic knight, his own great axe slick with blood.

Then came the shout that all had dreaded.

'Stanley rides!'

365

The host of horsemen were careering down from their watching, waiting place, their stag's head banner whipping above them in the wind raised by their speed. The brightness of their armour still shone in the August sun, the scarlet of their surcoats as yet undefiled by the filth of battle. Their trumpet call rang in the shimmering air.

'They come to join us at last. Now they see we nearly have Tudor.' The King's voice was hoarse.

'Dickon, no! You know they come to destroy you. We must withdraw.'

'Never! I live or die this day rightful King of England!'

And the charge slammed into the chaos of the fighting.

I saw it though I was not there. I felt the shock of the heavy horses smashing into, overwhelming the King's forces, though I was not there. I heard the crash and the cries carried to me on the battle wind.

I saw the white boar banner go down. It did not rise again.

And a single word resounded in my head.

'Treason!'

21

Milestones

Another milestone. And another. And another.

It was all I could do to stop myself falling asleep – and then falling to the ground.

Another milestone. Another mile closer to London.

Closer to sleep.

I could barely remember the last time I'd slept. Well and long, at least, not in fitful starts. Afraid to close my eyes.

The night before the battle, perhaps.

Before the waking nightmare began.

In truth I had hardly known whether I was sleeping or awake as I stumbled down from the church tower. As calls dropped from above, warning me to take care. As, in the half-light below, a kindly woman handed me my pack and the leash she had tied to Murrey's collar.

Her royal collar.

Should I take it off and hide it?

Murrey had whimpered, her liquid eyes gazing up beseeching, as my hesitant fingers reached out – then grasped the collar to pull her with me. The leather was rough, the gilt fleur-de-lys upon it cool to my touch.

I had to get out of there, had to get on my way. I had a job to do.

Astride Bess, I had ridden away from the village, back the way I had come. Seeking the old road.

Watling Street.

To the south, King Richard had said.

The King —

To the west hung a heat haze – and clouds of crows and rooks, circling.

Everywhere men were hurrying. Mostly north or east, some south as well.

Some were on horseback, most on foot, all rushing as fast as they could – if they could rush – often looking back over their shoulders. All were filthy, sweaty, bloodied – their own or others'

367

blood? Torn clothes, ripped mail, some struggling out of armour even as they ran, tossing it aside.

Once, in the neighbouring field, riders hunted down a man, thrust their lances into him as he lay writhing on the ground. Dismounted to search his body. One cheered as he stripped him of his boots and held them up for his fellows to see.

I turned away, urging Bess on. But I took my sallet from my bundle and threw it down under a hedge.

More stragglers coming towards me, one limping, another clutching a bleeding shoulder, others with dazed eyes.

In those eyes I saw my own.

Then, between them —

'Make way, make way!'

I knew that voice.

A rider on a light grey horse. Armour encasing both – dirt and gore encrusted, but burnished. Murrey and blue livery.

My heart leapt.

The horse was Storm.

Cantering towards me along the lane. Scattering the trudging, defeated soldiers.

I raised my hand and called, 'Your Grace!'

The stallion skittered to a halt.

But —

The knight was too tall.

He snapped up his visor.

'Matthew?'

Lord Lovell's face. Smudged with dirt, dark dried blood, an ooze of fresh red at his temple. He stared down at me.

'Matthew – for the love of God, flee!'

'I thought you were King Richard.'

I could not hide the misery in my voice.

'He's dead, Matthew. Hacked down by the traitor's men in front of me.'

I had known it – of course I had – but to hear the words...

'Where is he, my lord?'

'Back on the battlefield, where he fell. The fighting moved on, till our men could fight no more. And then we broke...'

'But Storm —'

'I found him loose on the field and took him to save my skin.' He grimaced. 'You wonder at it perhaps – loyal Lovell fleeing? But we are all branded traitors by this new "king" – they

368

say he proclaimed himself such as he set foot on Welsh soil. They are butchering all they catch – no quarter given. Not to flee would be self-slaughter. Would that Richard had left the field when he had the chance.'

He told me of those last moments in few words: the charge, the King killing Tudor's giant standard bearer with his own hands, the carnage as Stanley's cavalry ploughed into their rear... the names of men who died. The Duke of Norfolk, Masters Ratcliffe, Brackenbury... Kendall.

'What will happen to him?'

'The King? His body will be despoiled – stripped of all he has, like any common soldier. Then, when Tudor has found him – if they can still recognize him – he will be taken... I know not where. Leicester, London? To be put on display so all know he is dead.'

My stomach turned over. Thank the Saviour I had eaten nothing since early morning.

'But Matthew, did not the King give you a message to take? Why are you here?'

'I could not... go – without knowing.'

'You must take it – and swiftly. It is of utmost importance – especially after... You must not fail Richard, even now. Wait —'

As though uncertain, he paused. Glanced – left, right – over his shoulders.

Few straggling soldiers were to be seen now – and no pursuers. For the moment.

With difficulty, he dismounted and began to unbuckle his armour. It was slow work and he murmured his thanks as I helped. From time to time he winced as a plate brushed against his wounds.

As we worked, he explained.

'You shall take Storm – no, don't protest. Your journey is more urgent than mine. For me, young Lincoln, Richard's nephew, is the new king, not this traitor. I will find him when the time is right. He will need followers. Rally to his cause yourself, Matthew, one day, if you can. But meanwhile, you can carry your message more quickly aboard Storm. See, we can remove his finery too. Throw it into the ditch for some scavenger to find. Switch his saddle and bridle when you have a chance, or muddy these when you reach water. He will always be a fine horse, but it may help you escape notice.'

He broke off, looking around.

'As for me, I have only what I now stand up in. If you will give me your pony and bundle, it may be that I can make my way across country as a simple pedlar.'

'There is food, too, in the pack.'

'Then we will share that if you are willing – we will both need it on our journeys.'

He reached down to pick up his sword and scabbard. Then, hesitating, he kissed it on the hilt before handing it to me.

'Take my sword too. It may be of use to you – and it is a thing that no pedlar would have. Keep it safe, if you can – and return it to me if ever we meet again. Richard himself gave it to me when I was made viscount.'

He watched as I clumsily strapped it on, his mouth curling in a humourless smile at the way it hung loose about my waist. Then he spied something else.

'Is that Richard's boar upon your chest?'

'Aye, my lord. And I will always be proud to wear it.'

'Your loyalty does you credit, boy, but if you value your life, hide it.'

'I'm not afraid —'

'Maybe not, but your task is more important than your pride. Here...'

He deftly unpinned the badge, turned back the collar of my doublet and refastened it within so it was nestled against my undershirt.

'Now, be off with you.'

He boosted me into Storm's saddle and raised his hand to clap him on the hindquarters.

'I thank you for what you are to do. And do not worry, Matthew – I will take care of your pony. You look after yourself – and do your duty to Richard.'

One slap and Storm was cantering again along the lane, Murrey bounding after.

Another milestone. Then another.

My eyes desperate to close, desperate to sleep.

There had been a village. A well.

I had raised the bucket, drunk gratefully.

370

While Storm bent his head to the water, I mixed mud pies in the soil like a child and smeared them on his fine saddle and bridle. Plastered them over patches of congealed blood on his coat. Took out my knife, scored lines on the leather, rubbed in more filth.

Murrey growled.

Raucous laughter, shouts and catcalls.

Many hooves. Marching feet.

Round a corner, a procession of soldiers. To the front, banners that had flown among Tudor's forces on the battlefield.

Too late to melt away without drawing their notice. No villagers were about, all doors and windows shuttered against the uncertain times.

I pulled Storm into the shadow of a nearby building, threw the sword belt down and kicked dust upon it. I prayed we would not be seen and my attempts at disguise tested.

But these soldiers had no interest in a boy cowering in a corner. Laughs resounded around the empty street, coarse oaths, ribald jests thrown from man to man. They were having fun, perhaps hoped for more.

Their watchful captain, riding at their head, called to remind them.

'No more, lads, no more. You heard what His Grace the new king said.'

At his words, I had to check myself – must not step forward to catch the rest.

But they too were pausing for water on this warm day.

As they clustered around the well, both horsemen and footsoldiers, the leader finished his warning.

'Don't touch his face, lads. They must be able to recognize him when we get to Leicester.'

There among them, as they jostled each other for water, was the body of a man slung over a horse.

Naked, covered only in dirt and dried blood. Hands and feet hanging down, tied with rope under the horse's belly.

But I knew who it was.

I buried my face in Storm's neck to stifle my cry of horror.

Another milestone flashes by.

Can I reach the next?

Thirty-seven more to go.

Can I hold on? Can I make it?

I followed them. Until they came to Leicester. Turned away from my own road, to follow his.

All the long way back to the town that I – we – had left yesterday.

I followed him, leading Storm, as the sorry procession filed over the old stone bridge and through the western gate.

News had reached the town before us. Messengers. Victorious soldiers.

'Tudor has won!'

'King Richard is dead.'

And crowds flocked to see him as they had the day before. As he had ridden, confidently, to battle, his crown, his armour aflame in the morning sun.

Silent crowds. They stood lining the roads and watched.

Some turned away in sadness and disgust. Others thronged to support the victor.

Mingling amongst them, soldiers. Men at arms.

Job done, horrors faced, comrades killed, wounded.

Death escaped.

Wine bottles clutched.

And so the jeers began.

As I trudged, yards behind, I heard them.

The French I knew, though it was not the French of courtly romances or love songs.

The Welsh, Breton, I could guess.

Sometimes English – it hit me like a blow to hear what was said.

Local voices too, now, egged along by the soldiers. After all, what was a King but a man? And one King is much like another to any common person.

Most held back, kept a respectful distance as he passed. But one or two stepped forward – and before the captain's men could push them away, spat at his body.

'That's for those poor little princes,' one man yelled.

The captain's man just laughed as he shoved him back into the crowd with his pikestaff.

My anger rose. But I could do nothing. Not now, not yet.

Then, as I watched, trailing all those yards behind, a single soldier stepped into the road, urged on by those behind him.

Unsullied scarlet surcoat over mail. Open helmet burnished bright.

Unsheathed dagger in upraised hand. Poised to strike. The August sun glinting along its length.

'This is for all those beatings you —'

A moment's hesitation – by both him and me.

A familiar voice and smirk. Then surprise.

'Look, he's a crookback!'

And in the instant before he drove his shining blade into the lifeless body, I knew him.

Hugh Soulsby.

A moment later it was done, to the jeers of the crowd.

A fresh wound. But no spurt of blood now.

Hugh swung away, triumphant, to the acclaim of his companions, his knife held high.

I recognized a flash of blond hair, a white brow, among them, before I flung myself forwards, my hand grasping at the sword hilt hidden under my cloak.

But before I had gone three paces, kind hands pulled me back.

'Don't get yourself killed, lad,' said one man.

'There may be another chance to honour him,' said another.

Another milestone.

Twenty more to go.

Sweet Jesus, let my task be worth this.

They had carried him into a church – a church! – and strung him up by his wrists to put him on display. And encouraged local people to come and gawp at him as he hung among the tombs of Tudor's Lancastrian ancestors. And kept guard in case any thought to cut him down and spirit him away.

I would have done it if I could. Or even just covered his naked body.

But they kept guard outside too. And I could not leave Storm and Murrey alone.

So I hid in alleys and watched and waited. For I knew not what.

For two days and two nights.

For two long days and two long nights he hung there on display.

Another milestone. And another.
So close now.

On the third day, in the grey of the evening, the good friars had come to ask for his corpse.

They cut him down and rolled his battered body in a shroud. No coffin for this King. And they carried him away to his final resting place.

I followed them to their priory.

I had coins for them, and they let me, a boy only, no threat, enter their church.

I held the stoup as they sprinkled holy water.

My voice breaking, I sang his favourite *lauda* as they lowered him into his swift-cut grave. Too short it proved to be. His head twisted awkwardly, the cloth falling away from his bloodied face, his dark shadowed eyes.

They had had little time to prepare, they said. The new King had been impatient. Take him, dispose of him, let him be seen by living eyes no more, be no rallying point for rebels.

They glanced over their shoulders in worry that soldiers would come.

We prayed together, before the earth was thrown in, the floor tiles relaid.

No monument here for this King.

Let the people forget him.

Storm's hooves clattered across the London cobbles. We reached Newgate minutes before sundown, minutes before the gate would be locked for the night.

News of the battle had already come, the gatekeeper said. His voice was heavy with dread. But what would the council do when Tudor himself came? He shook his head.

Everywhere men's, women's faces were full of fear. People wondering what the future held.

But I didn't care. Not now. I only knew I had a message to deliver – at last.

When King Richard handed it to me, I had thought it just a ruse to keep me from the battle. But Lord Lovell's words had made me think again.

Yet still I had delayed...

Strong horse though he was, Storm had given everything to get us here so swiftly. As we turned into Master Ashley's courtyard, he was trembling beneath me, his flanks heaving and lathered.

I slithered down from his back, my knees almost buckling after my long ride, and stood waiting for a groom to come. To take him and rub him down, feed and water him.

But no one came. The courtyard was deserted. No torches blazing by the doorway.

Murrey sniffed around, her tail aquiver.

I called.

Still no one.

I led Storm to the stables.

No one there.

Only rustlings, stamping of hooves, a gentle whicker, another in answer. The horses shifting uneasily in the darkness.

I tied Storm in a stall and found him oats and water. Then, dread rising like searing bile in my throat, I made my way to the main entrance.

I did not need to knock.

The heavy oak door was ajar, and its iron lock had been smashed to pieces.

22

Old Friends

I pushed the door open.

All was darkness. Silence.

I stepped across the threshold and rummaged in my pouch for my tinderbox.

But I didn't strike it. Danger might be waiting and I must not give myself away.

Murrey whined. I quieted her with a finger on her nose.

I listened again.

Still nothing.

Reaching forward with my hands so as not to stumble, I made my way across the dark entrance hall. Still no chink of light anywhere.

Where to go first? Where was my master? I had come all this way to give him my message, only to find no one at home. No servants even.

But why was no one here?

I stepped with care, my hands still before me, towards Master Ashley's study door at the far end. Once there might I find a clue? If there was still no sight or sound of anyone, I would risk striking a light to see by.

The scent of newly snuffed candle drifted into my nostrils.

How? If no one was there?

One hand moved to my sword hilt.

The fingers of the other touched the smooth wood of the door and nudged it softly open. The smell of smoke was stronger here.

A dog whimpered. I moved to quieten Murrey, but...

The noise had come from inside the pitch-dark room. A panicked voice shushed it. A light, female voice.

Murrey yapped once in reply before I could stop her.

'Murrey?' whispered the voice.

A sharp crack as tinder was struck, and the sudden flare of a candle lit up two scared faces.

'Alys! Elen!' My own voice emerged as a strangled squeak.

'Matthew!'

Alys thrust the candle into Elen's hand and threw herself across the room to fling her arms around me.

'What are you doing here? I mean, why were you *not* here? We heard the horse, the calls. We were afraid – we doused the lights. Was it you?'

Her whispered questions tumbled out as we held each other. Then she broke away and stepped back hurriedly. In the glow of the other candles that Elen was now kindling, her face was flushed and confused.

I looked away so she could compose herself. At my heel Murrey was touching noses with her sister, Shadow, who was more like a ghost in the dim light. I fondled both hounds' ears.

'How did you know it was Murrey?'

'She sounds just like Shadow, and I knew she hadn't barked.'

Alys sounded more her old self now, though as I turned back, it was clear how much she'd changed since last we'd met. Taller, less boyish, she had grown into a young woman while I had been away. Had I altered as much in her eyes?

Questions for another time, perhaps. For now —

'What's happened here? Where's Master Ashley? All the household?'

A shadow crossed Alys's face despite the candle light. She stepped to one side and waved her hand.

Behind her, on the floor, swathed in a blanket and head propped on a cushion, lay my London master. His face was deathly white and his breathing laboured. Fresh blood oozed from a jagged gash on his temple and was matted in his sandy hair.

Elen was on her knees beside him now, dabbing at the wound with a cloth.

'How... ? Who...?'

More questions racing through my brain, I knelt down too and took his hand. It was cold, but the pulse was regular.

'He was like this when we came,' murmured Elen. 'We couldn't move him so we tried to make him comfortable here. His wife had been beaten too, but not so badly. I've settled her in her chamber with a sleeping draught.'

'Beaten? Mistress Ashley? But —'

'Matt, where have you been?' interrupted Alys, abandoning any attempt at keeping quiet. 'We came here to look for you as soon as we heard about –' she swallowed, 'about the battle. Then we found – this! Where were you?'

'I was there,' I said, barely audible.

'What?'

'I was with the King. And then —' My voice failed me.

Alys's eyes grew larger in the flickering light.

'Is it true? That he's – dead?'

I couldn't speak, just nodded.

Elen turned her face away.

Alys fiercely dashed the tears from her cheeks.

'Then Tudor —'

Anger and sadness jostled for supremacy in her face.

'Then Henry Tudor will be King. Elizabeth will have to marry him, and...'

'He's on his way here now. Tudor. I saw him set off from Leicester before I left. I stayed to see the King—'

'What?'

'Buried.'

I could not tell them of all that I had seen.

'Tudor was marching at the head of his army. They were cheering, many still drunk, driving wagons of spoil stolen from the King. It was easy for me to overtake them.'

The small roads, across country, before – before Watling Street and the milestones.

'But I came here with a message for Master Ashley. From King Richard.'

'A message? What does it say?'

'I have no idea,' I snapped, indignant. 'It's sealed, and for him alone.'

'Well, he's in no state to see it now.'

'He has woken once or twice,' said Elen.

'But he's scarcely been lucid, has he?' Alys retorted. 'The message may be important. We should open it.'

I was shocked. I had forgotten my first suspicion that the message was just about me.

'But it's the King's business. Between him and Master Ashley alone.'

'Matthew, if the King is —' She gulped, as though her tears were choking her, and brushed her hand again across her cheek. 'If that is so, perhaps it's important. Perhaps it would explain this.'

She spread her hands wide. My glance followed hers around the room. In the trembling candlelight, I saw that not only was my master battered and on the floor, but so were all the contents of his study. Chairs were upturned, tables on their sides, papers, quills, books scattered everywhere.

'The whole house is like this. Mistress Ashley, when we could get any sense from her, said that armed men came, broke down the door and attacked her husband. While some shouted questions at him and the steward, others ransacked every room. The servants all fled or were taken away, along with the steward. She said she thinks they believed Master Ashley was dead.'

'Who were they? What did they want?'

'I don't know,' she cried in exasperation. 'Except that I think they must have been Tudor's agents. Perhaps they got word of the battle even before we did. But maybe the message will tell us what it's all about.'

I reached in my pouch for the small square of folded parchment that the King had handed me – oh, so long ago now. He had been smiling as he gave it.

As I turned it in my hands, deep within the memory, Murrey growled. A scraping as of feet on flagstones came from the hallway behind me, then a loud halloo.

Elen scrambled up and lunged towards the candles, while Alys grabbed for Shadow's collar, terror scrawled across her face.

I spun round, my hand clapping to the sword hilt at my hip, my fear crushing at my chest.

Whoever was there was making no attempt at stealth. Another holler, and the glow of a blazing brand approaching across the hall.

Elen stopped quenching the candles – it was too late for that. Out of the corner of my eye I could see the remaining lights glittering on a drawn knife in Alys's free hand.

Still, silent, we waited.

The footsteps, two sets, moved closer.

Another call, softer now.

Then Murrey let out a muted whine of welcome and paced forward, and Shadow, still in Alys's whitening grip, sat down and licked her paw, unconcerned.

And into the doorway, lit now by the flame of the torch he held, stepped —

'Roger!'

His name tripped from my mouth in a laugh of relief. But Alys was less forgiving.

'Roger! You idiot! You scared us half to death. What do you think you're doing?'

Roger's face fell at her assault.

'I've come to help. If I can.'

His gaze scouted around the room, coming to rest on the prone form of Master Ashley.

'What's happened? Simon said the house was in uproar, but...'

He ground to a halt.

'Simon? Where...?'

As I asked, the head of my fellow apprentice peered around the door jamb. Seeing me, his eyes lit up.

'Matt? You've come back. Where's Mistress Ashley? She sent me for aid when those men broke in, but there was none there. Only —'

He caught sight of Master Ashley and the colour bled from his face.

'What...?'

Alys took charge.

'I don't know who you are, but if you are of Mistress Ashley's household, can you tell us who did this? And why?'

But Simon only shook his head, his mouth working as though he might be sick. Elen went to him, drawing him in to the room and turning up a stool for him to sit on. She knelt next to him, stroking his arm as his head hung down towards his knees.

'Simon is an apprentice here,' put in Roger before I could say anything. 'He came to Baynard's Castle for help because Master Ashley is a friend of the King, but of course most of the men at arms are with the King's army, or...' He stumbled to a halt, his face crimson. 'I mean, they were with the King. King Richard, of course.'

Alys's lips tightened.

'He's dead, Roger. King Richard is dead.'

He nodded, his eyes lowered.

'I know. That's what they're saying. When the news came to my parents, I looked for you at the castle. But the servants said you were not to be found. No one could be spared to search for you because the rest of the men at arms had gone to join the defence. Then Simon turned up.'

'You were at Baynard's Castle?' I asked Alys.

'Of course. Where did you think I'd be?'

'But —' I thought back. 'I thought you were at Sheriff Hutton with Princess Elizabeth.'

She shivered, shaking her head.

'No. I was, but I travelled down two or three weeks ago. To stay in the King's mother's household to prepare for my wedding. That's why Roger's here too. He came so he could attend me and visit his family while he was in London.'

'Your wedding! But I thought —'

'You thought what?'

'That King Richard... That the old Queen...'

Her face twisted.

'Dame Grey saw me herself when I arrived. She said that I must prepare myself to be married. That King Richard had asked her to reconsider, but ... but that he needed the loyalty of all his subjects. That after the coming battle Lord Soulsby must be rewarded. And that Lord Soulsby...'

She bit her lip, then rushed on,

'That Lord Soulsby would be fighting with Lord Stanley for the King. But then we heard that Lord Stanley and his brother... that they...'

Of a sudden, she rounded on Roger.

'What defence?'

Roger rocked backwards on his heels, startled.

'Defence?'

'You said the men at arms – those who hadn't gone with the King – weren't at Baynard's Castle because they'd gone to join the defence.'

'Oh, that. Yes, word came that men of fighting age were mustering. In case... in case the city council decides to refuse Tudor entry to the city. Like they did with old Queen Margaret. All the men, well most of them, had gone to join the militia.'

My mind went back almost two years to when I had tried to do just that. When the city had held firm for King Richard at the time of the great rebellion.

Tears shone in Alys's eyes.

'They won't refuse him entry. How can they? What would be the point? Matt says Tudor's marching here at the head of his army. He won his victory. King Richard... Well, Lord Lincoln would be his heir and he's far away in the north. There are hardly any knights with him. Even if he... even if he chose to march against Tudor... even if London...'

She shook her head again.

'They cannot change what's happened, what God has willed. Whysoever he has willed it... But what use did you think you could be?'

'I...' Roger was crestfallen. 'I don't know. But a serving woman said that you'd had a letter delivered by one of Master Ashley's servants. She said you'd been worrying about it for days.'

'My letter?' I asked Alys. 'Saying I was going to the King?'

'Of course. I couldn't believe you'd be so daft as to do that.'

'The serving woman said that when news came of the battle, you and Elen disappeared,' Roger went on. 'So, when Simon arrived, asking for help... Well, I thought you might have come here. I thought I should perhaps come – to check that you were safe and find out what help I can offer.'

'Well, I, for one, am pleased to see you,' I said before Alys could respond. 'And of course you will be of help.'

He threw me a grateful glance – although in truth I had said it as much to reassure me as him.

'I don't know how,' Alys shot back. 'Unless he can read that message without opening it.'

'Message?' asked Roger.

'From the King to Master Ashley. Matthew brought it. From the battlefield.'

'What does it say?'

'We don't know. And Matt doesn't want to open it.'

'But it may be important.'

Both of them were staring at me. Alys's eyebrow arched.

'That's what I said.'

The creamy parchment, the thick blob of scarlet wax upon it, was still clutched in my hand.

Alys's quick eyes were watching as my fingers turned it over and over.

'It doesn't bear his signet.'

'No,' I said slowly. 'Perhaps it was to be secret. He said I could travel more easily than one of his men if...'

I hesitated.

Her face was set firm.

'That decides it, then. A secret message, sent when he was thinking – thinking that he might lose the battle. And he did. And now Master Ashley...'

She took the message from my hand, glancing at my face. When I didn't move or speak, she deftly broke the seal and unfolded the parchment.

'It's in code.'

Disappointment tinged her voice.

'Then it isn't just instructions to keep me from the battle.' I tried to smile.

Alys skewered me with a glare.

'What?'

'Nothing. It's just...' It was my turn to bite my lip.

Roger was squinting over her shoulder at the scrap of parchment.

'If it's in code, surely you can break it? You made it seem so easy when we were at Middleham.'

'That was different, Roger. We had a book to help us.'

'As the King wrote it, he was consulting a book,' I said. 'I think it was the cipher book Ed found at Middleham.'

'The same book? There were code tables written in it. Perhaps he used one of them. It's in proper letters.'

'It didn't take him long to write.'

'Then maybe it's a substitution code like ours was.'

Roger and I placed Master Ashley's desk back upon its feet while Alys fetched a candle. By its light the three of us pored over the message.

It was just four lines long.

Clyayvbdkl cypluk, Hsz hsslz nvlk nhha zsljoa, olypuuly tl ola wshu. Ullt kl qvunluz hhu tpqu gbz vw Tljolslu. Hsz ql uvkpn olia vu, b rbua clyayvbdlu Thaaold gvukly adpqmls.

Kpjrvu

'Do you think that's a signature, there at the bottom?'

'He'd usually sign letters Ricardus Rex – King Richard in Latin – but this is just one word.'

'Could it be "Richard"?'

'The two Rs would be a useful clue... but no, it's six letters, not seven.'

'So not "Gloucester" either then.' I remembered the single word he had signed on the paper on the day of my beating,

'He was King, Matthew, not just Duke any longer. I wonder if it could be "England" in Latin – "Anglia"... No – the first and last letters are different. Perhaps it isn't a signature after all...'

Tiredness was stealing back over me now after my ride, but a name wormed its way back into my brain.

'How about "Dickon"?'

'Maybe. I remember the Queen and Lord Lovell calling him that...'

Alys fished some parchment, a pen and a pot of ink up from the floor and scribbled letters on it.

'You know, it might be. If the K is a D, and the P an I, and it is a simple substitution code... then, counting back... Matt, I think you're right. D – I – C – K – O – N. There. But how strange that it is so straightforward. If I've broken it so quickly, how long would it take one of Tudor's spies if they'd got hold of it?'

As she traced out the rest of the cipher and then started to decode the message, dread clutched at me. If it were so easy, perhaps it was just a note to keep me safe away from the battlefield. Had all my horror at betraying King Richard's instructions and the terror of my ride from Leicester been in vain?

'But it's nonsense.' Alys broke through my thoughts.

'What?'

'It means nothing. Unless it's a code within a code.'

I peered at what she'd written. Two words only. *'Vertrouwde vriend.'*

'It's not nonsense,' I said. 'It's Flemish.'

'Really?' said Roger, craning his neck to see.

'I picked up some in Bruges. Master Ashley is fluent in it. That means "Trusted friend".'

'And the King was exiled there when he was young,' recalled Alys. 'Perhaps he knows – knew it as well.'

'And how many of Tudor's spies would? Most Flemish merchants switch to French or English when abroad – they don't expect anyone to learn their language.'

Excited now, Alys worked on, deciphering the rest of the message and soon laid before me the words –

Vertrouwde vriend, Als alles goed gaat slecht, herinner me het plan. Neem de jongens aan mijn zus op Mechelen. Als je nodig hebt on, u kunt vertrouwen Matthew zonder twijfel.
    Dickon

With the little Flemish I knew, it was a struggle to translate it, but eventually, with some guesswork, I had it.

Trusted friend, If all goes wrong, remember the plan. Take the boys to my sister at Mechelen. If you need to, you can trust Matthew without question.
    Dickon.

'The boys?' asked Roger.

'His nephews,' I said. The pale faces from my dream swam before my eyes. 'The princes that were.'

'Edward and little Richard? Then they're —'

'Alive.'

Tap, tap, tap.

'Of course they are,' snapped Alys. 'Did you ever doubt it?'

'But the rumours. During the rebellion.'

'About King Richard? Matt, surely you can't have believed them!'

'No, of course not,' I protested. 'But —'

'But what?' She stared at me, exasperated. 'Matt, those rumours were put about by Henry Tudor and his mother – to turn unthinking people against the King.'

I ransacked my memory. Where had I first heard them? Of course – from Hugh. And he from his uncle. And his uncle had fought for... Lord Stanley.

What a fool I'd been to even think twice about them.

To my relief, Alys had moved on.

'But where are they? Still in England?'

A groan from behind us. We turned.

While we had been talking and working on the code, Elen and Simon had been sitting next to Master Ashley, and it struck me now that for some minutes Elen had been making small soothing noises. The patient's eyes were open and he was struggling to sit up. Elen propped another cushion behind his shoulders.

'Bring me the message,' he croaked out.

My cheeks were warm with guilt as Alys took him the unfolded parchment, its seal broken in two.

He squinted at it, then waved it away.

'Not that – the other. Matthew?'

He coughed and pain racked him. Elen held the cloth against his head until the spasm ended, then dribbled water from a flask into his mouth.

'What other?' asked Alys.

'Did they find it?'

She gestured about the room. 'How can we tell?'

'Not here. Matthew? I didn't tell them.'

My master was seized by a fit of coughing again, but this time was able to reach for the flask himself.

Alys glanced at me, her eyebrows raised.

I stepped forward.

'I can find it, sir, if you can tell me where.'

Master Ashley nodded with effort.

'He said I could trust you, boy. That day he first brought you here. And now again. Was he right?'

'Aye, sir.'

'Richard wasn't always a good judge of men. But sometimes I think he saw in them something of himself. Something he could place his trust in. I have failed him in this, but will you serve him one more time, Matthew?'

'Of course, sir. If I can.'

'Then go to the print house. The upper case. The box of letter Rs. Behind there. If they didn't find it...'

They hadn't. In minutes I was back bearing a morsel of parchment, scarce bigger than the plain seal it carried. But I also brought ill tidings.

'Master, the printing press.'

'What of it?'

'They've wrecked it. Torn it apart.'

His eyes closed an instant, as though immensely weary. Then they blinked open again.

'No matter, boy. A press may be mended – or bought anew in Flanders. People, however... The message, Matthew. Open it.'

It contained one word, in King Richard's own hand.

'Gipping.'

'So,' said Master Ashley, 'You must ride into Suffolk.'

23

'Ever My Uncle's Man'

They allowed me two hours to snatch some sleep while they prepared for the journey. That was all we could spare – more perhaps than we should.

Master Ashley, regaining some of his strength with a mouthful or two of wine that Simon brought for him, had spent it on worrying that Tudor's men would return. Or that Master Lyndsey would break down under questioning and talk of people and places connected with his business.

'It seems Tudor has spies everywhere, maybe the Stanleys too. Perhaps more even than Richard suspected, for all the many agents he had himself. Those agents may all be targeted. That may help us if it spreads their men too thinly. Though they may of course be more concerned with finding out how the city will receive Tudor.'

Alys shot a look at Roger and me, a faint shake of the head, a warning in her eyes.

Master Ashley took another sip of wine from the cup Simon held to his lips, before continuing.

'But if they still suspect me, they may keep watch on all my contacts too in case they will lead them to the boys.'

'Why would they be so desperate to find them?' Roger asked.

'Tudor cannot afford to let the boys live. They say he will overturn the law on young Elizabeth's illegitimacy so that he can marry her and make her his queen.'

'If he does that, then surely Edward would be the real King,' said Alys. 'Both he and Prince Richard have a better claim to the crown.'

'Aye,' agreed Master Ashley. 'And he will not stand for that. From all I've heard, he intends to rule, not place young Edward back on the throne. He will not offer the boy his oath of lifelong loyalty, for all his declarations against his bastardy. Tudor is an ambitious man – he will not put aside his desire to be king. If he finds them, he will kill them.'

His words stunned us all into silence. Alys, of course, was the first to speak again.

'If the boys are in such danger, why did King Richard not send them out of the country before?'

'I imagine he remembered his own time of exile, and perhaps not fondly, though it was then that we met, in his moments of respite with his brother in Bruges. And with the shifting politics on the continent, the boys might fall into the hands of his enemies, like Tudor himself – one moment in friendly Brittany, the next in France.'

He paused a moment, thoughts scudding across his weary eyes like clouds in a storm-filled sky.

'I think perhaps he hoped they could live anonymous lives out in the country until they were old enough to move to loyal households as squires like any other noble lad – when the rumours and threat of rebellion had withered and died away. Like old Henry Bolingbroke did with the Mortimer heirs many years ago. And it was working. After Buckingham, what talk had there been of them? And once Tudor was gone...'

He shook his head, his face pale and drawn, showing his age for the first time since I'd known him.

'Now no more talking. Sleep, boys, while the girls make things ready for you. You have a long dangerous ride ahead of you.'

Another one, I thought morosely as I settled myself in a borrowed blanket.

To my surprise, when Elen shook me awake, I found not only Roger, as agreed before I slept, but also Alys kitted out ready for the journey.

'You're not leaving me here,' she said when I tried to object. 'Ralph Soulsby will be coming to claim me in marriage. Nothing will make me forget that he and his father rode with the Stanleys. Princess Elizabeth may have to resign herself to marrying Tudor, but no duty to Dame Grey could ever make me wed a traitor.'

'We spoke of it while you slept,' said Elen. 'Master Ashley agrees it will be for the best.'

'I offered to give up my place to her,' said Roger, smiling more broadly than he had a right to do at that time of night. 'But your good master said I might be useful to you both on the road. Though for the life of me, I cannot think how.'

'Safety in numbers, perhaps,' muttered Alys darkly. 'What other use you may have escapes me too.'

He bowed his agreement.

Unsure though I was that the plan was a good one, I knew there was no point in arguing with Alys if she had made up her mind. And in truth, I would be grateful for her company as well as Roger's. Perhaps it would be almost like those days long ago in Middleham when the three of us had often ridden out together on the moors as the Order of the White Boar. Although one other member of the Order would always now be missing...

Shaking away the memory, I turned to Elen.

'What about you? What will you do?'

'Oh, I'll stay here and help Master Ashley and his wife. I'd only slow you down if I came too – I'm not so good a horsewoman.'

'You will be careful? It may be dangerous here. With Tudor on his way...'

She placed a hand on my arm to quiet me.

'Don't worry, Matthew – of course I will be careful. And Simon will be here with us. He tells me he has been training with you all summer in case of emergency.'

To my surprise, Simon blushed to the roots of his hair at her words and hurried off into the hallway, murmuring something about fetching our bundles.

It was well after midnight when the three of us set out. Sometime while I slept, Roger and Simon had helped Master Ashley at last to his chamber, but Mistress Ashley had emerged from hers – to find out what was happening, then to make sure we had all we needed for the journey.

Her eye was blackened and her cheeks cut and bruised where she had been struck during the attack. She embraced me as I stood dumb in shock at her appearance, then leant on both Simon's and Elen's arms on the entrance steps to see us off.

Master Ashley had insisted we take fresh horses from his stable and Simon and Elen had swathed their hooves in cloth to muffle the noise as we rode out of the courtyard into the dark deserted streets. At our heels slunk the two hounds, mirror images of dark and light against the cobbled roadway.

The moon, just past full and sinking towards the west, cast crazy shadows from all the buildings nearby. If there were any spies lurking in those shadows, we did not see them.

How, then, we came to be pursued we didn't know.

*

It took many hours of hard riding to reach our destination. But as I had hoped, King Richard's boar badge still commanded loyalty in these early days after the battle. The country was waiting, watching, hardly breathing in this twilight between the golden sun of Yorkist rule and the dark unknown of the Tudor future. We trusted that the dragon symbol of the victorious usurper would not be welcomed so readily – if we were pursued.

Some had not had news of the battle and questioned us before we could leave them and hasten on our way. Others waved us on with a good will and long faces.

As Master Ashley had advised, we made our way north from London first using the system of post-horses that King Richard had put in place when he was still Duke, to send his brother news of his wars in Scotland. In this way, at every post-house we had fresh horses. When we turned off that route, the final pair had to take us far further – to Gipping Hall itself. Though fine horses, we had pushed them so hard that they were dripping with sweat and lather as we clattered on to the cobbles of a wide stable yard.

The sun had long since retired, and darkness pressed upon us, as, dazed with exhaustion and filthy from the journey, and following a few words of explanation, the three of us were ushered towards the nearby mansion, as the grooms came to lead our mounts away.

With the uproar of our arrival in the stable yard, a messenger must have been sent to the house. Lady Tyrell herself was at the main door to greet us, surrounded by serving men holding torches aloft. Several were armed, and all rather elderly.

'Alys! Alys Langdown! What are you doing here?

A formidably tall woman, Lady Tyrell pushed her way past the servants and rushed forward to embrace Alys. As she took her arm and led her into the house, she said,

'You mustn't worry about the men, my dear. Since we heard the terrible news, we're having to be extra careful. But of course all the younger men went to fight for the King. Most of them haven't yet returned.'

She glanced askance at Roger and me, but said nothing to us so we simply followed them into the great hall. A fire was blazing there despite the warm evening, and Lady Tyrell ushered Alys to a seat beside it.

'Sit down, my dear, take some wine. Some bread and cheese, perhaps – or I can ask the cooks to bring something hot, though it is so late? You look fit to drop, my dear. Tell me why you are here. I haven't seen you since we were last at court together. After poor Queen Anne...'

Her busy words ran to a halt as Alys accepted the proffered wine-glass and gulped gratefully. Shadow sidled up and sat down, alert, at her side, as Alys replaced the glass on a nearby table.

'Thank you, my lady. It has been a long day, and a long ride. We have come all the way from London.'

'London! But —' Lady Tyrell drew back a fraction. 'But isn't Tudor...?'

'He had not arrived before we left. We have been sent with a message.'

'Then I'm only sorry that Sir James is not here to greet you. He is on the continent in service for...' She hesitated, her eyes again flickering over Roger and me, 'for King Richard.'

'That is why we are here, Lady Tyrell,' said Alys. 'On the King's service. The true King.'

'Indeed? And who are "we"?'

Alys shrank back from a sudden sharpness in Lady Tyrell's words and her own voice wavered.

'This – this is Matthew Wansford, my lady, and perhaps you remember Roger de Kynton?'

My lady inclined her head as both Roger and I bowed our most courteous bows, but her face was still suspicious. When she didn't speak, Alys stammered on.

'Matthew was sent by... by King Richard from the battlefield with a message to Master Ashley.' A flutter of recognition in Lady Tyrell's eyes, but it was blinked away in a moment. 'Master Ashley – he has been prevented from coming here himself by agents of Henry Tudor. So... so we have come instead.'

'Why?'

The force of the word finally bludgeoned Alys into silence. She took another gulp of wine, her free hand reaching across to fondle Shadow's ears.

Her ladyship's glance darted from her to me and back again.

Roger stepped forward into the breach and bent his knee in a flouncing, ceremonious fashion, whisking off his cap and sweeping it to his heart as he was used to do in dancing classes at Middleham.

'My lady, we have travelled far to bring you greetings from —'

But Lady Tyrell cut him off.

'Not you – the other boy. Speak! Why are you here?'

As Roger retreated, I seized my courage in my hands and took a pace forwards, sensing Murrey hugging close to my thigh and drawing strength from her presence.

Now was a moment for plain speaking – and our task was urgent.

'To take Edward and Richard, the – the princes to safety, my lady. If it will help you trust us, I have this.' I thrust my boar badge, outside my doublet once more, towards her, and then reached inside my pouch. 'And also this.'

She took the scrap of parchment I held out, that I had hoarded since the road to St Albans.

After peering at it, she said,

'That is indeed his signature – the King's I mean. And,' she looked again at the parchment and up at me, 'And Edward's too. Do you know him?'

'Yes, my lady. At least – we have met. I – I was his page once – when he was newly King. On his journey to London. Before...'

'When he was King?'

'Aye, my lady.'

'And yet you are King Richard's man?'

'Yes, my lady.' My voice sounded firm, though my insides roiled. 'More recently I was apprentice to Master Ashley. It was he who sent us.'

'And what do you intend to do with the – boys?'

'King Richard said they were to be taken to his sister in Flanders. Master Ashley told us we should go by boat from

392

Lowestoft – that would be the nearest seaport and the safest crossing to the continent.'

Much of the tension in Lady Tyrell's features seeped away, but doubt still shaded her eyes.

'And you say you know young Edward?'

'Aye, my lady. We rode together one Christmas-tide, and then again towards London. We became friends – almost.'

For so I had believed.

She motioned to one of the old servants, all of whom were standing silently nearby, and in a few moments two figures appeared in the doorway.

Alys and Roger exchanged glances, and for the first time it occurred to me that my friends had perhaps never met these boys.

But I knew them of course.

Edward and Richard. The boys who had been princes.

They advanced a pace or two into the hall, their faces pale, fear in their dark shadowed eyes. I smiled, hoping Edward and I could pick up our friendship across the distance of those two long years. But of a sudden my dream on the morning of the battle burst into my mind – with a shock as powerful as the blast of one of those monstrous cannons that had bombarded the armies facing each other that day.

I quavered inside at the memory, but I stood my ground. It was just a dream after all, nothing solid, nothing that would sway Edward's reception of me. Surely, if he recollected me at all, he would recall our closeness during those days at Northampton and St Albans, how we chatted, joked, laughed together amidst the cares of his uncles' business – how he had clasped hands with me warmly as we took our farewells and urged me to visit him in his royal apartments at the tower. Yet so much had changed in the days and weeks that followed. And now, as though I was being put to a test, the boys and I stared at one another across the cold grey width of the hall.

Would I pass? Would they remember me and know they could place their trust in me and my friends?

After an eternity waiting, to my surprise Edward dropped to one knee, dipping his hand into his pouch.

'Murrey?'

My hound's eyes beseeched me and I gestured to her to go. She bounded across the stone-slabbed floor and, as Edward drew out his hand, performed her usual perfect pirouette for the scrap he held. He threw it to her, waited till she had wolfed it down, then clapped his hands. She fell to the ground, unmoving, as though she had been shot, and stirred again only when he whistled.

Laughing, he slipped her another morsel, ruffling the fur on her head.

Then he glanced over to me and his expression changed. He drew himself up, looking very much like my memory of his father, the old King Edward.

'Matthew? Murrey has not changed, but you – you look – older.'

So he had recognized me – if only through the antics of my hound. Would it be enough to persuade him to trust me?

Crossing the expanse of cold stone flags, I knelt before him.

What should I call him? Two years ago he had insisted on 'Edward'. But now...?

I lowered my head.

'Your Grace, it has been more than two years since last we met.'

'Oh, yes, it has. And a great deal has happened in that time. Then I was King. Now...' He paused. 'And you were ever my uncle's man.'

What was that emotion in his voice? Was it fear, scorn – or anger?

Whatever it was, the greeting I had hoped for would not be mine. Perhaps I should not be surprised after all that had passed. I brushed away the stab of disappointment. The matter at hand was too important to dwell on my own emotions.

I got back to my feet and looked him in the eye – though he was still taller than me.

'Aye, Your Grace, I was and ever will be. And now I have come to take you to safety with his sister, your aunt.'

'Safety!' He spat out the word as though it brought evil tidings. 'And I'm to believe you? After what my uncle did? And now that Henry Tudor has come to restore us? When I was lodged at the Tower, Lady Stanley said he —'

I raised my hand. Whatever he saw in my face caused his words to fade away.

'Listen to me, Edward.' Now was no time for niceties. 'No matter what you may think of your uncle, of what he did, Henry Tudor is the more to be feared. He wants the crown for himself –

he won't restore it to you or your brother. The moment he stepped ashore in Wales he called himself King. He has issued proclamations from Leicester in the name of King Henry. He swore to marry your sister and if he makes her legitimate, it will mean you are too – and therefore the rightful King. But he will not bend his knee to you. He won't rest until you are dead.'

Little Richard gasped and his hand crept to clutch his brother's. Edward was silent, but shock was scored across his eyes. Yet I had to go on, to tell them the truth.

'No matter what she said to you, Lady Stanley is Tudor's mother. And her husband, Lord Stanley, betrayed his anointed King on the battlefield. Who would you rather trust?'

I fell quiet myself at last, amazed at the words that had forced their way out. I had perhaps never uttered so many all at once before.

Then, as the boys remained motionless, I drew cool air deep into my lungs and, releasing it slowly, bowed my head to them both.

'We will take you to your aunt Margaret and your friends in Flanders. They will keep you safe. One day, if you wish it, maybe they will help restore you to the throne.'

.

24

A New Morning

'Matt. Wake up.'

Tap, tap, tap.

Someone knocking.

'Matt? Did you hear me? Wake up. We must be off.'

Alys.

Groggy from sleep – the first sound, dreamless sleep for days – I grunted without words. Her quick footsteps faded away along the passage.

I swung my legs off the feather bed, splashed myself awake with the basinful of water placed ready and, dragging on my doublet, went to the window.

Outside a grey dawn was breaking. Threads of mist were floating across the flat fields beyond the stables, the wide fishponds, the chapel, its cut-flint walls lustrous in the half-light.

Something tugged inside me. The sun would be rising soon over the familiar moors high above Middleham, clothed now in the purple velvet of heather. Dew would form chains of sparkling diamonds on cobwebs adorning the golden bracken. The mist would linger in the dale perhaps for hours yet.

I turned away.

Upon a chair were my cloak, my new bundle of things for our journey, and Lord Lovell's sword. I had kept it closely hidden since that first day at Leicester, had not even unsheathed it.

I drew it from its scabbard now. It was a fine-wrought weapon, well balanced, its hilt a simple cross bound with lightly worn leather.

I weighed it in my hand, then skipped to one side, whirling it about me as I had learnt, to parry the blow of an invisible enemy and turn the defence into my own attack. It felt comfortable in my hands, though I had never wielded a true sword before.

As I slid it back into its leather sheath, my eye was caught by some dark red specks where burnished blade met hilt. Lord Lovell had cleaned his weapon after the battle, but in a hurry. I rubbed the stain away with a corner of my cloak.

Downstairs, in the main entranceway, a slender figure was silhouetted against the growing daylight. It was Alys, staring out across the countryside, with Shadow a pale statue at her side.

Hearing the clicking of Murrey's claws and the hesitant scrape of my footsteps on the stone flags, she swung to face me.

Something about her had changed.

'Alys – your hair!'

She threw me a quick smile as her hand crept up to her head.

'Lady Tyrell cut it for me. She says, if I must go, it may be safer if I travel as a boy. In case we are followed. They will be searching for two boys and a girl, not three – or five – boys.'

She gazed back out over the waving fields of corn and barley, touched to gold now by the first shafts of sunlight.

'And if I'm not to be married soon, no one will notice if I don't have long hair just now.'

We stood side by side in silence for a few moments. Then she said quietly,

'Matt, will you tell me all that happened? There was no time to ask at Master Ashley's. All we heard was that Lord Stanley...'

I turned to her, as she stood upright in the pinkish twilight, her ragged hair sticking out all-ways out from under her boy's cap, her eyes catching the rays of the sun and melting into liquid emeralds.

But my heart seemed to force its way into my throat. All I could croak out was 'No – not today', before I buried my face in the shoulder of her doublet, and let out all the sobs I had held in for days, and all the tears.

She embraced me for some minutes, wordless herself, her arms tight around me as my body shook in distress. Then, as the sobbing died away, she loosened her hold and pushed me a little away from her.

'We must carry on. We must finish this.'

Her voice, though broken, was fierce, determined.

I nodded and, wiping my face with my sleeve, followed as she led the way back into the great hall, the two hounds trailing behind.

Roger hailed us from where he was helping himself to bread, cheese and ale at a long trestle table, cheerful as ever, despite all our troubles and the early hour of the morning.

Sitting a little way along from him, and similarly dressed in rough travelling clothes, Edward and Richard were also breaking their fast. They didn't speak as we joined them, but again in Edward's face was that mixture of anger, fear and defiance I'd seen last night. But also perhaps a new respect. Richard, as I discovered, followed his brother in most things, though there was still more of fear in his younger eyes. I neither knew nor cared what they could read in mine.

I had hardly time to chew a first mouthful of bread and cheese, and drop some down to Murrey, before Lady Tyrell came hurrying in.

'You must leave at once. Strangers have been seen in Stowmarket asking questions. There's no time to waste. Horses are being saddled in the yard.'

As we each swallowed a last draught of ale and snatched up our bundles, she carried on, addressing me apparently as the leader of the party.

'Remember what I said last night. Cut across country until you reach the River Waveney. It may be slow going, but safer than the roads. Follow it until you come to the sea. The town there is Lowestoft. You should be able to buy your passage in the harbour there.'

She ushered us out to the stable yard where five lean ponies were waiting patiently while grooms finished harnessing them. As Alys and the boys went to sling their packs across the ponies' withers, Lady Tyrell's hand on my shoulder held me back.

'Be careful who you show your badge to, and don't tell anyone who you really are. The ships' captains are fiercely independent like all men of the sea. They may not want to become entangled in affairs of the English crown.'

I nodded, but she didn't release her grip on my arm.

'And, Matthew, my husband does not know the boys were here. He is so often away on business. To him they were just two new pages – he was never at court with them and they have been sworn to secrecy. It was thought safest. If you should meet him abroad...'

'Of course, my lady. I understand.'

At last she let me go. A minute later the five of us and two hounds were trotting along the lane away from the hall, turning east towards the rising sun.

25

Lowestoft

Our journey that day might have been a pleasure in less troubled times. For all my yearning to be home in Yorkshire, even I could have found beauty in the slow-moving, meandering river, fringed by gracious willows and warm sunlit water meadows. As herons leisurely took to flight on their great grey wings at our approach and flocks of geese paddled honking away from the river bank.

But as we drew nearer to the sea, the trees thinned and the lush grassland became scrub, and the feeling crept through me that we could be seen for miles across this flat, almost featureless landscape.

Lady Tyrell had assured us that she and her people would tell any pursuers that we had headed north-west, as though towards King Richard's northern strongholds. But how long would that keep them from our trail?

Darkness was falling as our ponies' hoofbeats echoed along the main street of Lowestoft. There was little more than this one paved way, with scatters of houses along alleys climbing on our left-hand side and tumbling downhill towards the harbour to our right. The swell of the sea reached my ears from far below and lights twinkled on the masts of ships and from lanterns on the quayside – a black mass now against the dark grey of the water. A mist was rising in the cool of the evening, carrying the salt tang of the sea to my nostrils.

Roger and I left Alys and the boys with the horses and made our way to the tavern on the corner where Lady Tyrell had said sea captains might be found. I glanced up at its swinging sign as we entered and nudged Roger. The sign of the silver lion. We were in the country of the Dukes of Norfolk and I took it to be a good omen.

The first two or three captains only laughed at the sight of us, despite the coins we offered, but within minutes we had made a down payment on a passage across to Friesland, the rest to be paid on our safe arrival.

'It's a boat called the Falcon, though its master is Friesian,' Roger told the others on our return to the dark, misty corner where they had waited. 'It sails just after midnight on the ebb tide.'

'Can we go aboard now?' asked Richard.

Of all of us, he had found the day most tiring, though his complaints had been few. I was sorry to have to shake my head.

'Not until an hour or so before. The crew are still loading their cargo of wool and we'd just be in the way.'

'Let's get some hot food,' suggested Alys. 'Shall we try that tavern?'

'We passed a quieter one on the way back – the Fleece. It might suit us better and there was stabling.'

The Fleece laid on a fine stew of lamb and aromatic herbs and mugs of good ale, and we arranged to leave the ponies there until Lady Tyrell's people could claim them. At last we were closing in on our goal. I almost began to relax.

Richard was nodding in the corner of the settle and the rest of us were in the middle of a spirited debate about the latest French romances when I realized Alys had fallen quiet.

'What's wrong?' I asked.

Her usually clear eyes were troubled.

'I'm not sure anything is. But... a few minutes ago a man came in, talked to the serving man and left again almost straight away. I noticed him because he seemed familiar. He's just come back in and I think... I'm not sure, but I think he's watching us. No!' The word came out as a squeak as Roger began to turn round. 'Don't look his way. That will just alert him – if it is anything to worry about.'

'Everything is something to worry about,' I said grimly.

'What do you think we should do?' asked Roger.

Alys shook her head. 'I don't know.'

'Perhaps,' I said, thinking quickly, 'perhaps if we go out separately – maybe you two and Richard through the main door, Edward and I through the stables, as though we're checking on the ponies. He's only one man – he can't follow all of us.'

Roger looked doubtful.

'But if there are more watching outside?'

I shrugged.

Edward said, 'I think we should try it. What if he's the only one now? He may be keeping an eye on us in here while waiting for others to join him.'

'That's possible,' said Roger. 'Well, you're the —' I kicked him under the table; he smiled, 'the one who's used to giving orders.'

'Not any more,' Edward said, darting a look at me, but Roger forged on.

'Are we to go, then? Shall I wake Richard?'

As Richard rubbed the sleep from his eyes, I reminded them all what had been arranged.

'Captain Hans said his boat is the first tied up along the quay – it has a hawk as a figurehead. Also he said any of the alleyways opposite, back along the road we came along – he called them "scores" – they lead down to the harbour. You three head for one of them. We'll wait two minutes after you've gone, then leave through the back door.'

Alys, Roger and Richard, his eyes more haunted than ever, took up their bundles and, with Roger making much of calling his farewells to Edward and me, made their exit through the front door, Shadow hugging close. A second later, a fair-haired young man in dark travel-stained riding gear set down his mug, cast a hurried glance at the two of us, then stood up, threw coins upon his table, and followed them out.

I cursed under my breath.

'Richard and I have our swords,' said Edward. He half-unsheathed his – I caught a glimpse of curlicued words inscribed darkly on the well-honed blade.

'I hope it won't come to that.'

We didn't need to wait any longer. Without another word, we rose, gathered our things, and soon we were out on the main street, Murrey a silent shadow at our heels.

At first the place appeared deserted. The sea-fret was coiling everywhere, grey and ghostly in the darkness. It deadened our footsteps on the cobbles as we trailed first one way, then another, squinting to see where our three friends or the strange man had gone. From a few house-fronts lanterns were hung, but they shed pools of light that hardly penetrated the murk. There was no sign of anybody.

Edward opened his mouth as if to speak, but then the silence was shattered.

A shout, then another. A man's voice, urgent.

Thirty, forty yards away, maybe more – it was hard to tell in the fog.

Edward and I exchanged glances, then began to run, he drawing his sword as he did.

In a moment, in the light of a single house lantern piercing the fog and the dark, we spotted who had called.

The man from the tavern.

His back against the house wall, his face turned away from us, he was cursing quietly now. Then he raised his voice again.

'Put down your sword or I'll cut his throat.'

A few yards in front of him stood Richard, his sword in his hand. He was panting heavily, staring wide-eyed at the man. Another sword was lying on the cobbles between them, three bundles abandoned nearby. Roger was crouching off to one side, his face glimmering white with terror in the swirling mist, his arms wrapped round a squirming, whimpering Shadow.

And then I saw who else was there.

The man held someone close against his body with one arm, while his other hand pressed the glittering blade of a dagger to their neck.

It was Alys.

She was rigid in his hold, her head forced back against him, fingers clutching his arm, eyelids fluttering, her throat curving back as though straining away from the sharp steel.

Edward darted to his brother's side, all the while keeping his gaze fixed on the young man and his captive, and his sword at the ready.

'What happened?'

The man twitched round a little at his movement. The point of the knife was dark now against Alys's pale skin. Her hands tightened convulsively on his wrist.

My fist clenched Murrey's collar, as Roger inched towards me, tugging the other wriggling hound with him.

'He came at us with his sword,' Richard said hoarsely, his eyes not leaving the man's face for a second, 'I disarmed him with that trick Father taught us – remember? But then he drew his knife and grabbed her.'

'Her?' the man cried in surprise. 'What do you mean?'

'Let her go!' I yelled.

His head snapped towards me. Knowing Alys would hate me for it, I shouted again, 'She's a girl, not a boy!'

His grip must have faltered in his astonishment. Sensing the blade no longer so close to her neck, Alys took her chance to drive one elbow into his stomach while tearing his knife-hand from her throat, then stamped on his foot and flung herself away from his flailing grasp. Her stumbling strides cannoned her into Roger and Shadow, spilling all three into a sprawling mess at my feet.

But as the man buckled under her onslaught and himself staggered forward, his hand snatched at his sword and, rolling over to the side, he was back on his feet in an instant. There he faced Edward and Richard, standing now shoulder to shoulder, their swords upraised before them.

His eyes flicked sideways to where I was hauling Alys and Roger to their feet, the hounds milling about us, whining. He clearly saw that we were nothing to worry about and turned back to the two armed brothers.

'Two against one,' he said, a mirthless grin unfurling across his handsome face. 'But two little ones. I've had worse odds.'

And he attacked, throwing himself towards the boys, both his sword and knife slicing and stabbing through the greyish eddies of mist.

Alys gasped, catching at my arm at the ferocity of the onslaught. But if the man had thought he'd have an easy time of it with boys, he was wrong.

For all his superior height and weight, he was matched against brothers who, as sons of a King, must once have had the finest weapons masters available. Perhaps they had never fought in earnest before, but an onlooker could not have guessed. Had my fellow pages at Middleham displayed such footwork, Master Fleete would have burst with pride, and their anticipation and skill in attack and counterattack was as good as I'd ever seen.

Stroke for stroke they began to get the better of their adversary. The sea-fret muffled the clang of swords on sword and dagger as, between them, step by gruelling step, they battled him back to the wall again.

But still they could not overmaster him.

Tiredness and despair were creeping on to young Richard's face, and Edward's frustration was likewise written in his eyes. Though on the defensive, did the man also see it – or feel a waning of their attack? Or was he simply desperate, like an animal forced into a corner, with nowhere to go? Whichever was the case, he both redoubled his efforts and sought for a way out.

And found it.

In a moment of respite from Richard's attack, the man flung his dagger at him. Though Richard parried it with his blade, knocking it away, the man, with his free hand, caught up Alys's pack from where it lay abandoned on the ground and swung it at both boys. Richard took the brunt of the impact, his sword spinning out of his hand, but the move also took Edward by surprise.

His opponent saw his advantage and leapt at him, landing a blow that the boy could barely parry. His sword glanced off Edward's blade and struck the boy deep in his shoulder. Edward staggered back, blood spurting from the wound, while the man, also tipped off balance by the force of his deflected blow, fought to keep his footing.

As, twisting about, he regained it and started to raise his sword for the killing thrust, Roger and I threw a terrified glance at one another. Then, he drawing his knife and I my sword, we rushed forward yelling, Murrey and Shadow bounding barking at our side.

We caught the man unawares, so focused was he on Edward. And, with Richard also recovering his sword and his balance, somehow, between us – three boys and two hounds – we charged him to the floor, Roger and I toppling upon him in our onrush.

He fell beneath us like a sack of grain tossed from a wagon, heavy and awkward. With a sickening thud, his head hit the timbers of the house-front, knocking him cold. His eyes were sightless as Richard's sword point swung down to his throat and his own sword fell from his unconscious hand. It lay on the ground, dark blood seeping from it into the dust.

Roger and I dragged one another to our feet and while he scurried to catch hold of the gambolling hounds, I hurried across to Alys. Crouched down beside Edward, she was busy tearing her cloak into strips.

'How is he?'

'Not good,' she said, starting to bind his wound. 'It's deep. I may be able to stem the bleeding for a while, but he'll need a surgeon.'

Richard shoved the fallen man with his toe and when his head lolled to one side, he sheathed his sword and ran over to his elder brother.

'Ned? Can you walk?'

Edward's face was pale with shock and pain, but he nodded.

'I think so, Dickon. Once I've caught my breath.'

Alys finished tying her makeshift bandage, then relinquished her place to Richard. He knelt down and, propping Edward against himself, stroked his head, murmuring to him all the time in gentle tones.

Alys came over to where I now stood, my sword pointing at the unconscious man's chest – just in case.

She said quietly, 'Matt, I – I think he's Ralph Soulsby.'

'What?'

'I thought I recognized him in the tavern, but it's been so long since I saw him. He was just thirteen or fourteen then. It was only when he grabbed me and called out that I realized.'

'You knew his voice?'

'Yes.' She hesitated. 'No. The name he called. It was Hugh.'

All my insides turned to ice.

The shining blade, the cowardly stab.

The jeers.

The horror. The shame I'd felt at doing nothing.

The anger. The desire for revenge. Now more than ever.

But not for me. For my King.

And the ice melted to fire.

Alys caught at my hand as my sword tip wavered closer to the prone man's chest.

'Matt, we have to get out of here. If Hugh is in the town somewhere, there may be others too. We can't afford another fight. Now is not the time.'

She was right, of course. I knew it. I could no more hope to fight Hugh and gain my revenge now than at any time when we had met before. Even with Roger or young Richard alongside me.

And I had my duty still to do. And perhaps all of this could have been avoided if I had done that on the day of the battle...

My betrayal of my master vivid in my mind, the flames died down.

Roger was hovering close by, a hound grasped in each hand. The expression on his face told me that he had heard Alys's whispered words.

'What should we do?' he asked. Alys only stared at me.

Not for the first time since the evening at Master Ashley's, they were looking to me to decide.

I resheathed my sword.

'You three take Edward to the boat. I'll tie this one up so he can't make more trouble and then I'll join you once I'm done. Go carefully. If Hugh is out there...'

Alys hissed through her teeth.

'I'll stay with you, Matt. Shadow and I can —'

'No,' I said, firm, though my stomach was churning now at the thought of Hugh perhaps nearby. 'Go with the others.

'Then Roger —'

'Richard will need his help with Edward. And Captain Hans knows him.'

Relief flooded across Roger's face, though he tried to hide it, turning away towards Richard and Edward.

'Take a couple of the bundles if you are able, Alys. And tell Richard to carry his sword ready if he can.'

I peered back the way Edward and I had come, through the confusion of mist, darkness and glimmers of occasional lanterns.

'I think the third score back was the widest and best paved. There was a lantern at its entrance and I think I saw another further down. That may be the safest way to go.'

She nodded, then glanced up at the lantern flaring in the seething mist above our heads.

'Lady Tyrell was right about local people not wanting to become involved. You'd think that with all this racket going on in the street...' She shook her head. 'Come after us quickly, Matt – and take care.'

I watched as Roger and Richard helped Edward to his feet, then half-supported, half-carried him as they walked slowly away. Alys hefted two of our packs and followed after with Shadow. They all soon disappeared into the mist like wraiths at the tail end of a dream, leaving me alone with Murrey – and the man lying senseless before me on the ground.

Pushing to one side my thoughts of him and his cousin, I set about my task, gathering the rest of the strips Alys had torn from her cloak and tying his wrists and ankles with them. He groaned as I wrenched one binding tight and his eyelids flickered. Duly warned, I wound the final strips of cloth into a thick gag and somehow forced it between his teeth.

406

Sticky blood darkened my hands as I drew them from beneath his head. Gulping back a retch, I wiped them clean on his doublet, then stood, keen to escape from the scene and the memory of what had happened here.

Picking up the remaining bundles, I whistled to Murrey, who was sniffing about among the shadows of the still-empty street, and together we headed off back into the veil of mist, clammy and chill against my skin.

Had I miscounted the alleys as I passed them, or had Alys? Or, despite Edward's injury, had my friends travelled faster than I thought possible?

Whatever the reason, when I reached the entrance of the wide, paved score, I could see and hear no one ahead of me in the darkness.

True, the lantern at its mouth threw little light into its black throat, and the sea-fret gathered closer here. It was seeping and creeping all around, spectres crowding close upon me from the shadowy depths of the passage. Even the familiar clicking of Murrey's claws upon the cobbles sounded damp and heavy under its weight.

I paused a moment. But I had to go on, I knew. Time was passing and soon we had to be aboard the ship. The tide and captain would not wait. And I had promised to help the others find their way.

I patted Murrey's head and said, 'Good girl.' The words were more to comfort me than her and their sound was deadened by the fog. She gazed up at me, letting out the slightest whine, her eyes small sparks in the gloom. Then, side by side, we plunged into the alley.

In the instant it took to cross the pool of lantern light, strange details imprinted on my mind.

Our shadows stretching thin before us.

Crumbling brick walls curving in and out before my eyes.

Pebbles of every colour pressed into pale bands of mortar.

Cut faces of flint gleaming, glassy dark.

Tiny blooms of purple toadflax clinging on for grim death.

Then we passed into darkness and the grey swirl of the mist.

Black branches of trees, overhanging, looming out of the fog.

Beyond the wavy walls, the mewing of a cat, the rattle of a chain and whine of a tethered dog.

The sweet smell of rotting vegetables wafting. Woodsmoke from a high chimney.

I glanced back. The glow of the lantern still shone, reassuring, through the tendrils of sea-fret, through the murk.

We walked on.

A plaintive hooting. A swoosh of air as the owl swooped over and was gone.

The dull clump of my boots on the ground.

The walls – rippling spans of brick – closing in on us. The alley was narrowing. Ahead, veering to the right.

And there through the drifting strands of mist was the faintest glimmer. That second lantern I had seen? At the corner of the alley?

But something warned me to stop, forced my hand to my sword hilt. What was it?

The light.

It was moving. Moving towards the corner. Towards us.

A grumble deep in Murrey's throat.

The scrape of boots on cobbles.

The swish of my blade being drawn. The thud of three bundles being dropped.

The reek of sweat – and of fear. Was it mine?

Around the corner came the lantern, held high in someone's hand. A tall, broad figure. A burnished open helmet above a familiar face.

Hugh.

26

The Score

The lantern crashed to the ground as Hugh reached for his sword.

Glass shattered, oil spilt. Flames flashed across its surface.

Flaring, they lit up the narrow alleyway, casting demonic shadows across my old adversary's face and up the high brick walls. The sharp blade of his sword glittered only inches from mine.

My heart hammered against my ribs, echoed by the fast rise and fall of his chest. But he recovered more swiftly.

'I should have known it would be you,' he spat.

Yet he hadn't attacked.

Relief swept through me. For all that I had grown and filled out in recent months, he would always overmatch me in size. But I was also bemused at his words. Playing for time, I said, 'What do you mean?'

A sneer spread across his broad face.

'When we called for Alys and found she'd gone to that man's house. That merchant. I remember Roger telling us when he became your master.'

'What of it?'

'He thought you'd done so well for yourself,' he scoffed. 'Going to London, becoming an apprentice.'

'Better than you have,' I shot back. 'Son of a traitor, riding with a traitor.'

His smirk slipped, twisting into a darker expression.

'What do you know of my father? And my uncle is no traitor!'

'He fought with Lord Stanley.'

'Who will be right-hand man to the new King.' He rallied, his face smug once more.

'Only because he betrayed the old one.'

'Old Dick had no right to be King. Everyone knew it.'

'That's not true,' I retorted. 'King Richard had more right than Tudor ever will. Even he knows he must marry Princess Elizabeth before the people will accept him.'

'He's doing it to unite the houses of Lancaster and York and put an end to all these wars.'

'Is that what you truly believe?' I asked. 'What war has there been in our lifetimes – until Tudor came?'

He was silent, his eyes hooded, the flickering shadows from the lantern playing across his stony features.

How strange was this talk, in a dark alley, between two such enemies? But I forced myself to speak on, to gain time to decide what to do.

'Why are you here anyway? Why did you follow us?'

'We have our orders. They come from King Henry himself.' Pride was blazoned across his face and voice.

'Which are?'

'I don't have to tell you.'

I pushed on again, thinking desperately.

'Why did your cousin try to kill us?'

'What? Where is he?'

He flicked his gaze from side to side, chary of taking it away from my sword, but seeking into every shadowy, mist-shrouded corner of the score.

'Don't worry, he's still alive,' I said. 'But he won't be coming to help you. He shouldn't have tangled with Alys.'

'Alys? What's she doing here?'

'She rode with us, of course.'

'We thought she'd stayed at Tyrell's place. Our informants said five boys. That her companions had ridden on just with the princes and a guide.'

My insides lurched at his words.

'So you know who they are.'

'The princes? Of course. Why do you think we're here? To hunt you down and kill you? You're not worth the effort!'

Despite all I'd heard from King Richard and Master Ashley, and repeated to Edward and Richard at Gipping, until that moment I had perhaps only half believed it myself – that Tudor really would seek to murder Elizabeth's brothers in cold blood. But Hugh's mocking face didn't lie.

I forced myself to carry on.

'And you knew they were at Gipping?'

'Not until we got there. Then we put two and two together. As Ralph said, what other two boys would Yorkists go to so much trouble to hide – and then smuggle away when Henry Tudor came.'

'And it's just you and Ralph here then?'

He didn't answer with words, but his expression as he realized that he was now alone was reply enough for me. My decision was made.

I hurled myself at him so suddenly that he could do no more than roughly parry my blade, and then I had a chance to pivot and land a blow on his body before he had recovered.

But my heart sank at the crunch as my sword struck him. He was wearing mail beneath his doublet. I had hoped to take him by surprise, that it might give me an edge. But instead he had the edge – of being armoured while I wore only a jack.

Yet my blow had at least winded and bruised him, if it had done no more damage. It gave me a little time to think again as we circled each other warily in the narrow score, he grimacing with the pain.

'You wretch!' he snapped. 'Think you can best me, eh? You never have before.'

That I knew well. But my mind had to stay in the present, not the past, if I were to have any chance at all.

He flung himself at me with a snarl, but I skipped out of the way, at the last moment twisting and striking out as he passed. The flat of my blade caught him hard on his upper arm. His flinch told me he wore no mail there.

He was stronger than me, more skilled, better armed. But was I more agile, lighter, quicker? Might his greater height and weight work against him – however unlikely that seemed?

These thoughts flitted through my brain as we circled once more, slowly, carefully, watching one another, each with heaving chest, catching our breath. All talking was now over. Silent again, Hugh fixed his eyes on me, no longer scouting for his cousin, for help, focused only on me, searching for any warning sign, for any movement, any action. And I did the same – quietening my breathing, ignoring the pounding of blood in my ears, praying I would be ready for his next move – forgetting who else was there in the score with us.

With a flurry of deep red, glinting in the lamp's glow, Murrey darted in to snap at Hugh's ankles, then danced away, yapping sharply as he lashed out with his boot. A growl, a twirl around, then another swift, scarlet rush into the fray.

411

As Hugh kicked again at my hound and she spun away, I took the chance she gave me. I catapulted myself at him, lunging with my sword and aiming this time for his unprotected, bull-like neck.

He roared in anger as he drove his own blade up in response and our swords clashed and sparked. My blade snagged on his hilt and, with a fierce twist of his wrist, he forced it down and then away, wrenching it from my hand. It clanged as it hit the wall while I, thrown off balance, sprawled to the floor.

As my hand flailed in a grab at my sword – too far! – he whipped round and followed through, and I rolled to the side just in time for his sword to smash down on the cobbles instead of my head. I tried to scramble to my feet, but wasn't quick enough. He kicked me back to the ground, winding me, and before I could rally, his heavy boot was on my chest, pinning me down.

I struggled for breath, and writhed to left, to right, but he only stamped down harder until I could not move for the crushing pains in my ribs. And as I stared up at him, helpless, he brought his sword down, down, until the tip almost touched my nose.

Motionless now, but for my straining chest, I gazed along the shining blade, its point unwavering between my eyes, its polished length reflecting flickers from the lantern flames on to the dark, looming walls of the score. Into my terrified mind crept unbidden a memory from our time at Middleham. Weapons training, two years or more ago. When Hugh had beaten me like this before. Then the sword had been wooden, not tempered, sharpened steel – but the hate in his eyes was the same.

Those eyes narrowed now, black slits in the devilish red of the flaring lamplight.

'Runt!' he taunted. 'Upstart!'

I had never felt so alone, so defenceless. A gaping hollow yawned inside me like the mouth of hell, a pit of sheer terror so deep I would never fall to its end. The faces of my friends, my family – my long-dead mother – images of my short life, all chased through my head as the cool sword point traced across my chin and down the length of my neck.

It rested there a moment, its razor edge against my skin, then he lifted it and delicately tapped it on my throat – once, twice, three times – as though playing with me.

Then his eyes and mouth tightened, and he clasped both his hands upon the hilt, raising his sword high to plunge the point deep into my neck.

But before he could ram it down, a ferocious snarl rang out, and Murrey, in a flash of red, launched herself at his sword arm, sinking her teeth deep into the flesh.

Hugh screamed, dropped his sword and thrashed at her with his other hand. But she would not let go and hung there, teeth clamped on his upper arm as he hit her and hit her to no avail.

His falling sword missed my head by no more than an inch and I plucked it up and flung it to the far side of the score before I rolled over and over, out of the way of his now tramping boots. I grasped the wall and hauled myself back to my feet, gasping one pain-filled stabbing breath after another. How many ribs had Hugh's boot broken?

One hand pressed to my side against the pain, I bent to reclaim my own sword. Hugh's curses were echoing round the alley together with the clatter of his boots, and my only thought now was to dash back to help my loyal hound.

But as I swung round, Hugh's left hand dragged the dagger from his belt. The lamplight flashed on its upraised blade, then he jabbed it sharply down, thrusting it deep into Murrey's flank.

I heard her strangled yelp, saw bright blood gush from the wound, saw her grip loosen. Though Hugh's face was contorted by pain, a smirk lurched across it. He shook her from him before slumping to his knees, his hand clutching his arm.

A howl of rage smote my ears and before I realized it came from me, I had charged the half-dozen paces to where Hugh knelt and dealt him such a blow on his jaw with my sword hilt that he toppled to the ground.

In an instant, all was reversed.

He lay sprawled on his back on the cobbles, gulping in great gasps of air, staring at my sword point lined up unwavering between his eyes.

Such hate had never seized me before, or such fury. As I stood there, enraged, with Hugh at my mercy, Murrey whimpered once, twice, a gurgling breath, then she was silent. And I knew my loyal, royal hound would never dance again, or come back to life at a whistle.

My eyes stung, but I dared not tear them away from Hugh. A moment's distraction, a split second's indecision, and for all his bites and bruising, he would throw me off him and finish what he had begun.

Yet, staring down at him now, I sensed fear in him for the first time – fear of me, of what I, a runt and an upstart, would do. And power surged through me, the power of life or death over a fellow human being.

'Traitor!' I hissed at him. I saw again the stab. First one, then another. 'Coward!'

And in that instant I wanted to hurt. To hurt that cringing cur at my feet.

Murrey had never cringed, never once in all her life. In all her oh-so-short life. My loyal, courageous hound. What had King Richard called her? A brave little thing? Little she may have been, a runt even, but she had always been brave. Never a coward like this creature before me, pleading for his life.

For out of his mouth came choking sounds, barely words, entreating.

'Please, Matthew... please... I beg you... My uncle... Lord Stanley... They will...'

But those words were not the ones to help him. He must have seen it in my face. His voice faltered, died away.

For again into my mind came the sights and sounds of that fateful day, the banners whipping in the wind as the traitors charged, the screams, the horror, the stench of blood – in my nostrils again now. The jeers, the insults – the stab.

And I wanted to inflict pain on him as he had on Murrey, on me. To stab him as he had her – as he had my King.

And my sword point edged closer to his throat.

'Matthew!'

Alys's voice broke into my thoughts.

'Matt! What —'

Roger's too.

Hugh's eyes darted to the sound, but mine didn't move, didn't dare leave his.

Into the darkness on the fringe of my vision, the pale ghost of a hound trotted, bent its head, nudged the unmoving dark shape that lay there. Shadow.

Roger, raising a ship's lantern above his head – casting light upon the whole scene.

Alys, her cropped hair stark in the harsh light. Clutching –
what? A sword. Glinting. A glimpse of scrollwork inscription on
the blade. Edward's.

'Matthew. What happened?'

Her voice was soft, softer than I'd heard it before. Before...

'He stabbed...' A croak. Me? 'He killed...'

Roger peeled away, moved further up the score.

'I'll go check the main street. See what —'

He disappeared into the murk, the swirling mist.

Alys's hands clasped mine, still clenched upon the sword
hilt. Warm fingers on my cold.

My eyes didn't waver. The sword point inched closer.

'He —'

'I know, Matt, I know.' Her words were barely a murmur,
so close to my ear. 'I see her. I see what he did.

'I have to —'

'No, Matt – no, you mustn't.'

'But – but he would...'

He would do it, wouldn't he? Finish it. He wouldn't flinch
from it – wouldn't stay his hand – if this were reversed.

'But, Matt – you're not him. You never will be.'

Her hands pressed tighter, closed over mine. Her voice as
firm.

'Matt... Matt, tell me. What – what would King Richard
do?'

And I knew then. That was all it took.

Those words. Those memories.

Of all those times when I had watched, listened, learnt.

All that the Duke, the King, had ever said to me, done for
me. His half-smile, his gentle mockery, his firm handshake in
farewell, the final promise I had made. And when I had betrayed
his trust and his memory. Once. But not now. Never again.

I knew then that I wouldn't kill Hugh – wouldn't thrust the
sword home. Wouldn't do to him what he would have done to me
without a second's thought. I couldn't. No matter what he had
done.

And Hugh saw it.

His eyes narrowed, his lip curled, his face relaxed. The
fear had fled. Now only contempt remained.

But the tip of my sword pressed still against the soft base
of his throat. As I unbuckled my sword belt with my other hand

and passed it to Alys. As she slipped it out of the scabbard and threaded it beneath his booted legs, strapping it round them as tight as she could. As I ordered him to turn on to his face and raise his wrists behind him.

Next Alys held her sword to his neck while I unfastened his own belt and, ramming my knee into the small of his back – ignoring his cry of pain – I pulled his injured arms up to tie them fast. Then Alys's deft hands tore a strip of cloth from his cloak, fashioning a gag.

Soon we had finished, and Hugh lay trussed and helpless on the cobbles in the guttering light cast by his smashed lantern. He struggled and strained against his bonds, but he could scarcely move, and not so much as a whimper escaped from his stopped-up mouth.

I brushed the dust and grime from my doublet as best I could, before slipping my own old belt through Lord Lovell's scabbard and resheathing his sword. I silently offered up my thanks to his lordship for his gift on that dread day that now seemed so long ago.

Footsteps pounded down the alley towards us. Shadow crouched low, a small growl in her throat. Alys stood ready, her sword raised, though I had no heart to draw my own again.

The glow of a lantern approached the corner and rounded it. It was Roger, of course. Out of breath,

'They've found Ralph. The villagers. They're untying him. We must go.'

Hugh recommenced his writhing with renewed hope. But a swift kick in his ear from Alys's booted foot quietened him.

She leant down close to his face.

'Count your blessings, Hugh,' she whispered. 'You're still alive. Next time you may not be so lucky. We all had a good master, a good teacher. Not everyone is so ready to forgive. And lessons don't always last.'

She stood back up and collected one of the discarded bundles, while Roger scooped up the other two.

'Come, we must be off. We'll be safely away long before they find him. All of us. Long before – and far away.'

I gathered up Murrey's lifeless body. She weighed heavy in my hands as she had never done in life, and her bloodied head lolled against my chest.

Alys, calling Shadow, slipped her free arm through mine. And, with Roger raising his lantern to light our way, together we three walked down the score towards the midnight harbour, to where the ship awaited us and the tide had begun to ebb.

Here ends THE KING'S MAN, the second book in the sequence called THE ORDER OF THE WHITE BOAR. The third book, KING IN WAITING, will continue Matthew and his friends' adventures in the years that follow.

Author's note to *The Order of the White Boar*

Richard, Duke of Gloucester, born in 1452 and brother to King Edward IV, ultimately became King himself as King Richard III, perhaps England's most controversial monarch. The second book in the *Order of the White Boar* sequence, *The King's Man*, tells the story of his road to the throne and his reign through the eyes of Matthew and his friends. This story was distorted, twisted out of shape, by his enemies after his death, for their own purposes. I have gone back to the earliest writers of the history of those events to try to piece together a more accurate version of Richard's life than is usually presented in traditional history books.

Since the discovery of King Richard's grave in 2012, 400 or more years after it was lost, many more people have become interested in the real man, rather than the caricature that was created by his enemies. I have also drawn on the findings of the archaeology in my story. For instance, we now know that Richard suffered from scoliosis, a condition that affected his back, though not enough to prevent him being an active, successful warrior and general, as Matt discovers.

Matt and his friends, and many of the events in this first book, are fictional (see 'Cast of characters'), but as in all historical fiction, they offer a way for us to see and interpret the 'facts' of history that we possess – which cannot always be fitted together to make up a single, complete picture of what 'really' happened. Perhaps there will always be at least one piece of the jigsaw missing – leaving us with some kind of puzzle. Maybe Matt is that missing piece – allowing us to see a full picture, if not *the* full picture, once he's slotted into place.

This book is dedicated to Philippa Langley and her colleagues in the Looking for Richard Project – John Ashdown-Hill, Annette Carson, and David and Wendy Johnson. Without their painstaking research and immense dedication, patience and perseverance, King Richard would probably never have been found – and this book might never have been written. My thanks to them all and to the many Ricardians and others who have helped in numerous ways.

Author's note to *The King's Man*

Within days of the battle at which King Richard III died (which came to be known as the Battle of Bosworth), members of the council in Matthew's home city of York wrote that 'King Richard late mercifully reigning upon us was through great treason . . . piteously slain and murdered to the great heaviness of this city' and called him 'the most famous prince of blessed memory'. Two years earlier on his coronation tour of England, the Bishop of St David's had said of him: 'He contents the people where he goes best that ever did prince' and a Scottish ambassador remarked that 'Never has so much spirit or greater virtue reigned in such a small body.' Dominic Mancini, reporting back to his French master on events in England in 1483, said of the new King, 'The good reputation of his private life and public activities powerfully attracted the esteem of strangers.'

But more than a hundred years later, in a play by the great playwright William Shakespeare, King Richard was described as 'deform'd, unfinished, sent... Into this breathing world, scarce half made up... that bottled spider, that foul bunch-backed toad... determined to prove a villain... the bloody king', being portrayed as a tyrant with a hunchback and withered arm.

It's often said that history is written by the winners. This is perhaps particularly true in the case of the history that was created during the Tudor dynasty after the first Henry Tudor was victorious in battle and took the crown from King Richard. He reigned for twenty-four years as Henry VII, his son for more than thirty as Henry VIII, his grand-daughter for more than forty as Elizabeth I. And it was under her rule than Master Shakespeare provided the most famous condemnation of King Richard – and the one that sticks in most people's minds more than four hundred years later.

This book is one of an increasing number seeking to roll back those centuries of misinformation by going back before the creation of the Tudor myths about King Richard, to the records of his time, and considering them with an open mind. The first to do so was written by Sir George Buck in the early 1600s, almost as soon as the last Tudor monarch was dead – and no longer had to be reassured of her rightful place on the throne by slandering her dynasty's predecessor.

I've tried to stay as close as possible to the scant information we do have from the months of turmoil after the death of King Edward IV – the period from April to June 1483 that is covered in the first chapters of this book. Scant information, but major events and conflicting views on them. These first few chapters may be confusing to some readers – but no more confusing than they must have been to the people living at the time. Some of this confusion I've tried to communicate through Matthew and his friends in the Order of the White Boar, themselves trying to make sense of it all, perhaps without much success. If you've reached as far as this note, I hope that means you've read all the way through that – and beyond – to where I was able to focus again on the relative simplicity of Matt's own story – and how it touches and weaves more closely again about that of 'his' Duke – now 'his' King.

All history is interpretation, and historical fiction too. And where reliable evidence isn't available – as for much of the period covered here – gaps have to be filled in. One of the most gaping holes in history is perhaps the mystery of what happened to the two sons of Edward IV, who have become known as the 'Princes in the Tower'. No matter what Shakespeare says – or many historians down to the present day – no one alive now actually knows for certain. All that can be said is that they weren't officially seen in public again after the summer of 1483.

Tudor-era propagandists proclaimed that the boys were murdered in the Tower on the orders of their uncle, by then King Richard III. Interestingly, Henry Tudor himself, their mother Elizabeth Woodville and their sister Elizabeth of York never made such an accusation. No one did during Henry Tudor's reign as Henry VII – almost twenty-five years; at least we don't have evidence of any accusation – and records are relatively numerous and complete from that period. The story only grew and became widespread over the following decades – until, repeated and embellished often enough, it became accepted as 'true history'. This of course suited Elizabeth I, only England's second crowned queen (a woman on the throne?!), and a Protestant one at that, in a period of religious turmoil. She didn't want there to be any doubt that she was on that throne by right, and that her grandfather, Henry Tudor, had won that right to rule – and from a ruthless, usurping, child-murdering tyrant, as Richard was now made out to be.

History is written by the winner... even, or perhaps particularly, when they themselves usurp the throne illegally...

So what did happen to the 'Princes', Edward and Richard? Today we can only speculate, which is what I have done in the latter part of this book – and also all that any historian can do, given the lack of evidence. Rumours, hearsay – it's all we have. And as Duke Richard says to Matthew, rumours are 'dangerous beasts'.

However, it is possible that a project underway since 2015 may one day find the answers. Philippa Langley, who led the search for King Richard's grave with the Looking for Richard Project, has turned her efforts to the 'Missing Princes Project', seeking evidence from anywhere in Britain and Europe that may shed some light on the mystery. If you can offer help in any way, for example investigating local archives, please contact http://philippalangley.co.uk/missing-princes-project.php.

Many others aim to look again at the real Richard III. In 1924, the Fellowship of the White Boar (which of course influenced the title of my books) was set up to do just that, and was subsequently renamed the Richard III Society, which can be found at www.richardiii.net. More recently another international society has been founded, the Richard III Loyal Supporters, www.r3loyalsupporters.org. Memberships of these groups run into the thousands, and there are many more 'Ricardians' worldwide who may be members of neither.

I have had help and support from, and valuable discussions with, many of them – too many to name individually here without risk of missing any out – but I hope they know I am grateful for their contribution. One or two may even spot themselves somewhere in these pages. I would, however, particularly like to mention historian Matthew Lewis, whose meticulous research and rational blogs have been an excellent guide along the way, and to thank him for one especially apt metaphor! And also Deborah Willemen @MamaMoose_Be for her help with the Flemish. Whatever its faults, social media does a wonderful job of bringing likeminded people together!

Is it strange that a man who has been dead more than five hundred years stirs such interest, even passion in some? For me, it's the continuing injustice of the smears against him, when he's unable to respond or fight back – and when indeed he had few friends and family left to do it for him – that spurred my interest and sympathy.

By what seemed an incredible coincidence, 12 September 2012, the day of the first press conference at which it was announced that King Richard's grave had possibly been discovered, was also the day on which was published the long-awaited report into the tragic deaths of 96 football supporters at Hillsborough in April 1989. The false stories about what happened that day in Sheffield began immediately, with modern tabloid media swinging into action, and they were made 'official' by repetition in the UK Parliament and by apparently 'upstanding' police officers. Those stories sought to place the blame for the tragedy on the Liverpool supporters, to shift the focus away from the failings of those who were really at fault – the authorities, the police themselves. The ones who had control – the ones who could get the 'official' story out there to the public.

Those supporters had family and friends to fight for their good name – and fight they did. Tirelessly, for almost twenty-five years – the time it took for the 'official' story to be overturned and shown to be the lie it was. Such injustices can be reversed – by people with extraordinary courage and determination such as they showed.

This book is dedicated to those people – the families of the 96.

About the author

A Ricardian since a teenager, and following stints as an archaeologist and in publishing, Alex now lives and works in King Richard's own country, not far from his beloved York and Middleham. Much of this book was 'seen' and 'heard' while striding over the nearby heather-clad moors with a loyal hound, 'rescued' in the golden summer of 2012 and named, indecisively but Olympically, Milli Mo Ennis Ohuruogu Murray – Milli for short.

Since publishing *The Order of the White Boar* and *The King's Man*, Alex has also edited two anthologies of short stories by authors inspired by King Richard III: *Grant Me the Carving of My Name* and *Right Trusty and Well Beloved...*, both sold to raise money for Scoliosis Association UK (SAUK), which supports people with the same condition as the king.

The third book in the *White Boar* sequence, *King in Waiting*, was published in 2021, with the fourth, *Sons of York*, following in 2022.

Please review any books you've enjoyed and follow Alex at:

Website: alexmarchantblog.wordpress.com
Amazon: www.amazon.co.uk/Alex-Marchant/
                  e/B075JJKX8W/
Facebook: www.facebook.com/AlexMarchantAuthor/
Twitter: twitter.com/AlexMarchant84
GoodReads: www.goodreads.com/author/show/
                  17175168.Alex_Marchant
Instagram: www.instagram.com/alexmarchantauthor/

Translations of coded text

Qcas og gccb og dcggwpzs – Ozmg
[trans.] Come as soon as possible – Alys

Nyrk r nzkty!
[trans.] What a witch!

Qb eia ijwcb epmbpmz bpm jwga apwct/ . . .
[trans.] It was about whether the boys should be moved from the Tower. I thought it was to stop them being a focus for rebellion, like they have been – but maybe it was about their safety. And with the Duke of Buckingham as Constable of the Tower . . .

Fqp'v vgnn Oqvjgt!
[trans.] Don't tell Mother!

Qtdfqyd gnsix rj!
[trans.] Loyalty binds me

422

Also by Alex Marchant

King in Waiting

1486. These are dangerous days for the Order of the White Boar.
King Richard III has been betrayed and killed. Victorious Henry
Tudor sits uneasily on the throne of England. Richard's loyal
friend, Francis Lovell, plots revenge. Alys Langdown, ward of the
Queen, awaits an unknown fate. And ever-loyal Matthew
Wansford serves his new master, Edward Plantagenet, true King of
England – who now must seek his own road …
From exile in Flanders to an uncertain welcome over the sea –
what challenges lie ahead for the Order and for the King in
Waiting?
Follow Matthew and his friends' adventures in Book 3 of *The
Order of the White Boar*

'Evocative and intriguing… brings the uncertain and dangerous
times after the Battle of Bosworth to life' – Wendy Johnson

Time out of Time

Welcome to the golden summer of 1976. Year of the Heatwave,
year of the Drought. Normally sun-starved and grey, England is
plagued by endless blue skies – no rain for months, the country
scorched and parched, standpipes in the street.
But 12-year-old Allie has other worries. When her family moves to
ancient, ramshackle Priory Farm – far away from her friends and
everything she has ever known…
Then she discovers a doorway into history – and her adventures
begin. What secrets will Priory Farm reveal?
An exciting timeslip adventure, *Time out of Time* whisks the reader
off to explore one small part of England through the ages…

'Absorbing and thought-provoking. I absolutely loved this book!'
Wendy Johnson, Looking for Richard Project

Available from Amazon, all good bookshops or direct from Alex:
AlexMarchant84@gmail.com

Printed in Great Britain
by Amazon